THE CHILDREN OF CTHULHU

By H. P. Lovecraft

Bloodcurdling Tales of Horror and the Macabre:
  The Best of H. P. Lovecraft
Dreams of Terror and Death: The Dream Cycle
  of H. P. Lovecraft
The Road to Madness: The Transition of H. P. Lovecraft

Other Lovecraftian Collections:

Tales of the Cthulhu Mythos
Cthulhu 2000

Shadows over Innsmouth

THE CHILDREN OF CTHULHU

CHILLING NEW TALES INSPIRED BY
H. P. LOVECRAFT

Edited by John Pelan

and Benjamin Adams

The Ballantine Publishing Group · New York

A Del Rey® Book
Published by The Ballantine Publishing Group
Introduction and Compilation Copyright © 2002 by John Pelan and Benjamin Adams

www.delreydigital.com

Library of Congress Cataloging-in-Publication Data
The children of Cthulhu : chilling new tales inspired by H. P. Lovecraft / edited by
John Pelan and Benjamin Adams. — 1st ed.
p. cm.
1. Horror tales, American.   2. Horror tales, English.   3. Lovecraft, H. P.
(Howard Phillips), 1890–1937 — Parodies, imitations, etc.   I. Lovecraft, H. P. (Howard
Phillips), 1890–1937.   II. Pelan, John.   III. Adams, Benjamin.
PS648.H6 C46 2002
813'.0873808 — dc21   2001043930

ISBN 0-345-44926-6

Manufactured in the United States of America
First Edition: January 2002
10 9 8 7 6 5 4 3 2 1

CONTENTS

Introduction: The Call of Lovecraft John Pelan and
Benjamin Adams ... vii

Details China Miéville ... 1

Visitation James Robert Smith ... 21

The Invisible Empire James Van Pelt ... 33

A Victorian Pot Dresser L. H. Maynard and M. P. N. Sims ... 57

The Cabin in the Woods Richard Laymon ... 85

The Stuff of the Stars, Leaking Tim Lebbon ... 109

Sour Places Mark Chadbourn ... 125

Meet Me on the Other Side Yvonne Navarro ... 141

That's the Story of My Life John Pelan and Benjamin Adams ... 161

Long Meg and Her Daughters Paul Finch ... 181

A Fatal Exception Has Occurred At . . . Alan Dean Foster ... 243

Dark of the Moon James S. Dorr ... 261

Red Clay Michael Reaves ... 275

Principles and Parameters Meredith L. Patterson ... 291

Are You Loathsome Tonight? Poppy Z. Brite ... 325

The Serenade of Starlight W. H. Pugmire, Esq. ... 331

Outside Steve Rasnic Tem ... 345

Nor the Demons Down Under the Sea Caitlín R. Kiernan ... 355

A Spectacle of a Man Weston Ochse ... 371

The Firebrand Symphony Brian Hodge ... 389

Teeth Matt Cardin ... 437

Notes on the Contributors ... 463

INTRODUCTION: THE CALL OF LOVECRAFT

John Pelan and Benjamin Adams

Perhaps no other author has exerted as powerful an influence over twentieth- and twenty-first-century weird fiction as Howard Phillips Lovecraft. His view of a chaotic and hostile universe fused the genres of horror, science fiction, and mythology in a manner truly unique, resulting in a body of work still avidly read more than sixty years after his death. Like any brilliant popular literature, Lovecraft's tales spawned a host of imitators. Lovecraft encouraged others to add to and expand upon his cosmology, and young writers of the 1930s such as Robert Bloch, Henry Kuttner, and August Derleth contributed stories to the rapidly growing canon. More established authors such as Clark Ashton Smith and Robert E. Howard referenced Lovecraft's oeuvre in their own works, and thus the Cthulhu Mythos grew, and grew, and grew. . . .

It's probably fair to say that "If it ain't broke, don't fix it" is one of the most overused axioms in the English language. Ultimately, though, what does it mean? That one shouldn't try to improve something that already works? What a frightening, Luddite concept. The only way we grow and move forward is to continually fix what ain't broke.

In this case, of course, we're referring to the Cthulhu Mythos.

Much of the fiction that has been passed off as Lovecraftian in recent years has boasted purple prose offered as "style" and bizarre proper nouns trundled out as "atmosphere." We must assume the writers of tales such as these are seeing only the superficial elements of previous stories in the Cthulhu Mythos, rather than attaining a true grasp of H. P. Lovecraft's vision. What these authors see ain't broke, and they sure as heck ain't gonna fix it.

The stories written by Lovecraft in the 1920s and 1930s were rife with a terrifying vision of an indifferent and chaotic universe populated by beings that were, in their total alienness, completely inconceivable by mere humans. Lovecraft's fashioned cosmology dealt at length with the tragic results of encounters between frail individuals and the Great Old Ones or their minions.

Like so many bread crumbs, Lovecraft dropped names like Cthulhu, Yog-Sothoth, and Nyarlathotep throughout his loose myth-cycle, but the trail of crumbs leads nowhere. It was never meant to do so. His stories are frequently contradictory in their details about these monstrously alien beings that infiltrated Earth from the farthest reaches of space and time. The Cthulhu Mythos (so named by Lovecraft's protege August Derleth, but more properly referred to as "Yog-Sothothery" by Lovecraft himself) is full of dangling loose ends and tantalizing hints at vast cosmic truths.

The grand tradition of borrowing Lovecraft's concepts and, in many cases, expanding upon them led many later authors to add their own spices to the fictional stew, which as a result became more of a weak broth than a hearty meal. While it's true that some tremendously powerful material has been written by both the first and second generation of "Cthulhu's Children," there is also much that tries to explain the unexplainable and codify the infinite. Many authors have completely missed the point that the true horror in Lovecraft's fiction lies in the unknowable . . . the mystery of a vast and infinitely strange cosmos.

There have been numerous attempts to catalog the entities of Lovecraft's cosmology, to present a monstrous genealogy as it were; these attempts have for the most part exhibited a complete lack of understanding of his vision. And yet this literary calcification of Lovecraft's concepts has been so pervasive that these genealogies have been accepted as canon, leaving the whole structure that much more ossified and static, a vast, tottering monolith.

And many lesser writers have fallen victim to the tendency to merely throw a few Lovecraftian beasties and the Necronomicon into their tales. These pastiches aren't so much derivative of Lovecraft as they are of others who followed him, including Derleth. And as such the stories have fallen into hidebound rhythms: Seeker after occult lore discovers an unspeakable volume and conjures up Cthulhu, and all hell breaks loose. Many of the writers aren't even familiar with Lovecraft's own inspirations, such as Lord Dunsany, Edgar Allan Poe, Arthur Machen, and M. R. James.

For this collection, we asked authors to break past the "don't fix it" mentality and bring Lovecraft's original concepts kicking and screaming into the twenty-first century. The plain fact is that seventy years of literary conservatism have stripped away the awful power and hideous majesty of Lovecraft's creations. And while the elderly gentleman himself was terribly old-fashioned, what he wrought in his imagination was not. At their core, Lovecraft's stories are still among the most powerful and disturbing ever written. These stories have spoken to an entire new generation of authors, most of whom have rarely if ever essayed a Lovecraftian pastiche. What we have here is a book comprised of tales by authors who said "it may not be broken, but I want to fix it *this* way. . . ."

And so they have. . . .

The stories in this collection range from the historical to the futuristic. What they share is each writer's reaction to the vision of H. P. Lovecraft and an affinity for his core concepts. These stories are the literary Children of Cthulhu, and we hope you enjoy making their acquaintance.

JOHN PELAN—Midnight House

BENJAMIN ADAMS—Sacramento, California

DETAILS

China Miéville

When the boy upstairs got hold of a pellet gun and fired snips of potato at passing cars, I took a turn. I was part of everything. I wasn't an outsider. But I wouldn't join in when my friends went to the yellow house to scribble on the bricks and listen at the windows.

One girl teased me about it, but everyone else told her to shut up. They defended me, even though they didn't understand why I wouldn't come.

I don't remember a time before I visited the yellow house for my mother.

On Wednesday mornings at about nine o'clock I would open the front door of the decrepit building with a key from the bunch my mother had given me. Inside was a hall and two doors, one broken and leading to the splintering stairs. I would unlock the other and enter the dark flat. The corridor was unlit and smelt of old wet air. I never walked even two steps down that hallway. Rot and shadows merged, and it looked as if the passage disappeared a few yards from me. The door to Mrs.

Miller's room was right in front of me. I would lean forward and knock.

Quite often there were signs that someone else had been there recently. Scuffed dust and bits of litter. Sometimes I was not alone. There were two other children I sometimes saw slipping in or out of the house. There were a handful of adults who visited Mrs. Miller.

I might find one or another of them in the hallway outside the door to her flat, or even in the flat itself, slouching in the crumbling dark hallway. They would be slumped over or reading some cheap-looking book or swearing loudly as they waited.

There was a young Asian woman who wore a lot of makeup and smoked obsessively. She ignored me totally. There were two drunks who came sometimes. One would greet me boisterously and incomprehensibly, raising his arms as if he wanted to hug me into his stinking, stinking jumper. I would grin and wave nervously, walk past him. The other seemed alternately melancholic and angry. Occasionally I'd meet him by the door to Mrs. Miller's room, swearing in a strong cockney accent. I remember the first time I saw him, he was standing there, his red face contorted, slurring and moaning loudly.

"Come on, you old slag," he wailed, "you sodding old *slag*. Come on, please, you cow."

His words scared me but his tone was wheedling, and I realized I could hear her voice. Mrs. Miller's voice, from inside the room, answering him back. She did not sound frightened or angry.

I hung back, not sure what to do, and she kept speaking, and eventually the drunken man shambled miserably away. And then I could continue as usual.

. . .

I asked my mother once if I could have some of Mrs. Miller's food. She laughed very hard and shook her head. In all the Wednesdays of bringing the food over, I never even dipped my finger in to suck it.

My mum spent an hour every Tuesday night making the stuff up. She dissolved a bit of gelatin or cornflower with some milk, threw in a load of sugar or flavorings, and crushed a clutch of vitamin pills into the mess. She stirred it until it thickened and let it set in a plain white plastic bowl. In the morning it would be a kind of strong-smelling custard that my mother put a dishcloth over and gave me, along with a list of any questions or requests for Mrs. Miller and sometimes a plastic bucket full of white paint.

So I would stand in front of Mrs. Miller's door, knocking, with a bowl at my feet. I'd hear a shifting and then her voice from close by the door.

"Hello," she would call, and then say my name a couple of times. "Have you my breakfast? Are you ready?"

I would creep up close to the door and hold the food ready. I would tell her I was.

Mrs. Miller would slowly count to three. On three, the door suddenly swung open a snatch, just a foot or two, and I thrust the bowl into the gap. She grabbed it and slammed the door quickly in my face.

I couldn't see very much inside the room. The door was open for less than a second. My strongest impression was of the whiteness of the walls. Mrs. Miller's sleeves were white, too, and made of plastic. I never got much of a glimpse at her face, but what I saw was unmemorable. A middle-aged woman's eager face.

If I had a bucket full of paint, we would run through the routine again. Then I would sit cross-legged in front of her door and listen to her eat.

"How's your mother?" she would shout. At that I'd unfold

my mother's careful queries. She's okay, I'd say, she's fine. She says she has some questions for you.

I'd read my mother's strange questions in my careful childish monotone, and Mrs. Miller would pause and make interested sounds, and clear her throat and think out loud. Sometimes she took ages to come to an answer, and sometimes it would be almost immediate.

"Tell your mother she can't tell if a man's good or bad from that," she'd say. "Tell her to remember the problems she had with your father." Or: "Yes, she can take the heart of it out. Only she has to paint it with the special oil I told her about." "Tell your mother seven. But only four of them concern her and three of them used to be dead.

"I can't help her with that," she told me once, quietly. "Tell her to go to a doctor, quickly." And my mother did, and she got well again.

"What do you not want to do when you grow up?" Mrs. Miller asked me one day.

That morning when I had come to the house the sad cockney vagrant had been banging on the door of her room again, the keys to the flat flailing in his hand.

"He's begging you, you old tart, please, you owe him, he's so bloody angry," he was shouting, "only it ain't you gets the sharp end, is it? *Please*, you cow, you sodding cow, I'm on me knees. . . ."

"My door knows you, man," Mrs. Miller declared from within. "It knows you and so do I, you know it won't open to you. I didn't take out my eyes and I'm not giving in now. Go home."

I waited nervously as the man gathered himself and staggered away, and then, looking behind me, I knocked on her door and announced myself. It was after I'd given her the food that she asked her question.

"What do you not want to do when you grow up?"

If I had been a few years older her inversion of the cliché would have annoyed me: It would have seemed mannered and contrived. But I was only a young child, and I was quite delighted.

I don't want to be a lawyer, I told her carefully. I spoke out of loyalty to my mother, who periodically received crisp letters that made her cry or smoke fiercely, and swear at lawyers, bloody smartarse lawyers.

Mrs. Miller was delighted.

"Good boy!" she snorted. "We know all about lawyers. Bastards, right? With the small print! Never be tricked by the small print! It's right there in front of you, *right there in front of you*, and you can't even *see* it and then suddenly it *makes you notice it*! And I tell you, once you seen it it's got you!" She laughed excitedly. "Don't let the small print get you. I'll tell you a secret." I waited quietly, and my head slipped nearer the door.

"The devil's in the details!" She laughed again. "You ask your mother if that's not true. The devil is in the details!"

I'd wait the twenty minutes or so until Mrs. Miller had finished eating, and then we'd reverse our previous procedure and she'd quickly hand me out an empty bowl. I would return home with the empty container and tell my mother the various answers to her various questions. Usually she would nod and make notes. Occasionally she would cry.

After I told Mrs. Miller that I did not want to be a lawyer she started asking me to read to her. She made me tell my mother, and told me to bring a newspaper or one of a number of books. My mother nodded at the message and packed me a sandwich the next Wednesday, along with the *Mirror*. She told me to be polite and do what Mrs. Miller asked, and that she'd see me in the afternoon.

I wasn't afraid. Mrs. Miller had never treated me badly from behind her door. I was resigned and only a little bit nervous.

Mrs. Miller made me read stories to her from specific pages that she shouted out. She made me recite them again and again, very carefully. Afterward she would talk to me. Usually she started with a joke about lawyers, and about small print.

"There's three ways not to see what you don't want to," she told me. "One is the coward's way and too damned painful. The other is to close your eyes forever which is the same as the first, when it comes to it. The third is the hardest and the best: You have to make sure *only the things you can afford to see* come before you."

One morning when I arrived the stylish Asian woman was whispering fiercely through the wood of the door, and I could hear Mrs. Miller responding with shouts of amused disapproval. Eventually the young woman swept past me, leaving me cowed by her perfume.

Mrs. Miller was laughing, and she was talkative when she had eaten.

"She's heading for trouble, messing with the wrong family! You have to be careful with all of them," she told me. "Every single *one* of them on that other side of things is a tricksy bastard who'll kill you soon as *look* at you, given half a chance.

"There's the gnarly throat-tipped one . . . and there's old hasty, who I think had best remain nameless," she said wryly. "All old bastards, all of them. You *can't trust them* at all, that's what I say. I should know, eh? Shouldn't I?" She laughed. "Trust me, trust me on this: It's too easy to get on the wrong side of them.

"What's it like out today?" she asked me. I told her that it was cloudy.

"You want to be careful with that," she said. "All sorts of faces in the clouds, aren't there? Can't help noticing, can you?" She was whispering now. "Do me a favor when you go home to your mum: Don't look up, there's a boy. Don't look up at all."

When I left her, however, the day had changed. The sky was hot, and quite blue.

The two drunk men were squabbling in the front hall and I edged past them to her door. They continued bickering in a depressing, garbled murmur throughout my visit.

"D'you know, I can't even really remember what it was all *about*, now!" Mrs. Miller said when I had finished reading to her. "I can't remember! That's a terrible thing. But you don't forget the basics. The exact question escapes me, and to be honest I think maybe I was just being *nosy* or *showing off*. . . . I can't say I'm proud of it but it could have been that. It could. But whatever the question, it was all about a way of seeing an answer.

"There's a way of looking that lets you read things. If you look at a pattern of tar on a wall, or a crumbling mound of brick or somesuch . . . there's a way of unpicking it. And if you know how, you can trace it and read it out and see the things hidden *right there in front of you*, the things you've been seeing but not noticing, all along. But you have to learn how." She laughed. It was a high-pitched, unpleasant sound. "Someone has to teach you. So you have to make certain friends.

"But you can't make friends without making enemies.

"You have to open it all up for you to see inside. You make what you see into a window, and you see what you want through it. You make what you see a sort of *door*."

. . .

She was silent for a long time. Then: "Is it cloudy again?" she asked suddenly. She went on before I answered.

"If you look up, you look into the clouds for long enough and you'll see a face. Or in a tree. Look in a tree, look in the branches and soon you'll see them just so, and there's a face or a running man, or a bat or whatever. You'll see it all suddenly, a picture in the pattern of the branches, and you won't have *chosen* to see it. And you can't *unsee* it.

"That's what you have to learn to do, to read the details like that and see what's what and learn things. But you've to be damn careful. You've to be careful not to disturb anything." Her voice was absolutely cold, and I was suddenly very frightened.

"Open up that window, you'd better be damn careful that what's in the details doesn't look back and see you."

The next time I went, the maudlin drunk was there again wailing obscenities at her through her door. She shouted at me to come back later, that she didn't need her food right now. She sounded resigned and irritated, and she went back to scolding her visitor before I had backed out of earshot.

He was screaming at her that she'd gone too far, that she'd pissed about too long, that things were coming to a head, that there was going to be hell to pay, that she couldn't avoid it forever, that it was her own fault.

When I came back he was asleep, snoring loudly, curled up a few feet into the mildewing passage. Mrs. Miller took her food and ate it quickly, returned it without speaking.

. . .

When I returned the following week, she began to whisper to me as soon as I knocked on the door, hissing urgently as she opened it briefly and grabbed the bowl.

"It was an accident, you know," she said, as if responding to something I'd said. "I mean of *course* you know in *theory* that anything might happen, you get *warned*, don't you? But oh my . . . oh my *God* it took the breath out of me and made me cold to realize what had happened."

I waited. I could not leave, because she had not returned the bowl. She had not said I could go. She spoke again, very slowly.

"It was a new day." Her voice was distant and breathy. "Can you even imagine? Can you see what I was ready to do? I was poised . . . to change . . . to see everything that's hidden. The best place to hide a book is in a library. The best place to hide secret things is there, in the visible angles, in our view, in plain sight.

"I had studied and sought, and learnt, finally, to see. It was time to learn truths.

"I opened my eyes fully, for the first time.

"I had chosen an old wall. I was looking for the answer to some question that I told you I can't even *remember* now, but the question wasn't the main thing. That was the opening of my eyes.

"I stared at the whole mass of the bricks. I took another glance, relaxed my sight. At first I couldn't stop seeing the bricks as bricks, the divisions as layers of cement, but after a time they became pure vision. And as the whole broke down into lines and shapes and shades, I held my breath as I began to see.

"Alternatives appeared to me. Messages written in the pock-marks. Insinuations in the forms. Secrets unraveling. It was bliss.

"And then without warning my heart went tight, as I saw something. I made sense of the pattern.

"It was a mess of cracks and lines and crumbling cement, and as I looked at it, I saw a pattern in the wall.

"I saw a clutch of lines that looked just like something . . . terrible . . . something old and predatory and utterly terrible . . . staring right back at me.

"And then I saw it move."

"You have to understand me," she said. "*Nothing changed.* See? All the time I was looking I saw the wall. But that first moment, it was like when you see a face in the cloud. I just *noticed* in the pattern in the brick, I just *noticed* something, looking at me. Something angry.

"And then in the very next moment, I just . . . I just *noticed* another load of lines — cracks that had always been there, you understand? Patterns in broken brick that I'd seen only a second before — that looked exactly like that same thing, a little closer to me. And in the next moment a third picture in the brick, a picture of the thing closer still.

"Reaching for me."

"I broke free then," she whispered. "I ran away from there in terror, with my hands in front of my eyes and I was *screaming*. I ran and ran.

"And when I stopped and opened my eyes again, I had run to the edges of a park, and I took my hands slowly down and dared to look behind me, and saw that there was nothing coming from the alley where I'd been. So I turned to the little snatch of scrub and grass and trees.

"And I saw the thing again."

Mrs. Miller's voice was stretched out as if she was dreaming. My mouth was open and I huddled closer to the door.

"I saw it in the leaves," she said forlornly. "As I turned I saw the leaves in such a way . . . just a *chance conjuncture*, you understand? I noticed a pattern. I *couldn't not*. You don't choose whether to see faces in the clouds. I saw the monstrous thing again and it still reached for me, and I shrieked and all the mothers and fathers and children in that park turned and gazed at me, and I turned my eyes from that tree and whirled on my feet to face a little family in my way.

"And the thing was there in the same pose," she whispered in misery. "I saw it in the outlines of the father's coat and the spokes of the baby's pushchair, and the tangles of the mother's hair. It was just another mess of lines, you see? But you *don't choose what you notice*. And I couldn't help but notice *just the right lines* out of the whole, just the lines out of all the lines there, just the ones to see the thing again, a little closer, looking at me.

"And I turned and saw it closer still in the clouds, and I turned again and it was clutching for me in the rippling weeds in the pond, and as I closed my eyes I swear I felt something touch my dress.

"You understand me? You understand?"

I didn't know if I understood or not. Of course now I know that I did not.

"It lives in the details," she said bleakly. "It travels in that . . . in that perception. It moves through those chance meetings of lines. Maybe you glimpse it sometimes when you stare at clouds, and then maybe it might catch a glimpse of you, too.

"But it saw me *full on*. It's jealous of . . . of its place, and there I was peering through without permission, like a nosy neighbor through a hole in the fence. I know what it is. I know what happened.

"It lurks before us, in the everyday. It's the boss of *all the things* hidden in plain sight. Terrible things, they are. Appalling things. Just almost in reach. Brazen and invisible.

"It caught my glances. It can move through whatever I see.

"For most people it's just chance, isn't it? What shapes they see in a tangle of wire. There's a thousand pictures there, and when you look, some of them just appear. But now . . . the thing in the lines chooses the pictures for me. It can thrust itself forward. It makes me see it. It's found its way through. To me. Through what I see. *I opened a door into my perception.*"

She sounded frozen with terror. I was not equipped for that kind of adult fear, and my mouth worked silently for something to say.

"That was a long, long journey home. Every time I peeked through the cracks in my fingers, I saw that thing crawling for me.

"It waited ready to pounce, and when I opened my eyes even a crack I opened the door again. I saw the back of a woman's jumper and in the detail of the fabric the thing leapt for me. I glimpsed a yard of broken paving and I noticed just the lines that showed me the thing . . . *baying.*

"I had to shut my eyes quick.

"I *groped* my way home.

"And then I taped my eyes shut and I tried to think about things."

There was silence for a time.

"See, there was always the easy way, that scared me rotten, because I was never one for blood and pain," she said suddenly, and her voice was harder. "I held the scissors in front of my eyes a couple of times, but even bandaged blind as I was I couldn't bear it. I suppose I could've gone to a doctor. I can pull strings, I could pull in a few favors, have them do the job without pain.

"But you know I never . . . really . . . reckoned . . . that's what I'd do," she said thoughtfully. "What if you found a way to close the door? Eh? And you'd already put out your eyes? You'd feel such a *fool*, wouldn't you?

"And you know it wouldn't be good enough to wear pads and eyepatches and all. I tried. You catch glimpses. You see the glimmers of light and maybe a few of your own hairs, and that's *the doorway right there*, when the hairs cross in the corner of your eye so that if you notice just a few of them in just the right way . . . they look like something coming for you. That's a doorway.

"It's . . . unbearable . . . having sight, but trapping it like that.

"I'm not giving up. See . . ." Her voice lowered, and she spoke conspiratorially. "*I still think I can close the door.* I learnt to see. I can unlearn. I'm looking for ways. I want to see a wall as . . . as bricks again. Nothing more. That's why you read for me," she said. "*Research.* Can't look at it myself of course, too many edges and lines and so on on a printed page, so you do it for me. And you're a good boy to do it."

I've thought about what she said many times, and still it makes no sense to me. The books I read to Mrs. Miller were school textbooks, old and dull village histories, the occasional romantic novel. I think that she must have been talking of some of her other visitors, who perhaps read her more esoteric stuff than I did. Either that, or the information she sought was buried very cleverly in the banal prose I faltered through.

"In the meantime, there's another way of surviving," she said slyly. "Leave the eyes where they are, but *don't give them any details*.

"That . . . thing can force me to notice its shape, but only in what's there. That's how it travels. You imagine if I saw a field of wheat. Doesn't even bear *thinking* about! A million million little bloody *edges*, a million lines. You could make pictures of damn *anything* out of them, couldn't you? It wouldn't take any effort at *all* for the thing to make me notice it. The damn *lurker*. Or in a gravel drive or, or a building site, or a lawn . . .

"But I can outsmart it." The note of cunning in her voice made her sound deranged. "Keep it away till I work out how to close it off.

"I had to prepare this blind, with the wrappings round my head. Took me a while, but here I am now. Safe. I'm safe in my little cold room. I keep the walls *flat white*. I covered the windows and painted them, too. I made my cloak out of plastic, so's I can't catch a glimpse of cotton weave or anything when I wake up.

"I keep my place nice and . . . simple. When it was all done, I unwrapped the bandages from my head, and I blinked slowly . . . and I was alright. Clean walls, no cracks, no features. I don't look at my hands often or for long. Too many creases. Your mother makes me a good healthy soup looks like cream, so if I accidentally look in the bowl, there's no broccoli or rice or tangled up spaghetti to make *lines and edges*.

"I open and shut the door so damned quick because I can only afford a moment. *That thing is ready to pounce.* It wouldn't take a second for it to leap up at me out of the sight of your hair or your books or whatever."

Her voice ebbed out. I waited a minute for her to resume, but she did not do so. Eventually I knocked nervously on the door and called her name. There was no answer. I put my ear to the door. I could hear her crying, quietly.

I went home without the bowl. My mother pursed her lips a little but said nothing. I didn't tell her any of what Mrs. Miller had said. I was troubled and totally confused.

The next time I delivered Mrs. Miller's food, in a new container, she whispered harshly to me: "It preys on my eyes, all the *white*. Nothing to see. Can't look out the window, can't read, can't gaze at my nails. Preys on my mind.

"Not even my memories are left," she said in misery. "It's colonizing them. I remember things . . . happy times . . . and the thing's waiting in the texture of my dress, or in the crumbs of my birthday cake. I didn't notice it then. But I can see it now. My memories aren't mine anymore. Not even my imaginings. Last night I thought about going to the seaside, and then the thing was there in the foam on the waves."

She spoke very little the next few times I visited her. I read the chapters she demanded and she grunted curtly in response. She ate quickly.

Her other visitors were there more often now, as the spring came in. I saw them in new combinations and situations: the glamorous young woman arguing with the friendly drunk; the old man sobbing at the far end of the hall. The aggressive man was often there, cajoling and moaning, and occasionally talking conversationally through the door, being answered like an equal. Other times he screamed at her as usual.

I arrived on a chilly day to find the drunken cockney man sleeping a few feet from the door, snoring gutturally. I gave Mrs. Miller her food and then sat on my coat and read to her from a women's magazine as she ate.

When she had finished her food I waited with my arms outstretched, ready to snatch the bowl from her. I remember that I was very uneasy, that I sensed something wrong. I was looking around me anxiously, but everything seemed normal. I looked down at my coat and the crumpled magazine, at the man who still sprawled comatose in the hall.

As I heard Mrs. Miller's hands on the door, I realized what had changed. The drunken man was not snoring. He was holding his breath.

For a tiny moment I thought he had died, but I could see his body trembling, and my eyes began to open wide and I stretched my mouth to scream a warning, but the door had already begun to swing in its tight, quick arc, and before I could even exhale the stinking man pushed himself up faster than I would have thought him capable and bore down on me with bloodshot eyes.

I managed to keen as he reached me, and the door faltered for an instant, as Mrs. Miller heard my voice. But the man grabbed hold of me in a terrifying, heavy fug of alcohol. He reached down and snatched my coat from the floor, tugged at the jumper I had tied around my waist with his other hand, and hurled me hard at the door.

It flew open, smacking Mrs. Miller aside. I was screaming and crying. My eyes hurt at the sudden burst of cold white light from all the walls. I saw Mrs. Miller rubbing her head in the corner, struggling to her senses. The staggering, drunken man hurled my checked coat and my patterned jumper in front of her, reached down and snatched my feet, tugged me out of the room in an agony of splinters. I wailed snottily with fear.

Behind me, Mrs. Miller began to scream and curse, but I could not hear her well because the man had clutched me to him and pulled my head to his chest. I fought and cried and felt myself lurch as he leaned forward and slammed the door closed.

He held it shut.

When I fought myself free of him I heard him shouting.

"I told you, you slapper," he wailed unhappily. "I bloody told you, you silly old whore. I warned you it was time. . . ." Behind his voice I could hear shrieks of misery and terror from the room. Both of them kept shouting and crying and screaming, and the floorboards pounded, and the door shook, and I heard something else as well.

As if the notes of all the different noises in the house fell into a chance meeting, and sounded like more than dissonance.

The shouts and bangs and cries of fear combined in a sudden
audible illusion like another presence.

Like a snarling voice. A lingering, hungry exhalation.

I ran then, screaming and terrified, my skin freezing in my
T-shirt. I was sobbing and retching with fear, little bleats bursting from me. I stumbled home and was sick in my mother's
room, and kept crying and crying as she grabbed hold of me
and I tried to tell her what had happened, until I was drowsy
and confused and I fell into silence.

My mother said nothing about Mrs. Miller. The next Wednesday we got up early and went to the zoo, the two of us, and at
the time I would usually be knocking on Mrs. Miller's door I
was laughing at camels. The Wednesday after that I was taken
to see a film, and the one after that my mother stayed in bed
and sent me to fetch cigarettes and bread from the local shop,
and I made our breakfast and ate it in her room.

My friends could tell that something had changed in the
yellow house, but they did not speak to me about it, and it
quickly became uninteresting to them.

I saw the Asian woman once more, smoking with her friends
in the park several weeks later, and to my amazement she
nodded to me and came over, interrupting her companions'
conversation.

"Are you alright?" she asked me peremptorily. "How are you
doing?"

I nodded shyly back and told her that I was fine, thank you,
and how was she?

She nodded and walked away.

. . .

I never saw the drunken, violent man again.

There were people I could probably have gone to to understand more about what had happened to Mrs. Miller. There was a story that I could chase, if I wanted to. People I had never seen before came to my house and spoke quietly to my mother, and looked at me with what I suppose was pity or concern. I could have asked them. But I was thinking more and more about my own life. I didn't want to know Mrs. Miller's details.

I went back to the yellow house once, nearly a year after that awful morning. It was winter. I remembered the last time I spoke to Mrs. Miller and I felt so much older it was almost giddying. It seemed such a vastly long time ago.

I crept up to the house one evening, trying the keys I still had, which to my surprise worked. The hallway was freezing, dark, and stinking more strongly than ever. I hesitated, then pushed open Mrs. Miller's door.

It opened easily, without a sound. The occasional muffled noise from the street seemed so distant it was like a memory. I entered.

She had covered the windows very carefully, and still no light made its way through from outside. It was extremely dark. I waited until I could see better in the ambient glow from the outside hallway.

I was alone.

My old coat and jumper lay spreadeagled in the corner of the room. I shivered to see them, went over, and fingered them softly. They were damp and mildewing, covered in wet dust.

The white paint was crumbling off the wall in scabs. It looked as if it had been left untended for several years. I could not believe the extent of the decay.

I turned slowly around and gazed at each wall in turn. I took in the chaotic, intricate patterns of crumbling paint and damp plaster. They looked like maps, like a rocky landscape.

I looked for a long time at the wall farthest from my jacket. I was very cold. After a long time I saw a shape in the ruined paint. I moved closer with a dumb curiosity far stronger than any fear.

In the crumbling texture of the wall was a spreading anatomy of cracks that—seen from a certain angle, caught just right in the scraps of light—looked in outline something like a woman. As I stared at it it took shape, and I stopped noticing the extraneous lines, and focused without effort or decision on the relevant ones. I saw a woman looking out at me.

I could make out the suggestion of her face. The patch of rot that constituted it made it look as if she was screaming.

One of her arms was flung back away from her body, which seemed to strain against it, as if she was being pulled away by her hand, and was fighting to escape, and was failing. At the end of her crack-arm, in the space where her captor would be, the paint had fallen away in a great slab, uncovering a huge patch of wet, stained, textured cement.

And in that dark infinity of markings, I could make out any shape I wanted.

VISITATION

James Robert Smith

Only the few who sorcery's secret know,
Espy amidst these tombs the shade of Poe.
—H. P. LOVECRAFT

James Allyson received a postcard from E. A. Poe on October 28, 199–.

It wasn't a cruel joke or a hoax perpetrated by some acquaintance. He'd left all of those people behind. He had a deep feeling, a cold certainty that the card was real. He'd had the feeling before.

James stood in the red dust beside his mailbox near the unpaved road, and he held the card up to the light. The beams glowed through the yellowed cardstock, and it was like looking through a hardened sheet of beeswax. He gazed at the inkings scrawled there and felt the chill again.

He reread it, a spidery script style from decades ago:

> *James, I will be arriving soon. Travel is slow for me. I look forward to meeting you.*
> *Sincerely, E. A. Poe.*

The date scribbled on the card was two weeks old. James looked down the road and up, but there was no one to be seen between himself and where the gravel track bent east and west. He was alone except for the trees and the birds that flitted here and there in the warm October air. Still, a shiver crept the length of his spine, and he shrugged his shoulders to ward it off. How long would it take him? James didn't know, but he turned to hurry down the mile-long driveway to his house.

All along the way he kept glancing into the surrounding forests. But, though he jumped at each woodland sound, every rattle of blowing leaf, at the snap of tiny twigs beneath small feet, he saw nothing that should not be and arrived none the worse but for the odd chill that tickled his spine.

This was yet another misplaced gift from *them*.

James was alone. He had no brothers with whom to communicate, and no sisters were around to fuss over his welfare. His father and mother had died in that automobile accident. Police had told him the accident was caused by a road too wet and a night too dark. The pain of their loss was still not blunted; it was a sharp ache that he'd rarely forgotten in the months since they passed. He could not grow content in the home they had left in his name, in this secluded house in which he had lived the best days of his youth. And there was that unfaced hunger, so great that his life had become little more than a kind of slow struggle not to think about it.

His parents, always striving to give, to make him happy: He feared their deaths had been a deliberate act on their part, a way to free him from a life he hated. Perhaps it was true. Who else had known of his passion for the writer?

Coming at last to the end of the gravel drive, James made his way across the wide parking area. Standing alone in the open place in the forest, he gazed again at the oblong of cardstock pinched in his fingers. *Arriving soon.*

I look forward to meeting you. James would have wondered why, but he remembered his parents, and all that they had given and tried to give. Still trying, it seemed.

. . .

He had been quite miserable in the year or so before his parents had died. The constant rip and tear of competition once he was away from school had been almost too much for him. There had been times when he felt that there was nothing to do but kill himself. And though he had never voiced it to them, they must have seen it in his demeanor when they visited. The pressures had been too great for their protected boy, so they had acted this final time as they had acted so many times in the past. And while James had contemplated suicide, waiting to gather the courage, he had been informed of the accident.

Depression had gripped him for a time. Who else cared? Who else could now comfort him and hold him and keep him safe? There was no one. And when he dwelled on that single, cold fact, he almost had been able to act. And then he thought of retreat. As they must have known he would.

Around him he had solid walls: paid for. Beyond those walls lay hundreds of acres of post oaks and Virginia pines. His nearest neighbors were more than two miles away, accessible only by red clay roads; the closest phone was two miles past that. And there was money in the bank. More than he might have saved over a lifetime of hoarding and investing. He had his parents' savings and their life insurance policies: double indemnity for their untimely demise. His contentment and safety had been bought through the mortality of the only people with whom he had truly shared love.

They had always given him what he needed most, when his needs had been at the most severe. A trip to Baltimore as a teen, standing in a sunlit cemetery, gazing upon the tomb-now-shrine. "Oh, I would loved to have met him," he had told his parents, those givers of all.

And so he prepared for the arrival of Mr. Poe.

. . .

He put away his car and shut up the garage, so that the doors to it were stoutly locked and not liable to swing accidentally open. There had been a television in the den, which he rarely used. So he boxed it up and stored it safely in the attic. He went about the old house after that, searching for things that might disturb his coming visitor. When he had finished, he found he had several boxes full of appliances and electronic *necessities*. Poe and his fellows had done without, and so would James.

After that, he went through the house, from the attic to the basement, from one end to the other, searching for anything that might distract either of them from the other. And he almost, almost, missed it.

He opened up the liquor cabinet and hid the score of bottles in the back of a row of high shelves above the kitchen counter. James's father had once stored paints and stains there, and it had a door and a lock so that young James wouldn't be able to get into trouble. James found the key to it in a jewelry case that had belonged to his mother, and he locked it safely and forgot about it.

Later he went to his room, unpacking boxes of near forgotten books he hadn't read in years, and he filled the empty gaps where the electronic gadgets had taken up space. He arranged his bookshelves, making certain books easier to reach than others, some more obvious than their companions. His books covered the walls and filled the nooks wherever he could fit a shelf or customize a place for them.

James Allyson took out the card from where it rested against his chest in his shirt pocket. He fingered the stiff, yellow paper and felt at the sharp corners of it and ran his fingers over the faint, raised trails where Poe had scrawled his name. *I look forward to meeting you.*

He gazed up at the hardwood shelves that loomed to the height of the ten-foot ceilings: a wall of neat, well placed spines—a thousand authors facing out at him. Maybe the visit was a message to salve his guilt.

Days passed. He waited for Poe, sitting at the end of the drive near the house, his back to a smooth-barked poplar tree, a book to keep him company. The sun came up over the steep ridges that closed the house in its little valley, the brook below him trickling over polished quartz. He waited there, but no one came.

At last, tiring of the wait, James closed himself into the den that had become a library. The smell of pulp, of gilt-edged pages and leather spines, surrounded him. He drank it up, reading aloud, mumbling alone in the room until he fell to sleep.

In his sleep, he dreamed that he heard horses, that he heard their hooves clattering over stones and that iron-bound wheels were crushing scree into the earth. He dreamed he heard the hooves clop-clop their way to his house, and then there came the sound of a door opening wide, slamming soundly shut. Footsteps at his front door, and the fading retreat of shod horses vanishing into the twilight.

When he awoke, Poe was there.

His eyes were large and deep, like those of some huge, faithful dog, but flinty and hard. His face was pale, his cheeks standing out as if from some long fast, making his eyes look as if they were buried in shallow pits dug there in his poor face. But his mouth, below a thick mustache, was pleasant, turning almost into a smile as James roused himself, startled, his book falling from his lap.

"I apologize. I didn't want to awaken you, and since I was expected, I made my own way inside. I didn't mean to frighten you." His voice was solid, real, if somewhat faint, as if husked from lungs unaccustomed to such use.

After a while, James collected his senses enough so that he did not merely sit and stare. He eased to the edge of his seat and looked hard at his visitor, making certain that he was real, that he was not some phantom or a fever dream brought on by his lingering guilt or by his long seclusion from the world. When he felt he could, he asked the question.

"Why are you here?"

Poe remained where he was, stationed in front of one of the larger bookshelves that began at the doorway and ended at a spot less than two feet from the hearth. He turned his eyes from James Allyson and let them roam over the spines bulging out at him. His hand went up, feeling the fabrics and the inks, his pale skin stark against the darker colors of the volumes he touched. "I will tell you, James. But not yet, not now. For the time, I ask only for your hospitality, and that you allow me to read these works. . . . I wish to inspect them."

"The books." James looked at the small man who gazed stiffly up at the volumes.

"Yes. Will you allow it?"

There was no hesitation. "Of course."

And the stiffness went out of Poe, so that he seemed almost to wilt at the utterance. But quickly, quickly, he reached up, apparently at random, and he took down the first book that met his fingertips. He looked at the title, at the name of its author, and he sat back in the blue chair that was to his left, and he began to read in the failing light.

Before Poe could ask how, James went to the lamp that stood beside the blue chair, and he switched it on. Poe looked up at him, no words passing his lips, but the gratitude was there in his eyes.

After that initial exchange, Poe traded no words with his host. And as if understanding that nothing more was expected of him, James made little attempt to engage his guest, except to offer to share the meals James cooked and to indicate where the writer might sleep, should he feel the need for rest.

Both became like ghosts, neither speaking nor indicating a desire for communication. Allyson moved softly about the house, going from room to room, pausing to prepare his meals, from time to time checking to make sure that Poe needed nothing. Occasionally, he would go and stand expectantly at the threshold of the den, waiting for word from the mystery who had come to exist beneath his roof. Always, he would merely stand and watch, waiting for the words that wouldn't come. For Poe would only sit, unmoving except for his hands, which quickly turned the pages of the books that he consumed, going through them one long shelf at a time.

And he did read them. He went through that initial shelf more swiftly than James would have thought possible. His eyes darted over the pages, and his white-skinned fingers turned the papery leaves at a quickening pace that began to grow more and more bothersome to James as the days passed slowly by. And James began, bit by bit, to become annoyed with his guest.

If Allyson had to be host to this uncalled wraith, then he must certainly be allowed to know the why and how of this visitation. He tried to bury himself in one book or another, to try to forget that Poe was there until such time as Poe made good on his agreement to allow James to know the why. He decided to go to Poe's work, to drown himself in Poe's fiction, searching there for the reason behind it all. But he found nothing. No great revelation came to him, and the deep, dark melancholy of it all seemed to only increase his growing impatience, to begin to slowly turn it into something approaching anger.

And just when he thought that his patience was going to rupture, Poe spoke.

"Soon," he said. "Allow me just a little more time."

After that, James shut himself up in his room. He came out only to eat and to bathe, and he no longer made meals that were large enough for two. Before, Poe had shared the food with James. Now, though, James did not notice if his guest ate at all. And he did not know if hunger ever gripped the man, for he merely avoided the small figure so that the not-quite-welcome presence didn't turn James's emotions again toward anger.

James did notice when Poe had read all of the books in the den. For at night he would hear him as he left the room with its great bookshelves, so that he could go to the other rooms and retrieve the books that were stored in them. James bit down on his impatience, trying not to let the resentment turn to hate. He tried very hard. And then the image of his parents—that nagging question.

At last, he could not take any more.

One dark morning, James awoke. He didn't bother to bathe or to dress in anything more than the same rumpled clothes he had worn the day before. He had to get out of the house, he had to leave so that he could find some vent for his anger before it exploded in the face of his guest. A walk in the forest was what he had needed, some fresh air and a short time away from the one who sat reading in his home, wearing thin what welcome there had been.

It was dark out, but he had chosen quite an early hour to rise. He went to the front door and had his hand placed firmly on the brass knob there. Peering through the glass panes and into the darkness, he saw, and his hand froze on the tarnished metal.

Outside, it was snowing; but the silent fall was not of frozen water. Ash was falling silently from the sky, so that James could see little else but the constant flow of the sooty stuff. What trees he could see were half buried, their trunks bare poles standing amidst it all. The fall of it had near buried his house to a point above the sash of his windows but below the eaves of the roof. He turned the docrknob, and the click was so loud that it seemed a rifle shot in the silence.

"I would not do that," Poe said from behind, causing James's heart to skip a beat. "If you opened the door now, it would just get in. And then where would you be?"

Allyson took his hand from the door and leaned against it, his fingers to his mouth, trying to stifle the gasp that had come to him. Poe stood in the threshold of the den, staring at James with that same burning gaze with which he had arrived. James looked to the shelves above the counter, and he saw that the door there was opened wide, that the lock had been forced. There was the faint stench of liquor in the close air of the room. The drink. James had not thought that Poe would search for it.

James stared first at the broken cabinet, and then at the hardened eyes of the one who waited in front of him.

"Are you ready to know? Now?"

Although his lips fluttered as if he were speaking, no sound came from James's mouth.

Poe took another step toward him. "I thought not." He stopped and let the bottle drop from his grasp. "But I am going to tell you, whether you want to hear it or not.

"Sit down." Poe indicated one of the straight-backed chairs that sat about the table James's father had built long ago. Allyson did as he was told, looking up at who stood still in the doorway to the den. There was a long silence as Poe seemed to be waiting, as if listening to the silent fall of the earth outside the house, burying the pair of them in their cozy tomb.

"My life was a horror. From my birth to my death, it was a horror. You cannot know what it was like to be me.

"I attempted to tell the world what it was to struggle against what I faced. I wanted the world to know, just a little, what I suffered. I wanted it to know the failure, and I wanted it to taste the sorrow, and I wanted it to feel the complete sadness that filled my days.

"And, perhaps, I did that, to some measure. Perhaps some who read my work do know what I felt, what pain my art revealed. But . . ."

Then Poe's gaze was fixed on James where he cowered, his back against the wood, the dead man before him. "But I never was rewarded with seeing the actual horror written on another's face as life had written it on mine. I wanted them to feel it, but I never experienced their fear, their revulsion.

"And then. I learned of you. And that is why I returned, and that is why I chose you, and that is why I will see now what I could never see in life."

With each word Poe was a step closer, and with each step his flesh seethed and decayed until the thing that stood heaving, inches from James, seemed to be animated as much by the constant action of the maggots that writhed in its pudding flesh as from any commands coming from whatever brain lay in that dissolving skull. "Show me, James. Show me." And Poe's ripe hands clutched about his host's face, drawing it close to his lidless eyes so that he could see what was etched there as he planted a kiss upon Allyson's lips.

When James awoke, he was lying in his bed. He opened his eyes. His window was wide, the screen letting in the cool breeze that evening had brought with it. By his bed, Poe sat, looking whole again, and very sad.

"I am sorry, James. If it could have been another, so be it. But it was you, and you chose yourself as surely as we did."

James merely lay where he was, and the fear in his eyes must have been evident.

"Don't be afraid. I have done what I came to do, and now I will leave. I . . . I thank you. I realize it must mean nothing to you, but I thank you. It's all that I have." He rose then, and James could see that Poe held a book in his hands. James recognized the dark green jacket.

"There is one thing that I can give you. I should like to warn you that someone else is coming. There is another who is coming to visit you. He wrote rather well, and I can only imagine what singular visions he will conjure here.

"Good-bye, James. Don't hate them. They only told us of your admiration."

Even as Poe vanished, fading into nothing, James knew that he should flee. But night was falling, and there was some comfort to be had in the security of four solid walls. Outside, though, in the coming gloom, the forest was alive with the call of whippoorwills.

Gingerly, James reached out and felt at the book, peering through teary eyes at Lovecraft's name stamped there in black ink. Waiting, he cried softly as the bird noise increased to a scream. He thought of his parents, wondering if he should curse them.

THE INVISIBLE EMPIRE

James Van Pelt

What the beginning of my tale must do is to convince you that
a man of science like myself could do what I did at the end. I
don't know if I can. Some actions are too hard to explain.
Maybe it was the fever born of living in a foreign land. Maybe
Charlie Crump and his superstitions affected me. Perhaps I actually became insane for a moment. All I can tell you is that
the events are true, and for what it's worth, I did what I did.

It started with young Colonel Thomas Montgomery, eyes
bleary with drink, sitting on the edge of the vertical shaft that
stretched down into the Epitome. He was facing me as I
cranked the windlass that lowered a bucket carrying four Negro miners a hundred feet down into the tunnel.

When I'd arrived in the Colorado Territory two weeks earlier, Montgomery had squinted at me from under his hat.
"What kind of black boy are you?"

"I'm mulatto," I'd said a bit stiffly, *and quite a bit better educated than you*, I thought.

"Neither fish nor fowl, eh?" He scowled.

Now, only fourteen days later, the colonel seemed to have
forgiven me for my African mother. I believe he found in my

English accent a sign of kinship not present in my American cousins.

"Surly bastards," he said, gesturing toward the men, now vanished below. "Before I surrendered with the Western Army in North Carolina, Jonas, they were *properly* scared of me. Hell, Charlie Crump served as my houseboy." Charlie Crump was the crew chief, a likable man of twenty-five or so, about my age. He'd tipped his hat at a jaunty angle and grinned at me as I lowered the crew. Montgomery rolled a whiskey bottle between his palms. Only a swallow or two remained. I concentrated on holding the bar against the cable's tension. If the bucket jerked, it could spill the miners.

Looking into the shaft, he said, "I should have become a raider. There would be glory in that." He pulled a drink from his bottle. "For my service, the Confederate government gave me one Mexican dollar for food, and a mule to get home on. You know what I found there? Do you? Surly, superstitious, brown bastards from pantry to parlor. No Klan then. I should go back, you know. Give them a bit of the white sheet. Give them a bit of the ghost. You can scare a man into better behavior. Nothing like a little terror to keep him awake at night. Better than guns. Better than nooses." He sounded introspective suddenly. Very quiet. "Plant an imp in a man's head, and he'll walk always in darkness."

I nodded. Some variation of this story came whenever he drank, and he hadn't missed a day since I joined him. Now he was worse than usual, swearing more, slurring his speech.

But keeping the bucket ride smooth was my job now, not listening. They didn't warn me at Oxford's School of Mines about drunken, Southern expatriate owners who knew nothing about hard-rock mining. He tunneled on whims, overworked his crews, and stored blasting powder too near the machinery. Reading American authors—Nathaniel Hawthorne, Ralph Waldo Emerson, and Edgar Allan Poe—hadn't prepared me for this land either. Well, perhaps Poe, who wrote, "There are moments when, even to the sober eye of Reason, the world of our sad Humanity may assume the semblance of Hell."

Across the canyon, a puff of smoke billowed from the Daedelus. A few seconds later the explosion echoed sharply. Up and down the gulch, yellow tailing piles marked the slopes. Powder blasts resounded regularly, and when no wind rattled through the trees, the sound of hammers on drills filled the air. Below, tents and rude log structures occupied nearly every flat spot, and in the middle, Clear Creek oozed like muddy soup.

I wasn't thinking about the colonel, though. In my mind's eye, I pictured the shafts and drifts and crosscuts underground. One hundred and eighty feet down, we had hit water. If we were to go lower, we'd need pumps or a drainage tunnel.

More troublesome, however, was the cavity in Bernice, the middle of three coyote tunnels Montgomery had extended. A miner lost a hand drill while setting a powder charge the day before. He'd placed the drill, whacked it twice, and the third time it had disappeared into the hole. He'd fled, blubbering about witches and demons. Now none of the men would go into Bernice. I went down by myself and widened the cavity until it was large enough to extend a lantern into. When I did so, no light reached walls or ceiling, and when I pitched a rock through, it clattered once against something, then made no other sound as it fell. Suddenly I'd felt nauseated. My light dimmed, and I backed out. Bad air.

How could there be a natural cavern in granite? This was a conundrum more interesting than any story I'd heard from the colonel.

Still he droned on, "I didn't *have* a home to go to. That damned Sherman gave the land over for slave occupation. Camp followers, the whole cursed lot. I could see the Atlantic from my porch, you know, the clipper ships. I remember their sails, full of the sea breeze. It's been two years, now. You think they've grown a decent crop yet? You think they can care for themselves without proper direction? Might as well have burned the building to the ground."

"You did well with your dollar, sir," I said absently. The bucket would be nearly to the new shaft now. I waited for the signal. One bell meant "stop" or "lower the bucket." Two meant "bring it up."

"Investors," he said, leaning over the hole. From where he sat he would be able to see the men's candles eighty feet down, if the air was clear. "Not *everything* ended in Yankee banks." He flicked a pebble over the edge. I cringed. If it hit one of the men, it could sting. They were runaways who'd fled west during the war. That's all Montgomery hired. At first I thought it was because he could pay them less than white miners, but now I think it was his hatred of them. He relished the chance to make their lives miserable.

He swung his feet out of the shaft, and stood. "The air's too dry here. Too damn thin. The work's dangerous. The gold, what there is of it, is impossible to dig out, and what I ship to the stamper mill is stolen. I can't get a decent breath that doesn't smell of Chinese, Yankees, and darkies." He paced around the shaft, the empty bottle dangling from his hand, a dangerous scowl in his eye. "Did you see how they looked at me before they went down? Insolent. Pure disrespect. In Atlanta white women walk in the street because the Negroes won't give way, and the law, Northern law, protects them. Used to be they knew their place."

I watched the bell, a hammer strung next to a panning plate. When they tugged on the cord, the hammer struck the metal. They were working the new dig, and I didn't have the cable marked for the proper depth, so I relied on them to signal me to stop their descent.

After I'd explored the odd cavity down in Bernice, I'd spent most of the afternoon in the Epitome collecting samples from the shaft walls. Before I'd arrived, the colonel had found the main vein, much thinner than he hoped it would be. Several tunnels followed it through the mountain, the coyote tunnels, so named because they were exploratory, not like the engineered shafts I was used to seeing. The support timbers gave me nightmares, roughly hewn beams jammed haphazardly into place. A good nudge would knock any one of them down. My first day in the mine, while Charlie gave me a tour, a foot-wide support timber fell over, nearly smashing my foot. Neither of us had touched it. Charlie grinned and wedged it against the floor and ceiling. I'm not claustrophobic, but the Epitome gave me shivers. The mountain's weight hung over me. The ore was low grade, too. Colonel Montgomery hoped for better luck at other levels, which is why he'd hired me. "Expertise," he had said, "solves problems."

I'd noted the promising spots. The assay numbers were posted on a beam by the windlass. I studied them. The rock was thick with quartz, but it was difficult to tell with small samples what bore gold thread and what was worthless bull quartz. I ignored the colonel as he continued his rant. Work went better when he stayed in his tent farther down the mountain or rode his horse into Blackhawk where there was a proper saloon, with wood floors and glass in the windows.

The hammer clanged once. I leaned against the bar, stopping the bucket's descent. The colonel stood on the shaft's edge again, his back bent, looking down. At first I didn't realize what he was doing, his posture seemed so odd, as if he were praying. Then I saw: He held a rock the size of a human head. He swayed a little, from the weight or the drink I couldn't tell. I opened my mouth to speak—I have no idea what I would have said—but he lurched forward and pitched the rock into the opening before I could speak. Whatever I might have uttered stayed frozen in my throat. The colonel stood perfectly poised, his hands empty, while the rock—it must have weighed fifty pounds—hurtled down the shaft.

The retarding bar jumped out of my grip. I didn't hear the rock hit. Everything seemed silent, but I felt it in my hands, the vibration leaping up the cable and through the bar. The windlass spun a half turn before I grabbed the bar to stop it.

Stunned, I looked at the colonel. He never raised his eyes. If he had, the spell might have been broken, but he stood like a dusty statue, head down. Behind him the mountain rose steeply. Pine spotted the slope, clinging to gaps between dark granite outcrops. A lone bird, a hawk, glided overhead at a level with the ridge's top. I held the bar, the vibration no longer alive in my fingers, the metal a deadly still, cold weight against my hand.

Two bells. I watched the hammer, not believing it had moved. Two bells again, insistently.

I started the laborious process of bringing the bucket up.

The colonel stepped back, dusted off his hands, then strode past me. "I'm getting a drink. You tell those men I don't pay salary if they're aboveground." His voice was absolutely steady.

Time crept as I turned the windlass. They didn't ring the bell again, and they made no noise. I'd almost convinced myself that the rock must have missed. Maybe it clanged off the bucket's rim. They were just scared. The walls weren't steady if rocks were falling off, they'd be thinking. They wouldn't suspect the rock had been dropped intentionally. Who would toss a stone down a mine shaft on purpose? They were frightened and coming up to tell me we needed to stabilize the walls.

The buckle holding the bucket to the cable appeared, then the men. Three held one like a broken toy. Blood soaked them all. At first I didn't recognize what I was seeing. They've covered his head, I thought. Why would they do that? But his head wasn't covered. That *was* his head, not head-shaped any-more, and his shoulder hung awkwardly. They didn't move, the three men, they just held him, as if by supporting him they could put him back together.

I shifted my gaze down. On the bucket's edge a deep dent bent the metal. A single bloody drop and a clump of hair marked the dent.

"We need a mortician," Charlie Crump said. All the Ne-groes spoke with thick accents, but this was clear. He didn't ask for a doctor. He didn't ask what happened. He just held his dead companion. "We have to be burying," Charlie said. They carefully lifted the dead man from the bucket and laid him be-side the shaft. I covered the corpse with a tarp.

One of them said to another, "It's dat debil man again."

"This has happened before?" I said, unable to take my gaze from the lump under the tarp.

They nodded.

There was no constable in Veronica Falls, which wasn't a full-fledged settlement yet like Idaho Springs or Central City, so I walked along the cart trail to the jailhouse in Idaho Springs, about a five-mile trip. The air smelled of blasting powder and shook with explosions. Sawing, hammering, cursing.

Enduring their angry stares, I stepped aside for men on horseback or leading mules, hauling supplies in huge baskets draped over their backs. The farther west I'd gone from Boston, the worse this country had become. Boston, at least, had re-tained a sense of civility. A man wearing a jacket over a white shirt with starched collar would be considered properly attired. Here, I couldn't tell if it were the color of my skin or my style of dress that attracted so much attention. It cost fifty cents a shirt to have them laundered, which was what I paid for them new, but a person had to keep an appearance of dignity about him or be reduced to the barbaric. Men lying in open tents, waiting for their shifts, stared at me.

Signs advertising tools and dry goods hung from log buildings that weren't even chinked yet. I could see tables and chairs through the cracks in the walls.

"You're that fancy, European mining engineer Montgomery's hired on, ain't ya? Heard you were a bit of a dandy. Didn't know you were a black fella, not that you're all that dark," said the sheriff, sitting on a stool outside his cabin, which also served as a jail. "What are you, some kind of Arab?"

"I'm British," I said.

Like everyone else in the camps, he was desperately in need of a bath. Grease and dirt stained his shirt so heavily, I couldn't tell what pattern it was. I don't know why I thought I would get justice from a man such as this.

"Did anyone else see this happen?" he asked. "How 'bout the colored boys. They see it?"

I shook my head.

He rubbed his hand down his beard. "I've been out to Montgomery's claim before. Heard a rumor, but the darkies wouldn't answer questions. You being foreign, I reckon you don't understand how things work around here. We need proper, believable witnesses to make an arrest."

"I saw it," I said.

He rubbed his beard some more. "There is that," he said, "but it's just you. One witness won't do."

"That's outrageous! If Montgomery came to you saying I dropped a rock down the shaft, would he need a corroborator?"

The sheriff laughed. "Of course not. He's white, even if he is a Rebel."

My mind reeled at this turn of events. "I thought the War Between the States was supposed to emancipate the Negro race."

He seemed to think that over, then said, "We freed 'em. That doesn't make them the same as everyone else. I hear the plan is to round them all up and ship them back to where they came from."

"Are you going to arrest Montgomery or not?"

"Look, I don't like him any better than the next man, but there's no use in me going up there if there's no case. You could be mistaken. It'd be your word against his. If he's stupid enough to kill his own crew, then he won't last long out here. Anyway, miners die all the time. If I'd had any sense, I'd have bought a hearse instead of a mining kit. That way I'd be one of the few to *make* money from digging holes."

I left his cabin. By then the day was nearly done, and the tree stumps cast long shadows behind them. When I got to Veronica Falls, night had fallen, stars glittered in the dark blue sky. Lanterns lit mine entrances in the slopes above, while silhouetted forms sat in glowing tents along the creek. Woodsmoke filled the valley, carrying the smell of cooked beef and vegetables. It had been six months since I left London, and I missed the rain-washed streets, the pubs, the way boat lights reflected on the broad Thames, waiting for the tide to turn. I missed an enlightened city where even a street urchin's death deserved an investigation.

I made my way toward my quarters in Brown Town, where the Negroes, Chinese, and Mexicans pitched their tents. Montgomery's crew tent might have been made for ten men, but twenty-four slept there. Generally eight-man teams worked the Epitome in round-the-clock shifts, so we weren't stacked on top of one another all the time. Nonetheless, it made even the primitive conditions of the Pakistani gold dig where I'd worked with my Oxford mentors look palatial by comparison. No native servants taking our laundry in the evening here. No break for tea in the afternoon, even if field rationing had meant boiling the leaves twice.

Somewhere in the dark, a gunshot echoed. Then two more. I shuddered and drew my coat closer. Americans!

I'd spent nearly all my money to get to Montgomery's mine. In our correspondence he'd promised to reimburse my traveling expenses, but now he said I needed to "earn it out." If I quit his employment, I'd have no way to get home again. But I swore to myself then, as I wandered up the darkened cart path, Clear Creek gurgling in my ears, that I would stand in harm's way rather than let him hurt another miner. Accidents can happen both directions. There are many ways a man can be killed in the Colorado mine fields.

A strange scene greeted me in the crew tent. Rather than the still forms of men bedded down for the evening, I saw a circle of heads bent over an oil lantern. They chanted low, deep words that made no sense to me. It might have been nonsense, but it sounded like language. The lantern lit the faces nearby, serious, white eyes, flashes of teeth. Charlie Crump saw me. He pushed his way out of the circle, grabbed my arm, and took me from the tent.

"I must ask you this question," he said. Of course, it was in his Southern dialect that sounded to my ear like, "I mus' as' ya dis question. What kind of person is ya?"

This confused me. "I'm an academic, an educated man," I offered.

The men in the tent still chanted, and I could not shake the sense of unreality. He said, "No, I mean are you for Master Montgomery, or are you for us?"

I didn't have to think to answer. "He must not kill again."

Charlie nodded. "Master Montgomery is a devil." Charlie's voice dropped, and he moved closer, as if he was afraid to say the words loudly. "He is in league with the Invisible Empire. He boasts of it. If we are not respectful, if we forget that the white man is master, then we will be punished. He took tokens from all of us and made evil signs so we could not leave."

In the darkness outside the tent, I looked around. The stream still gurgled, and pans rattled against pans in another tent down the hill. Rough laughter came from the opposite direction. Everything still appeared real and definite. Even Charlie's hand grasping my arm felt solid, but it seemed as if I'd entered another world, where Satan and madmen coexisted. I shook my head in sudden understanding and said, "No, no. That's the Klan. Montgomery is part of a group that terrorize freedmen so that you will be slaves again. There is no invisible empire."

Charlie whispered vehemently, "I have seen its messengers in Carolina. Ghosts on horses with fire in their eyes and lightning at their hooves."

"Men in sheets," I said, a part of me wondering if it were true.

"He means to kill us all. The mine holds no gold, so he is returning home. Before then he will make a sacrifice to the empire. He's told me when he was drunk. He'll seal the mine with all the men in it." Charlie squeezed my arm harder. "We have his book of spells. He collects witchy papers that he keeps locked in a trunk, but I have the key. I've always had the key. If we are to beat a devil, we must use his own magic against him."

Charlie glanced around, and he spoke so nervously I thought Montgomery might jump out from behind a bush any moment. "While he was away at the war, a special book was delivered to the house. It came in the middle of the night. The courier wasn't human. I saw him. His cloak slipped when he handed me the book, and I saw his demon eye." Charlie shuddered, as if he faced the man now. "I have that book, but I cannot read it. Will you read it for us?"

So it was that I found myself back in the tent, crouched before the lantern, the black miners surrounding me as Charlie handed me the volume. Its cover crackled unpleasantly against my hand. The men hummed in their throats like huge bees, pressing against me when I opened to its first page. In the lamp's yellow light, I could barely make out the spidery writing. "It's in Spanish," I said. Fortunately I read Spanish well, along with French and Latin. Many of the best mining texts are in Spanish. I canted the book toward the lantern to show the letters better.

The title was *El Libro de los Normos de los Perdidos*, and below that was the date, 1579. "It says the author was Miguel Cervantes. *Upon My Captivity in Algiers*. Ah, not the author, the translator." I wondered if this was the same Cervantes of *Don Quixote* fame. I turned to the next page carefully, although the nearly two-hundred-year-old paper seemed supple. I only read a few lines before I came upon an epigraph, which I translated out loud, " 'That is not dead which can eternal lie / and with strange aeons, even death may die.' " The lantern guttered and nearly went out.

"Do not say the black magic words, Master Jonas," Charlie hissed.

His beliefs, which would under any other condition provoke incredulity, chilled me. The men leaned away, some with their hands over their ears, still humming. Their fear and sweat hung in the air.

I nodded my assent and read on silently. This was no Christian superstition. Nothing of witchcraft in this book. It was cosmology and history and strange references to monarchs or gods with unrecognizable names who existed as exiled sovereigns. Most of it I didn't understand, but my bile rose while reading, and I felt the same kind of nausea I'd felt in the Bernice. Is it possible that there is the equivalent of bad air in words? "There are incantations here for calling forth a creature known as the lurker at the threshold. See, there are notes in the margins." My finger shook while pointing. Charlie moved to where he could see.

"You will have to tell us how to speak it."

"The notes are a warning, not a translation but commentary from Cervantes. He says, 'Under sanity's blanket lies chaos.' Then he writes, 'The spell of summoning costs a human life. Yog-Sothoth consumes.' "

One of the men started shaking. His lips drew back from his teeth, and his teeth ground together. Eyes rolled back so there were only white marbles in his head. He collapsed, falling slowly between the men crammed so close together. No one paid him heed. They continued their moaning, rocking back and forth. I looked down at my hand on the page. For an instant, it seemed the spidery writing glowed black on the paper, as if the volume couldn't contain the letters anymore, and the ink wasn't ink at all, but thin slits to nothingness behind them.

I dropped the book and fled from the tent.

When the sun rose, I was still walking. My agitated pacing had taken me past Idaho Springs, past the stamper mills and abandoned sluice troughs. Down river, below the town, broken equipment sat in piles beside the path. As the sky lightened, I saw first the black holes opened into the mountain, lost claims, dead-end shafts that led to nothing, abandoned when their owners ran out of money or patience, left as futile evidence. In my exhaustion, I fancied the mountain was a great face and the mines were eyes. If eyes are the window to the soul, then the mountain's soul was blank and heartless. No compassion twinkled in those inanimate sockets. I thought about the tunnels burrowing through the canyon's sides, some beneath me, miles and miles of lightless passage stretching through the rock.

During my life in mining, I had never thought of mountains this way, not the way I did that morning after reading Cervantes's horrifying translation. For me, a mountain had presented itself as a beautiful, ages-long story. An open, striated cliff face, bands on bands of mineral and different colored rock told a geologic narrative, as moving as any of Shakespeare's greatest plays, as epic as Homer's *Odyssey*. But that day I didn't see them as lovely. The yellow tailing piles seemed pestilent, as if the mountain oozed with sores. From one end of the valley to the other, no trees hid the granite bones. Only stumps until just below the ridges, and if the mining continued, those would be gone, too. The creek splashed up ocherous, scummy water where no fish could live.

I would stop Montgomery, then leave this terrible valley, where black miners trusted frightening books and a crazy Confederate dropped rocks on his men.

But as the sky grew lighter, and the sun crept down the mountain wall, my fears lessened. Montgomery was evil, this was true, but last night's performance in the tent had had nothing to do with him. Perhaps I had a touch of fever myself. Who knew what diseases passed from man to man in these filthy conditions? Certainly nothing I'd seen in London, where a doctor was no more than a few blocks away, at the worst.

I'd deal with Colonel Montgomery, and I'd do it without "supernatural" aid. But I could use his own fears against him, his ignorance of the mines. What man would own a collection of witchcraft and superstitious drivel who didn't believe in it at least a little? No wonder he wanted to scare the Negroes. He was nearly heathen himself.

All I needed was preparation, and then to get him into the claim.

"You need to see the vein yourself," I said, holding the gold-threaded quartz in my hand. "It's the richest ore I've ever seen."

Montgomery lounged in his chair like a slothful cat, his arms draped back over the low top, his feet on the table next to the open bottle. Behind him, his travel cases lined the tent's walls, each with a huge clasp lock. Charlie told me that some contained liquor, but books filled many, his entire collection of supernatural studies. From what I remembered of American history, if Montgomery had been caught with the same books in Salem in 1692, he would have been hanged.

His feet came off the table.

"Give it to me," his whiskey-roughened voice growled. He found a hand lens in the desk's clutter to examine the pebbles. At length, he said, "This came from my mine?" The lens magnified his eye into a black ball as lifeless as those dead-end shafts I'd seen that morning.

"There's a cavity at the end of Bernice. I wanted to find out how deep it was, so I chipped a wider opening. It wasn't until I got to the surface that I thought to look at the stone I'd removed. I exposed a band the same as that at least six feet wide. It could rival anything in California." I tried to sound optimistic, but not overeager.

Montgomery bent over the rocks again. "We'll need to do an assay to be sure. I want to inspect it first, though. Get Charlie Crump to run the bucket. I don't trust any of the others."

He noticed my hesitation.

"Oh, Charlie has been with me a long time. I swore to him if anything ever happened to me, I'd haunt him. These African folk are big on hauntings. Very simple that way, so don't worry about riding down with me."

As we took the steep path to the shaft, Charlie bringing up the rear, Montgomery said to me, "You're not superstitious, are you? A man died in here yesterday. Lot more ghosts than him in this mine." He laughed, and I remembered what the sheriff had said about coming out to this claim before. How many other "accidents" had there been?

"Are *you* worried about ghosts, Colonel? I don't remember you in the tunnels before."

His hand went to his chest, feeling something under his

shirt. "I don't believe in ghosts, Jonas. A schooled man like yourself should know better. It's the coloreds who live in a spiritual world. That's why the Klan is so effective. Properly funded, they will win back the South." He paused, then said without irony, "Just in case, though, I wear a warding. My kitchen woman made it for me years ago. If there were ghosts, it would keep them off. Belts and suspenders is what I always say. Besides, the richest gold strikes in history are associated with tragedy. The Buluma deposits in Austria were discovered after a cave-in killed fourteen miners. The ancient Egyptian kings shored up their mine walls with slave bodies. The greatest treasures in the world were founded on death."

Charlie made no noise as he followed. I couldn't help but think of him last night, as I read from the book, eyes wide, too frightened for me even to read the words out loud. Belief is a powerful thing. Charlie and the others believed in haunts and witchings and ritual. I'd seen them pinch spilt salt to toss it over their shoulders. I'd seen one man spin counterclockwise three times after accidentally killing a spider. I'd seen the small sacks they wore round their necks, filled with little bones and bits of feather.

I'd seen mine owners, too, on a hunch pouring thousands of dollars into worthless projects in the belief their fortune resided only a few feet deeper. I'd seen prayers said over open pits, hoping divine intervention would place wealthy deposits in that day's diggings.

That's what I learned to resist during my geologic studies. Minerals congregated when the conditions were right. No belief or ritual would put gold ore where the geologic conditions weren't favorable. Science guaranteed success where faith could not. That was why I studied Earth's stony mysteries and turned away from men, like Montgomery, who were too puzzling to fathom. I longed to return to the classroom. Perhaps I could become a lecturer in England, where a man of learning would be respected for his education and not be relegated to sleeping in Brown Town because he wasn't white.

I reached for the square shape in my ore bag. The book was there. If this worked, the men would be rid of Montgomery one way or another. No matter what, when I left, their lot would be better.

If I'd felt my brow then, would I have felt fever? The plan was insane. The sheriff in Idaho Springs wouldn't arrest Montgomery, but there was law farther east. I could write to the magistrates in Kansas City. Still, we pressed on.

My memory of the trek up the hill is filled with garish color: igneous rocks so dark no shadow showed on them, clouds bleached as if the sky had been erased and the stark parchment of the universe shown through. More than once I stumbled. Granite scree imbedded itself in my palm. I put my mouth against the wound and sucked.

Charlie manned the windlass. Montgomery lit an oil lantern, a luxury he never allowed the miners. They carried shadowgees, tin cans or buckets shaped to hold candles. I stepped into the bucket beside him. Overhead, the noon sun beat down, but a cool draft blew from the mine. The cavity at Bernice's end must be vast indeed to push this much air from the tunnel.

I nodded to Charlie, and he unlatched the windlass. The headframe pulley creaked as the cable played out. Ground rose to our eye level as we started the long descent. Crudely carved granite walls replaced the sun-washed mountainside in our view. Montgomery bumped me when the bucket lurched. "Be more careful, you charcoal buck!" he shouted to Charlie. In the shaft's close confines, his voice resounded. The lantern smoked and stank. He hadn't properly trimmed the wick. He smelled of unwashed clothes and old liquor. I half hoped Charlie would drop a stone himself. Surely providence would cause it to hit him and not me. I looked up. The opening glowed like a white-hot coin.

"If this ore assays out, we'll hire more crew," he said. "Cornish miners who know what they're doing. Not this shiftless crowd of buffalo heads. My investors, my *Southern* investors, will be very happy."

"Always proper to turn a profit, sir," I said to keep his suspicions away. Would he notice the new timberwork in Bernice?

At seventy feet we passed the northward-wandering Agnes, the oldest of the Epitome's three tunnels and the only one with track for ore carts. As always, I grimaced at the few support pillars the light illuminated. They were ill-fitted, coarse beams that needed to be hammered back into place periodically as the uncured wood contracted.

At 110 feet, Charlie stopped the bucket with nary a jostle, only a foot shy of Bernice's floor. We stepped out. Montgomery's oil lantern cast a much brighter light than the candle in my shadowgee. I checked my pockets. There were plenty more candles there, not that I expected to use them all.

"You should lead, sir," I said.

Bernice bore northeast into the mountain, following quartzy rock in a zigzag fashion for hundreds of feet. We passed short exploratory adits, horizontal tunnels that petered out in a few yards. The farther in we went, the lower the ceiling became. I kept one hand above my head, running it across the rough rock. Something felt wet, and I brought my fingers down to the light. They glistened from seep. I'd seen no sign of water this high in the Epitome before. I rubbed my fingers together. The water was slimy, and the tunnel smelled fetid. I wiped my hand hard against my pants.

Soon we were bent at the waist. Even shrouded in glass, Montgomery's lamp flickered from Bernice's steady, moist exhalation. The light surrounded him in a circle, while his black form eclipsed the lantern itself. He passed two newly hewn timbers without pausing. I stopped. The cavity was only thirty yards farther around another bend. Over his head, fresh boards covered the ceiling for ten feet. He didn't even remark on the change. Perhaps he never had been in his own mine. I put my shadowgee in a niche on the wall, waited until Montgomery went past the corner, then kicked the first support under the new boards. It didn't move. I kicked it again. What if he heard? What if he discovered me at work? Maybe I'd miscalculated the weight. I sat, braced my hands behind me and kicked the beam again with both feet. It slid over a few inches, and pebbles dropped from between two boards.

"I don't see your vein," said Montgomery, his voice echoey and small. "Where the blazes are you, Jonas?" The turn in the tunnel brightened. He must be coming back. I scooted closer to the beam and kicked a last time with all my strength. The timber slid another half foot. A board cracked farther along. More dust dribbled from the ceiling. Montgomery's lantern came around the corner, and I reared back for one more desperate kick, but I didn't need it. With a loud pop, the center board snapped and rock roared into the tunnel.

Instinctively, I rolled away, covering my head. Rock on rock makes a particular sound, a crisp clack. For several seconds, lying on the stone floor, I heard the rocks hitting one another, clack, clack, clack. There was dust.

It took me a minute to light a new candle. Broken rock choked the tunnel closed from floor to ceiling, and shards reached to my feet. If I had not moved, the cave-in would have killed me. The flame bent toward the shaft. My blockage hadn't stopped air flow. If my calculations were correct, there was no more than twelve feet between Montgomery and myself. Of course, he wouldn't know that. He'd have no way of knowing if the entire drift had collapsed.

"Montgomery," I called. "Are you still alive, Montgomery?" I placed my hands on the jumbled rock.

"Thank God!" came his answer, his voice clear through the breakdown. "Jonas, is the drift clear behind you? Can you get help? My leg . . . I'm hurt."

I didn't say anything for a while. He had stood on the edge of a mine shaft and dropped a stone on four men, killing one. I remembered his eyes when he looked up, no different than if he'd stepped on an insect. The breeze blew cool air through the rocks beneath my hands. I let it play off my face. "Who would come to help you, Colonel? Should I call Charlie Crump? How about the other men on the bucket yesterday? Do you think they'll come down the shaft for you?"

No answer.

You may think at this point that surely I meant to kill him, but I didn't. I'd loosened the ceiling, but only enough to fill the passage. Montgomery could dig his way out in a day or two, all the while without light, an unknown cavity looming behind him.

I sat on the floor, extricating the book from my ore bag. It seemed even more repugnant than when I'd held it in the tent the night before. Perhaps the moist air penetrated its cover, or maybe the environment—my heightened senses—affected me, but the tome felt heavier, more gruesome.

"How much oil do you have for your lamp, Montgomery?" I knew exactly how much he had: no more than half an hour's worth.

Rocks rattled on the floor. He grunted in pain. I imagined he was trying to remove the fall. Had he seen the cavern at Bernice's end? Even a man of limited imagination might conjure up a monster from such a place, and Montgomery was far from limited. I wondered, too, if the bad air had cleared out. The air's movement was brisk enough, but there could still be patches. If they were concentrated enough, they might render him unconscious, possibly kill him.

The book rested on my lap. My single candle cast enough illumination for me to see a few feet of tunnel back to the shaft. All tunnels look the same when you are by yourself. The walls around glow with light, the tiny minerals catching the flame, reflecting it in glisters, but the light fails so soon, and the circle's middle, the tunnel's center stretching in both directions, is darkness like an eye's pupil, surrounded with color, centered in black.

I began reading the words. Somehow they were different underground. Even a rational man like myself can be affected by the mine's solitude, by odd echoes and tinkly drips tapping into unseen pools. Any miner can tell you that a mine is not a quiet place. The silence itself creaks.

"What is that you say?" Montgomery shouted. He sounded frightened and continued to struggle. Stones clattered on his side.

I spoke a bit louder. For this to work, he had to hear what I was reading and realize what it was. The sentences hurt my throat. Saying them was like vomiting.

When I reached the spell's end, I started over.

I finished the second time; there was no sound on the other side. Either Montgomery was resting, or he was listening. He'd said to me once, *Plant an imp in a man's head, and he'll walk always in darkness.* If he was scared to the bone, so scared he'd flee the mines, then his men would be safe.

"Is that the Spanish book?" he yelled.

I took up the chant. Somehow it was easier to say now, and the rhythm fell more naturally.

"Don't read from that one, Jonas! It's not safe, Jonas!" He swore vehemently.

My eyes no longer strained to see the words on the page. Without stopping, I looked up. The candle flamed brighter, unnaturally radiant, and the wax gave way before the assault. It wouldn't last a minute at that rate. Shaking, I drew another from the bag. When lit, it, too, burned like phosphorous. By the light of the twin suns, the pages became transparent, and the text hung suspended, all the words visible at once, but it didn't matter; I wasn't reading anymore. My voice became powerful, not my own, and the spell boomed the tunnel's length.

Montgomery screamed through the stone, his imprecations no longer coherent.

Then, suddenly, all became still. The chanting stopped; I did not stop it. It was as if a presence that had taken me had left. Montgomery cut off a curse in mid-utterance. Since I'd entered Bernice, the candles' flame had bent toward the entrance as the breeze exited the mountain. Now they stood straight up. Then they tilted the other way, as if a new tunnel had opened on Montgomery's side, pulling greedily at the air.

Something was coming.

Montgomery screamed again, a pathetic whine like a kicked mongrel.

"Let me out, boy! Let me out, you goddamned nigger!"

The wind pushed at my back and whistled through the rubble. Whatever lived on the other side drew everything toward it. Fine sand peppered my neck, then disappeared into the broken rock. The first candle went out.

Fear gripped me. The entirety of my being demanded I run away. I felt it in my muscles and bones, an instinctive aversion, but I forced myself to stay. The thing that approached could not be of this world. I imagined it rising from the cavity, flowing into the opening I'd made, filling the small shaft. By lamplight, what did Montgomery see? He uttered a nonhuman screech, then a soggy gasp. Green-limb snapping. Hollow slurping, and Montgomery continued to scream, a mindless, noisy babble.

Finally, there were only wet noises. Moist rippings. Damp slaps.

Rocks slipped from the top of the pile, and the jumbled stack lurched toward me. Twelve feet of rock, four feet wide and high, chocked tightly against the mine's wall slid a foot toward me. There were two or three tons of rock blocking the mine, and it moved!

Frantically, I turned and scrambled down the tunnel on all fours, stood too soon, whapped my head against the ceiling, reeled from wall to wall until I collapsed at the mouth of the tunnel. Behind me, rocks tumbled. The thing beyond was dismantling the blockage. I reached the bucket and climbed in. Weakly I pulled the bell cord twice and prayed that Charlie Crump could pull me up before the thing from the mountain broke through.

No trip in my life was ever longer. As the bucket crept up the shaft; the wind vacuumed me back, whistling by. Slowly, ever so slowly the light at the surface grew larger, while every second I expected a clawed hand or a tentacle to drape itself over the edge, and when I reached the top, I didn't talk to Charlie. Instead, I staggered up the slope to the powder cache.

The explosion shook the entire valley.

By the time I made my way to the tents, a crowd had gathered, a hundred miners, picks resting on their shoulders or shovels at their sides, expecting to hear the news.

"Was anyone in the mine?" someone shouted. "Do they need rescuing?"

I must have presented quite a picture. Blood from the bump on my head streaked my face, my fine coat was torn. Dark smudges marked my white shirt, from starched collar to the belt. They waited for my answer.

"The colonel was in the dig, but no one is alive," I said, finally. "There's no mine left."

Shaking their heads, they slowly dispersed. Soon only the Idaho Springs sheriff stood there, his hands deep in his unwashed pockets.

"I came by today to talk to Montgomery," he said. "Don't seem like I'll get the chance now." No purpose was reflected in eyes shaded under his hat, and I didn't care why he had come. My hands started quivering. My legs lost their strength. I sat on the ground. He sat beside me. A hundred yards downhill, Clear Creek roiled in sullen, muddy, sun-drenched muttering.

"Nobody will miss the bastard," he said.

I tucked my head between my knees, on the verge of sickness. I'd left a monster in the mines. Poor Montgomery. I'd only meant to scare him. What would happen when the next prospector broke through into the cavity? Did the lurker on the threshold always wait there, or did it only appear when someone read the spell? Had it gone back to the nether regions past the stars that Cervantes's book talked about? I could still hear it pulling rocks down, coming toward me.

In the meantime the sun pressed like a warm kiss on my shoulders. The sheriff sat with his hands wrapped round the top of his hobnailed boots.

Finally he said, "Guess you'll have to find another employer. Don't know what luck you'll have, being you are . . . what was it you said you were again?"

I looked up. There are awful things in the world, beneath it, beyond it. The sheriff waited for an answer. I'd thought of him as uneducated, unwashed, white American, but now his fingers laced firmly across his boots, and his hat shaded curious eyes. He had arms, legs, and a familiar torso. Our differences were small. Whatever he was, he wasn't claws or tentacles or a rending thing that rose when called. He wasn't a part of the real invisible empire.

"I'm human," I said.

A VICTORIAN POT DRESSER

L. H. Maynard and M. P. N. Sims

The girl took a deep breath to steady her nerves before approaching the room. Sixteen years old and dressed in a simple white cotton shift, she looked virginal, which appearance was accurate. Her long brown hair had been washed and brushed until it shone in the gaslight. Tonight she had been allowed a bath and, as she lifted her hand to knock on the door, she could smell the delicately perfumed soap on her skin.

Luxuries such as baths were rare in her home, an orderly institution run with a pious hand by her father, the village rector, who preached that cleanliness came from within and only by absolute devotion to God would purity be attained.

But the entire day had been special. She was awakened at five o'clock, when all the other family members were still asleep. The rector's wife, who had married him shortly after the death of the girl's natural mother, took her downstairs to the kitchen, and, instead of the usual breakfast of thin broth supplemented with a wedge of dry bread, she was given two boiled eggs with bread cut thinly and spread liberally with butter. This, she thought, as she dipped a piece of bread into the creamy yellow yolk, is true extravagance. Since then she had been spoiled to an extent that

exceeded all her birthday treats and surpassed even the extrava-
gances occasionally enjoyed at Christmas.

Now it was early evening, with the shimmers of dusk masking
the onset of darkness. She rapped on the stout oak door with her
knuckles.

"Enter," said a voice from within.

She opened the door and stepped into the gloomy interior of
the rector's study.

McQueen led me through the labyrinthine aisles between the
furniture stacked high in his cavernous warehouse.

"I think I might just have something to appeal to you," he
said, glancing back over his shoulder at me.

"You said that last week," I said. "And I wasted a two-hour
drive getting down here for nothing." The dust in the place was
swirling through the air, playing havoc with my sinuses. It
added to my sense of irritation.

"Well, we've done a couple of houses since then, and an
auction over Dorchester way. Picked up a few choice pieces."

Billy McQueen, like his father before him, specialized in
house clearances—buying furniture and other household items
for a pittance and selling them on at a high markup. He dealt
mostly with the antique trade and, over the years, had built
up a thriving business. Some of the finest pieces of furniture that graced the halls and rooms of some of the grandest
houses in the local area had sat gathering dust in the McQueen
warehouse at one time or another. For antiques dealers and
for interior designers like me the place was a treasure trove,
but to let McQueen know it would do serious damage to our
wallets.

We reached the end of an aisle and turned right into another, this one featuring mainly bedroom furniture.

"Now what do you think of this?" McQueen had stopped beside an art deco dressing table—a nice piece, classic deco style, finished in a swirling walnut veneer.

"Very nice," I said. "Can you move those?" I said, pointing to the wardrobes that leaned against one another in precarious support behind the dressing table.

Without hesitation McQueen put his shoulder to one of the obscuring pieces of furniture and pushed it aside. It looked as if my suspicions were about to be confirmed and I felt a tingle in my fingertips. It was a familiar feeling, one I always get when I come across a piece of furniture that's exactly right for my purposes. They need not be valuable pieces, or rare, not even antique, so long as they are *right*.

The second wardrobe squealed and grinded its way across the concrete floor, and the hidden gem was revealed in all its glory.

"Victorian pot dresser," McQueen said. "Brought it in on Wednesday."

A thick layer of dust covered its richly polished oak, and spiders' webs hung from the intricate carvings of corn dollies. The centerpiece, an elaborately carved effigy of a Green Man, was coated with grime, years of wax polish and dust mingling to form a crust that obscured the finer details and flattened the wrinkles and lines, giving it a bland, almost featureless appearance. There were three drawers, all decorated with engraved German silver escutcheons depicting rural scenes. These held the handles, fashioned from the same metal and worked to represent twisted stalks of wheat.

A half-eaten sandwich sat on the dresser in its plastic container, the ham looking decidedly green, the bread showing signs of extreme distress. "Don't you ever clean this place?" I said critically.

" 'Pile it high and never dust.' That's what the old man used to say. The punters like it like this. Makes them feel they're getting a bargain, no matter how much they pay over the odds for it. Now what do you think of the dresser?" He didn't mention that he had stretched his father's concepts a little with a website for the business and sales done over the Internet, as well.

What I thought was that the dresser was exactly right for the kitchen of the house I was currently working on. However, there was no chance I was going to let McQueen know it. "It's okay." I strived for enigmatic nonchalance.

"Six hundred," he said.

I started to walk away, back down the aisle, returning my interest to the art deco dressing table. As diversionary tactics go it wasn't that original. I doubt McQueen was fooled for a moment, but he expected me to play the game. Victorian pot dressers don't come up on the market that often. Over the years they have been used for all manner of purposes in people's houses, but they were originally designed and built to store and display pots. Which was precisely why its place in the kitchen I was currently creating was important to me.

"Five-fifty. That's my bottom line." Suddenly he looked distracted. He turned his head to one side and cupped a hand to his ear. "Can you hear music? Sounds like someone playing an organ."

I ignored him for a moment, then, with a frown, faced him again. "It's not original," I said. "And no, I can't hear a thing."

McQueen looked affronted. "Now, Colin, don't try pulling that one. Of course it's an original. It's got a maker's label, and the original bill of sale is in one of those drawers. So don't give me the old it's-a-fake cobblers."

He pulled at one of the drawers, grasped a piece of paper lying within, and then swore heatedly. The hand he held in the air for my inspection dripped blood from a ragged gash on the knuckles. Blood smeared the dusty surface of the dresser.

"Here, take this." He thrust the paper into my hand. "I'm going to find a sticking plaster."

I walked back over to the dresser and studied it again. It was tall, more than six feet high. "I didn't say it was a fake. I just said it wasn't original. Victorian pot dressers were made without a back to the shelves. This one has a back, and if you look closely you can see that there is still sap seeping from one of the knots. Ergo, it's not original. Two hundred."

I was concerned the blood would mark the wood, so I put the paper into my jacket pocket and took out a handkerchief and leaned over to wipe the dresser clean. But the surface of the wood was untouched. It was still covered in dust, still as grimy as before, but the blood had gone, without leaving a mark, as if it had soaked into the wood.

"Five hundred, and that's my last word." McQueen was back.

The bargaining went on for another ten minutes until we agreed on a price that suited me. With an agreement to have the dresser delivered the next day, I left McQueen grumbling into his beard. I had no sympathy for him, as both he and I knew that he'd made a healthy profit from the deal. As I climbed into my car he was standing in the doorway of his warehouse, head to one side again, hand again cupping his ear. Then he shook his head and disappeared back into the gloom.

Sally Roberts lived in a fashionable part of Islington; in a large, three-story Edwardian house in a quiet mews, which she shared with her husband, Milos, a Czech émigré theatre director, and two Irish wolfhounds called Gielgud and Richardson. It was she who had commissioned me to design her a new kitchen and dining room. I arrived at the house early the next morning so I could prepare the kitchen for the arrival of the dresser. Sally greeted me at the door with Richardson, who nuzzled the pocket of my jacket, sniffing out a roll of mints, the tidbits I had been feeding the dogs throughout the duration of my work at the house.

Sally, as always, looked freshly scrubbed; her English rose complexion flawless and beautiful, all this without a hint of makeup and at seven-thirty in the morning. It was a face that had made her the darling of the tabloid press and society magazines during her brief but sensational career as a fashion model. She had retired from the catwalk at thirty when she met and fell in love with Milos, but even now, five years later, she would have no trouble launching a comeback. Not that she had any desire to. She loved domestic life and was more than happy to play the devoted wife to the man who had stolen her heart.

I followed Sally through to the kitchen. In my absence the day before the electrician had been there to finish wiring the lights and to fit the industrial-size oven chosen by Milos in order to indulge his culinary enthusiasms. The kitchen, as I had designed it, was an eclectic mixture of old and new: an antique pine refectory table with matching settles occupied a place in the center of the quarry-tiled floor, setting off the sleek, modern designs of the cooker, the fridge, and other appliances.

I learned a long time ago that the key to good interior design is sympathetic lighting. I held my breath as I flicked the switch down, praying that my plans for the lights in the kitchen would live up to expectations. I was not disappointed. There were no harsh, flickering fluorescent tubes, no glaring tungsten bulbs, just soft, concealed halogen lights that infused the kitchen with a glowing ambience. The cooking area was brighter and more practical, but the overall effect was calming and restful. I was delighted, as was Sally, which was the main thing.

"We tried it all out last night, after the electrician had gone. Milos cooked me a Czech dish with lamb and rice—it's got a name but I can't pronounce it. You should have seen him, Colin. Like a child with a new toy." She went across to the kettle and switched it on. She moved with an almost feline grace, an economy of movement that made her appear to glide over the quarry tiles. "Tell me about the dresser. I can't wait to see it," she said. "You sounded very excited when you phoned me yesterday." As she stood by the kitchen window, the early morning sun kissed the top of her head, making her short blond hair glow like a halo. Milos was a very lucky man, and I needed to be careful if my feelings were to remain cloaked.

The gloomy interior of the study obscured the corners of the room, but didn't shield the girl's perception that there were other people present. She could see her father standing behind his desk, and seated at it, in front of her father, was the squire.

Like everyone in the village she had heard the stories about the strange things that were said to happen at the Grange, the squire's house. She'd heard the children gossip in hushed tones about the bright lights seen hovering above it at certain times of the month; about the music and the chanting that were sometimes heard; about the misshapen creatures that were said to stalk the grounds after dark and to dwell in the vast cellars beneath the house.

"Martha," her father said, quietly. "A special day has arrived for you. A day on which you can fulfill your destiny."

The girl had received little in the way of education and had scant knowledge of what destiny was. What she did know though, was that the shadows in the corners of the room were pulsating now, and moving closer.

The squire stood and put his hand on a red brocade cloth that was draped over a large object to one side of the desk. With a practiced flourish he pulled the drapes away to reveal a pot dresser—not a plain, ordinary one such as she had seen before, but an ornately carved one with a huge Green Man at the top and other large, blasphemous creatures crawling over the rest of it, as though trying desperately to prise themselves away.

Martha became aware of organ music playing, and she saw

*her father was softly playing a tuneless dirge on the instrument
he kept by the window.*

The dogs heard the van arrive outside even before we did and
began barking furiously.

"Gielgud, Richardson, that's enough!" Sally shouted as she
went through to open the door. Before doing so she grabbed
both of the dogs by the collar and pulled them into the study,
shutting the door behind them.

McQueen's sparkling, new Mercedes van was parked at the
curb. McQueen and a young lad disembarked and opened the
van's rear doors. I watched from the doorway as they removed
the top section of the dresser and set it down in the road. The
bottom half, which contained the drawers, was taken out next
and McQueen and the lad made heavy weather of carrying it
through the front garden and up the concrete steps to the
house. "Don't strain yourself, Colin, will you," McQueen muttered as he carried the piece past me. Sally had gone ahead of
them, opening doors and moving objects that might be in the
way. She kept glancing back at the lower half of the dresser, a
delighted smile on her face.

By the time the top half was carried through, McQueen was
sweating profusely, but the boy had taken off his shirt and was
proudly displaying his muscles, occasionally glancing at Sally
to see if she had noticed. I went into the kitchen to supervise
the positioning, and Sally put the kettle on. When we were
satisfied it was exactly where we wanted it, the lad went to
lock the van up, Sally took the tea and biscuits through to
the lounge, and McQueen and I went into the garden for a
smoke.

A cry of pain and a loud volley of expletives shattered the
tranquillity of the morning.

In the kitchen we found McQueen's lad, Tom, sitting on the

floor, doubled over, his hand pressed to his shoulder. Blood was trickling out from between his fingers.

"What on Earth happened here?" McQueen said to the boy.

"Bloody thing scratched me," Tom said, jerking his thumb at the dresser. When he moved his hand we could see the extent of the damage to his shoulder. There were four parallel scratches running from the top of his arm to the shoulder blade. They were quite deep and dribbling blood.

"It looks nasty," Sally said. "I'll get the first-aid kit from the bathroom."

McQueen was looking at the dresser, rubbing his chin and running his fingers over the smooth wood. "What do you mean, it scratched you?" The skepticism in his voice was a sham, as the sticking plaster on his hand bore witness.

Tom looked up at him, his face still creased with pain. "I was giving it a polish, cleaning it up. I was crouched under there. . . ." He pointed to the space between the drawers and the base. "Next thing I know, something scratches me. Felt like I'd been bitten at first, then I saw the blood."

Sally returned to the kitchen and, crouching down next to the boy, opened the small first-aid kit. "I'll just clean it up," she said to him, pouring some antiseptic onto a ball of cotton wool.

As the antiseptic was applied and the boy swore again, I joined McQueen in his examination of the dresser. "There's nothing sharp here," he said, running his fingers along the wood beneath the drawers. "Nothing, certainly, that could make marks like that."

McQueen went back to the hall, picked up the boy's shirt, and tossed it to him. "Come on, get dressed. We've got a long drive back."

With a groan Tom pushed himself to his feet. He thanked Sally and walked back to the van. With a promise to call me the moment anything interesting came in, McQueen joined the boy in the cab and set off.

When I went back to the kitchen Sally was standing, staring up at the dresser. She had let the dogs out and they were sniffing the piece curiously.

"Well?" I said. "What do you think of it?"

She was silent for a moment, her hand reaching down and stroking Gielgud's ruff. Then she turned to me. "It's perfect, Colin, absolutely perfect. Milos is going to love it." She pulled open the center drawer, running her fingers across the bottom of it, and bringing them up thick with dust. "Young Tom was right. It needs a clean and polish." She stared up at the face carved in the top panel. "I'm not too sure about him though."

"It's a Green Man," I said. "It's meant to be lucky. And the corn dollies are a symbol of—" My display of knowledge about the myths and legends was interrupted.

"Fertility. Yes, I know. I don't think I'll tell Milos that. It might give him ideas."

I heard the front door close, followed by Milos's booming voice calling hello.

"In the kitchen," Sally called back.

Milos bounced into the kitchen followed by a raven-haired girl in her early teens. Milos embraced his wife, planting a kiss on her cheek, then stuck out his hand to me. "Colin, good to see you," he said, pumping my hand enthusiastically. "You haven't met my daughter, Martina." To the girl he said, "Martina, this is Colin Gould, the genius who has designed this wonderful kitchen."

The girl was crouching down, petting the dogs, which were responding by nuzzling her and licking her hands. "Hello," she said to me brightly. Unlike her father's, her voice was pure Home Counties with no trace of an accent, a product of the expensive boarding school she attended. I remembered Sally telling me that Milos had brought his daughter to England after the death of his first wife, the girl's mother, some ten years ago.

"Martina's on holiday from school and is staying with us

for a few days," Sally said, and I noticed immediately that something was wrong. There was a flatness to her voice that told me she didn't approve of this change to their domestic arrangements.

"We'll have a good time together, yes?" Milos boomed, but his enthusiasm seemed overstated, perhaps to make up for Sally's obvious lack of it.

"Martina, don't let the dogs lick your face," Sally said.

Martina giggled and said something in fluent Czech to her father, who laughed and replied in the same language. The girl looked up at Sally, saying nothing, but the expression on her face was a challenge.

I looked at my watch. I had an appointment to discuss a new commission with a prospective client in Stanmore, and I didn't want to be late. I said to Milos, "Before I go, tell me: what do you think of the dresser?"

He came over and wrapped an arm around my shoulder. "Colin, it is a beautiful piece. Very . . . macho, yes? Perfect."

Martina was looking up at the carvings on the dresser. "It's ugly," she said. "And he's evil." She pointed at the Green Man. "Pure evil."

"Don't be so stupid," Sally snapped at the girl. "You always have to dramatize everything."

The girl smiled to herself. Satisfied at having finally provoked a reaction from her stepmother, she sipped her water and wandered into the lounge.

Sally watched her go, shaking her head slightly, then turned to me. "I'll see you out, Colin."

She walked me to the door. "I'm sorry about Martina," she said when she was out of earshot. "Fifteen years old and sometimes she can be so incredibly childish."

"Don't apologize," I said. "She was trying to goad you, not me."

"Damnit, I know. She used to be so sweet. A year ago we

were getting on so well, then suddenly she changed into this nascent superbitch."

"Hormones," I said. "And I think she sees you as a rival for her father's affections. My two girls went through the same thing not long after Jackie and I divorced. Gave her hell for eighteen months, then suddenly switched their loyalties and started to give me a hard time. They're twenty-one now, and thankfully they've grown out of it." I rarely spoke about the twins and their mother to my clients, but over the weeks I'd been working on her house, I had become very fond of Sally. We had an easygoing and fairly candid relationship.

"Twenty-one! God, that's six years away. I'll be in the madhouse by then." She laughed at her own dramatics and kissed my cheek. "See you Monday?"

"Bright and early. My last week," I said. "You'll soon be rid of me."

A shadow seemed to pass across her face, or perhaps it was just wishful thinking on my part.

Then there was an indistinct noise from behind her, but fear kept her attention focused firmly upon the dresser. More noise caused her to turn her head, and as she did so, she caught sight of a mass of inhuman shapes, huddled together, tentacles breaking free from the cluster to wave sightless in the air, lolling heads barely able to stay upright on molten bodies that seemed to merge into the darkness and be carried by it.

The squire grabbed her arms and pulled her toward the pot dresser. The wood seemed to hold her as if it were alive, and she felt tiny cuts tear into her back.

The music stopped and she was sure she could hear her father praying, but the words contained more syllables than sense to her and were not the words she had learned so devotedly at Sunday lessons.

The swaying mass of shadow separated into a crowd of individual creatures that had bodies such as she had never seen before. Above her head the wood was pulsating, liquid sap dripping onto her forehead in a parody of her baptism, her body held tight so that she was powerless.

She had seen cheap engravings of Satan—it was part of her upbringing within the church—but nothing she had ever witnessed was as indescribably monstrous as the beasts she saw crawling toward her. She screamed, but her screams were ignored. She heard rather than felt the wood behind her rip and splinter, and then two bands of extraordinary strength tightened around her chest.

She was unconscious before the creatures were upon her.

Unlike a lot of interior designers I favor a hands-on approach to my work. It isn't enough for me to draw my ideas on paper, present them to the client, and then hire experts to transform the ideas into reality. I still hire experts in certain fields, but much of the work I do myself, and, as in the case of Sally's kitchen, I remain on site for the duration of the contract.

The final week was to be a rounding-up operation, as I liked to call it. It would give me a chance to test all the appliances, correct any design faults, and make sure the kitchen was working the way I had designed it.

I arrived on the Monday morning full of optimism that the week would be a breeze, and encountered the first of what would prove to be many problems.

"I don't understand it," I said as I examined the patch of mold just above the granite worktop. "This is an internal wall. It's the original plaster, and I don't remember there being any mold there before."

"There wasn't," Sally said glumly.

I dealt with the mold on the wall, but it puzzled me because it was unlike any mold or mildew I had encountered before. It didn't seem to be fungal; more like a moss than a mold. Still, I cleaned it off, bleached and repainted the area of wall, and when I left the house that evening there was no trace of it.

Returning the next morning, I was horrified to see that the mold had not only come back, but had spread to the size of a dinner plate.

Martina met me at the door. Sally, she informed me, was still in bed with a headache. To me the girl was perfectly charming, making me a cup of tea and toasting some bread, which she served with a choice of honey or marmalade. We sat at the kitchen table drinking our tea. "Have you noticed how it smells in here?" she asked between mouthfuls.

I sniffed the air but could smell nothing but fresh paint and toasted bread. "Can't say that I have."

"Oh, yes, it's quite a definite smell," she said. "Earthy. Like the forest floor after a shower of rain."

"It's your imagination," Sally said from the doorway. "We went through all this nonsense last night. And why didn't you wake me when Colin arrived?" She was clearly furious.

Martina shrugged. "I thought you could do with the rest," she said.

Sally grabbed at the girl's shoulder and spun her around in the chair. "Don't you dare patronize me!" she said.

"Sally . . ." I said ineffectually.

"Keep out of this, Colin. I've taken just about all I'm going to take from this little—" Her words were cut off by Gielgud and Richardson, who had bounded into the kitchen at the sound of Sally's raised voice and were now barking furiously at her. "And you two . . . out of here!" she said, but the dogs did not move. Their barking quieted, but they continued to growl threateningly at Sally. She reached for Martina again and the growls became more menacing; both dogs bared their teeth at her. Sally froze, hand outstretched.

"Martina," I said quietly, trying to restore some order to the chaos into which the morning had erupted. "Take Gielgud and Richardson out to the garden, there's a good girl."

She did as she was told without argument. I watched from the kitchen window as she picked up a ball from the lawn and threw it to the end of the garden. The dogs chased after it, tails wagging. I looked around at Sally. She was crying, tears streaming down her cheeks.

"Do you want me to phone Milos, get him home?" I said.

She gave a short, brittle laugh. "He's why I'm upset. He always sides with Martina, never backs me up. Now he wants the dresser moved to his study."

I was astonished. "What on Earth for? Surely it belongs in the kitchen. Doesn't he like it?"

"Oh, he loves it. Says it reminds him of 'dark European nights, of moonless seas, and the bottomless abyss that surrounds us.' You know what nonsense he can talk when he gets creative. He's researching the origins of the carvings on it."

I was horrified that the dresser might be moved from the kitchen. Apart from my design being meddled with, and the need to replace it, I felt an indefinite unease about the interest Milos was taking in it. When I watched Sally busying herself in the kitchen I only hoped my feelings weren't turning to jealousy.

The mold or moss on the kitchen wall refused to go away. Despite several scrubbings and liberal doses of bleach, and even a mold killer, the mark remained. I mentioned the difficulty with it to Sally, but she just looked at the mark with tired eyes and said, "I shouldn't worry about it, Colin. It hardly matters now, does it?"

But worry about it I did. With the mold there I couldn't finish the job, and until I finished the job I could not submit my bill, and my bank manager was breathing down my neck about an overdraft that was pushing its limits. I used my cell phone and contacted a builder friend who specialized in damp and rot problems, and he agreed to meet me at the house later that day.

Dave, the builder, scraped some of the greenish black growth from the wall with a penknife and rubbed it between his fingers. He sniffed his stained fingertips and said, "It's not mildew, or any kind of mold I've ever encountered."

"Great," I said. "Which leaves us precisely nowhere." I shook my head in despair. "Well, whatever it is, it's spreading." The patch had grown since the morning, not so much in diameter, but thread like filaments were reaching out from the edge of the mark, some of them more than a foot long. I rubbed at them with my finger.

"I don't want to worry you. . . ." Dave said. He had walked to the other end of the kitchen and was crouching down beside the dresser. "But there's more here."

It was a spot the size of a penny, greenish black, exactly the same as the larger mass. Then we pulled the dresser away from the wall. The back of it was covered in the green, pungent-smelling stuff. It took an age to clean and it still looked like a temporary job to me.

Later that day Milos came back to the house to see Martina. Sally had gone into town to the hairdresser and beautician, feeling that she needed to be pampered; she probably did. Milos came into the kitchen, looking unutterably sad. He looked around at the new oven, the dresser, and the granite worktops. "A dream kitchen," he said. "Sally's present to me. So sad, such a shame she cannot feel the passion for this. . . ." His open arms indicated the dresser, looking forlorn in its current state.

I said nothing, concentrating on painting over the latest stain. I had decided to give it one more try before calling in a structural engineer. Milos brightened when Martina entered the room. He hugged her and held her close.

"Colin," she said to me, completely ignoring her father, "would you come and have a look at Richardson? He's got something on his back."

The dog didn't seem to be in any pain, but something was irritating him. He was sitting, head twisted back over his shoulder, nibbling at something. I got down beside him. He looked at me with his lugubrious brown eyes. Gielgud pushed his snout against my hand and Martina took him by the collar and pulled him away.

Just above Richardson's shoulder blades, coating the fur, was a greenish black patch, the touch and smell of it terribly familiar. I pulled aside the fur and was horrified to see that the stuff not only covered the hair, but was also spreading out across the skin. Like an iceberg, the part that was visible was just the tip. A patch of skin about six inches square was covered by the stuff, and where the dog had been worrying it with his teeth he had drawn blood. It didn't look good.

"I think we ought to let the vet check him out," I said calmly, not wanting to alarm Martina.

"I'll take him," Milos said. "Martina, you can come with us. It will give us a chance to talk, yes? We need to talk."

Martina shrugged and went across to Gielgud, who was lying on the grass chewing a large cow bone. I saw she was going over his fur carefully, looking for any sign of the mold or whatever it was.

Milos went to fetch Richardson's lead while I ruffled the dog's neck and spoke softly to him. "Soon have you right, old fellow," I said, but I didn't believe it for a moment.

. . .

Milos and Martina arrived back from the vet's without Richardson.

"They kept him in for tests," Martina said. "The vet seemed completely baffled by it. He's bringing in a skin specialist from the veterinary hospital at Brookman's Park."

"It will be expensive," Milos added. "But I told them I'd pay any amount of money to ensure Richardson's recovery."

When Sally returned she invited me to stay for dinner. I accepted, but reluctantly—I had a ton of work to be getting on with at home, but I felt that to refuse would seem churlish. I also noticed that Martina's attitude toward Sally had softened considerably. Over dinner I learned that, surprisingly, Martina agreed with Sally about the dresser and Milos's new obsession with it. That development, at least, was welcome. Milos didn't join us for the meal, engaged as he was in what he called his "new research."

What wasn't welcome was a telephone call from the vet to tell us that Richardson had passed away. The details were sketchy, but it seemed that they were performing a small exploratory operation to take samples of the growth on his skin, when the dog went into shock. A cardiac arrest followed. They failed to save him.

At the news Martina burst into tears and ran upstairs to her room. Sally cradled the receiver and stared blankly out through the window to where Gielgud, Richardson's brother, was asleep on the grass, enjoying the rays of the early evening sun. She looked around at me. "It's all falling apart, Colin," she said, a tear slipping down her cheek. "All falling apart."

I touched her shoulder, and without hesitation, too quickly in fact, she melted into my arms and we were kissing guiltily, but with vigor.

. . .

When I arrived home later that night the answering machine light was blinking frantically. Six messages. I swore. I needed some time to think about what had happened. Although it had been some years since my divorce I realized that an involvement with Sally would be life-changing, and I wasn't sure if I was ready for that.

Of the six messages, three were from prospective clients, so I noted those; one was from the bank, giving me the personal touch; and two were from Billy McQueen—the last of which sounded desperate: "If you can't ring back then check your bloody e-mails!"

I switched on my laptop and logged on. There were a few messages but only one of importance, only one from McQueen.

It's Tommy, my boy. The cut got worse so I took him to hospital. They kept him in because the wound seemed to be infected, they said. They've just rung me. He's in a coma. They don't think he's going to come around. Ring me, Colin. It's about the dresser.

I swallowed some brandy and dialed McQueen's number.

Fear skulked in the rector's face, but he fashioned a mask of eager devotion to hide his true feelings. It was no more than he had spent a lifetime doing. The refuse of their feasting was now littered about the floor. Martha was a good girl, a daughter to be proud of, but what was pride beside the quest he had set himself for an immortal place amongst the banished ones of his desires? The chance meeting he had witnessed between the squire and the brittle monstrosity on that moonless night had led him here to this nirvana. Tonight he had glimpsed the promised land of his dreams, and it was not the Holy Land enshrined within his Scriptures, nor any heaven promised to those who led a blameless life or repented. It was a dark fantasy of vibrant colors, filled with oddly shaped beasts that crawled and slithered, that murmured incoherently yet with a language he knew would have meaning if only he were given access to the secrets he craved.

The squire stood up and adjusted his clothing, dishevelled from the enjoyment he had taken from the rector's daughter. He had known she would make an excellent sacrifice, and if his own base pleasure could be satisfied at the same time, then so much the better. The human form he had adopted might be impossible to discard after so many centuries, but there were a few human vices that dulled the constant yearning to return to his natural existence.

The creatures around him were still basking in the youthful enjoyment they had partaken. If only they knew how few of them would survive to join their ancestors in the perpetual struggle against infinite banishment. Let them seek a few moments of carnality before they were lured back to their cellar and their darkness.

It was the beast that had come to be celebrated as the Green Man that needed his attention now. It was too soon, even after so many years, for it to seek escape, and so he had to bind it once more to the Earth. With wood ripped from the pews of the now desecrated church he had arranged for one of his men to fashion the pot dresser. When it was completed the squire had slit the man's throat, allowing the blood to act as a binding agent to the images carved into the wood. Now that same agent was required to lure the inhuman creatures back. In a fluid movement the squire pierced the artery of the hapless rector, pushing him onto the dresser so that the rich blood adorned the wood, as though anointing a new believer.

The pillow was damp from her tears. She rolled from the bed, went to the dressing table, and blew her nose on a tissue from a box decorated with teddy bears. The bedroom was the same uncertain mix of child and young woman. Lacy underwear lying next to a nightgown with cartoon rabbits on the front. Soft toys on a shelf, above which a pop star poster boasted bare chest and hard eyes.

She had cried when her mother had died, but she had been so young it was difficult to know whether the tears came from deep knowledge or raw emotion. She had cried today when she heard about the death of her dog. Then she had seen Sally kissing Colin, and she didn't know what to think. Her first instinct had been to tell her father, but his study door was closed and—she found—locked. Shut out, she was confused.

Martina went across to the window and looked out at the darkened garden. After a short while her eyes grew accustomed to the blackness and she could make out familiar shapes. Then a movement caught her attention. It was a large garden, divided into almost separate sections by clumps of bushes and trees. A small stand of fruit trees sat at the end of the garden, and hanging from the bough of an old Bramley apple tree was a swing, an old wooden one that had been there when they had bought the house. They all liked it.

Sitting on the swing was a girl about her age, long brown hair swishing in the night air. Her loose cotton smock was well past the summer's fashion trends. She was swinging gently, almost in slow motion, but all the time staring up at Martina's window.

Martina ran across the room and switched out the light so that she could get a better look at the girl. When she returned to

the window the swing was still in motion, but it was empty. The
girl had gone.

At the far corner of the garden Martina thought she could see
a flash of white cotton, perhaps the girl's smock dress, but there
was insufficient light to be sure. Then she thought she could see
other shapes in the garden, different from those she could re-
member from the daylight. It was as if the garden at night had
become a playground for things that hid during the day. Almost
as if the girl on the swing had drawn Martina's attention to
her so that the nighttime creatures could slip into the garden
unseen.

There was something attractive about the unrestrained jerking
of the creatures, something that seemed to draw Martina down
to them, to want to join them. She pulled on a fleece for warmth
and ran down the stairs. She reached the kitchen, then the back
door, and turned the key in the lock.

McQueen answered the telephone on the second ring.

"Colin. Thank God." He sounded desperate.

I began to mumble an apology for not calling sooner but he
cut me off with "Tommy's dead. He never regained consciousness, and they switched off the monitors about an hour ago."

"Are they saying what he died of?"

There was a mirthless laugh from his end. "Heart failure.
Cause unknown. Christ, I laid into that doctor, not his fault,
but a strapping lad like that. It isn't right a small cut should
lead to this."

The cut. The dresser. The dog. The dresser. The mold, and
the way the blood faded into the wood when McQueen himself was cut. Selfishly I thought about Sally, and then ridicu-
lously of the contract money I was still owed. I was so far into
selfish thought that I was missing what McQueen was saying.

". . . still got it?"

"Sorry, got what?"

"The bill of sale we took from the dresser drawer when you bought it off me. Surely you remember?"

I had forgotten about it completely and had to think carefully where I'd put it. I roamed back in my mind to the day I saw the dresser for the first time, I had gone to see McQueen by appointment, and I was wearing . . . I dashed for the wardrobe, leaving McQueen hanging on. The jacket I had worn that day was hanging inside the wardrobe and the bill of sale was still inside. A little crumpled, already torn and ink faded from the years, but it was there and it was intact. I couldn't decipher the writing or understand the language in which it was written, but my scant knowledge of old mythology was enough for me to recognize what I thought it was. It certainly wasn't a bill of sale.

The night was a quiet lake of still calm. There were tranquil pools where a sly moon splashed puddles of light. All was peaceful and all was enticing. Martina stepped outside, and the coolness of the air touched her young skin, raising slight goose bumps on her body.

The girl was on the swing again, her bare legs flashing like pale moonbeams in the silent garden. If there was rustling in the bushes Martina was deaf to it. If shadows formed behind her, with shapes that were less than natural, she was blind to them.

Martina had thought she would have to search the garden to find the girl, so she was delighted to see her. Then the girl jumped down from the swing and for a moment Martina thought she was going to run away again. Instead the girl stood erect, her head pushed back, her arms outstretched, her eyes closed yet staring up at the moon.

Walking toward her Martina became aware of muted music in the background, the organ from a church service. A small breeze played on the girl's neck, sweeping her hair over her eyes. She made no attempt to brush it away. Then she turned her neck toward Martina and opened her eyes. For the first time Martina felt cold reality drench her dreamlike state. The girl's eyes were as white as the moon, the milky white of blindness, and yet it was clearly evident that she could see and that she was directing things around her with liquid movements of her arms. Things that lumbered out of the darkness, pallid countenances draped with cunning and anger. Noises emanated from them that had the form of words but sounded into the night air like evil thunder crashing from below as well as from above the earth.

Screaming with an intensity that shocked even her Martina ran back to the house. The door opened and she sobbed with joy to see the secure figure of her father standing there.

"Martha, your special day has arrived," Milos said.

The kitchen was awash with light when I arrived. A distraught Sally finally answered my frantic knocking at the door. She had obviously just jumped out of bed wearing only a cotton nightgown, her hair dishevelled.

The door to the garden was wide open and cool air played into the house from outside. It was impossible to tell if the discordant organ music was coming from outside the house or was playing in one of the rooms, possibly Milos's study. Sally thought he was still in there. He had refused to join her and Martina for supper and locked himself in. Apparently he had been shouting to himself earlier, strange words that sounded like a contorted version of his mother language, but which she instinctively knew wasn't.

A foul stench wafted in from the garden, a mixture of the earthy smell Martina had complained about and rotting flesh.

It was the smell I would expect if a centuries-sealed pit were opened up.

When we came to the kitchen the scene was worse than I had imagined. With Sally beside me in the doorway to the hall I could see the whole of the kitchen. The pot dresser was swaying. The wall behind it was covered in the green mold, pieces of plaster flaking off and falling to the floor. The dresser itself seemed alive with a pulse of its own, swaying with an ancient rhythm that matched the music and the noises from the night.

Martina was trapped against the dresser. She didn't appear to be tied to it, but her arms and legs were held firmly against it and only her head seemed capable of movement, and that only to mirror the awful motion of the dresser. Her clothes had been ripped off and her fragile nudity added to her vulnerability.

Sally was wrong; Milos was not in the study. He stood in the doorway to the garden, facing out, chanting. He was holding a drawer of the dresser in his hands, and he seemed to be searching it for something. He was clearly distressed that the drawer was empty. He was beseeching something that I could not see.

The dresser suddenly stopped moving, and my attention fell to it. The mold had streaked out so that it covered the whole ceiling in fine irregular lines, as though someone had randomly flicked paint there. Martina was almost unconscious; her head slumped onto her shoulder. Then I noticed the Green Man carving was gone. In its position at the top of the dresser was a gaping hole, as though a huge bite had been taken from it.

Milos turned. He shouted at me, "Have you seen it? Do you have it?"

At first I thought he referred to the carving, but his continued search of the empty drawer told me what he was looking for.

I held aloft the piece of paper we had once thought was an innocent bill of sale. "Is this what you're after, Milos?"

He glared at me, and the force of fury that controlled his mind behind those eyes was as strong as it was evil. "Give it to me," he demanded.

"So that you can bring them back? What then?"

Sally tried to wrest the paper from my hand, but I pushed her away. "What is it?" she asked. "Give it to him if it stops all this."

I shook my head. "We have no idea what this is, Milos." I looked again at the ancient and crumbling paper, dry and cracked from the centuries. I glanced quickly at the indecipherable words upon it, words that meant little to me, but despite that I was certain that if Milos got his hands on them, sure catastrophe would follow.

The windows shattered and a huge green leg broke through. The foul stench of decay accompanied it, and the door was ripped from its hinges as another huge shape smashed against it.

Suddenly Martina let out a great cry and fell to the floor. The dresser began to shake. Sally cupped Martina in her arms and both of them closed their eyes.

I began to tear the paper into pieces.

Milos started shouting in desperation. "The sacrifice is ready. The untouched maiden is yours. Make me like unto you. Please." He ran to the door and the wind whipping into the room lashed at his clothes as if they were sails on a ship.

Martina was crying and laughing at the same time. Sally clearly thought it was hysteria and hugged her all the tighter. But I guessed why she had been able to escape from the dresser and the sacrificial rituals.

"You're not a virgin, are you, Martina?" I asked, almost laughing out loud myself.

"It was only once—but it was enough, wasn't it?"

The green leg lifted away and the roar that filled the night scared the moon.

The paper was in tiny pieces now and I flung it at the

dresser. It stuck to the mold, and where it touched the wood began to smolder and smoke as if about to burst into flames.

It wasn't easy and my hands and shoulders got badly burned, but I maneuvered the dresser out of the kitchen into the garden and shut the door, pushing the table and chairs against it by way of flimsy defense.

Through the shattered window I was able to see Milos as he was taken. There were bulbous heads lolling on shrunken bodies, and willowy tentacles that adorned bodies shaped like animals. An outline of a large human shape, with a headdress of leaves, dominated all the restless creatures, directing them all, even the ones with limbs like rope and insect heads.

As the tumult diminished the last thing I saw was the swing at the bottom of the garden. There was a young girl on it, sitting perfectly still. Her eyes were open, yet she seemed to be sleeping.

THE CABIN IN THE WOODS

Richard Laymon

1

After the sun goes down, I never leave the cabin. I secure the shutters and barricade the door and sit close to the fire.

I have no doubt, however, it can come in if it wants.

So far, it hasn't tried.

I've been living in fear of the night that it does, for the feeble shutters and hingeless, unlocked door will stand no chance against an onslaught by the horrible thing.

I would escape if I could . . . flee from the cabin and these desolate hills . . . lose myself in the crowds and bright lights of a metropolis and never again set forth into the wilderness. I dare not, however, attempt it.

I have no means of transportation other than my own two feet, you see, and the nearest town is many miles away. Even if I should begin my journey at the very first hint of dawn, I fear that night would find me still hurrying through the vast, wooded wilderness.

And *it* would come for me.

Certainly, I might be lucky enough to stumble upon a refuge for the night. A hunting shack, perhaps, or another cabin. Or I might happen upon a road; a vehicle might stop for me and a kind driver might offer me passage to a place of safety.

If such a refuge or road exists in this region, I have not yet found it.

Time after time, at first light, I have left the feeble safety of my cabin to stalk through the woods in search of a neighbor, an abandoned dwelling, a road. I have roamed in every direction . . . never, however, for more than six hours at a time.

You've no doubt heard the old mind-teaser: "How far can a dog run into a forest?"

The answer, of course, is "Only halfway. Then it's running out."

I am much like that dog.

Knowing I must return to my cabin before the arrival of night, I can search only *half* the distance I might be able to travel in the course of a full day of hiking.

Over the weeks I have been trapped here, I've gone greater distances by quickening my pace. Not long ago, I actually ran from the cabin at the break of dawn in order to cover as much ground as possible. I ran until overcome by exhaustion, then walked, then ran again. By this means, I traveled perhaps twice my usual distance.

No place of sanctuary, however, presented itself to me. Nor did I come upon any roads.

At last, with half the day gone, I turned back.

Dear God, not soon enough.

In my worn-out condition, I hurried as quickly as possible but soon realized that I stood little chance of regaining my cabin before dark.

It felt like a death sentence.

Worse than that. Our criminals are mercifully hanged or electrocuted or shot, not torn from their feet and carried off in the talons of a monstrous creature, flown away to confront a fate so hideous I cannot bear to think of it.

I did, however, possess Arthur's double-barreled shotgun.

While it was hardly capable of destroying the creature, it could certainly destroy me. I vowed to use it on myself rather than allow the monster to snatch me away.

With the promise of a shotgun blast to console me, I continued my journey to the cabin. My race against darkness had begun shortly after the noon hour. I dodged trees and bushes, waded streams, climbed over deadfalls, chugged my way painfully up steep slopes, bounded down hillsides, sometimes fell, stopping to rest less frequently than my body called out for—but more often than seemed wise.

In the late afternoon, the sunlight took on a rich golden hue and cast long, long shadows. Once, this had been my favorite time of day with its deep, melancholy beauty. Now, it filled me with dread, for it signaled the approach of dusk . . . and darkness . . . and the hideous flapping thing that would come down for me out of the night sky.

Soon came dusk, silent and dim, gray and blue. My legs felt like pillars of stone. My arms were leaden, my hands barely able hold on to the shotgun. My lungs burnt and my heart felt ready to explode. And yet I ran on, and on.

At last, as night spread across the hills, I saw my cabin in the distance. Though my legs could hardly carry me at all, I struggled forward, wheezing for air. I left the trees behind and trudged across the clearing. Closer. Closer to my cabin. Then came the cry of the ungodly beast and the *whup whup* of its enormous wings. Raising my eyes, I saw it sweep across the night, its massive shape blotting out the stars.

It wasn't coming for me. Not tonight.

Instead, it was no doubt busy on some other unspeakable errand.

But it would be back for me. If not tonight, then tomorrow night or the next.

It will never let me leave this place alive.

It needs what I have.

2

Arthur Addison, my brother-in-law, was the first to go. Though I am appalled by his fate, I cannot help but feel a certain wry satisfaction.

He had, after all, accompanied us into the wilds against my wishes.

I'd been looking forward to a time of solitary intimacy between myself and my new wife . . . not to a threesome including her brother.

We couldn't keep him away, however, because he was half owner of the cabin. It had been in my wife's family for well over a century, being passed down from generation to generation and finally to Emily and Arthur following the sudden deaths of their parents in a train disaster.

Though they owned the cabin, they had never visited it. Their ancestor, Garrett Addison, had apparently built the structure in the most wild and desolate region he could find in order to elude . . . no one is quite sure who or what he hoped to elude. According to family tradition, he was an "odd one." Even his wife and three small children, left behind in Providence, were apparently glad to find themselves abandoned by him.

I have neither the time nor inclination to relate all I know about the history of Garrett's cabin. Let me simply say that its location eventually became known to the family, it was visited and photographed by subsequent generations, and passed down through the family until the property came into the hands of my wife and her brother.

To me, it seemed like an ideal place to while away a fortnight before resuming my attempts to finish the collection of dark and brooding stories on which I'd been working for the past two years.

When I proposed the adventure to Emily, she said, "Smashing idea! Let's do it!"

Soon, however, Arthur learned of our plan. "You're mad," he said. "The old place is virtually inaccessible." Their father had apparently journeyed there as a young man and had very nearly been turned back by the distances and the rough terrain. After persisting and eventually reaching the cabin, he'd stayed for only a single night before hurrying away. "He never told us what happened that night," Arthur explained, "but he warned us never to go there. I think it would be wise to heed his warning."

"But Arthur," said Emily, "that was ages ago. Though I can't imagine what might have distressed Father so much, it surely wouldn't be a problem this many years later."

Arthur continued to argue, protesting that such a trip would be arduous, uncomfortable, and quite possibly dangerous. But we were not to be dissuaded. At length, Arthur said, "All right, then. If you *must go* out to that godforsaken cabin, *I'll* go with you."

"Don't be silly," Emily told him.

"I insist. I won't have you traipsing off into such a region with no one to protect you except Dexter." When he uttered my name, he wrinkled his nose as if sniffing a foul aroma.

"I'm quite capable of seeing to Emily's welfare," I informed him.

He said, "Hogwash."

In consideration of his size and propensity for violence, I refrained from punching him in the face.

Emily tried several times to talk him out of accompanying us, but to no avail. Nor could we simply strike out and leave him behind. Aside from being half owner of the cabin, Arthur was in sole possession of the only map detailing its whereabouts.

He refused to allow us so much as a glimpse of the map.

Though I was tempted to call off the entire enterprise, Emily had grown so curious about the cabin and its environs that she wouldn't be talked out of it.

"It'll be fine, dear," she assured me.

"Arthur's an oaf."

"Oh, he's simply overprotective of me. He is my big brother, after all."

"But I had my heart set on being alone with you."

"I know, dear. I'm disappointed, too, but Arthur has made a solemn promise to allow us privacy whenever we ask for it."

"Ah, splendid. We're doomed to be asking his permission."

"It won't be so bad. Really."

"*You* deal with him, then. I can hardly see myself requesting him to walk off so that I can engage in dalliance with his baby sister."

Laughing sweetly, she said, "I'll take full charge of shooing him off."

She proved to be as good as her word.

3

After departing from the train at Brattleboro, we hired a car to take us as close to the cabin as roads would allow. After requesting the driver to pick us up at the very same spot a fortnight hence, Arthur consulted his map for the umpteenth time and we set off over a woodland trail. All three of us carried backpacks loaded with clothing, equipment, and food for our adventure. In addition to his pack, Arthur bore his rather large shotgun, which he rested on his shoulder as he strolled along.

Our hike from the road to the cabin took the better part of five days. Though we suffered from exhaustion, aching muscles, mosquitos, numerous scratches, bruises, and blisters — though we found ourselves ever more uneasy about the utter isolation of our surroundings and the strange noises we sometimes heard in the night—we completed the journey without major incident.

This surprises me somewhat, looking back on it. Surely, the creature must've been aware of our approach. The noises in the night, at that time unidentifiable, I later realized had been the flapping of its giant wings and its uncanny screams of rage or glee.

Why it refrained from attacking us, I don't know. Perhaps it had reasons of its own for allowing us to continue on our way to the cabin. Perhaps it *wanted* us there.

By the time we arrived, weary and battered, we were ill-suited for further travel. Otherwise, I doubt we would've spent a single night at the place.

It appeared somewhat brow-beaten and ramshackle from the outside, but that came as no surprise. After all, the dwelling had stood abandoned for a great many years. If anything, I suppose we might have expected it to look worse than it did.

Overall, the cabin appeared to be intact except for its front door. The door, smashed from its moorings, lay flat on the floor a few feet inside the cabin.

We stood on the porch, looking in at it.

"I wonder how *that* happened," said Emily.

"Perhaps a bear wanted in," said Arthur.

"Oh, dear."

"Nothing to worry about." Arthur removed his backpack and lowered it to the porch floor. "No doubt our intruder is long gone. However." He readied his shotgun. "Wait here," he said, and stepped into the cabin.

After only a few strides, he very nearly vanished in the gloom.

"Do be careful," Emily called to him.

"It's quite all right. Though I must say, there is a rather foul odor. A smell of *death*, I'm afraid." A few moments later, a match flared. Its glow illuminated Arthur near a far corner of the room, his back to us, a match pinched between the thumb and forefinger of his upraised hand.

"I say," he said.

"Arthur?" Emily asked. "What is it?"

"A chap," he said.

"A *what*?" I asked.

"A dead chap."

"Oh, dear," said Emily.

"Quite without his noggin, I'm afraid."

"*What?*" I asked.

"Come and take a gander for yourself, Dexter. Quite up your alley, the sort of drivel you're so fond of scribbling. Unless, of course, you're too timid to experience the genuine article."

I started through the doorway, but Emily clutched my arm.

"I'll just take a look," I told her. "Wait here."

"Be careful, darling."

As I made my way through the cabin, Arthur's match died out. I was engulfed by blackness. Stopping, I explained, "I can't see."

Arthur chuckled softly. "Follow your nose, old boy, follow your nose."

"Arthur!" Emily chided him from the doorway.

He chuckled again. A few moments later, another match flared. I hurried toward Arthur while he sucked the flame down into his briar. The aroma of cavendish quickly joined the stench of rotted flesh.

The match still burned when I came to a halt beside him.

Sprawled on the floor just in front of a rocking chair was all that remained of a human body. Arthur, in his droll and faux-British way, had called this person a *chap*. Unless he was considerably better-versed in anatomy than myself, however, the attribution of maleness to the cadaver was a matter of pure supposition—or wishful thinking. Its clothes were shredded rags. So was most of its flesh. Little more than bones was left, and the skull was gone entirely.

As I stared down at the horrid stranger, Arthur's pipe died. The air, bereft of his sweet smoke, suddenly choked me with its stench. Gagging violently, I ran for the door. Emily leaped out of my way. I jumped from the porch. In the fresh air and sunlight, I managed to halt the spasms and avoid the further embarrassment of vomiting in front of my darling wife.

Arthur was vastly amused. He spent the next ten minutes or so chuckling and shaking his head at me and making comments such as, "Cast-iron stomach there, Dexter?" while he went about removing the cadaver. He carried it out of the cabin with his bare hands. It took him several trips. He threw the bones into a bushy ravine about a hundred feet from the cabin.

Done, he grinned at us and brushed his hands together like a man who has just chopped a good load of firewood. "That's that," he said.

"But where's the poor man's head?" Emily asked.

"I suppose he lost it somewhere."

"Perhaps it's still in the cabin."

"Awfully dark in there," I added.

"I'll open the shutters," Arthur said. "The place could use a bit of an airing out. Whiffy in there. Quite noisome, actually." Laughing, he trotted up the porch stairs and entered the cabin.

A few minutes later, he came out.

"No sign of the chap's head, I'm afraid."

"I don't believe I'll sleep in there tonight," said Emily.

4

It was then we discussed quitting the cabin altogether. I was in favor.

"Let's get away from here now," I said, "while we still have light."

And our heads, I thought, but kept that part of the argument to myself, not wanting to appear unmanly.

"But we've only just arrived, dear fellow."

"There was a dead man in the cabin," I reminded him, going along with the prevalent assumption that the victim was indeed a male, though I had no reason to believe it so. "By all appearances," I went on, "he did not succumb to old age. I don't want to subject Emily to whatever it was that . . . *destroyed* that poor man."

"Oh, Dexter," said Arthur, "he's been dead for ages."

"Hardly ages. He still had meat on his bones."

"None worth mentioning," said Arthur with a grin.

Squeezing my arm, Emily said, "I'm done in, darling. I think we *all* are. Besides, it'll soon be dark. Let's remain here at least for tonight. We'll sleep under the stars. When we're all fresh and rested in the morning, we can decide whether to stay on here or begin our trek back."

"Bravo!" said Arthur. "The voice of reason."

"I still don't think we should stay here," I protested.

Chuckling, Arthur patted me on the shoulder with one of his soiled hands. He said, "Don't be frightened, poor boy. I'll protect you."

5

I was fast asleep late that night when Emily, in her bedroll beside mine, shook my arm and whispered, "Dexter! Dexter!"

"What is it?" I asked.

"Do you hear that?"

I listened and heard a quiet, heavy *whup . . . whup . . . whup*, like the slow beating of gigantic leather wings. During our trek to the cabin, we'd heard such sounds many times in the night but they'd always seemed far away.

Now, they were nearby and coming closer.

I put a hand on Emily and whispered, "Don't move. Don't speak."

"I should warn Arthur."

All three of us had spread our bedrolls in an area in front of the cabin. To allow us a modicum of privacy, however, Arthur had settled down some twenty feet away from us.

In the brightness of the moonlight, I could see his dark shape on the ground. He didn't appear to be stirring.

The flapping of the creature's wings grew louder, louder.

"Oh, dear God," Emily murmured.

I shouted, *"Arthur! The skies!"*

He bolted upright, gasping.

We all looked to the skies.

Though I gazed toward the flapping sounds, I saw little more than the dark shapes of trees. Then something crashed through the upper branches.

Crying out, *"By Jove!,"* Arthur shouldered his shotgun.

The monster's squeal pierced my ears.

A huge shape of blackness descended upon Arthur.

KRAWBOOM!

The flash of his muzzle blast lit the night . . . lit Arthur and the creature.

Emily screamed.

Arthur fired off his other barrel. In the darkness following the second brilliant flash, I was too blind to see what became of him.

Sobbing and shuddering, Emily clung to me.

Some time later, holding each other, we struggled to our feet. We staggered over to Arthur's bedroll. His shotgun lay on the ground, but he was nowhere to be found.

6

Emily and I spent the rest of the night inside the cabin. I smoked Arthur's pipe, every so often, to mask the remains of the stench and also in an effort to prevent myself from drowsing off.

We'd closed the cabin as much as we could: fastened the shutters, propped up the door in its frame and barricaded it with various articles of furniture.

Emily lay on the floor, her head on my lap. I sat with Arthur's shotgun ready by my side.

During the long, seemingly endless hours of waiting for sunrise, I thought of many things. Along with so many other thoughts, it occurred to me that I'd been granted my wish to spend time in the cabin with Emily . . . sans Arthur. How ironic, I thought; now that he was gone, I didn't feel the slightest inclination toward romance.

I also considered the possibility that my "wish" might have been the cause of Arthur's misfortune. The notion plagued me with guilt for a while. However, I realized that no power of mine could have drawn such a beast to Arthur. I also knew that, if I'd had control of Arthur's fate, he never would have accompanied us on this journey in the first place. Even now, he would be safe in Providence.

Throughout the long hours of the night, I had ample time to wish that Emily and I had remained in Providence ourselves.

We'd known of the cabin's reputation. Like children eager to play, however, we'd chosen to ignore the dangers and make our journey anyway.

Oh, how I wished we might travel back in time, heed the warnings so apparent throughout the history of this hellish place and shun it. But we couldn't make such a journey. We were here for better or worse.

Soon after the first gray light of approaching dawn showed in the cracks around the door, sleep overtook me.

I have no recollection of my dreams, only that they horrified me and I woke up with a scream in my throat.

Emily, on the floor beside me, took me in her arms and soothed me with gentle words and caresses. "It's all right, darling," she murmured. "It was only a bad dream. You're fine now. Everything's fine."

"We . . . we must get away from here."

"We will," said Emily, her warm fingers stroking my cheek. "We'll leave immediately. As soon as we've found Arthur."

"But Arthur . . . the creature took him."

"We don't know that."

"It took him, darling."

"Perhaps. But neither of us saw it go off with him. I saw nothing of the sort, did you? We were both blinded by the brightness of the gunshots. All we truly know is that the creature descended upon Arthur, and we were unable to find him afterward."

Looking my beloved wife in the eyes, I said, "I believe it bore him away."

"Perhaps he ran off and hid in the woods."

"But he hasn't returned."

"Perhaps he's lost. Or injured. He may be in desperate need of our help."

Even now, I thought, he's likely dead in the stomach of the beast.

"We can't simply abandon the area," Emily said. "Not without doing all in our power to find him."

"Oh, darling," I said.

Seeing the anguish in my eyes, she kissed me gently. Then she said, "Arthur may very well have perished last night."

I was both glad and saddened to hear the words . . . confirmation that she hadn't lost touch with her common sense.

"It's . . . very likely," I told her.

"If that *is* what befell him, we must find his body and take it away from this hideous place."

"We won't be able to . . ."

"We cannot leave here without him."

Good God, I thought.

7

We unbarricaded the cabin door, removed it from its frame, and stepped outside into the sunlight. Having little knowledge of the nature of the winged beast, I couldn't be sure it was entirely nocturnal. Therefore, I stood with Arthur's shotgun, watching the skies and listening while we made a search of the immediate area.

I neither heard nor saw any sign of the creature.

As for Arthur, we studied the ground near his abandoned bedroll. We discovered nothing unusual there, not even any drops of blood.

Narrowing her eyes, Emily gazed into the woods. "He's out there. I know he is."

"But the forest is . . . it's huge, darling. We might search it for *days* without . . ."

"We'll find him," she said. "I'm sure we will. We must."

"At the risk of our *own* lives?" I asked.

"If need be."

"But, darling . . . Do you think for one moment that Arthur

would want *you* to be . . . taken by the beast . . . for the sake of retrieving his body?"

"I'm sure he would never choose to be left behind as carrion in this godforsaken wilderness."

Not wanting to incur her displeasure, I nodded in agreement.

"Then find him we shall," I said.

8

And find him we did.

After our initial search of the area, I stood guard while Emily prepared our meal.

We'd risen late. It was well past noon by the time we renewed our search for Arthur. Staying close together, we circled the cabin again and again in an ever-widening spiral outward.

To me, the search seemed hopeless.

It also seemed foolhardy. We should have been making our way toward safety, putting as much distance as possible between ourselves and the cabin before nightfall . . . not circling it in the hope of finding Arthur's remains.

We came upon him late in the afternoon.

I can hardly claim that we *found* him, however. On the contrary, he found us.

Trudging through the dense forest, we kept our heads low. For the most part, we watched the ground and the areas in front of us, not only looking for Arthur's body but taking care not to bump into trees or trip over roots or stumble over fallen branches or injure ourselves in any other way.

We didn't see Arthur at all.

As if to confirm Emily's opinion that he preferred not to be left behind, Arthur's fingers had snagged her hair as she walked beneath him.

"Oh, drat," she muttered.

A few paces in front of her, I looked back in time to watch her reach up with the intention of freeing her hair from a low-hanging limb.

I saw that it was no tree limb, but the hooked fingers of a human hand.

Before I could warn Emily, she touched the hand and screamed. She stumbled backward. A banner of her blond hair remained with the hand for a moment, then slipped free. She fell onto her back.

We both gazed upward at the hand.

It belonged to a muscular, hirsute arm that extended downward through the fork of a heavy branch some seven or eight feet above the forest floor. The arm appeared to be as stiff as the branch itself.

9

Emily had been clutching onto the hope of finding her brother alive. Upon seeing his arm, however, the hope fled. Though she sat up, she remained on the ground and shuddered with sobs as tears spilled down her face. I went to her and held her for a while.

At length, she recovered enough to speak. "Will you . . . will you bring him down? Will you?"

"Of course."

And so, leaving Emily weeping on the ground, I climbed the tree.

I averted my eyes from Arthur until I stood upon the heavy branch that bore him. To say that he lay facedown . . . No. His back, torn and draped by the shreds of his clothing, was skyward. He had no head whatsoever. The remainder of his body appeared to be intact though horribly torn and gouged.

Several broken branches higher on the tree revealed the course of his descent.

At the time, I considered the possibility that Arthur had scurried into the tree in an attempt to escape from the creature, and climbed to its uppermost regions before it took off his head and he fell.

However, I later realized it hadn't happened that way at all.

The winged creature, flying above the forest, had simply released its hold on Arthur's decapitated body and let it fall where it might.

"It is Arthur?" Emily asked from the ground. Asked, though she knew full well.

"I'm afraid so."

"And he's . . . dead?"

"I'm . . . yes. I'll bring him down, but . . . perhaps you shouldn't watch. He's . . . much the worse for wear."

"I'll step away," she said.

She turned her back. As she slowly walked off, I called down, "Don't go far, darling."

I then made my way onto the limb with every intention of lowering Arthur to the ground. At first, I was loath to touch him. But Arthur himself, I realized, would have laughed at me, mocked my squeamishness. He would have *relished* the job, had our positions been reversed. This fortified me for the task (and gave me not a little satisfaction).

Setting to work, I quickly succeeded in freeing Arthur: I tumbled him sideways and gravity did the rest of the job. A large man, he landed upon the ground with quite a wallop. I'm afraid I must've smiled, but the outcry from Emily tore the smile from my face.

She hadn't gone off, at all; she'd hidden nearby and watched.

Now she rushed forward, squealing, her arms outstretched. She seemed about to drop to her knees and wrap her arms around Arthur, but suddenly she halted. She stood above him, arms out, knees bent, back bent, head down, and made quick little gasping sounds.

"Arthur?" she asked.

She hunkered lower as if listening for an answer.

"Arthur, where's your head?"

My stomach twisted tight.

"Arthur, what have you done with your head?"

"Emily?" Though she didn't respond to my voice, I continued, saying, "I'm afraid the creature must've . . . taken it."

For a while, she continued to stand over Arthur, hunkered like a wrestler about to wage battle, hardly moving at all except for her back and shoulders and head rising and falling ever so slightly as she gasped for air.

Then, as if speaking to Arthur, she said, "This simply won't do."

Finally, she straightened her back and lowered her arms and tilted back her head. She stared up at me in the tree and the look in her eyes chilled me to the bone.

"We must find Arthur's head."

"But . . ." If the madness in her eyes was an indication, she would have us searching the woods forever. "We'll never find it, darling."

"We *shall*."

"We'll never find it because . . . I have no doubt the creature ate it."

In a low, cold voice, Emily said, "Then we shall kill the creature and rip Arthur's head from its belly."

10

Never before had I seen such furious, mad rage in Emily—or in anyone else. Trembling, I made my way down from the tree.

Emily clutched my arm. Glaring into my eyes, she said, "We'll do it tonight. We'll lie in wait and . . ."

"I think we should *leave*, darling."

Her grip tightened. Her fingernails dug into my flesh.

"Leave if you must, Dexter. *I* leave when the monster that did this to my brother is slain and I hold Arthur's head in my two hands."

I simply gaped at her.

"Are you with me?" she asked.

"I really think . . ."

And there I halted my words. Though I had no doubt that Emily's sanity had been knocked askew by her grief, I also knew this: I would lose her love forever if I chose not to stay with her and deal with the beast.

"We'll stay," I told her. "We'll kill it."

No sooner had the words escaped my lips than her mouth was planted there. She kissed me with a fierce and wild abandon, and embraced me, and soon, overwhelmed with passion, we found ourselves upon the ground not very far away at all from where Arthur lay sprawled.

Utter madness, I thought.

But utterly splendid, and Arthur made no complaint.

11

That night, Emily spread her bedroll on the ground in front of the cabin in the very same spot where Arthur had lain himself down the previous night. It was Emily's plan. To me, it seemed foolhardy. Though I'd gently urged her time and again to abandon such a coarse of action, she remained no less determined than ever.

To my everlasting regret, I took no action to stop her.

Though I'd feared the worst, I'd told myself that perhaps we would prevail. The alternative, subduing Emily by force and taking her away, would have cost me her love.

Far better to have lost her love, however, than . . .

Let me tell it as it occurred.

Soon after the fall of darkness, I took my position and Emily took hers. She lay on her bedroll, a blanket over her body, a bowie knife clutched in her hand. I lay stretched out on the ground a few feet away from her, Arthur's shotgun resting on top of me, my entire body hidden beneath a scattering of leafy limbs—a method of concealment I'd discovered while reading accounts of the Apache chief Geronimo.

I knew full well that Arthur's shotgun, fired at point-blank range into the winged monster, had failed to save him. However, a study of his two empty shells revealed that they'd been loaded with a light birdshot. Arthur had been well prepared for shooting ravens from the sky, never guessing he would find himself attacked by a monster the size of an aeroplane.

In his pack, I found other cartridges, many containing heavy loads of buckshot. Several were armed with solid lead slugs. I slipped two of the slug-bearing shells into the shotgun and filled my pockets with more ammunition.

The heavier ammo gave us a fighting chance. Or, more accurately perhaps, the frail hope of a fighting chance.

Countless times as I lay on my back waiting, I told myself, *Of course the birdshot didn't harm the damn beast. But the slugs certainly will. The slugs will knock it silly, blast it dead. They're bound to. Only a fool would throw birdshot at such a creature. What was Arthur thinking? If he'd had his shotgun properly loaded for the occasion, he'd still be with us.*

I told myself those words so many times, probably, because I hoped to make myself believe them.

I hoped they were true, but doubted it.

Time and again, as we lay there silent in the dark, I imagined myself leaping up, casting the foliage aside, and rushing over to Emily, grabbing her arm, pulling her up, blurting, *Enough of this madness! We'll spend the night in the cabin and be away from this godforsaken place first thing in the morning!* I imagined Emily trying to struggle free from my grip. I imagined shaking her roughly by the shoulders. *Enough! I won't have us throwing our lives away for the sake of Arthur's damned head—a head that was of questionable worth even when it still resided atop his neck!*

But perhaps the slugs will stop it this time, I told myself.

Or perhaps the monster is elsewhere tonight, somewhere far away, and we'll get through the night unscathed.

I had little hope, however, for any such outcome.

Finally, near the end of my tether, I was about to leap up and call a halt to the plan when I detected the faint *whup . . . whup . . . whup* of the monster's flapping wings.

"Arthur?" Emily asked.

"I hear it. There's still time. Shall we make for the cabin?"

"Never," said Emily.

The flapping of the terrible wings grew louder, louder.

In a gentle, coaxing voice, Emily said, "Come along, darling. Come to Emily."

I thought for a moment that the words were meant for me.

Silence. Then came the noise of the beast smashing through the nearby treetops as it soared down at us. Then WHAP WHAP like boat sails snapping in a gale.

I bolted upright, shouldered my weapon, thumbed back both the hammers, and swung the shotgun toward the sky—a sky obliterated by the black shape of the monster.

I fired off both barrels.

KRAWBOOM! KRAWBOOM! The muzzle flashes ripped the night like lightning bolts.

In their glare, I glimpsed the beast—its red eyes, its horrid beak.

Then darkness, utter blackness.

Emily screamed.

Oh, God! Does it have her?

Blinded by the flashes, I broke open the shotgun. I flicked the spent shells from the chambers. With hands that quaked, I struggled to insert two fresh shells. One fell to my lap. But one went in and having no more time, I snapped the breach shut and thumbed back the hammer.

I could tell by the sounds of Emily's voice that she was no longer on the ground where she'd spread her bedroll.

And so I swung the barrels in the direction of her voice.

Upward.

And fired.

In the sudden flash, I saw Emily in the talons of the beast, squirming and kicking—driving her bowie knife into its breast as it bore her into the night.

After the flash, they both vanished in the black.

But I still heard Emily's voice through the ringing in my ears and the squeals of the beast and the flapping sounds of its giant wings. She shouted, *"There! Die! DIE!"* She kept shouting those same words again and again as her voice faded in the distance and finally disappeared.

12

The next day, I searched the woods.

I hoped against hope that Emily had stricken the beast with mortal wounds and had somehow escaped from it.

I found no sign of the beast or Emily.

13

That night, I was the bait.

I lay all by myself on Emily's bedroll in front of the cabin and waited, the shotgun resting along the length of my body but concealed by the blanket.

That night, I had no illusions about the shotgun.

But perhaps if I should strike the beast in *just the right place.*

Late in the night, I heard the *whup . . . whup . . . whup* of its approach. My heart quickened. I cocked the shotgun.

I'll either have my vengeance or the beast will have me!

As the flapping sounds grew nearer, nearer, I expected to hear the beast come smashing down through the trees.

But it didn't.

High above the tops of the trees, it glided overhead, blocking out the moonlight.

I led it, shut my eyes for an instant to save them from the night blindness, and fired a single barrel.

Through the deafening explosion came an ear-splitting *SCREEEK!* I opened my eyes in time to see the beast flinch in the moonlight.

Something fell from it.

Fell from underneath it, making me suspect that perhaps my slug had indeed struck a sensitive region, causing the beast to drop whatever it was bearing away in its talons.

Gazing upward, I watched *two* objects falling toward the ground.

The monster ducked and whirled as if to retrieve them.

I fired again.

The second shot seemed to change its mind. It swooped upward and flapped off and vanished.

14

The next morning, I searched the woods near the cabin until I found both the objects lost by the monster.

They stand side by side on the table as I sit alone in the cabin, penning this narrative of my hideous adventures.

They are oblong cylinders, perhaps a foot in height, constructed of a strange, metallic substance unlike anything I've ever seen before. The cylinders are shiny like silver. They both have lids . . . lids that may be rather easily unscrewed and removed, but which will never again be removed by me.

If and when I attempt my escape from this unholy region, I shall take both cylinders with me.

I shall keep them both with me always, if I live. Emily would want it that way; God knows, she would not wish to be separated from her brother.

If I fail to make good my escape from the beast, I will no doubt end up in just such a cylinder. Perhaps the three of us . . .

It doesn't bear contemplating.

The worst part is not that Emily is dead. Nor that some loathsome creature beheaded her. Nor that her brain was removed and placed inside this bizarre cylinder. The worst part is that when I hold the cylinders containing the brains of Emily and her brother, I feel warmth. I feel subtle tingling vibrations and know without any doubts whatsoever that *their brains continue to live.*

THE STUFF OF THE STARS, LEAKING

Tim Lebbon

There was a clear dividing line between grass and sand, as if the beach advanced further inland night by night and, as yet, no breeze had come to blur the latest step. Shrubs held their baleful heads above the golden tide, and the shells of dead things surfed long, drawn-out waves.

Yet Brynn saw little of this. He passed across that sheer border between land and water with his mind elsewhere. His wife had died a thousand miles from here, but she was never far away, and as he imagined her car plunging into the sea, he smelled seaweed and brine and rotting things. Gulls screamed in the waning light, mourning further losses. The sea always made him maudlin. As death edged closer day by day, it was a state with which he felt content.

Sometimes he imagined her waiting for him, wherever she was now.

Brynn's legs ached from the walk down the cliff path, and he was already beginning to dread the climb back up. Glancing along the beach to the west, he could see the sun dip into darkening waters. It caught stray clouds as it fell, bleeding pink across their backs. He paused, looked back at the cliffs, wondered whether he should leave this until morning.

But the path seemed quite safe. And of course there was the dead thing on the beach, past the dunes, down near the sea.

From the clifftops it had been barely visible, little more than a smudge across the sands, a shape losing clarity to distance. Even through binoculars the image had been unresolved, though it had presented a disturbing insinuation of size. Brynn was awed but dissatisfied. He knew he would need a trip down to view it firsthand.

He mounted the last dune. In the soft light of the setting sun he could see the shape just above the waterline. He made a trail across virgin sands, each step a gentle hush against the soporific sigh of the sea. Sometimes he wondered whether, if he succumbed to the ocean's hypnotic charms, he would wake up even when the waters rushed into his mouth.

Approaching the thing, he realized it was far larger than he had thought. A whale, perhaps? The local newspaper had called it a monster, but of course it would. Good for tourism. Building sand bridges was their main concern.

He stopped fifty paces from the corpse, close enough to view it in some detail. It lay on the beach like a huge lump of wax melted and congealed many times over, picking up imperfections with each burn and set. Mottled and split though its surface was, however, there were no barnacles suckered to its leathery hide, no seaweed hanging from its appendages. It was as though all life had eschewed this creature.

Brynn knelt in the sand and took his camera from the backpack, imagining what Helen would have thought of this. She'd have created a million stories about this thing's final hours, drawing in all manner of inconceivable ideas and waterlogged fantasies to construct her own version of events. . . .

Perhaps she'd been daydreaming when she died. Living stories in her head, while death crept up from behind, pushed the car over a cliff, and drowned her.

As he began taking photos, changing position every couple

of shots, the stench hit him. It must have been there before, but shock had obviously dulled his senses. It wasn't putrefaction, exactly, nor was it the tang of insides exposed to the elements. He held a handkerchief over his mouth with one hand as he snapped photos with the other.

The size of the thing stunned him. It was so big, he could not conceive what might have killed it. Could it really just die, something this magnificent, and wash up on this innocuous beach? As he circled the creature he saw tentacles buried in sand, surfacing a dozen feet further on, dipping in again, giving the classic sea monster silhouette.

He nudged one tentacle with his shoe.

There was a sudden shrill cry that startled him so much he dropped the camera, stumbled, and tripped over his own feet. Several seagulls descended as if to alight on the shape, but they only circled there, unable to land, repulsed by something, screeching in agitation until they flew away.

Brynn gasped and instantly wished he had not. The smell was even worse. He gagged, sought control of his stomach, then puked anyway.

Afterward he grabbed his camera and left, walking faster than he would have cared to admit. He did not look back.

In his caravan, waiting for his soup to warm, Brynn wondered why the prickly feeling on the back of his neck wouldn't go away.

Darkness tried to sneak through cracks in the windowpanes. Its pressure was almost discernible, pressing in like gas at a vacuum. He shivered and drew the curtains. It did nothing to hide the massive outside. He did not want to look out, in case he saw someone looking in, their face bathed in light borrowed from the moon. Their eyes unlit, even from without.

He sagged into his chair and sighed. He was acting like a

kid. He'd always been cautious of the dark. That's what he told people: cautious. Never really afraid, even when he was young. Cautious. Like he was around electricity or acid. He treated them with respect lest they hurt him, and he respected the dark equally.

He thought it was the reaction most likely to be welcomed by whatever lived there.

As the soup plopped and blubbered in the saucepan he examined his camera. The damp sand had buffeted its fall, but grains had somehow worked their way into the mechanism. He removed the batteries and put the camera away, searching through piles of notebooks and scraps of paper for his cheap spare.

The smell of artificial tomatoes hung heavy in the air. Brynn had a fleeting, aromatic memory of eating with Helen in an Italian restaurant in Cardiff—

—and then he was on the floor.

Throughout it all he knew what was happening, but he had no control. His arms and legs buffeted the cheap carpet. His heels beat hard, shaking the whole caravan. His head lifted, fell, lifted and fell again, as if an invisible hand gripped his hair, its owner determined to shatter his skull. His fingers flicked at the floor as his arms rose and fell, and he heard his nails cracking. His back arched, then jerked straight. He tried to grit his teeth against the pain, but they crunched together, and he tasted blood and the gravel of chipped enamel.

He thrashed like a landed fish.

And he saw things. His eyes turned up in his head to view the terrible fantasies he had created, the images of what Helen suffered during her final few moments of life. Violent waters surged, snapping things flitted in and out of the waves, then there was a cool, dark deepness promising only a cold death . . . and something down there, waiting.

Shock held him and whipped him around, but one thought

swept insanely around his head throughout the whole episode: *I won't piss myself, I won't shit myself.* Again and again. In that respect at least, his determination held out.

It was seconds or minutes before the fit subsided, instantly and without warning. As he lay still on the floor, panting and sweating and scared of the silence, Brynn's muscles continued to twitch and knot.

Something sighed against the outside of the caravan. Through a chink in the curtains, silhouetted by a tentative half moon, he saw a breath fading slowly from the cool pane, revealing the stars to him once more.

Eventually he made it to bed. He hid beneath the blankets and did not sleep.

In the morning, in the light, things seemed different. Brynn knew it was foolish, but the sun seemed to titillate the logical side of his mind. He'd had a fit for the first time in his life. He was scared, but thankful that he had not badly damaged himself. His fingers were sore, his head was bruised and thumping, but there were no broken bones. He would go to the doctor as soon as he was back in Cardiff.

Everything was normal.

As he arrived again at the edge of the cliff and began his descent, a dreadful smell assailed him. It was worse than the stink of the day before, far richer, more *gritty*. It reminded him of the color brown and of white noise, as if he was smelling everything at once. He gagged, sure he was going to be sick again, but somehow he kept control of his guts. Leaning over, staring down at the rough path, he watched a string of saliva stretch from his mouth and darken the soil where it made contact. *Stuff of me in there,* he thought. *Cells from my body, the stuff of stars, that's what we're made from.* He wondered who else he was looking at in the muck around his feet.

He stood, shaded his eyes against the sun, and stared down at the beach. The tide was out and he could see the thing lying there, a great black hump on the smooth golden sands. Its tentacles seemed more abundant this morning—longer, more numerous—although it could simply have been that the sands had shifted in the night.

Brynn tied a handkerchief over his mouth and continued the descent. He tried to remember coming back up the cliff last night—it had been dusk, the shadows deceptive—but he could not recall the climb. He must have been on autopilot. He was surprised he hadn't fallen.

He followed his own footprints back to the thing on the beach. As he came to the dunes, he realized that he was following more than the single trail he had laid yesterday. There were other disturbances in the sand, strange whipped prints like those of a snake, and more resembling the footprints of birds, though a hundred times bigger. They might have been carved there by the breeze or left by seaweed that had been blown away. Perhaps they were caused by thousands of burrowing worms blowing bubbles through the damp sand.

None of these options explained why all the trails led to the dead thing.

Brynn approached, trying not to step on the other prints, afraid he would sense what had made them. As a child he avoided cracks in the pavement. . . . *Step on a crack, break your mother's back.* Perhaps old habits never died at all, but just lay in wait eternally. Seagulls still buzzed the corpse, and as they turned and spiralled away they still called out in distress. The distress was echoed in his head, a phantom throb like someone else's pain.

The sun was hidden today, but it wasn't cold. A warm breeze blew in off the sea, carrying with it hints of the deep and desert islands. As Brynn came to a standstill he kicked a bottle washed up the night before. He picked it up, expecting a message, but it was empty of hope.

He squatted on his haunches and wondered what the thing had seen, where it had been. Six miles down on the ocean bed perhaps its mate waited even now, moving through unimaginable pressures in a vain search for its companion. Or maybe there were more of them, a whole community. Searching. Rising from the bottom. Air sacs inflating, flesh billowing out as the pressures decreased.

He shook his head and stood again. The sand was soft beneath his feet, still wet, but drying now that the tide had left it for a while. He stepped forward, ready to touch the hide of the dead creature, run his hand along its tattered mass and look for signs by which he could identify it. Great clots of flesh hung from its torn skin, bulging, dried up in the sun.

He reached out. He was within one step of the thing. The sand became softer, as if hollowed out from below.

But something grabbed him and turned him around, an inherent sense of self-preservation, and before he knew it he was walking back along the beach. His spare camera banged against his leg, unused. His head pulsed with the headache that had been plaguing him since last night.

He'd had a fit. There had been a shadow at the window. Yet he felt more alone now than he ever had since Helen's death.

Brynn did not want to climb back up the cliff path—that would have felt too much like defeat—so he headed to the base of the cliffs instead. Sand gave way to rocks, which protruded like the petrified remains of unknown creatures. A seagull landed nearby, glanced at him, and then took flight again, cawing its way out to sea.

Nursed among the rocks were pools, darkened by the sea

plants clogging their edges. There was an occasional pink flash of a sea anemone feeling at the water, and secret scamperings hinted at crabs and other creatures hidden in their own temporary ecosystem. Brynn wondered what it felt like to be trapped like that every day, and he squatted next to one of the pools, swishing the water and watching the reflection of the sky distort above his head.

He clambered over the rocks for a while until he found a spot out of sight of the beach. His jacket provided adequate protection from the damp sand, and he lay with his hands behind his head, eyes closed. He relished the cleansing warmth of the sun on his face. The steady beat of the sea was soporific, and he felt time drifting away from him, his senses withdrawing. Sound came to the fore, the sea singing different songs depending on where it struck the shore: from behind him, the soft hush of the salt waters shifting tons of sand; nearer, a roar as it stroked patiently at the receding land.

In ten million years, this would all have changed. The sea would have eaten this place. The sea ate everything in the end, wearing it down over massive expanses of time, which it alone could afford to expend waiting. Eventually, like a salmon to its birthing pool, everything went back to the sea. Somewhere in there was all of history, way beyond simple human understanding.

Helen had died in the sea. Her body was never found. Perhaps there were bits of her in the massive dead thing on the beach, atoms she had owned now given over to something else.

She died a long way from here, Brynn knew. But something that size could swim forever.

He had always hated himself for not hearing her final words, and the nightmares he had were guessed-at versions, guilt trying to fill in the blanks. The worst times were when she blamed him. However much he tried to convince himself that it could never have been his fault, the words followed him into waking and set terrible seeds of doubt in his mind.

Time passed, the sun moved, Brynn slid slowly into sleep.

When he stirred it was late in the afternoon, and the sun was already bedding down for the night. He stood stiffly, brushed himself down, shivered, and wondered why the cold had not awoken him. His head was still thumping, and his body had begun to ache even more from the battering it had received last night. His fingertips were bruised blue.

He picked up his backpack and noticed how far in the tide had come. Creeping up on him, patient, unhurried. One day, if he wasn't careful, it would have him. Just as it had taken Helen.

He made his way back along the beach until he came to the top of the dunes. The thing was still there. He was tempted to approach again, but something warned him off. He tried to convince himself that it was a simple matter of not wanting to invade its grave privacy.

He climbed the cliff path, panting, breathless, his knee joints burning and his sides stabbed with an ice-cold stitch. He had to stop three times on the way up, and for the last fifty feet—when the sun had truly set and he felt he was navigating by memory alone—he constantly expected to feel nothing beneath his next step, a wide, black nothing that ended with him broken on rocks a few frantic heartbeats below.

At the last, he was gripped by an incredibly clear urge to turn around and go back down. In the dark. Along a path that would certainly spill him to his death.

Sense and logic prevailed and he found his way back to his caravan, where something that had been working at the back of his mind for the entire climb came to the fore: the memory of what he had seen in the setting sun. The dead thing lying there with its tentacles — barely visible before — spread out across the sand like the spokes of a giant wheel.

Just lying there and waiting to turn.

Brynn tried to prepare something to eat, but his eyes were constantly drawn to the window. He kept imagining a face there, staring in at him, a face made of the same stuff as the dead thing on the beach . . . the stuff of unknown stars . . . so he closed the curtains.

It did not work. The outside was only hidden from view, allowing anything the opportunity to approach unseen. And seeing slivers of night through the threadbare curtain was worse than seeing a whole pane of glass: One eye, bloodshot and reflecting his own fear, would be more dreadful than a complete face.

Soup burned to the side of the saucepan, blackened, and coagulated into something barely resembling food. Brynn cursed and began to eat.

Later he took out his notebook and began to jot observations of the dead creature. He made rough sketches of the corpse, estimated its size and weight, and frightened himself in doing so. He was writing *The Book of the Sea*. He had been writing it ever since Helen died, but every chapter seemed to increase the distance between him and her memory. Still, he hoped a resolution would reveal itself soon, a twist in the forked tail of his grief—

He arched off the seat and hit the floor, pen and notebook sent flying. A groan of despair escaped him as he realized what was happening, then nothing else, because his neck was in tension as his head banged against the carpet once more.

This time the fit lasted longer and was more extreme. Light seemed to flee the caravan, scared by his thrashing, and the sounds of various parts of his body impacting the floor, doors, and cupboards faded to a whisper. Something stank, something worse than burned soup, more rancid than the chemical toilet he had not been tending properly. Faintness snowflaked his eyes. He vomited and felt the warmth across his face and neck. The thump of pumping blood filled his ears, sounding vaguely like the sea, and as coherent thought retreated he was sure he heard words in the rushes.

More ideas of Helen came in, but this time they were new visions of what she had suffered. So new, so detailed, so obviously heartfelt, that Brynn could not have possibly created them himself. They were put there for him to see. Helen in the car, shattered windscreen shards opening her to the seawater and spewing dark clouds as she sank, trapped, toward the ocean floor. A final breath held dearly, going stale inside of her, slipping murderous fingers through her lungs to clasp her heart as she saw . . . below, down past the car's hood . . . a total darkness. Not just a lack of light but something more.

And she kept on falling.

And Brynn would never know when or where she struck bottom because, as her lungs expelled their last, the image and the pain faded away to nothing.

His senses crawled back like whipped dogs seeking succor. He gasped at the air, moaned, tried to scream but puked again instead. This time, he was able to turn on his side so that he did not have to swallow it.

The caravan door was swinging in the morning breeze. The place stank, and he was rolling in his own filth. He must have been out all night.

After much struggling he stood and peeled off his clothes. His arms, legs, back, and buttocks were tender and bruised; his head throbbed as if his skull had been shrunk to compress his brain; he had bitten his tongue and the insides of his cheeks. Yet he took solace in the pain each breath gave him.

He found some clean clothes, dressed, made a pot of tea over the primus stove.

The cold hit him all at once, retrieving memories of last night like hypnotic suggestions. He suddenly needed to leave the caravan. The smell of vomit and shit hung heavy in its stale atmosphere, and he could make out dents and scrapes where he had been flipping about during his fits. To stay there would be to tempt fate. And though fate was about as believable as malignant demons, given a choice Brynn would tempt neither.

So he left the caravan and headed to the cliffs, and on the way he saw trails in the dew-laden grass, slick sweeps of disturbed moisture where something had passed by not too long ago.

Soon he found himself at the head of the path leading down to the beach. Daylight, fresh air, the eternal hush of the sea onto the rocks below, all helped to clear his mind of what had happened, both the fear of the fits and what he had seen while he was incapacitated. The pain felt good, because it was good to be alive.

The thing was even darker than before, almost black, and its tentacles were once again stretched out in dead abandon. Some were buried, others snaked along the sand as though seeking a comfortable resting place. From this high vantage point, the dead creature looked like a huge drift of oil on the beach.

On the way down, Brynn wondered yet again at how he had navigated this path in the semi-darkness. It was so narrow at times that his shoulder brushed against the cliff face as he passed, and showers of stones and sand snickered down onto the rocks below. And still the sea mocked his fears with its incessant song.

He had not brought his camera with him, nor his notebooks. He had left his jacket in the caravan, and now he shook and shivered as he waited for the sun to purge the shadows he was descending through. The path was slick with dew.

On the beach, a line of seaweed indicated high tide. Brynn thought it was further up the beach than he had yet seen it. He knew about tides and surges and seasonal highs—the sea had been his obsession since Helen had been lost to it—and he knew that there was nothing extraordinary about last night.

Really, he thought. *Nothing at all? What about that fit and those dreams? What about the trails in the grass?*

The sea was rough today, whipped into a frenzy by westerly winds, and where it struck the rocks near the base of the path it threw sheets of spray into the air. The wind carried it to Brynn, cooled his face, spotted his clothes. He opened his mouth and closed his eyes, wondering if some of Helen were splashing across him now, bits of the stuff that had made her spread across the oceans after so long.

He would touch the thing today. It must have been here for several days and decomposition was splitting it and venting its gases and melting its insides, but he would run his hands across those tentacles, feel its hide. Feel the truth of it.

He walked through the surf so that he did not leave a trail in the sand. It seemed the right thing to do. Because there were other prints there already, strange snakelike patterns winding across the beach. And as he neared the thing, he saw that it had begun to change. It was flattening, settling down into the sand, spreading a dark stain and becoming a new bridgehead between land and sea, between known and unknown. The tentacles stretched further than ever, but even they were breaking down and giving themselves to the beach.

Brynn fell to his knees and scooped up a handful of the darkened sand. It was sticky and heavy, warm and sweet smelling. He stopped himself from tasting it . . . though he yearned to know its true scent.

He fell on his back next to the corpse and stared up at the

new day. He could almost hear the thing rotting, a series of rips and tears over and above the constant hypnotic surge of the sea. He closed his eyes.

His muscles clenched, then shook in the grip of a sudden, violent fit. His eyes turned up in his head. Senses drifted away like breaths in a storm. A gust caressed his skin and then he was gone, a berserker in the dawn, flopping and flipping in the sand like a thing of the sea.

Black grit entered his mouth and eyes and ears, worked its way beneath his clothes, trying to make him a part of the beach just like the dead thing. He saw darkness, felt unbearable pressure and the icy cold of unknown depths. Helen was in his head—or he in hers—and he finally knew what she was thinking at the moment life left her body to its doom. He knew but it did not comfort him, not as it should have. It scared him. Even in the depths of his strange fit, he wondered how her final wish would come to be fulfilled.

She never wanted to leave him. Someday she would be with him again.

Her last thought had been of him.

Brynn opened his eyes, blinked rapidly, and rolled onto his side. His bones felt brittle and liable to break at the slightest impact.

The thing had all but gone; it was now little more than a hump in the sand. It had spread as it came apart, and as he stood, Brynn saw that most of the beach had taken on a dark tint. He walked across and tried the path to the clifftops, but he could not climb. He willed his limbs to take him up but they rebelled, showing him instead the trails in the sand that led down to the edge of the sea, and further. He doggedly sought other routes to the ground above, shambling along at the base of the cliffs, looking for handholds and cracks. But all paths were lost to him now.

The gale increased, driving the sea into angry white breakers, going from nowhere to nowhere with ferocious intent. He was sure the wind started on the beach and ended on the beach . . . he could see a horizon, but it seemed false, a trick done with mirrors.

The top of the cliffs looked a million miles away. He felt like crying but the tears would not come.

It was only as he finally followed the trails to the water—felt the sea close around his thighs, tasted brine on his tongue, sensed new depths opening up to him as he moved further and further out—that he felt truly in control once more.

SOUR PLACES

Mark Chadbourn

Ten years under foreign skies should be time enough to leave the past behind. Yet when I returned to Sheffield it was still there, staring out from the dusty, broken windows, watching from the side streets where yellowing newspapers and smashed syringes were thrown about by the merciless wind. For a city built on the backs of men toiling away in hellish steel foundaries, Sheffield had known good times and bad, but like all British cities—maybe all cities worldwide—there was one area that remained resolutely bad. And that was the place where I grew up.

Why those areas remain unredeemed in the face of the hardest efforts of councillors, charities, and do-gooding businessmen has never been clear to me. But whatever's there gets under the skin of the residents like ringworm. You never lose it.

I tried harder than most, but however many miles and years I had put between my home patch and me, I still felt sick in the pit of my stomach when I saw the crumbling, weather-stained tower blocks rising up like jagged teeth against the grey sky. Despite the time of day, the concrete shopping centre seemed deserted. Too many stores had been boarded up or plastered with posters, and that familiar unpleasant smell of urine still hung in the air.

I hadn't summoned the nerve to go back to the house, so I sought out the tiny café that had been a home from home for a few of us in the dismal days of our teens. The glass front was opaque through steam, but at least the place was still open. Amid the oppressive atmosphere of fried food, one man sat with a cold cup of tea at a Formica table scarred with the names of a generation of young lovers. He didn't give me a second glance.

When the door closed with a bang, Molly came out from the kitchen at the back, cheeks hollower, face lined, but unmistakably Molly. It took a second or two for the pinched expression laid on her by life in that part of town to be replaced by a smile of recognition.

"Bobby, is that you?" Her eyes narrowed slightly. "What are you doing back here?" It was an accusation of failure, filled with the disappointment of someone who had vicariously enjoyed the idea of someone escaping forever. The real reason dawned on her a few seconds later and she looked unconscionably relieved. "It's your dad, isn't it?" Not a failure at all. I *had* escaped; there was hope for all of them.

I nodded. "I haven't seen him yet."

She leaned over the counter and took my hand. "Oh Bobby, you poor thing. He's in a bad way."

"I heard. I don't know the details." I spread out the crumpled telegram next to the sugar bowl. "They just said he'd had some kind of breakdown. Couldn't look after himself anymore. Do you know what happened?"

She winced, looked away. "The old place has gone downhill since you were last here, Bobby dear," she said, as if that explained it all. Her words almost made me burst out laughing. *Gone downhill.* As if it could. "But look at you!" she continued. "You look wonderful. Where was it? France?"

"For a while. Then Rome, and Milan."

"Oh, you lucky bugger!" She gave my cheek a pinch. "It's nice to hear a success story, you know—" she motioned around the room "—with what we normally get in here." She brushed down her overalls, suddenly aware of my local celebrity status. "Listen to me rabbiting on. Let me get you a cup of char while you tell me what it's like working for all those glossy magazines." She winked. "Photographing all those beautiful women."

As she bustled around in the steam, a melancholy air seemed to come over her, and when the cup of milky tea was in front of me she said, "You know, I never thought you'd get out of this hole. I'd watch you with all those mates of yours on a Saturday morning, sitting at that table by the window." She nodded toward *our* place. "Nice lads, the lot of them, but no prospects, if you know what I mean. You were different. I could see it in you even then. You'd make us all proud, given the chance."

There was the key phrase. No one in this place ever got any chances. Unless they made their own.

"Then when that girl—Marie, was it?"

"Mary."

"Pretty girl. Lovely, really. For round here." She gave a weak smile. "She was even quite clever, wasn't she?"

"She was." *For round here.*

"But it was easy to see what she wanted. To get married, have kids quick, like her mum, and her mum before. And then—"

"And then I would have been stuck here forever, in some hopeless job, fat and old by thirty."

She nodded slowly. "I know your dad—and your mum, God rest her—they must have put a lot of pressure on you." She searched my face, the extent of the understatement known but unspoken. "They didn't really want much out of life, did they?"

"Not really."

"It would have been a shame if they'd stopped you getting what you wanted, all that potential gone to waste. All the girls here, we thought you'd be announcing the engagement once you'd finished school. And then one Saturday you didn't come in, and the other boys said you'd just upped and gone." She gave a relieved smile. "Good for you, I say!"

I sipped on the insipid tea; I'd forgotten how awful it tasted.

"That Marie—"

"Mary."

"She must have taken it hard."

I winced, the memory still raw, like all the memories of this place. "Yes. She did. And I didn't speak to my mum and dad for months after. Mum . . ." I took another sip; horsehair for the mouth. "She was three weeks buried before I knew she was dead."

She rested a comforting hand on my forearm.

I finished the tea and made to pay, but she waved me away. "Give my love to your dad." And then as an afterthought: "When you see him, try not to take it too hard."

It was midafternoon before I found the courage to wander up the drive of the horrendous Victorian dump they euphemistically called "the home." When I was a kid it had the kind of reputation you saw in old films about gothic insane asylums; everyone hoped it would go with the NHS cuts, but with the new *caring* policy it had earned an undeserved lease of life. That was ironic. In a particularly bitter way.

The past was still watching me from the trees so I hurried into the smell of antiseptic and stale tobacco. Incongruously, the nurses all wore crisp white and tried to smile most of the time. That got quite unnerving after a while in that oppressive place. They led me down labyrinthine corridors to my dad's room, which looked out over the grounds; it would have been a pleasant view if it wasn't so dismal out.

When I entered he was in a chair with his back to me, so I was spared the full shock of what had happened to him. As I skirted the room the revelation came to me in tiny fragments so I was prepared for the full-on view. He was sixty and looked about a hundred, his face sagging in the cheeks and hollow around the eyes. His hair, which had been steely grey the last time I saw it, had almost entirely fallen out, and what did remain was the colour of snow. But it was the awful haunted expression continually gripping his face that affected me the most; he looked as if he'd had a vista onto hell.

"Dad?"

He didn't look at me. I don't know if he could even hear me. His rheumy eyes shifted constantly across the rolling lawns and shadowed trees, as if he was constantly searching for something just beyond his field of vision.

"Dad? It's Bobby." I dragged up a chair and sat just off to one side, where he could look at me if he wanted. I can't say that we were ever close, but even if we'd been the worst of enemies it would have broken me to see him that way. It was five minutes before I could bring myself to talk to him again, but however much I tried I couldn't get any response from him. I slumped back in my chair, covered my eyes, tried to comprehend what could possibly have done that to him. When I looked up, he was staring directly at me. And what I saw in his eyes made me so sick I knocked over my chair in my hurry to get out of the room.

"What happened to him?" I tried to mask the break in my voice, but I guess the doctor had heard more than a few overly emotional relatives. Even so, his expression seemed unduly troubled.

"Have you spoken to the police?" He was in his forties with the kind of studious, sensitive face that marked him as an outsider.

"Why the hell should I talk to the police?"

He looked uncomfortable discussing the matter without any preparation. "You could—"

"No. Tell me now."

"There was an incident in the street where your father lived. Several bodies were found in one of the houses. By all accounts, even by the standards of such a thing, it was not a very pleasant sight." His choice of words almost made me laugh; it must have been the strain. "There had been a degree of mutilation. Whoever was responsible hasn't been caught—"

"And Dad?"

"When the police were going from house to house questioning the few people who were left in the street, they found him, well, as you saw him. He refuses to talk, barely eats. There has been some suggestion his condition is a response to stumbling across the atrocity, perhaps even witnessing it. The police were understandably very eager to talk to him, but so far he hasn't found the desire to communicate."

"Shock, then. So given time he could come out of it?"

"He could." His eyes gave the lie to his words.

Keeping one step ahead of the past is a difficult thing and I'd spent the last ten years doing it. Sometimes I'd failed and those were the worst times, unbearable, and the simple act of attempting it had taken the sheen off my new life. Nothing had worked out quite like I'd hoped.

Going back to the old house was almost more than I could bear, but I *had* to go back; it was a fishhook stuck in my life. Despite the memory hanging in my mind like a lowering cloud, I almost had trouble locating the street. Molly had been right; the place had changed and not for the better. It was now surrounded by a vast swathe of wasteland like some medieval battlefield, where the old redbrick back-to-backs had been bulldozed. All the familiar landmarks were gone. No great loss. I picked my way among the rusting washing machines, oil drums, and twisted wire with the smell of some industrial pollutant hanging in my nose. The wind rustled the scrubby yellow grass so it constantly seemed things were moving just below eyelevel all around. Twilight was coming in hard; I didn't want to hang around there any longer than I needed.

The old street looked incongruous in the new landscape, just two long rows of houses facing each other in the middle of nowhere. I suppose there were still a few residents hanging on to their familiar misery to prevent any further demolition; I know my dad would have died before he moved. The redevelopment wasn't so surprising. Nobody could get any price for the houses in that area anyway. There were rumours of them changing hands for just £150 in the local pub, any amount so the occupant could get away and start over. If they were anything like me it wouldn't have done much good; our sort carry our misery with us.

The lights in the city beyond were winking on as I crossed the last stretch of muddy ground. Before me the backs of the terraces were all in darkness; it didn't look like there was anyone left.

As I came up to the graffiti-scarred brick walls that bounded what passed as rear gardens, the doctor's brief description of the atrocity in one of the nearby houses came back in force. Bad things always happened round here, but nothing like that. Had it been some junkhead freaked out on dust? A gang killing? A part of me perversely wondered if it was just one of the locals who had finally had enough of living round here, snapped, gone wild with his former neighbours, and then stalked off to oblivion. It was disturbing to think that actually made sense.

In the same instant I became aware of a terrible atmosphere which permeated that place. It lay beyond the usual brand of social despair, although it was certainly despairing; there was an abiding sense of sickness and misery that felt uniformly spiritual. You might think it was a simple reaction to considering the murders, but I know it was palpable. A queasiness dabbled with my stomach and my throat felt like it was constricting. For some reason I couldn't quite explain, I suddenly felt very, very frightened, as if I had plugged in to the primeval part of the brain that instinctively responded to subtle dangers in the environment. I couldn't help glancing round at the lonely, darkening landscape, the silhouetted bulks of discarded fridges, old washing machines, and the bare bones of ancient sofas, the constantly waving yellow grass. It was only then that I realized the wind had dropped. But the grass was still moving.

My anxiety continued to rise beyond the reach of reason. With pounding heart I watched the gentle swaying. If I could only see what was in there: a dog, rabbits, an urban fox. Soon it would emerge.

Seconds passed, and the more I waited the more the strangling sensation of fear rose in my throat. My irrational response to that mundane sight took complete control of me and suddenly I knew I *didn't* want to see. I was in fear of my life; I had to get away from there.

"Quick! Over here!"

I started at the hissed words as if I'd been shot. A shadowy figure was beckoning to me frantically from a splintered wooden door leading into the nearest backyard. Before I had time to react, the figure had hauled me into the yard, bolting the door behind. My uncontrollable fear made me lash out wildly, but the grip on me was tight and I was propelled into the dark house. I stumbled onto a carpet that smelled of damp and urine and was on my feet in a second, but the figure was ignoring me. The back door was bolted several times and heavy drapes drawn across the window before a light was put on. The sickly bare bulb illuminated a man I recognised from my childhood, although like my father he looked much older than his true age. He was an American, his grey hair long and wild and matted with grease around a face that looked like it was made of leather. He'd always kept himself to himself as if he was afraid of being discovered, but on one occasion he'd let slip that he'd once lived in a place called Red Hook. I had no idea where that was, but the name was so evocative it had piqued my imagination for months after.

He didn't seem to recognise me, though: barely paid me any attention at all. He simply stared at the drawn curtains as though he could see through them, constantly kneading his hands together to stop them trembling.

By that stage I'd calmed enough to feel my earlier reaction was a little ridiculous.

The American seemed to know what I was thinking. "You always feel like that when you're near them. Sick in your stomach. Terrified. It's 'cause a part of us knows they shouldn't exist. Or maybe it's 'cause we recognise our natural predator."

"I don't know what you're talking about." His words had once again started that buzz of anxiety in my gut.

He looked at me suspiciously for a moment, then silently led the way up a darkened stairway to a stark bedroom that stank of vomit. Standing on either side of the window where we couldn't be seen, we looked out across the wasteland. Where the yellow grass was swaying, I could now see dark shapes moving back and forth, tracing out strangely disturbing patterns on the landscape. At first I thought they were people crawling slowly. Then I returned to my earlier guess of beasts; pigs, perhaps. Finally, and to my horror, I realised they seemed to be some sickening combination of the two.

"What are they?" I croaked.

Shaking his head, the American wandered back to his stairway. "Areas like this always have their infestations. I can't work out if those things cause places to turn bad or if they're just drawn here because they like the air." His chuckle turned into a phlegmy cough. "Places that God's given up on."

My head was spinning. I wanted to run out of there, get out of the city and back to where the decent people lived, but I was terrified of crossing the wasteland while those things were out there.

The American was mumbling again. "You know what I think? Spots like this draw people who *deserve* to live here. People like me." He looked at me with cold, hateful eyes. "And people like you."

Night had fallen completely and out in the wasteland the creatures were circling closer to the houses. The moon made their hides appear creamy white. Occasionally I caught glimpses of yellow pinpricks, like distant stars; their inhuman eyes glinting. Were these what had caused the atrocity? What had driven my father to the brink of insanity?

"It doesn't make any sense!" I said pathetically. After the events of the day, the strain of coming back, everything seemed too much, but that tough streak which had got me out of there in the first place stopped me from breaking down.

The American was roaming the room, yanking at his hair. "I can't leave here. That's the terrible thing. I can't leave!" Tears sprang to his eyes, but he made no attempt to blink them away.

Despite his age, I grabbed him roughly by the shoulders and threw him against the wall. "What are they?"

He started to cry weakly, his voice turning into an irritating whine. "They live underneath here! They've burrowed tunnels up from somewhere . . . somewhere . . . In the day I can hear them singing under the ground! It makes me want to kill myself!"

"Calm down." I shook him a little too hard.

"You know what they do? They feed on people! First they used to feed on emotions, all that bitterness and despair and hatred. But in the end that wasn't enough. They wanted—"

I shook him again until his head cracked on the wall. "How do you know all this?"

He looked away guiltily. "I just know."

"They killed those people?"

"They hadn't finished with them. But the cops came, disturbed them. They lay low for a while. I saw them disappear down the tunnel under number eighteen."

Ice water washed through me. "My house?"

He blinked, as if he was seeing me for the first time. "You're the Kirk kid?"

"My house!" My fear was suddenly replaced by a terrible rage. I threw the American across the room. He sprawled over the bed and landed hard on the floor.

"What do you care? You got out—"

"Shut up. You've got to show me."

"We can't go out there—!"

"You've got to show me!"

We hurried across the street like rats keeping to the shadows. The front door hung jaggedly on smashed hinges. I'd expected a little twinge of nostalgia for some of the good days—the few—when I was a kid, but all I felt was a deep fatigue. I'd never wanted to see the place ever again.

The American led me through the front room to the kitchen at the back; there was a ragged black hole in the middle of the floor. That gave me a brief feeling of relief, but when I looked out into the back garden I saw the deep furrows of disturbed earth that confirmed my worst fears.

The house itself was just as I remembered: cheap furniture, too few home comforts; nothing out of the ordinary. With a queasy sense of things spinning out of control, I knew my only hope was to check in the hole.

The American realised what I was planning before I spoke. "What's wrong with you? You don't have to go in there!"

I peered into the sucking darkness, not even thinking what those things I'd seen crawling around could possibly be; somehow it didn't seem important. I gave the American a hefty shove and followed him into the hole.

I don't know how long we slithered and slid around the tunnels; they were more extensive and confusing than I'd ever imagined, and I was so lost in my own awful thoughts I barely noticed the passage of time. Nor did I have any fears for my own safety; I was single-minded in my determination. But at least there was a faint luminosity to the walls that prevented us journeying in complete darkness. On closer inspection the illumination came from a thin coating of slime like the trail slugs left behind; I wondered if it was some filthy residue from those creatures.

The American had started mewling like some kind of animal and I honestly feared he was losing his mind. He had been under tremendous pressure, even by the yardstick of my hometown, where pressure was a daily constant. There was no going back, though. There hadn't been for very many years.

As we progressed, the burrowed tunnels emerged into ones that were stone-lined, although at first glance it was hard to tell they had actually been *constructed*; the walls were so rough-hewn they almost seemed natural. Certainly no human hand had ever touched them. The air, too, took on a disturbing quality. All I can say is there was a *pressure* to it, but of an emotional kind; despair welled up inside me, and fear, and anger, and all sorts of emotions that civilised people tried to keep buried.

Just as I was about to give up my search we came to a chamber lying off the main tunnel, and it was from here that the disturbing atmosphere seemed to be emanating. The American started to whimper, refusing to enter. I soon changed his mind.

The walls of the chamber were scarred with a chiseled writing, but of a kind I'd never seen before. It was incomprehensible, runic in form, but though inexplicable it filled me with an irrational dread. On one side there was an alcove made important by strange, twisted carvings that nauseated me the moment I laid eyes on them. Within the niche was a rock covered with more glyphs and runes. The American seemed drawn toward it. His whimpering died away as he inspected it from different angles. I hissed at him to leave it alone, but he was oblivious to my warnings. My instincts proved correct, for the moment he laid his hands on it, his body grew rigid, his head slumped backward and his eyes rolled up until only the whites were showing. The air itself suddenly grew electric.

"*G'a'Restlig Tharn.*" His mouth contorted to form alien syllables. The timbre of his voice made it sound as if he was praying. "*G'a'Restlig Tharn,*" he said again, and this time the entire wall that housed the alcove grew opaque. The milky surface shifted like mist, gradually clearing to reveal a vista across space. Stars flared in the infinite, icy void. I only had an instant to take it in before I realised there was something else out there, something alive although not in the terms of reference we knew. And as that thought entered my head I had the terrifying sensation that it had seen me, that it was suddenly hurtling toward me at a speed that defied reason.

In a blind panic I jumped forward and knocked the American away from the rock. The image on the wall cleared in a second, leaving me wondering if it had ever been there. But the sensation of that cold, alien intelligence focusing on mine still filled every fibre of my being, and I knew I would never, ever forget it.

"What's going on?" the American moaned. "What does it mean?"

Sickened, I pushed past him toward another chamber I'd spotted at the back of the room, wishing I could leave, drawn on by sick memories. The oppressive fruity smell emanating from the dark doorway told me what lay within before I saw the mutilated bodies of some of my former neighbours. Even so, I continued, immune to the horror as I had been for a long time. Here were people who had lived in the now-demolished streets. I wondered briefly if the authorities knew what lay beneath our depressed little patch and had simply tried to obliterate it, knowing they could never put it right.

But a pile of my father's closest neighbours lay there too; fresh kills. And among them was the thing I had been searching for yet feared finding. I ducked down and plucked a piece of glinting metal from the decomposing pile.

How hardened was I? Not as much as I believed, I suppose, for after that moment of revelation my mind seemed to wink on and off like a strobe light, barely able to contain the terrible thoughts passing through it. I vaguely recall the American shouting, "Something's coming!" and turning and seeing movement. I remember a sea of those creamy-white human pigs and me kicking and flailing like a madman. There was one moment when I looked into the face of one of the beasts and saw traits that echoed the stagnant gene pool of my hometown, not knowing if the beasts had become people or the people beasts, or if it was something infinitely worse.

The American was screaming for me to save him, and I almost considered it, but self-preservation took over, as it always had. I was blind and stupid with panic, but somehow I managed to break away. And then I was running along deserted tunnels for what seemed like hours and hours, eventually emerging in another house at the end of the street just as dawn was breaking over the dingy tower blocks.

My rational thought processes only really came together once I had crossed the wasteland and by then I wished they hadn't. Somewhere at the heart of it all was a bitter joke I could barely put into words. The place I had grown up in was damned, the people feeding on their own misery, feeding on one another, in a vile cycle that never ended. And what was that terrible alien power that focused its incomprehensible intelligence on me for the merest instant, yet scarred me forever? For all our pretensions to order and evolution and superiority, everything I'd experienced suggested we were truly meaningless, existing in a universe that was indifferent to us, where acts of kindness and humanity amounted to nothing. Goodness wasn't rewarded, evil wasn't punished; there was no overarching order. We lived and suffered and died and that was it.

But then I already knew that.

In my hand was the cheap, tarnished engagement ring I'd bought under duress, offered in despair. You can never leave the past behind. Those crawling things had unearthed the body I'd frantically buried in the back garden on a night of madness and jubilation, freedom that turned to slavery for as long as I lived. It was a desperate act of escape, my one chance—but here I was back home again. It was finding the body, that awful realisation, that had destroyed my father and that I had seen in his eyes when he gave me his final look of contempt.

I searched the fringes of the wasteland until I saw her, staring at me with those accusing eyes that had followed me for ten years. The past, always with me, to make sure I really didn't leave the old town behind.

And then I thought back to what the American said about these sour places attracting the people who deserved to live there. And you know what? I think he was right.

MEET ME ON THE OTHER SIDE

Yvonne Navarro

"I'm not sure I heard you correctly," Macy said. "What was that—some kind of Israeli name?"

"*Bethmoora*," Paul said. "And no, it's not Israeli. Actually, the roots aren't traceable to any specific language or dialect. But it's still . . . foreign."

"And you want to go there on vacation," she said, looking thoughtful. "You know, I'll have to check the expiration date on my passport—I didn't realize you were thinking about traveling overseas. It's where, exactly?"

Paul looked at her, and his deep green eyes never wavered. "I don't know."

"I never knew you had an interest in this," she said as she helped him finish with the last of the packing. Outdoor equipment, all of it—small camping stove and dried food, utensils and first-aid kits, lightweight survival clothing that would keep them warm and dry no matter how severe the rainstorms they ran into, all packed into roomy, sturdy backpacks that would, above all, hold plenty of water. After all, Paul was leading them into a stretch of the Arizona desert that could just as easily fry their brains inside their skulls as dump a monsoon-induced flash flood over them . . . then chill them down to their souls when the sun sank below the horizon. "When—"

"Brand new," he said, answering her question before she could ask it. Another woman might have found that annoying, but it didn't bother Macy; she and Paul had been doing stuff like that since the first day they'd met thirteen years ago. "I ran across this weird-looking little book called the *Encyclopedia Cthulhiana*, picked it up just because it had this whacked-out illustration on the front—curiosity, nothing more."

"And?"

He shrugged, but there was nothing self-conscious about the movement. "I'd never seen anything like it before, never heard of the stuff it talked about, so I shelled out a few bucks. Skimmed through it, asked around a bit. There's a lot of hype, but not much *real* info. Still, I kept coming back to the entry about Bethmoora, kept wondering about it. I did some poking around on the Internet and found out there was a *lot* more stuff around than I thought about this Cthulhuism, or whatever the hell it's called. Entire cults."

Macy considered this. "So you've done your research."

"More or less. It's not like we're going to Egypt, you know. Hell, we've been hiking in worse places than the Arizona desert."

She couldn't argue with that, and the truth was, she had no inclination to do so. They had this thing, her and Paul, a hunger for excitement, a not-very-well-hidden taste for danger. It was what had drawn them together and kept them that way, surviving through dozens of friendships and even an affair or two on both sides—odd, experimental things that had been born only to test the limits of their senses of self and their marriage, the what-if-I-did-this factor, and the strength of their affection for each other.

The thought of traipsing through the scorching Arizona

desert didn't scare Macy, but it did start a tickle of anticipation in her gut, the same thing that had been present during their two or three trips a year, trips that had included an illegal archaeology hunt in Egypt, a jungle trip in Burma where they'd entered a forbidden underground temple, a weekend of drugs and nearly unspeakable sex in Bangkok, other things done in Russia that were better left unsaid. Their jaunts around the home country were nothing more than minor stress-busters, two- or three-day getaways to hold them over until their work schedules and budget would allow them to seek bigger and better entertainment. This proposal of Paul's was a rarity, with a sense of adventure seldom offered in the short term. Each trip had given her some memento, a trinket to tuck away and savor now and then; only the Burma trip had gifted Macy with something she wore all the time, an irregularly shaped ruby half the size of her little fingernail and with a slash of black deep at its center. They had stolen it from the temple's altar, and it now hung continuously on a heavy gold chain around her neck.

For other couples in their income bracket, marriage held the promise of more normal things—a house in suburbia, fancy cars with leather seats, a kid or two who would give them a double decade of agony. No thanks: Macy had five brothers and sisters, and her mother—who was one of twins—had eight siblings, including yet another set of twins. Macy and Paul had talked about this before they'd ever said their vows, and Macy had no desire to raise a duo or two of screaming kids—twins routinely skipped a generation and so, as one of her sisters had already proven, Macy could pretty well expect at least one set of her own. Again, no thanks: she had opted for a kid-free existence, and she and Paul were the happier for it.

On the surface, the Arizona desert trip seemed inconsequential, but as she bent over the half-dozen poorly rendered maps he'd scrounged up on the Internet, then paged through that book of his, it began to sink in just how much he *didn't* know about this Bethmoora place—the truth of it was, the city might not even exist. All the odds seemed against it; according to what Paul had found out, Bethmoora was a city that existed in something called the Dreamlands, which in turn, existed in a realm accessible, perhaps, only in the mind. Yet the maps and notations he'd found here and there pointed to there being . . . *something* out there, a point at which they might find the entrance to the Dreamlands, and from there continue on.

But to what?

It was a wild concept, but there were things they'd seen, experienced, and learned in so many parts of the world that made her, *them*, believe many things could be accomplished that others, normal people, would dismiss out of pure ignorance.

She and Paul would not be so foolish.

The other books—the maps, the notes and perhaps the so-called encyclopedia—were full of half-truths and inconsistencies, clues that led to nowhere. There wasn't much solid to go on, other than the opinion that Bethmoora, once bustling and presumably beautiful, was now inexplicably abandoned by its inhabitants. But Paul, since he'd first run across this stuff, had this feeling about it, and now she had it, too.

Bethmoora was out there, all right. Just waiting to be rediscovered.

Revitalized.

And they were just the people to do it.

Even though it was late in the afternoon, above their heads the sun was a ball of blistering heat. They were smack in the middle of something their map indicated was the Palomas Plain in southwestern Arizona, and for as far as either of them could see, there wasn't much beyond the cacti and scrub grass poking up here and there through the rock-littered and sandy soil.

They'd stopped on the shaded side, which wasn't saying much, of a small pile of boulders to eat a semblance of lunch and consult the maps.

"What do you think?"

Paul gazed at the papers spread on the ground, then looked dreamily out across the desert. "I think we're doing good," he said. "A couple more hours that way." He pointed vaguely northwest.

"We're going to have to find it soon." She hated to remind him of this, but they had only so much time and water left— if they didn't hit their goal, they'd have to turn and retrace their route to the car, left parked along the side of an unpaved road near the Sundad settlement the day before yesterday. It wouldn't be the end of the world, but it would be a damned disappointing end to this adventure.

"We will," he promised her, and there was something in his eyes that told her he believed it. "We've got a couple of good hours of daylight before we have to make camp. We'll use those, get an early start in the morning, and go for, say, four or five hours. That'll be our turnaround point."

Macy nodded but she knew Paul well, so well. He was organized and efficient, but also arrogant; there was no mistaking the tone of certainty she heard in his words, the unspoken statement: *But we won't turn around, because we're almost there.*

And when she looked past him to where the open desert shimmered with heat and a thousand deadly creatures seen and unseen, she knew, without a doubt, that he was right.

Nightfall on the Palomas Plain was a spectacular thing to experience.

In English, Macy was pretty sure that *palomas* meant white-caps, and it was a fitting description. The fiery reds and purples of the sinking sun had an odd effect on the light-colored desert spread out before them, broken in the distance by small mountains. Instead of darkening the ground, it turned the lumps and bumps of distant rocks, shrubs, and barrel cacti into something that vaguely resembled small waves breaking over an unnamed ocean. She didn't know if this was what had inspired the area's name, or if the tiredness brought on by days of hiking in the heat-soaked desert was skewing her vision, but Macy enjoyed the sight anyway—it was kind of like walking on the surface of a sea filled with scorpions, giant desert centipedes, blister beetles, and tarantula hawk wasps instead of sharks and poisonous jellyfish.

"There," Paul said suddenly. Her gaze followed his pointing finger to a pile of beautiful, sunset-washed boulders at the bottom of an incline that led up the side of a small mountain, just one of dozens that remained anonymous on their maps. There were darker shadows amid the huge rocks, deeper crevices that begged for exploration but were likely already occupied. As if to confirm this, they heard the high-pitched wail of a coyote somewhere on the mountainside. "That's where we'll sleep tonight."

It took another twenty minutes to get there, with nighttime slipping in and greedily sucking away the last of the evening's light and the final traces of the day's heat as well; it was as if someone had opened a cosmic refrigerator and they were caught in the escaping wash of frigid air. Still, the desert was anything but done for the day—there was a sense of expectation in the chilly, creosote-scented air, and she knew from the expression on Paul's face that he felt it, too. It didn't matter that they were exhausted to the bone, because sleep would be a long time coming.

Macy gratefully released the buckles on her hiker's backpack and shrugged it off, sweeping the ground with one hiking boot to make sure she wasn't setting it on top of something alive, and listening for the warning rattle of a snake. But there was only the quiet; the coyote's cry had dwindled away and nothing had moved in to take its place—even the desert grass seemed reluctant to make noise in the occasional stingy breeze.

"Let's eat," she suggested as Paul pulled himself free of his own pack and let it drop. He nodded, and it wasn't long before they'd made a little dinner, working in sync to fire up the camp stove and pull together a no-frills meal of reconstituted beef stew and crackers, a pot of decaf coffee. Afterward they sat in silence, gazing unseeingly at the desert. Its blackness surrounded them, nearly smothering beneath a moonless sky that would have melted into the horizon had it not been for the mad paintbrush sweep of stars overhead, crystalline points of light in the unpolluted air. She was fatigued, yes, but she was . . . excited, too, full of the desert's odd sense of expectation and that deep heat that she always got around Paul when they were "out in it," as they sometimes called their treks into the dangerous unknown. She could see him watching her across the last flames of the small can of fuel, his eyes as dark as the crevices in the rocks at his back, his hair a layer of blackness that made the white of his skin almost shocking.

Macy rose to meet him, ready when he stood and reached out to her. When he would have lowered her to the ground she jerked him toward her instead, pulling hard until she fell back against the gritty surface of the boulder behind her. They yanked away each other's clothes and he took her upright, with her spine scrapping against rock that was still warm from the day's sun, and their mouths locked as tightly as their bodies. The orgasm that hammered through her was astounding, ten times deeper than anything she'd ever experienced; it seemed to go on and on, as though it had become a living thing on its own, something wild and wonderful with a thousand fingers that could reach into every fiber of her body. Even her teeth seemed like they were vibrating inside her mouth as she gasped for air and held on to her husband as best she could. She thought she heard him cry out with the immensity of his own climax, but maybe it was just her own voice, or maybe it was the two of them shouting together. Then they were slipping and she felt the skin on her back and rear end scrape all the way to bloodiness as they went sideways between two huge rocks and fell into darkness.

Macy woke within the safe circle of Paul's arms, but she had no idea where she was, or how they'd gotten there.

A cavern of some kind—she had the sense of an immense domed ceiling above them although she couldn't really see it. Stalactites and stalagmites were everywhere, flowing from where the walls sloped away into darkness, inverting into multi-colored, layered cones that crept upward from the floor and were as beautiful as any she'd ever seen. There was light, but it was an unsteady red and purple, as though the evening's spectacular sunset had somehow made its way into this place and become trapped. It moved restlessly and without pattern, shifting here, touching there, starting to blossom in one section of the cavern, only to wink out and appear at random somewhere else.

"What is this place?" she asked Paul as she sat up. Her voice echoed eerily as cool air washed her breasts and she realized she—they—were still naked. There was a red stain where the flesh of her back had pressed against Paul's chest and arm—she must have ground herself up pretty good during their coupling . . . and yet she felt no pain. If anything, her body tingled, the leftover effects of the unimaginable pleasure of a short time ago. "How did we get here?"

"I don't know how we got here," Paul answered slowly, "but I think I know where we are." He tilted his head at something high up and to the right, and when she peered into the shadows above her head she could just make out an oversized carving, letters she recognized from the book etched deeply into the multicolored rock wall in an arching pattern above a dark and pitted wall of solid rock.

BETHMOORA

"But *how?*" she whispered. "We were just outside, we—"

Paul reached out and pulled her back against his chest. "Maybe we're dreaming," he suggested softly. "Everything the book and the maps said about Bethmoora indicated it was in the Dreamlands. You could only get there in your sleep, remember? Maybe when we fell?"

Macy thought about this as she gazed around the cavern, or whatever it was they were in. She *felt* awake, lucid, healthy—yet every bit of intelligence suggested she ought to be feeling a damned good sting from the lost skin on her back and butt. Paul, too—she could see painful-looking scrapes and bruises along his knees and elbows, yet he didn't appear to even notice them. "But I feel awake," she said. "This doesn't have the sensation of a dream, it's not fragmented like that—I mean, we're having a coherent conversation here."

"Sleepwalking, then."

Macy raised an eyebrow. "Both of us? At the same time, and talking to each other?"

Her husband gave her an I-don't-understand-it-either shrug, then released her and clambered to his feet. "Let's find a way out of here," he said, and held out a hand. She let him pull her up, but only reluctantly; the truth was, she didn't feel any inclination *to* leave, and maybe that was a telling thing in itself. If they really were awake, wouldn't she want to find their way back? She didn't know about Paul, but for her it was quite the opposite—leaving was really the last thing she wanted, although she couldn't exactly say why.

Macy felt something bump against her collarbone as she stood, and her fingers found her black-slashed ruby, the one she had pilfered from the temple in Burma. Funny that the necklace was the only item she was still wearing. Even her socks and boots were gone, although she hadn't so much as unlaced them during the bout of sex. The precious stone felt warm against her skin, almost uncomfortably so, and suddenly she realized Paul was staring at her—no, at it.

"What?"

"Your necklace," he told her thoughtfully. "It's *glowing.*"

"Really?" She scrunched her chin down and could just barely see what he was talking about. It was, pulsing in heated hues of scarlet just above the dip between her breasts. The sight of it sparked something deep in the pit of her stomach—a flutter of excitement or, more likely, anticipated danger. The sensation made her lick her lips. "Damn."

Whatever was in the air, Macy could tell Paul felt it, too, could see the evidence of it in the way his eyes sparkled in the light shifting around them. Was it her imagination or did even that seem to be moving more rapidly now, bouncing back and forth around the rocks with an almost frantic energy?

Her husband looked at the ruby for a few more moments, then shrugged again. "Come on," he said. He gestured toward an area that looked like it might lead to a corridor of some kind. "Let's try over there."

"Okay." She let him take the lead and followed, feeling the cool currents of the cavern's air slide across her bare skin as they stepped gingerly along the rock-strewn floor. Their path took them next to the wall of rock beneath the Bethmoora sign, and Macy stumbled as she passed its center, threw out a hand to balance herself and fell sideways anyway. She twisted at the last second so that the back of her right shoulder hit the rock, and by the time Paul had turned to see if she was all right, she'd straightened herself again.

And once more, she found her husband staring at her.

"What now?" she demanded, then realized he wasn't gaping at her but *past* her, at the rock wall against which she'd stumbled. She turned, then froze.

Where her skin, its surface bleeding from a half-dozen tiny cuts, had brushed against the rock, a small whirlpool of light had started. It spun counterclockwise, like a smeared, deep scarlet rose being painted by an insane artist, around and around. At its center was a spot of compact blackness as dark and mysterious as a hidden tar pit.

Paul eased up beside her. "Do you see it?" he whispered. "That spot—it looks like your necklace. Same size and shape."

Macy leaned in a little. . . . Yes, she *did* see exactly that. Coincidence? Unlikely, and she found herself instinctively reaching to undo the clasp at the back of her neck. She wasn't even sure what she was going to do until the stone was in her palm, then she reached out and pushed it into the center of the swirling mass of light.

And, like molten lava sliding down the side of a mountain, the rock wall melted away.

Beyond it was a different world, a place that belonged in neither the underground cavern in which Macy had thought she and Paul were trapped, nor the desert they had presumably left somewhere above. The vista in front of them seemed more suited to the tropics—Hawaii, perhaps, or Tahiti. Verdigris copper gates were thrown wide on each side of the gaping hole, and everything about the stone entrance had a sort of liquid look at the edges that made it impossible to tell where the stone ended and the copper metalwork began. Palm trees and long, lush grasses swayed beneath a bright sun, and Macy could smell something fruity—pineapples, maybe—on a hint of warm breeze that danced over her face.

"My God," Paul breathed. His voice was actually trembling. "Macy, it's Bethmoora. It really exists, and it's *beautiful*."

And so it was. There were buildings perhaps a quarter mile away through desert spotted with tall, proud cacti, perfect specimens every one. Beyond that began a slow spread of hills, rolling gently into far-off, grass-covered lumps for as far as they could see. Intrigued, the two of them stepped cautiously through the gate, then clasped hands and ran forward, closing the distance and welcoming the soft grass beneath their feet after the cave's rock-filled floor.

The city itself was small and quaint, picturesque in every respect, a medieval version of perfection uncrowded by the small, meticulously maintained houses and shops sprouting between the larger inns and city buildings built along its cobblestone streets. Birds flew among the palm fronds, tiny geckos blinked at them and skittered up the walls, now and then something small and furry—desert jackrabbits perhaps—scampered between the neatly trimmed hedges. It would have been a lovely place to live, Macy thought, except—

"Where are the people?" Paul asked darkly.

She didn't know the answer and didn't try to speculate. There was an aura of abandonment to the small metropolis, a stillness in the air *beneath* the pleasant breeze that spoke more of a place centuries unoccupied than the surface sort of pretty that lay before them. Fingers still entwined, they wandered through the clean, flower-festooned streets, and Macy felt a little as if they were Adam and Eve in a modern but deserted Garden of Eden—no clothes, no supplies, not even a single piece of jewelry now that her necklace was gone. Everywhere they turned, around each corner and into each new street, the scene was as lovely and unblemished as the one before it. . . .

But all good things, so they say, must come to an end.

"Over there," she said suddenly and skipped on ahead, pulling Paul along as she changed directions.

"What?" he asked. "Do you see someone? Where—Jesus."

He jerked to a stop next to her and they both stared. Farther down this street, this particular one that might have been just another clean and nameless little avenue in Bethmoora, the daylight was . . . *disappearing*. There, maybe a hundred feet away from them, it stopped and a pervasive sense of shadow began, narrowing in on itself in a funnel shape until it came to a doorway, open to nothing but thick and utter blackness.

And, waiting in that doorway, was something just as nameless as the streets they traveled.

Not quite visible, it radiated an undeniable *presence*, a sense of menace that was both dreadful and, for them, full of the familiar forbidden anticipation. So many places they'd been to, yet almost all had ultimately fallen a bit short in fulfillment. That moonless night in Burma had been the exception, the temple with the stolen jewel that tied them to this city in a land of nowhere . . . yes, that temple, with its huge, black creatures, beings inexplicably chanted into existence by the bloody-garbed guardian priests, which had then chased them from the temple and damned near caught them.

Hair-raising and nearly deadly.

The best adventure they'd ever had.

Now the couple hesitated and looked at each other. "What do you think?" Paul asked, squinting into the wedge of darkness. "I can't see it very clearly—I guess it could be a man. . . ."

"No," Macy said softly. "I don't think it's human at all. Remember Burma?"

He nodded as they stared at the vague shape in the doorway, and it stared at them. "I found something in the book," he told her in a low voice. "That I thought might connect Burma to the Cthulhu stuff. If I'm right, those things that chased us were called the Dark Young, the offspring of this female fertility god with some twisted, unpronounceable name."

Macy's fingers automatically went to her neck, but of course the necklace wasn't there—funny, but until it was gone, she hadn't realized how used she was to fondling it. "Really," was all she said, but it was nothing more than an automatic response. Her pulse was racing and with no warning at all, she suddenly felt warm, way overheated for their nearly utopian surroundings. She started to say something else but forgot the words, nearly forgot how to *breathe*, when the thing in the doorway stepped out and into full view.

"What the hell *is* that thing?" Paul asked hoarsely.

She had no answer, just gaped, became more incredulous with each step forward it took. First it looked like a tall, anemone-shaped black plant that could, absurdly, walk like a man—one that stood at least seven feet high. Then the upper half of its body suddenly lifted upright, like a mass of hair rising on an updraft, except it wasn't hair at all. Instead, Macy realized they were seeing tentacles, a mass of them, waving and probing the air like some kind of mutated octopus out of a cheap undersea horror flick.

It cut the distance between them to less than twenty feet and stopped, and Macy felt Paul's hand tighten painfully around hers, his hold digging in until she couldn't separate the hammering pulse in his fingers from her own. And in her peripheral vision, she saw the best of all possible things on his face, that thing that made her know to her soul that she had chosen the perfect mate.

A dark and slightly crazed smile, the grin that more often than not meant he wanted, more than anything, to experience what would happen next.

An expression that matched her own.

And his smile only widened when another of the creatures stepped out from behind the first.

Twins.

Without asking her, Paul started to step toward it.

Stop.

He jerked back and looked at her. "What did you say?"

"Not me." She tilted her head and studied the creatures a few yards away. "Them, I think. In our minds, somehow—I heard it, too."

"Macy, is this *real?*" Beyond his excitement, Paul sounded on the edge of desperate. "Are we really here, awake—or are we sleeping in the desert somewhere? Maybe even dead?"

"I don't know," she answered honestly. Everything he'd just suggested could be true—hell, any one of the natives at the roadside trading posts had a tale to tell about some bush you shouldn't burn in your campfire, or some water hole that you avoided at all costs. Maybe they'd burned just such a bush and gotten high or something, cracked their heads on the way down. Even now coyotes and night creatures might be scavenging food off their cooling bodies.

It is real.

Macy shuddered as the voices, two of them and simultaneous, rippled through her thoughts, knowing instinctively that what she heard, her husband did, too. She found her own voice and asked the first thing that came to mind, blurting out the words before she had time to consider whether or not the things in front of her might find them insulting. "What are you?"

The beasts swayed back and forth. The tentacles that comprised their upper bodies were long and graceful, weaving with nearly hypnotic regularity.

We are the twins Lloigor and Zhar. We are brothers.

In unison, the twins suddenly slid forward, cutting the distance between themselves and the couple nearly in half. Now they were close, *too* close; Macy had a way too personal view of those tentacles and the suckers running along the length of each one. She thought she saw tiny teeth embedded in each.

Paul must have noticed, too, because this time he took a

step backward, dragging on her hand until she came with him. "Why are we here?" he demanded. "What—what do you want?"

For a long moment, their minds were silent. When the answer came, it had a longing, singsong quality that had been lacking in the creatures' previous words.

We need the woman, the twins whispered to them. *She is . . . our destiny. And we are hers.*

Paul scowled as this sank in. "That's it," he said. "We're out of here." Still holding firmly to Macy's hand, he started to turn and head back down the street, no doubt toward that copper-gated entryway. But he didn't get far—a foot was all—before Lloigor, or maybe it was Zhar, shot out an appendage and coiled it tightly around his neck.

It is not your choice. You are . . . disposable.

While the half-second that it took for Macy to register what was going on seemed to stretch in her mind like an eternity, Paul's face went instantly scarlet as the blood was compressed above his neck. The next instant, she was grabbing at the thing wrapped below her husband's jaw line, trying desperately to work her fingernails between it and Paul's skin, to find for him, somewhere, a little breathing room as he flailed at the attacking beast. When that didn't work, she outright clawed at it, gouging with her fingernails, punching and tearing. "*No—let him go!*"

No good. Paul's eyes were rolling up in his head now, his movements growing weaker as his body used up its oxygen reserve. The monster holding him seemed absurdly complacent, standing there and swaying gently next to its brother.

"I won't stay if you kill him!" Macy cried. "I'll leave—go back where I came from!"

For another two seconds nothing changed, then the tentacle released Paul and let him drop. Macy went down with him, barely managing to get an arm between his head and the ground before it hit. Her husband gasped for air and tried to sit up, finally found enough strength to do so. His neck was ringed with tiny, bloody circles. Enraged, Macy bared her teeth at the grotesque twins. "Damn the both of you," she snarled. "Abominations!"

If she'd thought her insult would hurt them somehow, she was wrong. The creatures simply stood there, patient and implacable.

"I'm all right," Paul rasped. He held onto her hand and made it to his knees, then staggered back to his feet. "I'm fine."

The woman.

Macy scowled. "Why?" she demanded. She swept an arm around her. "What's the story on this place, and what do you want with me?"

A thousand years ago we were en route to Bethmoora, destined to mate with a woman chosen by the high priests of the city. Bethmoora is a city of cycles, and as it has been since the beginning of time, the offspring of our pairing would have enslaved the city and ruled in depravation for five centuries. Then our children would sleep, and Bethmoora would rebuild and flourish as it had countless times before.

But we were betrayed by a temple acolyte who desired the chosen woman, and our coming was revealed. The residents of Bethmoora panicked and fled, disrupting the cycle and leaving the city abandoned, frozen in time.

Forty generations later, you are the last descendant of that woman. You, therefore, are the chosen one, our mate, who must reestablish the cycle and break free the wheels of existence. This is why you have been drawn to this place, to Bethmoora.

If Macy hadn't been so horrified, she might have laughed. "Mate?" she asked incredulously. "You can't be serious. You're not even *human.*"

"Besides," Paul put in, "if doing that will unleash five hundred years of destruction and misery, why the hell would she *want* to?"

"I'm not even from your world," Macy added. "I . . . *exist* somewhere else." She looked around a little helplessly, trying to orient herself back toward those elusive copper gates. "Back . . . there."

Species does not matter. Physical bodies can be altered to accommodate what is necessary. The thousand years of solitude has changed the fabric of the barriers between our dimensions, and they are ready to be broken down, the twins intoned. *Now the two worlds will be merged as one.*

For a few seconds, neither Paul nor Macy could speak. Then Macy found her voice. "So this would destroy not only Bethmoora, but everything . . . on the other side, as well? All life—*people*—would die?"

Not all. It will be a struggle, but the strong will survive.

"And me?" Macy asked softly. "Would I?"

Perhaps . . . if you are strong enough to survive the birthing of the twin gods, stronger still to endure the new world that will emerge.

Twins, Macy realized with a start. Of course. It was all coming together now—the history of multiple births on her mother's side; her own unquenchable taste, matched only by Paul's, for adventure and danger; even their irresistible urge to steal that keystone ruby from the temple in Burma. As the beasts in front of her claimed, it was, it had to be—

Destiny.

You will be changed, the voices echoed. *Forever.*

She glanced at her husband and found him looking at her. Was that a hint of the familiar hungry grin at the corner of his mouth?

Macy faced Lloigor and Zhar again. "And what about my husband?" she asked slowly. "What will you do to him?"

Nothing. Whether he survives the coming catastrophe depends solely on him.

"You would let him leave Bethmoora."

The mating will take three days, the birthing another seven. If it is your wish, we will send him to the gates and beyond, back to that place in the desert where the two of you joined and entered the Dreamlands. He will have those ten days to prepare.

"More of a head start than the rest of the world," Paul said dryly. "I guess I should be grateful." He shot the beasts in front of them an ugly glare, then pulled her close. "Macy, you heard what they said—you might not survive. You don't have to do this."

She laughed then, feeling the tropical breeze and, already, wondering what it would feel like to have a hundred or a thousand of their tentacles sliding over her skin, entering her, *altering* her in unspeakable ways to enable her to bear their young. The thought brought heat with it, deliciously decadent curiosity about what was to come, that craving, as always, for the dangerous and the unknown. What would she be like afterward? Would she still be . . . human? It didn't matter.

"I don't have a choice, Paul," she said. She cupped his face in her hands. "I never have—you know that."

"I love you," he said, and kissed her deeply.

Macy savored his touch, taking it inside herself where she could treasure it during the hardships to come. Her times with him, she knew, would be the memories that would see her through. "You, too."

"Sundad," he said suddenly. His arms tightened around her. "Be strong—I *know* you can—and meet me there on the other side. I'll make ready, and then I'll come back for you."

"You'll have a hard enough time staying alive," she said.

But Paul just grinned. "What the hell," he said with a shrug. "Life sucks without a challenge anyway."

He let go of her reluctantly. As he stepped back, she tried to burn his image into her mind—his lean and muscled body, the dark hair and ocean-green eyes, the softer hair that sprinkled his chest, pelvis and legs, the well-known scars that pocked his skin here and there, reminders of their past escapades. The thought of saying good-bye made her hurt nearly as much as the nearly constant rushes of pleasurable fear that were firing through her limbs. What new scars would she see on her husband's body the next time they met? For that matter, what new marks would he find on hers?

Or would he find her at all?

Yes, she swore to herself. *He will.*

On the other side of a changed world, perhaps, and it would be a fight, but it *would* happen, dammit.

Macy reached out and their fingers brushed a final time, then she turned and watched Paul as he walked away, keeping her gaze focused on him until he was out of earshot.

"The gateway to the Dreamlands," she said. "Do what you promised."

As you wish.

She saw her husband glance upward in surprise, then a circle of red and purple light spun open above his head and suddenly dropped and engulfed him. Then he, like the rest of whatever semblance of a normal and human life she had once had, was just . . . gone.

While at her back, in form nearly unimaginable, awaited her future.

No, she thought firmly and balled her fists. Not her *future* — only another adventure, the most dangerous and challenging of all, a temporary destiny. But she would prevail, because no matter what Lloigor and Zhar claimed, she would never believe that she was meant to be with anyone or any*thing* other than Paul.

"Meet me on the other side," Macy whispered.

And turned slowly to face the waiting beasts.

THAT'S THE STORY OF MY LIFE

John Pelan and Benjamin Adams

I've heard it said that family is the only thing you can count on in a crisis. Now, I've known my own strange family long enough to know that's not particularly true.

The Jeffisons of Arkham are a strange batch and were as far back as we could trace our ancestry, with a family tree filled with madmen, revolutionaries, and dire occultists. There were still secrets to our background that my eldest brother, Collis, refused to tell me; since our parents had died when I was only three months old, he had raised me as his own.

I'd left Arkham — or rather been dragged away during my freshman year, a sudden romance followed by an even more sudden move to the West Coast. I was married to Gwen and enrolled at U Cal Berkeley before I realized fully the extent of the choices that I'd made. Everything seemed wonderful for a time. . . . They say that most marriages today end in the first seven years; we didn't make it that far. Four years and I was watching Gwen drive away, her car filled with things that we'd bought together but I somehow no longer had any connections to. My marriage had just foundered on the rocks of cuckoldry, and in San Francisco I was utterly alone. I'd made no friends during the few years Gwen and I had lived there; everyone I'd known had either been a coworker in the Public Health building or part of Gwen's coterie of neopagans.

The only people to whom I knew I could turn were my family. They'd made their own attempts to venture forth into the world, but no matter their personal successes—and some of the Jeffisons had quite phenomenal triumphs in their chosen careers—all had wound up moving back to the Arkham area. Collis had traveled extensively across Asia in his youth and was now an instructor in ancient history at Miskatonic University. My brother Morse, who always seemed to have a drink in his hand, had done quite well for himself in real estate around New England and had controlling interests in several businesses in Arkham. His twin sister, Duana, had studied at the Sorbonne and now made a living as an artist, drawing, etching, and painting disturbing images with the same black sense of humor as the two Edwards: Pickman and Gorey. She shared a joint interest with Morse in a downtown New Age and pagan bookshop, The Golden Gallimaufry.

All of my siblings had left Arkham but had found themselves drawn to return to its aged, gambrel-roofed neighborhoods.

Just as I now found myself returning.

My brother Collis, a huge wall of a man, waved his right hand before him in a manner mocking game show hostesses. "So what do you think, Keiran?"

I glanced around the apartment Collis had thoughtfully procured for me. Prefabricated and rather soulless, it was like another two hundred of its ilk in Miskatonic Heights: a twenty-year-old complex built to house students from the nearby university who were either too well-off to live in the dorms or simply too antisocial to endure close proximity with a roommate.

I glanced around the apartment and saw my exile from Gwen in its every corner.

Collis must have seen the cloud cross my face. "Buck up, little brother. You're free now."

"Free." I snorted. "Yeah. It's great."

"You'll get over her in time."

In time. In time. I could imagine vast expanses of time, yawning dusty epochs of time, bloody great ages of time, and in all of it I could never envision forgetting Gwen. My heart, my soul still lay in bondage to her whims. I could physically separate myself from the cause of my pain, but I couldn't sever my ties to her.

"It's a fine apartment, Collis. Truly," I said. "I'm very pleased with it. Now let's get my stuff brought in."

Collis smiled, a sight that likely would make many bold men pale. "Good."

But as we lugged in the boxes, I knew that before the week was out I would be calling Gwen on the telephone, trying desperately to make something—anything—work out between us. Damn me, I was weak. Weak in conviction and weak in will. The woman had cheated on me, breaking a sacred covenant of trust. But the anger and pain I felt at her betrayal were nothing compared to my anguish at my separation from her. At that moment all I wanted was to see Gwen's face once again.

Gwen. Guinevere.

I fell asleep with her name like honey on my hungry lips.

I phoned her not just once, but at least five times during the first ten days of my return to Arkham. Sometimes pleading, sometimes weeping, often cajoling; using every psychological trick in the book to get her to admit that our separation hurt her as much as it did me.

Was she lonely?

"Oh, I have my friends. I know it must be hard on you, leaving everything behind and trying to start over."

Did she miss me?

"Of course I do. I wish you'd stayed here in town; we could both have had our distance and privacy and still hung out together."

Hung out.

"Like best friends."

Was there a chance we could ever get back together?

Silence. "You're putting me in a corner. What do you want me to say? You made it very plain that you didn't approve of my choice in lifestyle."

But we were married, and that meant neither one of us had a lifestyle. We were a "we."

"Well, maybe I'm just not cut out to be part of a 'we.'"

She had no problem being part of a "we" with that bastard who'd fucked her.

"Keiran, if you're going to keep bringing that up —"

What? It was the truth of the matter.

"No! Aren't you ever going to get it through your head? I wanted to do it. I slept with him, Keiran! And there've been others, *lots* of others!"

After that I didn't call her again.

I sat on Collis's back porch, enjoying the air. From the hillside where he'd built his home, the view across the valley was spectacular, as the lights of Arkham and the surrounding communities blinked on one by one. The Miskatonic River babbled softly to itself as it wended its way below us, and fireflies danced in the dim purple twilight.

Collis was inside, preparing dessert for us. Beside myself, my younger twin siblings, Morse and Duana, also sat at the glass patio table. Morse idly moved his half-finished zombie—his third of the evening—in damp circles on the glass as he told an anecdote about the hardware store he owned in Arkham, and his poor luck in finding an assistant manager who lasted longer than six months in the job. Duana, as usual, seemed bored with Morse and his tales, projecting an almost palpable ennui.

As Morse's reedy voice went on about the vagaries of the hardware business, my attention drifted to those points of light down in Arkham. Each one of those bright dots represented a life, I thought. And many of those lives were meeting, joining together in love and happiness and tenderness and Eros, as mine and Guinevere's lives once did. Would I ever feel such emotions again without her?

As had happened so often during the last three months, my eyes teared up. I dabbed at them with a paper napkin, hoping Morse and Duana wouldn't notice.

"Say, are you all right?" It was Morse. He reached out and gently laid a hand on my shoulder.

"I'm fine," I choked out. In my mind, the thought: *I'll call her tonight. I'll call her tonight. Perhaps she's changed her mind and is only waiting to hear from me again.*

"You're still thinking about Guinevere, aren't you?" There was no hiding the sour look on Morse's face.

"Why do you say it like that? I know none of you ever liked her, but I loved—*love*—her more than anything in the world. I threw away all I had just to prove some kind of stupid point by moving back here. All the happiness in the world if only I'd chosen differently. I could have made things work. I could have been happy. . . ."

"First," said Collis, who'd arrived bearing a tray filled with bowls of sorbet topped with wild raspberries, "we *tried* liking Gwen. But it was obvious from the start that she never liked us, and after a while the law of diminishing returns kicked in. We rubbed her the wrong way, so she rubbed us the wrong way. And then she dragged you off across the country, just so she wouldn't have to deal with us any longer."

My mood switched instantly from melancholy to mounting rage. "I don't have to listen to this crap—"

"*Shut up*," boomed Collis, his voice echoing down the hillside. "Yes, you do."

"Second," offered Morse, "she cheated on you and hasn't offered an apology. She shut you down and never even allowed you to really get angry with her, because she rationalized everything away. She's a great talker, that one—sometimes I wish I could have hired her as a negotiator—"

"Morse, get to the damn point," Collis ordered.

"Yes. Well. The point is, Keiran, you bought every word of what she told you. You even began thinking it might be your own fault that she had to go off and screw around with another man." He took another swig of his pina colada. Funny; I could have sworn that he'd been drinking a zombie just a few moments earlier.

"But our sex life could have been better—if I'd just paid more attention to her needs—"

"What about your needs, Keiran? Don't you deserve to have them fulfilled? Quit sitting around feeling sorry for yourself and get angry. Get angry and start *living* again."

I sat there, incapable of speech. Why were they doing this to me? Why were they trying to turn me against my beloved Gwen?

"Third," Duana finally said in her whisper-soft voice, "there's this. The latest issue; it just came into The Golden Gallimaufry." From beside her seat she picked up her large black leather handbag and rummaged around in it. Finally she produced a magazine. I knew it; it was called *Ambrosia*, and I'd often seen Gwen reading it. Once I'd picked up a copy she'd left on the couch, and found it to be a confusing mishmash of Wiccan Goddess-worship and Riot-Grrrlish propaganda, combined with amateurishly shot female-empowering pornography.

"What—what's so important about that?" I asked, dreading

the answer. In the months before we'd separated, Gwen had often talked of submitting material to *Ambrosia*, perhaps an article detailing her emergent interest in magick.

Duana brushed a wisp of black hair away from her eyes and silently flipped open the magazine. Once she'd found the page for which she was looking, she handed it to Morse, who handed it to me without even glancing down.

Collis stood at the rail of his porch, peering into the night sky. I looked at the article to which Duana had turned.

HOW TANTRIC SEX MAGICK

HELPED ME ACTUALIZE MYSELF

BY

GUINEVERE SKYCLAD

Cute, I thought. She'd already adopted a new, pagan name. And then I saw the photograph on the facing page.

My stomach lurched, and I felt a sensation exactly like having my feet slip out from underneath me on a patch of black ice.

The photo showed Gwen, naked, her small but firm breasts jutting forward proudly, astride a man (a different man! How many were there?), a circle of half-burned candles surrounding them. Her hands raised high in supplication to her Goddess; her eyes closed and the look on her face reflecting an ecstasy I'd never before seen in all the years I'd spent with her.

I glanced up and saw Duana quickly turn away from my haunted million-mile stare.

"Wait till you see the orgy sequence a couple of pages down the line," said Collis, still gazing out at the cold-hearted stars.

"I just read it for the articles, myself," Morse said blandly.

I don't recall how much I drank that night; I think that Collis must have carried me upstairs to his spare bedroom. The dreams came again that night for the first time in years, dreams of red rage and slaughter. My teen years had been so constantly disrupted by these nightmares that there was talk of giving me tranquilizers or sleeping pills.

I was in a wooded area near the ocean, somehow I sensed rather than saw that the woods were filled with my people, waiting, watching. . . .

The little men and their horses had no chance; we were upon them with cudgel and claymore before they were aware of our proximity. My club rose and fell, rose and fell and it shattered skulls, human and equine alike.

I awoke covered in a cold sweat and feeling the beginnings of a colossal hangover. I thought about telling Collis about the dream, but he'd always seemed strangely quiet when I'd brought up the subject before. Instead, I swallowed a handful of aspirin and returned to my bleak apartment.

After my family's intervention, I moped around for a while, still sad but thankfully broken of my illusions regarding Gwen. I dated a few women, mostly students from Miskatonic, but soon discovered that most of them had the mystical pretensions that I had once found so charming in Gwen. None of these relationships lasted very long. I pushed these women away like unappetizing dishes at a banquet of the damned.

And then I met Trista.

I sat nursing a Scotch at the Yellow King, one of the oldest pubs in Arkham. Its dim interior and musty air suited my melancholy mood. The folk there didn't bother me, and I didn't bother them, whereas in other bars I would have been greeted with stares incited by my hulking size, and maybe even drunken macho challenges from townies who felt they had to prove their manhood by taking down the largest guy in the joint.

The amber depths of my drink fascinated me, and I swirled it around in the cheap glass, watching the smooth contours of the melting ice cubes as they slid against one another. Like bodies they were, locked in the grip of Eros divine . . .

I dimly grew aware of a presence at the opposite side of the table, and glanced up.

The woman standing there seemed to have a nimbus of dark light around her shoulder-length, tightly ringleted black hair. Her skin was dusky and her eyes were large, dark green subterranean pools of surprising depth.

"Excuse me," she said, her voice a husky growl that immediately intrigued me. "I'm sorry if I bothered you."

Setting my Scotch down on the scarred table, I shook my head. "Not at all."

She stepped closer. "I was just wondering . . . are you a Jeffison?"

"Right the first time. How did you know? I haven't been in Arkham in years."

She smiled, a quick dark feral grin. "Family resemblance. I'm a student of Collis Jeffison's at Miskatonic."

"He's my older brother," I said. And then I surprised myself by inviting, "Please, have a seat, Miss—?"

She was sliding into the chair opposite mine before I was halfway through the offer. "Marsh. Trista Marsh."

"Keiran Jeffison." I reached over the table to shake her hand, which had an odd quality of both soft, tender areas and hard calluses. Hers was a hand that had done serious work in its time. "Funny, you don't look like a Marsh."

"You mean I don't have the Innsmouth Look," she said, referring to the odd, slightly repellent appearance many of the

Marshes in the area exhibited. Some bad blood had gotten into the Marsh line, traceable back to the small coastal hamlet of Innsmouth and a Marsh ancestor who had married an extremely strange woman from the South Seas.

"Ah, yes, that's what I meant. I hope I didn't offend. I've had a couple of Scotches and I'm not being as . . . politic . . . as I could be."

Trista Marsh laughed, a deep, soulful, and sexy laugh that entranced me. "Please, don't worry about it. I'm not related to the local Marshes, thankfully. My parents are from Scotland; they moved here to join the staff at Miskatonic when I was young."

"Where in Scotland were you from?"

"A small town near Galloway."

I blinked in astonishment. "Galloway? My family has roots there!"

Trista tilted her head and smiled. "Your brother's mentioned that. We've had quite a few long talks about Galloway. He thinks that perhaps your family and mine were . . . intertwined . . . long ago."

"That's unusual. He's usually very guarded about our family history."

"And just what secrets does your family have to hide?"

I chuckled into my Scotch. Not just at the boldness of her question, but at my odd desire to answer it. I wished I could, but apart from vague generalities about our place of origin and when the Jeffisons had come to America, there was nothing I could tell her. Collis had never told me anything more concrete. He'd implied that Jeffison was not our ancestral name, but had always refused to say any more about it. In the past I'd never thought much to press him on the subject. Now I resolved to ask him about it as soon as the opportunity presented itself.

"Well, that's something we can save for another time," I told Trista Marsh. "Listen — can I buy you a drink — ?"

"Absolutely not," said Collis. "You're not ready yet."

I'd bearded him in his office on the Miskatonic campus, in historic Armitage Hall. Collis sat at a desk that took up an entire end of the room, bracketed by overflowing bookshelves lining each wall from floor to ceiling. The office seemed far too small for a man his size, and with me in there as well, there was barely room to breathe.

"Dammit, Collis, I'm not a child any more. I'm ready to know our family's heritage, and I won't take no for an answer!"

"Actually, you will," he said calmly. "Your time away from family has left you fragile, and your behavior during the recent *l'affaire de Guinevere* shows that you're not ready for this."

"I resent that. I am *completely* over Gwen, thanks in part to your clumsily staged intervention — and I'm very grateful. I feel ready to fully reenter the family fold. What could possibly be so horrid about our ancestry that you can't tell me about it?"

Collis peered at me over pyramided fingers. "You'll be surprised, little brother."

"Please. Tell me."

For a moment it seemed as if he'd reconsider; I could see the struggle play itself out in the downward cast of his eyes and in the twitch of the muscles along his jaw. Then, finally, the words rolled out cruelly and inexorably: "No. Not yet. You're not ready."

With Trista, I found myself coming back to life. We prowled corners of Arkham I'd never known existed: Tiny curio shops and antiquariums revealed themselves before my startled eyes as she excitedly dragged me here and there. Musty old book-shops sparked her enthusiasm as much as they did mine, and with some bitterness I recalled how Guinevere hated going to such places with me.

In a small dessert shop near the campus we would often sip hot mulled cider and eat delicious cakes and pastries while comparing our finds. And at those times I silently marveled at how Trista had come to me, helping heal the wounds Gwen's betrayal had left in my heart.

More to the point: "You're in love," Collis said.

I'd met him for lunch on campus. The green quad had browned, and the last of the season's leaves twitched at the ends of skeletal branches, tore away, and spiraled in their death dance to the damp ground. Light puffs of mist burst in front of our faces as we spoke.

"Now, I wouldn't go that far," I said good-naturedly. I'd put aside my efforts at getting him to tell me about the skeletons in the Jeffison family closet, and the tenseness between us had mostly dissipated.

Collis pulled the collar of his jacket tighter around his neck. "I would. It's in your face, it's in your step, it's in the air around you."

"Sounds like the *Mary Tyler Moore* theme song."

He made a chuffing sound deep in his throat. "There's nothing wrong with admitting it."

I sighed deeply and felt the bite of the chill air in my lungs. "All right. Let's say I'm — enamored — of Trista. She's very special, Collis. I don't want to blow things with her by moving too quickly."

Collis laughed, a booming sound that echoed around the barren quad. "Keiran, the girl has loved you since the moment she first saw you. Why do you think she tracked you down at the Yellow King?"

"Tracked me down? I don't—"

"She already knew you were my brother. She'd seen you visiting me on campus and asked me who you were. I told her."

I stopped in my tracks. "You set me up?"

"I just aimed her in the right direction."

"You set me up!"

He drew an exasperated breath. "Yes, yes, okay; I set you up with Trista Marsh. Are you satisfied?"

I lunged toward him; startled, he stepped back as if expecting a blow. But instead I hugged Collis fiercely. "You damn bastard, I think you saved my life."

There was nothing he could say to that. For the rest of the day he wore his most ferocious grin, and I heard later that several freshmen in his afternoon course on the Lost Cities of Asia were so scared that they had to be sedated.

Trista impatiently pulled me down the sidewalk. "We're going to be late," she worried.

"The film doesn't start for another fifteen minutes, and we're only a block away from the theater," I pointed out. I wanted to relax and enjoy myself; the weather was warm and the late spring air smelled of flowers and promises. We were about to pass my sister's shop, The Golden Gallimaufry, and perhaps I'd give her a wave as Trista and I strolled by.

"All the good seats will be gone."

"It's only a revival of *All About Eve*, not the new *Star Wars* movie."

A moment later she nearly yanked my right arm out of its socket when I stopped abruptly to stare at a poster in the window of The Golden Gallimaufry.

"Keiran! What are you—"

Her voice trailed off as she saw how pale my face had gone.

I continued staring at the poster, thinking I had somehow stumbled into a waking nightmare.

"Oh, my—it's her, isn't it?" asked Trista.

I nodded, my throat gone dry as dust.

Guinevere's smiling face, larger than life, confronted us in black and white, a pale specter from my past. Beneath her ghostly visage, ornately flowing calligraphy announced:

GUINEVERE SKYCLAD

IN PERSON!

SIGNING COPIES OF

HER BOOK

EMBRACING SEX MAGICK

"She has a book," I mumbled. "She wrote a book. How the hell could she have written and published a book? It's only been a year since I left her."

"Keiran—"

"She must have been writing it before I left. And I never even knew about it. She never even told me. I can't believe this. I can*not* believe this."

"Keiran—"

"She always had me in the dark. I must have been like some kind of joke to her, some kind of Baby Huey lurching around the apartment while she was writing about *sex magick*—"

"*Keiran!*" Trista had grabbed the sides of my face and turned my face so that I had to look into her eyes. "She's *here*."

"What? Now? Here?" I babbled.

Trista gestured at the bottom of the poster, which bore today's date.

And now I noticed that The Golden Gallimaufry was packed full of people, all facing toward the rear of the shop. Because the people closest to us were standing, I couldn't see the object of their attention, but there was no doubt: Gwen was in there.

A mischievous light flashed in Trista's eyes, and I had the sinking feeling I knew what she was going to say next. A second later, she proved me right.

"I want to go in," she said.

Crowds have a tendency to part before me, a pleasant side effect of my size. When a man is six and a half feet tall, most people don't want to be in his way. I can only imagine the reasoning: *Oh, God, what if he falls on me? If I don't move, that guy's going to mow me down.* Perhaps they were afraid I would eat them.

The New Agers and Wiccans in The Golden Gallimaufry were no different. As soon as heads turned and people saw me, I had no trouble leading Trista into the center of the store. There was no sign of Gwen anywhere; merely a podium draped with a tapestry showing a crescent moon, around which the crowd had gathered in a circle. The early arrivals, lucky enough to be directly in front of the podium, were seated on the floor. The smell of patchouli was thick in the air, and I could hear the tinkling of tiny bells which had been sewn into loose-fitting, multicolored clothing.

I looked around and saw Duana standing by the sales counter. As usual, I couldn't tell what lay behind her inscrutable expression. She merely stared calmly into my eyes as I stomped across the room.

"Why the *hell* didn't you tell me about this?" I demanded, my voice trembling with anger.

"It was inevitable that you'd find out," she whispered. Then, to Trista: "Oh, I'm very glad to see you could make it."

Trista smiled ferally. "I wouldn't miss it for the world."

An unpleasant suspicion or two crossed my mind.

"*Hola!*" cried someone behind me. "Keiran, *mi hermano!*"

I turned to see Morse standing there, incongruously sipping on what could only be a margarita.

"I'm feeling a little festive tonight," he continued. "In a Latin mood!"

I resisted the temptation to knock the drink out of his hand, and instead whirled on Trista. "You knew Gwen was speaking here tonight. Everyone knew except me. I was set up. *Again.*"

Trista grinned and nodded, unafraid despite my barely contained Vesuvial rage. Near us, a group of black-velvet-clad Gothic types edged nervously away.

"Why have you done this to me? You—my *family*—"

And then I realized who was missing.

"Collis," I breathed. "Where the fuck is Collis?"

"He's around," said Morse. He took another big swallow of his margarita.

"Collis is nearby," agreed Trista. "Keiran, just wait and you'll understand. Collis has a very good reason for all this."

"Good enough that you *lied* to me," I spat.

She took the venom in stride. "It'll all be worthwhile, Keiran. Just wait and trust us. Look: The show is about to begin."

The lights had dimmed near the podium. An expectant hush fell upon the crowd, and even I found myself anxiously wondering what would happen.

And then . . . she came.

In a silent burst of white light and smoke Guinevere Skyclad appeared at the podium, smiling beatifically. A cheap stunt, but her crowd gasped and applauded as though they'd never seen the like before. Gwen had changed some: dyed her hair black, added a few new earrings higher up in the cartilage, and what appeared to be the tip of a much larger tattoo—the tail of a lizard—ran up along the left side of her neck and coiled around her ear. Maybe her New! Improved! style meant something to her, but to me it only brought home the point that I was over her.

I couldn't believe I'd ever been married to this New Age flake.

"Brothers and sisters," she said, "you do me a great honor by appearing here tonight, to listen to my insignificant words."

"Oh, brother," I muttered. Beside me, Trista took my hand and gave it a quick squeeze.

Gwen spread her arms. "I've come among you to tell you all of my experiences . . . of how sex magick has transformed me and lifted me nearer my full potential as a human being.

"Once I was like many of you. Trapped in a loveless, unfulfilling marriage—"

Trista gave my hand another, harder squeeze, and with great effort I kept my mouth shut.

"—with absolutely no sexual spark left—"

Squeeze.

"—no desire, no passion—"

Squeeze.

"—nothing but the empty shell of a passing fancy."

In the audience, heads bobbed in agreement with Gwen's words. I felt like rushing out there and ripping those heads off their toothpick necks.

I had never been so angry in my entire life.

Gwen's voice faded in my ears as the rushing of my own blood became all I could hear. I felt faint and closed my eyes for just a moment—

The ropes had been cunningly strung across the road at precisely the right height to catch the horses and send them plunging. Before the riders even hit the ground my family was upon them. With knives, clubs, and the few swords that we'd taken from our previous victims we dispatched them within seconds. We made short bloody work of hacking the meat into more portable segments as even the children helped by carrying stray limbs back to the caves. While the moon stared down at us, aghast at our feast that night, our friends from the sea came to join us, their women mingling freely with our men, and our men taking their pleasure with these strange women.

I tried blinking away the momentary vision. What was it? In my mind's eye I still saw the hapless bearded man, dressed in well-kept furs, as he backed away from me in fear. Behind him, a circle of similarly dressed warriors stood on a grassy ridge beneath a gloomy iron sky.

I could still see Gwen, standing at the podium, but behind her that stark landscape was also visible, as if the scenes were a photographic double exposure.

"Trista," I said softly, "I think I may be having a stroke."

"No!" she whispered harshly. "You're remembering. The anger is helping you remember."

"Remember? What—"

Squeeze. "Listen to that woman up there, Keiran," Trista insisted. "Listen to her. She's saying that your love for her was nothing but a sham. She's telling them how she betrayed you, and she's proud of it. She enjoyed it. She enjoyed cuckolding you—"

I saw the massive kettles glow a dull red as we tossed in the arms and legs of the little men who had foolishly ridden within our reach. The people from the sea enjoyed our feast as much as they enjoyed our coupling; they were like our clan, born to hunt these lesser creatures with their pathetic cities and their foolish religions.

I held the woman close as we shared the arm of one of the soldiers. I stared at her beautiful dark green eyes that stood out in such contrast to the red rivulets of blood that flowed down her chin and dappled her breasts. I saw my father tear off a chunk of meat from one of the women that we'd taken. Like my father, I saw no point in waiting for the meat to be fully cooked; fresh from the bone was tastier. I saw one of my sisters approaching with a steaming platter of brains—the best part. . . .

And then I knew nothing more.

I found myself sitting on the sidewalk in front of The Golden Gallimaufry. Trista's hand ran through my hair, rubbing away my anxieties. As well the wife of a warlord should. The cool night air helped sharpen my senses and bring me back to myself.

Offering his great, meaty hand, my brother Collis helped me to my feet. "Do you *remember* now?" he asked.

"Oh, yes, I remember," I said, grinning ruefully. "I can't believe I didn't for such a very long time."

"I told you that you weren't ready. Each member of our family, as we are reborn, must be brought to our heritage in a similar way, but you were too used to swallowing your anger and putting it aside, instead of embracing it. You'd become too much of a modern man.

"You needed to feel the bloodlust again. Only that would break through the blocks in your memory." His brows knitted together. "Um . . . how much *do* you remember?"

I remembered the dark caves near the sea. I remembered the larder, the cave where we smoked our meats and stored the treasures that we accumulated over three generations. I remembered our meeting and our melding with the people from the sea, the strange quiet folk with the large protruding eyes and the teeth as sharp as a shark's. And I remembered the ONE that spoke to us in our dreams, that promised an eternal undying as we would be born again throughout the ages if we coupled with the people from the sea. The ONE that gave us eternal life—lives to be lived to the fullest over and over again, reborn in each new age, seeking out the bonds of tribe and family and remembering who we were, all over again.

The sons and daughters of Sawney Beane.

"I remember *everything!*" I roared, sweeping my beloved Trista up in a bear hug and whirling her around. Morse and Collis beamed, and even Duana smiled slightly in her witch's garb. All my family and my wondrous, true wife, gathered together again, all of us with full knowledge of who and what we were.

Morse said it before I could. "This calls for a celebration." And in his hand was a stone mug that looked as if it were thousands of years old, filled to the brim with something that might have been wine.

"Yes, a celebration!" I echoed.

The door to The Golden Gallimaufry opened, and Guinevere Skyclad stepped outside. "Why, Keiran," she said with every ounce of sweetness she could muster. "I thought that was you inside. It's good to see you."

I smiled broadly. A *celebration!* And there was only one fitting way for our family to celebrate. . . .

"Gwen," I said, as Collis and Morse began circling behind her, "you remember my family, don't you?

"We thought we'd have you for dinner."

Reno/Seattle, 1997–2000
For Lou Reed

LONG MEG AND HER DAUGHTERS

Paul Finch

1

In the dream, he saw what he thought were the frozen ridges of ice-clad mountains. On second glance, however, he realized they were buildings . . . colossal in structure and jumbled chaotically together. It was a wondrous yet bizarre vision, all angles crazy, all symmetry absent. There was no order there, no apparent purpose hidden in the mayhem. Arches stood at random, towers leaned precariously; there were grand stairways that ended in midair, ramps that led to nothing, pillars that ran in colonnades, yet supported no roofs. On very edifice, the apertures of windows were visible, but of varying size and distortion and scattered blindly without thought to sequence or pattern. It was mind-numbing in its madness. The more he gazed at it, the more grateful he was for the opalescent mist that swamped the citadel like a milky sea, obscuring the worst of its alien excesses. . . .

"Nick?" said the voice on the phone. "Nick!"

"Mmmm . . ."

"Nick, it's Andy!"

"Andy," Nick mumbled, wondering who he knew called Andy. "Oh shit . . . *that* Andy!" He glanced across the darkened bedroom, and his sleep-sticky eyes widened in disbelief when they registered the neon numerals on his clock-radio. "This had better be good at five in the morning, Andy!"

"They've found Caleb."

Nick sat bolt upright. "Where?"

"Back in Cumbria, would you believe."

Nick swung his feet to the floor. He'd only been asleep four hours, but the name Caleb was more than enough to give any British police officer a wake-up call. "Where's he being held?"

"He's not."

"Don't tell me he's bloody escaped again!"

"Nick . . . he's dead."

Nick was in the process of pulling his jeans on. He paused. "Dead?"

"Up on the moors. They found him first thing this morning."

Nick sat down. "And he'd dead?"

"As a doornail, the local fuzz reckon."

"And this is up in Cumbria?"

"Yep . . . his old hunting ground. Apparently there are suspicious circumstances, too . . . so SCARS have copped for it. Detective Chief Inspector Beardmore's been on. It's me and you."

Five minutes later, Nick had thrown on his vest, a sweater, and a pair of old sneakers, and was in his cluttered bathroom, running an electric shaver over his stubble. The face that gazed back from the mirror was more weathered than it should have been for its thirty-nine years—old nicks here and there, a little on the pitted side maybe—but under his mop of black hair and with eyes once described by Amy as "laser blue," he wasn't unattractive. His mood soured a little when he thought about Amy. It seemed impossible that it was fifteen years since her death. Nick had been raised a Catholic, and at first he'd tried to handle the tragedy by picturing his wife and unborn son as two benign spirits who from that point on would watch over him, but after twenty years as an inner-city cop, it was difficult to have faith in anything in which goodness was the essential ingredient.

Evil, on the other hand . . . evil was a different matter. Nick Brooker had a very firm belief in evil.

2

"Sure this wreck's going to get us all the way?" Andy quipped, climbing into the front-passenger seat of Nick's old E-reg Citroën.

"Less of it," Nick replied, shoving a piece of toast into his mouth. He drove away from the curb. It was still quite early, but traffic was already pouring into the city center. "What do we know?"

Andy began to shuffle through the documents on his knee. He was slighter and blonder than Nick, and several years younger, but he, too, wore casual civvies. On "foreign soil" operations, SCARS always did.

"Somewhere called Barrowby," he muttered. He located a pad with directions scribbled on it. "About twenty miles northeast of Penrith."

Nick snorted. "What happened . . . Caleb get savaged by a flock of sheep?"

Andy continued to read. "Sounds like his body was found in the middle of the stone circle there."

"Come again?"

"Long Meg and Her Daughters . . . sort of an ancient monument."

"And that's it?"

Andy put the document down. "That's all we've got."

Nick shook his head. "I hope there's more when we get there, if they're sending us eighty-odd miles."

They made steady progress north, first along the M61 motorway, then on the busier but wider M6. By nine o'clock, they'd reached the Bowland moors, and Lancashire's central artery was slowly clogging up.

"How far?" Nick asked, as they ground to their third or fourth halt in five minutes.

"Forty miles," Andy muttered. "Shouldn't be so long now."

Nick glanced at the pile of paperwork. "I don't suppose there's a faxed medical report in there?"

Andy shook his head. "Things move pretty slow up Barrowby way. When this lot came through, a doctor hadn't even seen him."

"So who certified death?"

"No one. But according to the plod who found him, there was no doubt."

"Cryptic, eh?" Nick said, as he drove slowly on.

The eastern Lake District was very different from the high, rugged grandeur of the west. Whereas Skiddaw and Helvellyn had soaring fells, clad all over with pine and peaking in crags of spearlike granite, the forests of Lune and Milburn comprised rolling hills and verdant vales. While Cumbria's western mountains had a majestic, near-Alpine aspect, the area the detectives now cruised into was more classically English.

"You wouldn't believe there'd by *any* crime round here, would you?" said Andy.

To either side of them, fertile farmland was hedged in neat squares, interspersed with birch woods and threading waterways. Still further east, the Pennine uplands rose emerald green, slashed by gleaming limestone scarps.

"Don't know," Nick replied. "It's only eighteen years since that bastard was first on the loose."

"Yeah," Andy said after a moment, and his thoughts drifted. . . .

This lush and lovely area of northern England had been terrorized almost to death by the man called Alun Caleb, aka the Black Goat of the Woods. He was so nicknamed because he wore dark combat gear and a full head mask of black leather with zippered slits for his eyes and mouth; because he was a predatory rapist, whose sixteen victims were left broken both in body and mind; and mainly, because he signed himself that way in the gloating letters he wrote to the newspapers.

Andy didn't remember the investigation personally . . . he'd been at junior school at the time, but he knew Nick Brooker did. Nick Brooker remembered it better than anyone. The hardened detective-sergeant had been a rookie beat cop in those days, and only one of many young constables in the northern English forces who got drafted in for what was at the time the biggest manhunt ever launched by the British police. More than nine hundred officers, both detectives and uniforms, were involved, though of them all, Nick was the only one whose career it would make.

Even now, he played it down, maintaining that he'd only got his hands on the culprit through good fortune, and costly good fortune at that. There was no denying, though, that what the young bobby had done had taken tremendous courage.

In August 1982, he'd been part of a three-man detail on a Land Rover patrol on Alston Moor, quite close to a village where two of the rape victims lived. There hadn't been an attack for several weeks, and little progress was being reported. It was a hot, dry day, and by sheer chance, the unit stopped at Caleb's isolated farmhouse to ask for a jug of water for their overheating engine. The madman, however, having spotted them as they arrived, and assuming they were there to arrest him, charged out with his shotgun and fired at the officers with both barrels, killing the inspector outright and wounding the two constables. Nick had been the least badly hurt, though to this day there were buckshot pellets embedded in his sternum. He managed to overpower their assailant, knocking him unconscious with a blow from his staff.

The usual show trial had followed, sensation coming after sensation. News broke at an early stage that Caleb was a satanist whose home was filled with occult paraphernalia, and that he'd actively worshiped at a black-magic altar constructed in his cellar. As part of its material evidence the prosecution presented detailed notes written by Caleb himself, which outlined plans to attack a total of seventy women and offer them all "in bondage for the passing pleasure of the divine Shub-Niggurath." There'd been dramatic scenes in court. Several of the victims suffered breakdowns before they were able to give testimony, while others, perhaps understandably, had blocked out all memory of the incidents and were unable to give accurate accounts of what had happened.

Throughout the trial, Caleb—a strong, sullen man, whom his neighbors described as "a frightening loner"—admitted that he had abducted all the women in question, but insisted, bewilderingly, that he had not had sex with them . . . even though the medical experts made it clear that not only had each victim been forcefully and horribly raped: each had also been impregnated, suggesting a careful premeditation on the part of the madman.

"Barrowby, seven miles," Nick said, interrupting Andy's train of thought.

"Mmm." The younger detective nodded. "Nick, what did the judge say when Caleb got sent down?"

Nick considered. "I don't know . . . some drivel about him being the most evil man he'd ever met, et cetera. Gave him a full-term sentence, I know that. Said he should never be released."

"What did you make of all that weird stuff Caleb came out with—you know, the devil-worship bit?"

Nick shrugged. "Bloody headcase, wasn't he."

"Didn't he ask if he could take his books to prison with him?"

"Yeah . . . think so. Why?"

"Well . . . it just struck me. All this black-magic bit, and him being found in a stone circle . . ."

Nick glanced at him. "This is the twenty-first century, you know."

"Hey, pal, shit happens."

A moment passed, then Nick looked back to the winding country lane. "Yeah."

3

Barrowby was quaint.

It was centered around a village green with a duck pond in the middle, and consisted almost entirely of eighteenth-century stone cottages, all cleanly whitewashed. In keeping with the style, the Packhorse Hotel was ivy-clad on the outside, with a medieval shield over its door; on the inside it was all black beams, horse-brasses, and wooden Tudor benching. Its receptionist had long red tresses, buxom curves, and was very pretty, in a freckle-faced country girl sort of way.

"How long we booked in for?" Nick asked, as Andy filled the register.

"One night," the D.C. replied.

"That's optimistic."

"Nope," Andy said. "That's realistic. You know what the chief super's like when it comes to expenses."

"Any chance we can extend our stay if we need to, love?" Nick asked the receptionist.

" 'Course," she replied brightly. "It's early in the season yet."

The name tag on her smart pink jacket said that she was Miranda, and she seemed as efficient as she was attractive, handing them each a room key and a leaflet on the hotel and its general area, then pointing out the restaurant and the bar. As the cops went upstairs, they arranged to meet in the bar later.

Nick found his bedroom small but cozy. There was a plump quilt on the bed, a tray of tea things on the bureau, and a pleasing view over the green. There was also an en suite shower and toilet, both of which he thankfully used. A quarter of an hour later, he was back downstairs and in the bar, where Andy had a small Scotch and water waiting for him.

"Water!" Nick said, sipping it with a grimace.

"Absolutely . . . it's not even lunchtime yet," Andy replied, winking over the counter at Miranda.

She smiled back, then flinched as a bass male voice came crashing across the room: "*Cow . . . shite!*"

The two cops turned. At the far end of the bar slumped as surly an individual as either had ever seen, in early middle-age but huge of build, with a mop of graying hair over a tanned, craggy face. He was clad in bulky combat fatigues and a pair of old army boots muddied and scuffed almost to ruin. A big hunting knife was visible in a sheath at his belt, and beside him, propped against the fireplace, there was a narrow leather case, about three feet long and unbuckled at one end, from which the stock of a rifle protruded. A half-empty mug of ale stood on the bar top in front of him. It was clearly not his first; he was glaring drunkenly at the newcomers, and even made an aggressive lurch toward them.

"Jimmy, don't be daft," Miranda said nervously.

The man ignored her. His fat, hairy hand now stole to the hilt of his knife.

Nick leaned against the bar. "What have we got here, Constable McClaine?"

"Well, Sergeant Brooker, if he doesn't take his hand off that knife right now, I'd say wielding an offensive weapon in a public place."

Nick nodded. "Not to mention an unsecured firearm, which might, on police inspection, prove to be loaded and therefore unsafe."

"And of course," Andy added, "there's drunk and disorderly behavior."

Nick stared intently at the man. "So what do you reckon?" he asked Andy.

Andy sniffed. "Oh . . . I'd say a year and a half, maybe two."

The man gazed back at them, foggy-eyed, but clearly comprehending the error he'd just made. For several taut moments, it seemed he would approach them anyway.

"A whole year and a half," Nick repeated. "Unless you add to that . . . assaulting police officers."

"In which case . . . three or four years," said Andy.

"Plus, of course, he gets his fucking lights punched out," Nick added.

"Come on, Jimmy Kurns," came a new voice, "let's be having you."

The detectives glanced round, and saw a uniformed policewoman in the doorway. She was very young, twenty at the most, but had a firm tone. "Come on, Jimmy," she said again. "I don't want to arrest you this early in the day."

"Now seems as good a time as any," Nick interjected.

"I'd thank you to stay out of this, if you don't mind," the policewoman replied.

A moment passed, the bearlike Jimmy eyeballing them all in angry frustration. He swayed on his feet for a moment, then finished his beer with a swallow, grabbed up his rifle case, and shambled across the room to the door, which banged shut behind him.

Nick glanced again at the policewoman. "You know, if he goes and causes trouble somewhere else now, it's down to you."

"He won't cause any trouble," she replied. "He'll do what he usually does, go home to bed. He's been out all night poaching."

"And that isn't an offense any more?"

She turned to look at him. There was a cool, no-nonsense aura about her that Nick instantly recognized and admired. She might be out in the sticks, but this police officer wasn't to be trifled with. On top of that, she was quite a looker . . . red-lipped and blue-eyed, with soft blond hair which no doubt fell to lustrous lengths when unfurled. For the moment it was pinned beneath her smart Cumbrian Constabulary hat.

"Barrowby is a nice, quiet place," she said. "The worst we normally have to deal with out here is kids raiding orchards in September. We don't get tough with the locals, unless it's necessary." She paused for a moment. "You gentlemen are from the Serious Crime and Response Squad, I take it?"

Nick nodded, offered his hand. "Detective Sergeant Brooker. This is Detective Constable McClaine."

The girl shook hands with him. "Melanie Toomey. Well, I'm glad you're here, so long as you aren't going to pick a fight with *every* person you meet."

"Hey . . . do we look like the sort of blokes who pick fights?"

"You don't really want me to answer that, do you?" she said, walking outside.

Nick grinned at Andy, then they followed her out into the gravel lot, where a black-and-white cruiser was parked beside Nick's Citroën.

"So . . . where do you want to start?" Constable Toomey asked.

"Your station, if you don't mind," Nick replied. "I'd like to look through the paperwork."

She unlocked the cruiser. "I've got the paperwork in here. My station's ten miles away, in Lazenby. And it isn't much more than a desk and a coffeepot. Perhaps it'd be more constructive if I showed you the body?"

Nick glanced at Andy, and shrugged. They climbed in, and

five minutes later arrived on the village outskirts, next to another house of whitewashed stone, though this one was larger than the rest and freestanding in about an acre of flowering gardens. A plaque over its front door read: HAROLD CUSANI, M.D.

Dr. Cusani was a squat, pudgy man, with salt-and-pepper side-whiskers and a shabby line in gray tweeds. He also seemed irritable and was far from pleased that his morning appointments had to be cancelled because his surgery had been transformed into a temporary mortuary.

"It's most inconvenient," he said, leading them in.

Nick wanted to reply that murder usually was, though he didn't know for sure if it *was* murder yet. Instead, he scanned quickly through the situation reports, then looked down at the body.

It was naked, pale as wax, and lay full-length on a sheet of sterile paper. There was no obvious sign of injury, though Caleb's face had twisted itself into a ghastly cringe. Nick stared down at the legendary Black Goat of the Woods. The criminal didn't look so frightening now, having become emaciated through age, his frenzy of black hair withered to a few strands of silver.

"What did he die from?" Andy asked. "Exposure?"

Cusani shook his head. "I haven't done a full postmortem, but from what I've seen so far, froze to death."

Nick glanced round. "Sorry . . . what?"

"Froze to death," the doctor repeated.

"In May?"

Cusani looked aggravated again. "Look, I can't explain it, I'm just giving you the facts. When I first saw him, his arm and chest muscles had rigidified, which suggests extreme hypothermia. There was evidence of frostbite in his extremities . . . namely his fingers and toes. And on top of all that, he was coated in ice crystals. Now, to me, those symptoms are consistent with being frozen to death."

Nick turned to Andy. "Check with the Meteorological Office . . . what was the lowest temperature we had last night?"

"I've already done that," said Toomey. She took a notebook from her pocket. "The lowest temperature recorded in central-north England last night was eleven degrees centigrade."

"Wind chill?" Nick asked.

She shook her head. "This time of year . . . negligible."

"Is this even possible?" Andy wondered.

"I'd have said no," Cusani replied. "Of course, you can die from exposure anywhere, if your constitution's low enough. Hypothermia can set in at twenty degrees centigrade, if the wind's wet and strong. But it wouldn't explain this." He indicated the corpse. "I mean . . . we had to thaw him out."

"Okay," Nick said, "so he was murdered."

Toomey glanced at him. "He was?"

"He didn't freeze to death naturally, so it must have happened unnaturally—i.e., someone did it to him."

She smirked. "What, like locked him in their fridge for a few hours?"

"More likely hung him in a slaughterhouse somewhere . . . maybe an industrial freezer."

"Not around here," Cusani put in. "If there was such a facility, I'm sure I'd know about it, and he can't have been brought from any great distance away because, as I say, he was still coated in ice."

"A *mobile* freezer?" Andy suggested. "Like a butcher's van?"

Nick handed him the situ-report. "No tire tracks. At least, not inside the stone circle." He gazed at the body for a moment, knowing there had to be a logical explanation. "An airplane? Suppose he'd fallen from an airplane? That would explain the freezing effect, wouldn't it?"

Cusani didn't look convinced. "It might. But there'd also be extensive damage to the body. And, well . . . there isn't."

Nick considered. "Whatever, there'll need to be a full autopsy now." Toomey nodded. "And before you shift him to hospital," Nick added, "get your forensics lads here. Swab every inch of him."

4

Outside the surgery, Nick spent five minutes, staring at the hedgerow that stood opposite. It was already deep and luxuriant, and filled with hollyhocks . . . all the more bewildering of course, in these bizarre circumstances.

"Is Caleb's cottage still standing?" Nick asked.

Toomey shook her head. "It was burned down after he got convicted."

The detective smiled to himself. "Very convenient . . . for somebody." He glanced around at Andy. "Fancy taking the Citroën up to Durham?"

The D.C. looked nonplussed. "Why?"

"Go to the prison, bring back Caleb's books. We can have a look through them."

Andy shrugged. "Well yeah, but . . . you certain it's worthwhile?"

Nick nodded. "Let's get into the mad bastard's head."

"Can I help at all?" Toomey asked.

Nick turned to her. "Yeah . . . how many of the women Caleb attacked still live in the area?"

"One," Toomey replied. "She's the only one still alive. Barbara Maynard."

Nick tried to remember. "Wasn't she that well-heeled bird?"

"I wouldn't call her a bird. . . . She's more a middle-aged woman, now. A titled lady, no less. Her husband's dead, but he was Viscount Langdon."

"What was that big house called where they used to live?" Nick wondered.

"Halkin Grange. She's still there. Why?"

Nick paused to think. "I'm wondering if there's any value in going having a chat with her?"

Toomey raised a finely drawn eyebrow. "Not sure she'll thank you for raking it all up again?"

"I'm sure she *won't*," he replied, "but this is murder inquiry, after all."

"You want to go now?"

"Not yet," Nick said. "I fancy a look at Long Meg first. Any chance?"

"Sure."

Just then, a clap of what sounded like distant thunder came rolling from the northeast. Its booms echoed for several moments on the still, warm air. Nick glanced curiously around.

"Shot blasting," the woman constable explained. "That's Gilderdale Quarry. It's about eight miles away. There's an open-cast mine there. They're dynamiting."

Nick nodded thoughtfully, then tossed his car keys to Andy. "There you are, pal. Don't take her anywhere near Gilderdale."

Five minutes later, Nick and Toomey were cruising up a narrow lane. The woman handled the heavy vehicle smoothly, taking each sharp curve with deft precision. Nick wasn't sure which to be more impressed by . . . her driving skills, or the generous expanse of nylon-clad thigh now visible. He hadn't been with a girl for some time. The opportunity occasionally came along, but the memory of Amy always intervened. This policewoman, however, was a singularly desirable specimen.

"Doesn't this road go up to Halkin Grange eventually?" he asked, trying to put his mind on something else.

"Yeah," she said. "It's the long way around, though. It's much quicker across country."

Nick nodded. They drove on in silence for another two minutes, then pulled up by a stile in the drystone wall. Toomey climbed out. Nick did the same, stretching and breathing deeply of the fresh air. On the other side of the stile, a footpath wound uphill through a meadow deep in buttercups, then a copse of silver birch. The somber shapes of standing stones were visible beyond it. The place was astonishingly quiet.

"Do you get many people up here?" Nick asked, as they set off up the path.

"A few," the constable replied. "We're off the beaten track, but this is one of the largest stone circles in the country."

They passed through the copse. The circle was now clearly visible, constructed of boulders rather than pillars, each one spaced about twenty feet apart. As always with these ancient monuments, there was a stillness here, a peace, an aura of solemn antiquity.

"How many stones are there?" Nick wondered.

"They're supposed to be uncountable," the woman replied. He glanced at her. She chuckled. "It's a local myth. In answer to your question, though . . . I don't know. Sixty, seventy . . . something like that."

They now walked into the very midst of the henge. It occupied a wide area, three hundred square feet at least, and was more oval than circular; it even encompassed a stretch of country track, which led through to a cluster of farm buildings on the far side of the pasture. The boulders were of varying shape and size, some jagged, some smooth, all coated in lichen. Several had fallen over during the passing of the millennia, but remained in place; one or two of these had partially sunk and were visible only as uneven slabs of granite.

"What's that?" Nick asked, indicating a separate megalith a few yards outside the main circle.

"Long Meg herself," Toomey replied. "The rest of the rocks are 'her daughters.' According to tradition, they'd formed a coven and had gathered here to perform a Black Mass, but were confronted by a saint, who turned them all to stone."

Nick strolled toward the center, where a ten-by-ten square of ground had been fenced off with fluorescent crime scene tape.

"And what's the official line?" he wondered, gazing into the square.

"The usual," she replied. "It's neolithic, it was a calendar, or a giant sundial, or something like that."

"Which is bull, isn't it?" he said, turning to look at her. "Only a personal opinion, of course, but I prefer the more romantic view." He glanced back at the fenced-off square. "And I suspect someone else does, too."

"So what's your theory?" she asked.

He smiled. "I'm not here to come up with theories. All we were sent for was to establish that this is not a routine sudden death, which is clear enough from the outset. We'll need more detectives up here now, maybe a few local lads to do the legwork, set up an incident room, that sort of thing. . . ."

Just then, there was a crackle of static and a tinny voice came over the air: "Whiskey-Echo One to Seven-eight-two-two?"

"Receiving," Toomey replied, "go ahead."

"Shoplifter, Mel. At Langwathby . . . lady in the corner shop's caught some kid pinching sweets."

The constable rolled her eyes. "Roger. En route." She turned to Nick. "Duty calls."

"You go," he said. "Like I said earlier, I'll take a hike up to Halkin Grange, speak to Lady Langdon."

"Want me to call ahead . . . let them know you're coming?"

"No, it's alright," he replied. "Don't want to get them uptight or anything."

She nodded and moved away.

"There is one thing," he called after her. She turned. He indicated the spot where Caleb's body had been found. "We could use a tarp or something . . . over this. I mean, it's a murder scene now."

"I'll sort it," she said. "See you later."

A moment passed, Nick standing alone in the middle of the circle. Despite the serenity of the environment, pagan monuments like this always seemed to have an appeal for nutballs. Even if the crazies who came here weren't actually practicing magic, they might be deluded enough to *think* they were. No . . . Alun Caleb hadn't staggered half way across the country, to drop down dead here, purely by accident.

So thinking, Nick turned his steps toward Halkin Grange.

5

To either side of the gates there was a high brick post, and on each post, a gargoyle.

And such gargoyles. They glared down at Nick with an intensity that belied their ivy coats and granite stillness. In return, he regarded them warily. They weren't devils or dragons in the normal fashion, but ghastly hybrids . . . part insect, part mollusk it seemed, with tentacles rather than claws, mandibles instead of beaks, and multiple rows of eyes beneath odd crowns of thorns and barbs.

For all the ferocity of these guardians, however, the gates weren't locked, and Nick passed through them with ease. A few moments later, he was strolling up the long drive, hemmed in on either side by thick rhododendrons. He'd walked about half a mile, when he heard the *thrub* of an engine coming from behind. A second later a Toyota SUV, with mud splashed over its wheels and fender, came around the corner. It skidded to an immediate halt, the driver winding the window down. It was a woman . . . burly and thickset, with wiry black hair and a menacing frown.

"Hi," he began, stepping forward.

But she cut him off. "You're on private land."

Nick flashed his warrant card. "It's okay, I'm a police officer."

She shook her head. "Sorry . . . this is *still* private land."

"Not to me," he replied, unfazed. "Perhaps you could give me a lift up to the house?"

She seemed less sure of herself now. "What's it about?"

"I'd like to speak to Lady Langdon."

"Concerning?"

"Alun Caleb."

The woman eyed him for a moment, then opened the door. The moment he'd climbed in, she gunned the engine and drove on. Nick gazed out through the window. More rhododendrons drifted past, beyond them the green shadows of fathomless woodland.

"Isolated up here, aren't you?" he observed.

"That's the way we like it," she mumbled.

He looked at her with interest. "We?"

"Me and Lady Langdon."

"Just the two of you, then?"

The woman bit her lip, clearly uncomfortable answering questions. "No . . . Lady Langdon's daughter will be around somewhere. There's also a couple of village girls, who come up to help around the house."

"No men allowed, eh?" Nick gave a jocular grin.

The woman said nothing more, and eventually he looked back to the road. Bearing in mind the unhappy history, he'd possibly overstepped the mark there, but her reaction had been interesting all the same. Her body language was decidedly tense. When he'd first made the decision to visit Halkin Grange it'd been on spec . . . to cover all bases, so to speak; he hadn't seriously thought Barbara Maynard might be involved. Now he wasn't so sure.

The house was a rambling eighteenth-century affair, constructed from mellow sandstone. It had two long wings, each comprising tall Georgian windows, and a stepped frontage complete with the obligatory Ionic columns. Its windowboxes were full of spring flowers, while ivy hung in tendrils from the roof gutters. Nick was shown in and asked to wait in the lounge, a wide airy room with leather-upholstered furniture and a huge painting by Constable over its ornate fireplace. There was also a wall of shelves, each one crammed to bursting with books. Nick glanced at them as he waited. To a one, they were massive and weighty, bound with leather but ancient and splitting. Most bore lettering on their spines, though in the odd case where this hadn't faded to illegibility, it was unreadable . . . inscribed in some obscure alphabet he'd never seen before. Three of them, however, had modern labels attached. These read:

HSAN III   HSAN V   HSAN VII

"How may I help you, Officer?" came a polite but imperious voice.

Nick turned from the bookcase, and found Barbara Maynard standing in the doorway. He hadn't seen her for quite a few years, but he was certain this was she. A tall, willowy woman, she was perhaps fifty years old but agelessly beautiful, with flowing ash blond hair. She was dressed in jodhpurs, leather boots, and a brown tweed jacket, as if she'd just been out riding. Her poise and bearing were pure aristocracy.

"Sorry about this, ma'am. Detective Sergeant Brooker." He showed his warrant card again. "I need to ask you some questions."

Lady Langdon indicated the sofa. "Please sit. I've arranged some tea. I take it you'll join me?"

"Er . . . yes, thanks."

The pair of them sat, Nick on the sofa, Lady Langdon in the armchair. Several awkward moments passed as Nick explained the purpose of his visit, deliberately omitting the details and whereabouts of Caleb's death, though the very mention of the rapist's name brought a tinge of red to the woman's cheeks.

When Nick had finished, she delicately cleared her throat. "I presumed your visit would have something to do with this, I confess. But I can't say I'm sorry the man is dead."

"Well . . . you aren't alone in that," Nick replied. He looked up, as a red-haired girl in a bright summer dress came in with a silver tea service.

When Lady Langdon had thanked the girl, who departed with a smile, Nick resumed: "Er, the thing is, Lady Langdon . . . I won't beat around the bush. I'm a fella . . . I can't even begin to understand what it's like to be raped. I can only hope the fact it happened so long ago makes it easier for you to talk about." She calmly poured two cups. Nick scratched his jaw. "Er . . . you see, I need to ask you . . ."

"Go ahead, Sergeant," she said, handing him his tea. "I'm tougher than I look."

"Er . . . right. Yeah. I appreciate that it's eighteen years ago and all that, and I'm sure you've tried to blot it out of your mind, but—what actually happened . . . *that* night?"

She took a sip of tea, then began: "I was driving home from Little Salkeld. It was around eight o'clock. Clarence— my husband—was away on business, and I'd made an appearance at our annual Summer Show. Lady-of-the-manor sort of thing . . ."

"Were you on your own?" Nick interrupted.

She half-smiled. Nick could've kicked himself . . . as a rape victim, she'd be well-used to lines of questioning which seemed to imply she'd brought the attack on herself.

"I had a little MG, which I enjoyed motoring around in," she patiently explained. "We've never had many airs and graces up here, Sergeant. No chauffeurs, no bodyguards. Anyway, I'd taken the road through Barrowby. . . ."

"The one that goes past the stone circle?"

"That's right. It wasn't used very much, especially at night. As I say, I was on this road . . . when I came to a fallen tree. It was completely blocking my way."

For the first time, Lady Langdon's voice faltered. Her eyes glistened. Nick listened grimly as she spoke on. He still remembered certain details, himself . . . as far as he recalled, Caleb had cut the tree down, almost as if he'd known his victim was due along that route.

"Of course, I was stunned," the woman added. "I'd gone that way earlier and there'd been nothing there. It wasn't as if we'd had a storm or anything. . . ."

"Were you frightened?" Nick asked.

"Puzzled more than frightened. And foolish, I suppose. I got out of the car to have a look, and . . ." Now her words tailed off.

"He was there," Nick finished for her, as gently as he could.

She made an effort to steady her voice. "He came out of the bushes. He was dressed in . . . in black . . ."

"It's okay," the cop said. "I know the rest."

She dabbed at her eyes with a napkin from the tea tray. Nick waited for a moment while she did. During their careers, police officers were frequently assaulted, often very severely, but to them it was a hazard of the job, never something to lose sleep over. You were more likely to brag about it in the pub than be haunted by it at night. How different an experience like this must be . . . a young woman, alone on an isolated road, confronted by a masked man with an axe. Little wonder his other prey had all died young: The memory alone was a killer. It struck Nick that maybe he should feel strong and manly at this moment, proud to be the one who'd finally caught the maniac, but he didn't; he felt the way he usually did in the face of female suffering that resulted from male brutality . . . sullied, helpless, and mildly guilty.

"Excuse me," she said after a moment. "I'm—I'm alright now."

"Lady Langdon," Nick asked, "these last few days . . . did you know Caleb had escaped from prison?"

"I read about it, yes. It was all over the newspapers."

Nick was careful how to phrase the next question. "Were you concerned that he might come here?"

"It crossed my mind," she admitted, "but I'm not some foolish child. I also knew he was old and in poor health. I didn't expect to be attacked by him again, if that's what you mean."

"So you weren't worried by it?"

"As I say . . . it crossed my mind."

"Did you," he said, "by any chance, make any preparations . . . I mean, on the off chance he *did* turn up?"

"Preparations?" She seemed puzzled. "Sergeant, am I being questioned as a suspect?"

He held his hands up. "Of course not. I won't deny it, though. Caleb died in what we consider peculiar circumstances."

"I see. And you think that, as the only surviving victim, I may be responsible?"

"We have to consider every possibility, ma'am."

She appeared to understand this, and nodded.

Nick cleared his throat. "So . . . er, at the risk of being thrown out, where were you last night, between ten and twelve?"

"Here," she replied.

"Do you have any witnesses to that?"

"Two. Cora, my daughter. And Jenny—you've already met her. She's my estate manager."

Nick nodded. "And you were here all that time?"

"I was here all night. We played bridge till nearly midnight. Then we retired."

"Okay." The detective smiled and stood up. "Well . . . that's fine. That's all I needed to know."

Lady Langdon smiled politely. She also stood.

"Oh . . . there is one other question," Nick said. "You don't . . . have any sort of refrigeration unit here?"

She seemed bemused. "I—I have a deep freeze for frozen foods and such."

"No . . . I mean, perhaps something to do with farming. For hanging meat. Something like that?"

"This isn't a butchery, Sergeant. It's a family home."

"Of course," Nick said. "Just a thought."

She accompanied him to the front door. Outside, on the gravel drive, the estate manager's SUV was parked. Lady Langdon seemed surprised not to see a police vehicle there. "Are you on foot?"

"Afraid so," Nick said. "No worries, though. The exercise will do me good."

"I'd get Jenny to run you, but I don't know where she is at present."

Nick waved that aside. "It's alright."

Lady Langdon persisted. "Where is it you're going to?"

"Barrowby."

"Oh . . . well, that's not too far. You can even take a short cut." She pointed across the front lawn toward a wall of foliage. "There are deer paths through the coppice. Follow any one of them. They lead downhill to Croglin Beck. You'll have to get across that, of course, but it's only shallow and there are plenty of stepping stones. Should cut half an hour off your journey."

Nick thanked her and set off across the lawn. A few minutes later, he reached the outer cover of the trees, and glanced back. To his surprise, Lady Langdon was still watching him . . . as if to make sure he was really leaving. As casually as he could, Nick raised a hand. She raised her own hand in return. Then he plunged into the thicket.

For several moments, he fought his way through meshed branches, but at last he broke out onto a path. It was narrow and cluttered with fallen twigs, but it led clearly away in a more or less southerly direction. Nick started along it. On all sides, the leaves had that bright green, freshly painted look so consistent with spring. The undergrowth had yet to become thick and tangled, and indeed there were still swathes of blue-bells between the gnarled boles of the trees. The air was fragrant with blossom and bud. Above his head, a red squirrel darted like a streak of flame over a low-hanging bough. There was an aura of solitude that Nick found pleasant. In this May of the year 2000, there was much debate in Britain between country and town: Who had the right to go where? Should fences be put up or taken down? Was it really humane to ban blood sports when they provided jobs for a legion of rural dwellers?

Nick couldn't comment on any of this. He'd been born and raised in a dismal urban district . . . its grimy sights and smoky scent were second nature to him; without the clangor of shunting locomotives and factory sirens, he found the world oddly silent. Yet this vast tranquil acreage, which still made up so much of England, had a special place for him, too. He'd enjoyed enough countryside holidays to know how lulling it could be, how secret and secluded, how much safer than the concrete jungle.

Then a twig popped.

Nick stopped and turned. He saw nothing untoward. Mellow sunlight dappled the woodland floor, but among the budding twigs an eerie breeze was suddenly stirring. All at once, inexplicably, the cop knew he wasn't alone.

As casually as he could, he strode on. Another branch snapped—this one loudly, as if something of considerable weight had brushed past it. There was also now an odor, a rather sour odor, tickling at his nostrils. Nick sniffed the air. It wasn't so much an odor, in fact, as a stench . . . cloying, sulfurous. What was more, it seemed to be getting stronger.

Then there was a loud rattle of vegetation; more twigs crunched. Nick imagined the reckless trail an elephant might plough through the jungle . . . and all at once he didn't want to look behind him. Whatever it was, it was coming from that direction . . . *and it was coming fast.* Heavy boughs fell to earth. The smell had become intolerable. Nick wanted to gag, but now there was something else: a dank slithering noise, as if some moist bulk was oozing forward through the dry debris of the undergrowth.

Nick strode stiffly on, trying with all his will to steel himself. Was he going mad? This was an English coppice, not some lost tract of the Amazon. He now felt the urge to run, however . . . the *frantic* urge. He could sense something immense in pursuit of him . . . thirty or forty yards away at the most, and approaching rapidly. With a further ripping and thrashing, it tore through a dense patch of thickets. It knew that *he* knew, Nick realized. It wasn't trying to conceal itself any longer.

He made a wild dash. The terrain thinned before him but sloped downward. His speed increased accordingly. Veering sharply to avoid fallen logs, hurdling briars, he went at it like an athlete. But whatever was behind him, was also moving at pace and drove a deluge of sticks and leaf rubble before it, making it sound to Nick as if there was a landslide at his heels. The stink had become overpowering, all-engulfing. . . . Nick's head swam. More branches broke, loud as gunshots.

At six foot one and 196 pounds, Nick was hardly overweight, but he hadn't exercised properly in ten years or more. His heart slammed his ribs, sweat streamed off him. But he ran all the harder. He slid through banks of straggling ferns, turned an ankle on a loose boulder, but at last hammered down onto level ground and saw the airy light of open spaces not too far ahead. Yet if the stalking thing was perturbed by this, it showed no sign; in fact its blind charge grew in ferocity, for now it sounded as if trees were crashing down before it. Nick sucked in fresh air for one last effort.

Up ahead, the forest ended abruptly. Beyond it lay pastures, dotted with sheep and their lambs. If he could just make it that far, Nick hoped he would be safe; it was like the boundary between day and night, dream and nightmare. . . . Yet might the thing catch him at the very last moment? Could it be reaching for him now? *No* . . . the next thing Nick knew, he was out from the trees and staggering down a slope of wet pebbles. He tried to stop at the bottom but was catapulted forward by his own velocity . . . to land face-first in a shallow river.

Croglin Beck was only a foot deep at the most, but swollen with meltwater, and breathtakingly cold. Like a stinging slap from a hand, it shocked Nick out of his panic. Drenched and coughing up lungfuls of brackish fluid, he jumped up and still tried to stumble away, turning and glancing over his shoulder as he went, only to slip and fall again. At any moment, he expected something the size of a mammoth to burst out from the forest . . . and indeed something large and mobile was still fast approaching. With sharp rustles of foliage, and a dull thudding on the woody earth, a shape appeared far back under the trees, moving swiftly forward through the sun-flecked shadows. A moment later, it had resolved itself into two different shapes, distinct from each yet fixed together . . . though in no unnatural way.

It was a girl, quite a young girl, and she was mounted on a roan mare.

Once she reached the riverbank, the girl reined up and stared at Nick with a mixture of surprise and mirth. The detective gazed back from his sitting position in the middle of the beck. He was still too shaken up to feel as silly as perhaps he ought.

"You look as if you've seen a ghost, Sergeant," the girl said.

Nick rose slowly to his feet. "You . . . you know who I am?" he stuttered.

"I guessed," she replied, now allowing her animal to drink. "But it wasn't hard. Everyone in the village is talking about this business. I'm Cora Maynard, by the way."

Now that she said it, the resemblance to Lady Langdon was obvious. The girl's snub-nosed but rather pretty face was framed by tawny locks. She was tall and lithe, and fitted her riding slacks and white silken blouse very neatly.

"Hallo," he muttered.

"Are you alright?"

"Er . . . yeah. City boy, you see." He tried to smile. "Bit lost out here."

"You *do* seem like a fish out of water," she replied, steering her horse away from the river's edge. "I'd offer you a ride, but I don't think you'd fit in the saddle." And with a tinkling, minx-like laugh, she trotted away into the trees.

Nick gazed after her, more bewildered now than terrified, but shivering violently all the same.

6

Nick returned to Barrowby around lunchtime, plodding sodden through the village streets.

When he entered the Packhorse, Miranda gazed at him wide-eyed: "Dear me, whatever happened?"

"I could tell you," he said sheepishly, "but I'd rather not."

"Is there anything I can do?" she called after him as he went upstairs.

Nick gave it some thought. "I don't suppose there's any chance of a sandwich?"

"The lunchtime menu's on now." She smiled. "We do a lovely steak and Guinness pie."

"That'd be great," he said, going on up. "I'll be down in ten."

Once in his room, he swapped his jeans for tracksuit pants and his jersey for a sweatshirt. Then he sat on the bed and thought. He thought about the incident in the trees, and how it surely couldn't have happened the way he remembered it. Could he really have mistaken a galloping horse for that . . .

that prodigious *something*? It was inexplicable, but it was also unnerving. During the course of his career, Nick had faced down blackguards and gangsters, gunmen and knifers, terrorists, muggers, sex killers, wife-beaters . . . the worst criminal lunatics Britain could offer, yet he'd never been as frightened as he had during that two or three minute chase through the woods.

He checked his mobile phone and found it waterlogged and useless. Instead, he grabbed the bedroom line, punching out Andy's number. It was answered almost immediately. The detective constable sounded as if he was in a diner of some sort.

"Yeah, McClaine," he said, as he chomped on something.

"Where are you?" Nick asked.

"A Little Chef off the A688."

"Did you find anything?"

"Not a lot, to be honest." Andy swallowed his food. "Seems that about three weeks ago, Caleb started packaging and posting his books to a P.O. box in Penrith . . . presumably where he intended to collect them once he'd busted out."

"Or where someone else intended to collect them."

"Like who?"

"Not sure yet," Nick said, though he couldn't help but picture Barbara Maynard's shelves, impressively stacked with musty old tomes.

"There was one thing," Andy said. "I don't know. . . . This might be something." There was a rustling of pages. "It's a notebook of his, got left behind . . . dog-eared as anything, full of scribbles and diagrams and stuff."

"Anything in it you recognize?" Nick asked.

"Well, his handwriting's like spider shit, plus it's in some code or something. There's a couple of hand-drawn maps, though. One of them is that stone circle."

Nick stood up. "How do you know?"

"Well . . . it looks like it. There's a circle of seventy blobs and a separate blob a few centimeters away. Plus, there's some handwriting here I recognize. It looks like 'long' . . . you know, as in Long Meg."

"What do you mean 'it *looks* like'?"

Andy considered. "Well . . . it could be 'leng,' but what does *that* mean?"

Nick thought about it for a second. Leng? Leng Meg? Leng Meg and Her Daughters? For some reason, that had a disquieting resonance.

Andy was still talking. "It appears again a few pages on. . . . It's another map. God knows what *this* is. Looks like an island. Does 'M . . . T . . . Terr' mean anything to you?"

"No."

"It's a point on this map. How about 'M . . . T . . . Erb'?"

"No."

"Thought not. Anyway . . . this Leng is here, too."

"Hang on . . . whoa!" Nick suddenly said. " 'M T Terr' and 'M T Erb'? How about . . . Mount Terror and Mount Erebus?"

"Come again?"

"Two volcanoes," the sergeant said.

"Oh." The D.C. didn't sound much the wiser. "Where?"

"The Antarctic."

Andy almost laughed. "Well . . . that screws that."

"Not necessarily," Nick cautioned, having trouble believing what he was thinking. "How deeply frozen did the doctor say Alun Caleb was?"

"What?"

"Whereabouts is this Leng?"

"Well . . . if this is Antarctica, smack-bang in the middle. Probably on the Pole."

"Get that burger and chips down, and get your arse back here!" Nick interjected. "Quick."

"No probs," Andy replied. "Two hours tops." And he hung up.

Nick walked downstairs in a virtual daze. He met Miranda in the lobby. She smiled brightly. "Ready to order?"

"Er . . . maybe later," he said. "Tell me, is there a library round here?"

"Directly opposite," she replied. "Straight over the green. You can't miss it."

Nick thanked her, but when he opened the door to go out, found himself staring across the grass at a small country church . . . an old one, very basic, possibly Saxon in origin.

He turned questioningly to Miranda, who seemed to have been expecting this. She nodded. "That's right . . . in there."

"The library's in the church?"

"It isn't a church," she said. "It just looks like one. Barrowby doesn't have a church anymore."

"This town of yours is full of surprises, isn't it?"

"Is it?" she said. Her manner had altered slightly, as if the comment had offended her.

Nick nodded. "Yeah . . . yeah, it *is*."

Then he walked away over the green. It was now early afternoon, yet there was hardly anybody about. Cars were parked here and there, but there was little traffic on the move. For the first time, it began to strike him how odd this was. Almost hurriedly, he made his way to the library.

It clearly *had* been a church at some time or other. Inside, the glass in the tall casements was richly colored, each window depicting a famous Bible scene, while the ceiling was arched in vintage eccelesiastic fashion. Virtually everything else, however, had changed. In the alcove where the font had once stood, a librarian sat behind a desk; where once there'd been pews, now there was a maze of bookcases.

"May I help?" asked the librarian, standing. She was tall and slim, and wore her glasses on a chain. Unlike most librarians, however, she made no effort to modulate her voice.

"I was wondering where I might find Geography?" Nick said.
She indicated the nearest rack. Nick thanked her, then began
a quick search. Several of the books were weighty reference
works, with substantial sections on the Antarctic, but nowhere
in their indexes could he find any allusion to a place called
Leng. Even a quick scan through the general encyclopedias
and atlases failed. Disappointed, but knowing he couldn't afford to waste too much time, Nick strolled back to the main
door . . . only to stop in his tracks. Just to the right of where
he'd come in, sandwiched between two filing cabinets, there
was another desk, and on top of it a computer terminal.

Nick turned to the librarian. "Excuse me, are you on the
Net here?"

She looked at him over her glasses. "We are . . . are you
wanting to use it?"

"If I can."

She came cautiously over, eyeing his tracksuit pants and
sweatshirt.

"I promise I won't damage anything," he said, showing her
his warrant card.

She didn't seem convinced, but booted up the machine anyway. "I'm afraid we have to charge for this," she said, as the search
engine intro appeared on screen. "It's one pence a minute."

"Fine," Nick said, knowing he didn't have a penny on him,
but determined somehow to busk it.

He pulled a chair up and sat down. The moment the woman
left him, he typed in a general search on the word *Leng*.

Several seconds passed, then a single reference appeared. It
was a link to a website entitled Lost Places, Forbidden Cities.

Nick felt a surge of adrenaline. He followed the link, and a
moment later was staring at a wall of arcane frescoes. A variety
of additional links appeared across them. One of these read:
Leng. Nick clicked on it. At first nothing happened, but then a
chunk of text materialized:

LENG: Fabled seat of an ancient civilization, now lost. On a par with Atlantis, Lemuria, and Shangri-La, Leng was reputedly a city of awesome might and magnificence, and the capital of a thriving prehistoric empire, the traces of which exist only in scraps of myth and rumor. In keeping with the tradition, there are few certainties about where Leng was supposedly located, or even whether it existed at all. Scholars have placed it on a vast and otherwise barren plateau, in regions as far apart as central Asia, east Africa, and even the wild wastes of Antarctica . . .

Nick *knew* he was on to something, though it still seemed too incredible to be real.

According to legend, Leng was old even when the Minoans flourished, and was neither constructed nor inhabited by any of the ancient world's known peoples. Written references to it can be found on a papyrus dated to Egypt's Middle Kingdom (2000–1750 B.C.), in ancient Sanskrit tablets retrieved in the Indus Valley by Wheeler in 1944, and in the mysterious and tantalizingly incomplete series, the Seven Cryptical Books of Hsan, currently residing in the library of the Miskatonic University, U.S.A. . . .

Nick sat back. *Hsan!* He'd seen a reference to Hsan before. And he knew where. Again, he recalled the eldritch volumes on the shelves at Halkin Grange.

Just then, there was a deafening crash from the far end of the library, as if some huge piece of furniture had been thrown over. Nick whirled around in his chair. Deep shadows filled the library's farthest recesses; the stained-glass windows threw curious pink-and-green patterns through the aisles of dusty books. Nothing moved, however. Nick glanced toward the librarian's desk, but found it vacant, which meant *she* was probably the one who'd made the noise.

Nick turned back to the rows of shelves. "Everything okay?" he called.

The librarian didn't respond.

But something else did . . . something wet and squishing, like a person walking in sodden shoes, but a person of tremendous size and weight. Nick rose slowly to his feet, eyes scanning the vast chamber. With a sudden bang, an entire rack of books fell over . . . *and then he saw it.*

It was only a glimpse, but he felt his scalp start to prickle, because whatever it was, creeping stealthily forward, it was indeed an "it." Though it was nebulous in the shadows, still half-hidden by shelving, Nick had no doubts. . . . In his mind's eye, he perceived every inch of it: its massive trunklike body, the myriad arms that roiled about it in muscular, octopoid fashion. For an incredible moment, he thought he was looking at the hydra, the seven-headed monster from his favorite childhood film, *Jason and the Argonauts,* but this was no beast of heraldry or classical myth. This was something worse. Far worse.

Its sickly, sulfurous stench rolled forward to engulf him . . . and even as it did, books began to shoot from their shelves as if projected by catapults, not one or two; more a deluge. Telekinetic firepower launched volley after volley at him. They crashed across the desks with frightening force, slamming loudly into the wall. Those that struck Nick dealt painful blows. Even so, he was too transfixed by the swaying shadow-shape to duck or dodge. Only when something the thickness of a Bible smacked him on the nose and burst it wide open did he become alert to this second danger.

Almost drunk with shock, he stumbled toward the library door, but it slammed itself shut before he could reach it. He grappled with the handle, but it remained jammed upward as if by an invisible bar. Behind him, the slithering thing came closer . . . perhaps halfway up the library. Nick could sense its bulk, could hear its nauseating squelch. With a thundering roar, more cases of shelving overturned, more fluttering missiles precipitated forward. One hit the computer, dislodging the monitor from its plinth. It fell heavily to the floor, exploding in a shower of sparks and circuitry.

Nick beat madly on the door. A book struck the back of his hand with numbing force. Another caught him midthigh, inducing a dead-leg. He doubled over. He wanted to throw himself down, to shield his head with his arms, to whimper and scream. But to do that, he knew, would be to *invite* death . . . not only from the books, which still rained down like birds of prey, but from this blasphemous monstrosity, this daemonic invader that now filled the cavernous room from floor to ceiling. Its shadow was black as night, its stench a miasmic gas that choked off his air supply and glazed his eyes with peppery tears.

Another book—a huge ledger with a wood-reinforced spine— cracked him square on the temple. A bomb went off in Nick's head. He knew nothing more. . . .

7

The man was in a great and echoing hall, the distant ceiling of which was hung with icicles. A rolling carpet of mist obscured its immense floor, but he strode forward all the same; the chill, it seemed, held neither agony nor fear for him, even though he was naked. A high portal stood to his left, a casement, he realized. It was unglazed, and beyond it, snowflakes blizzarded over warped roofs and twisted towers. Beyond those lay only a searing glacial whiteness.

Even then, the man was unaffected by cold. He walked on, in zombie fashion. Lowering through the gloom toward him came a lofty archway. Again, it was misshapen, oddly angled, too ill-proportioned to be designed for human use, even a human of gigantic stature. The man passed through it all the same and sensed that he'd entered an even larger chamber, one to which there were no visible limits.

Even in this dream state, the man felt faint, heady, his vision blurring. Slowly, however, the frozen fog began to shift, so that a titantic throne—carved, it seemed, from purest ice—swam into view. And on that throne squatted an abomination from beyond the man's worst imaginings . . . something that was both squid and toad, yet mountainous in bulk. Glistening with odorous slime, it was punctuated by innumerable quivering vents from which brown, sulfurous steam exhaled. Folded to either side of it there were four sets of limbs . . . spindly, yet jointed and clawed and bristling with fibrous hair, like the legs of some loathsome, colossal spider.

At the first sight of it, the man felt his sanity reel. The horror of what he beheld was too appalling to conceive. Goose pimples ran over his skin, his hair prickled like thorns. . . . He wanted to shriek hysterically, to cry out so hard that his lungs might rupture, but a stonelike paralysis had seized him. He could only gape and stare, goggle-eyed, at the repellent being, and as he did, *it* stared back . . . one gelid orb winking open after another all over its miscreated form. More hideous yet, from some central lower portion of it, a grotesque object raised itself up in proud erection, a rigid shaft of blue-veined muscle, two feet long at least, nobbed and gristled and slick with mucus.

The man felt his gorge rise at the very sight of it, but now some force, some irresistible power compelled him forward . . . *good Lord*, to possess this abhorrent thing, to accommodate it, to nourish himself on its vile fluids. . . .

He awoke with a start, and immediately found himself under a restraining belt. Somewhere close by, there was a rumbling and rattling sound. Vaguely, Nick could sense motion.

"What . . . what the hell?" he mumbled.

"Take it easy," came a woman's voice. "You've had a nasty bump."

"Where am I?" Nick asked.

Even though he was lying down, his vision was fuzzy. It felt as if someone was hammering a spike into the side of his skull. The woman came into view. She was handsome and blond, wearing a white paramedic's smock. She also had rubber gloves on and was holding a wad of bloodstained cotton wool. "You're on your way to the hospital," she said.

"What . . . happened?"

"Try to relax."

Nick drifted back out of consciousness, and for several care-free moments was afloat in a void filled with crow-black feathers. Then he realized he was waking again. Daylight flooded his vision. Weakly, he tried to sit up, and this time he was able to; for some reason, the restraining belt had been removed, though by the looks of things he was still in the ambulance. It was a narrow, low-roofed compartment with double doors at one end. Woolen blankets had been laid over him; a tray, laden with medical equipment, sat to one side.

Nick probed gingerly at his wounded temple and found a thick dressing, held in place by surgical tape. A minute passed, then he swung his feet to the floor and shifted slowly along the bed to the doors, pushing them open. He'd expected to see a hospital parking lot, perhaps the entrance to an ER unit; what he actually saw . . . was Long Meg and Her Daughters.

The ambulance was parked in the very center of the stone circle.

Nick felt a thrill of fear. He climbed quickly down onto the grass, though he was still groggy and at first he almost toppled over. He grabbed at the ambulance door to support himself, but in that same instant the vehicle growled to life and pulled sharply away. Nick gazed helplessly after it as it drove out of the circle and bumped its way across the pasture to the farm track, whereupon it vanished downhill.

A few moments later, its engine faded away to silence. Nick didn't think he'd ever felt so lonely or vulnerable. He looked around at the obelisks. Beyond them, the late afternoon sun embossed the sward in dusty gold. Then he found himself searching for the crime scene, which by rights should now be roofed with tarpaulin and have a uniformed officer guarding it. There was no sign even of the pegs or tape. Only by chance did the cop glance down and spot the flattened grass below his feet. He was standing on the very spot where Caleb had been found. In knee-jerk reaction, he jumped backward, though it set his head spinning. Dizzily, he went down on one knee. Then he heard a voice . . . a very familiar voice.

"Our Ruler has returned him to us," it said, "the steel blade in the cloak of flesh . . . the hunter in the black night."

Nick looked up. Lady Langdon had appeared in front of the tall megalith known as Long Meg. She was wearing a white robe, tied at the waist with rope. Her arms were raised to the sky, her eyes shone with messianic zeal. One by one, from behind the other stones, other women appeared, all dressed in similar fashion, all as mesmerized as their priestess. Each one took a position in front of an obelisk. There were seventeen of them in total, and every woman Nick had so far met in Barrowby was present: Miranda, Jenny the estate manager, the librarian, Cora Maynard, the paramedic who'd tended to him . . . even Police Constable Melanie Toomey. As one, they gazed at Nick with near beatific smiles.

"What—what the fuck is this?" he stammered.

"You have been chosen," said Lady Langdon.

"Chosen for what?"

"To replace the one who went before you. The one who failed . . . for failure cannot be tolerated."

Nick glanced at the ground beside him. "Caleb? You mean Alun Caleb?"

"It was he who found and reopened the gate," the woman said.

"Gate?"

"The gate through which Our Ruler might at last return."

A slow realization was dawning on Nick. "It's this, isn't it . . . this circle?"

"It is always a circle," she replied. "It *must* always be a circle. As yet, though, our circle is incomplete. You must take up where the one called Caleb left off, for you were the one who mastered him."

"What is it you want me to do?" he asked.

"Continue the work. . . . Prepare the way for He of the Thousand Young."

"He of the Thousand Young," the other women muttered, heads fleetingly bowed.

In the face of such ceremony, it was impossible for Nick not to recall the symbols on the walls of Alun Caleb's ramshackle farmhouse, the altar in the cellar with its black drapes, its knives and skulls and pots of incense, and that bizarre phrase the madman had come out with in his statement . . . to offer those women *for the passing pleasure of the divine Shub-Niggurath*. In court, Caleb's barrister had quoted this as proof of his client's insanity. Now, Nick knew different. . . . He remembered the ice temple, and that . . . *that abhorrence* on the throne, that thing whose very appearance defied God, and of course, that monstrous phallus it had offered him! Caleb had always insisted he didn't rape those women . . . and he *didn't*. Because Alun Caleb was not the Black Goat of the Woods.

"He was the abductor," Lady Langdon said, as though reading Nick's mind. "As you will be."

An appalling picture of events began unfolding before him. Caleb had brought the women here, to this gateway, which connected with that place . . . *Leng*.

"He took them through, didn't he?" Nick said. "Only, the last time he went through . . . he was empty-handed. He sought to escape there, didn't he . . . where he'd never be found, but even Caleb couldn't go without an offering!"

"Caleb failed," the woman said simply.

Nick shook his head. "And his reward was . . . what? The Antarctic. And him without even his thermal undies on."

"Your words are profane," the woman said.

"Not so profane as allowing a man to freeze to death," Nick shouted, "as arranging the brutal rape of sixteen women . . . *wait!*" A new thought had struck him. He looked again at the women. He counted them. With the exception of Langdon, they numbered sixteen. "You're . . . you're the daughters, aren't you?" he said incredulously. "You're all its daughters! Those women who were impregnated by that thing . . . you're the off-spring! And yet . . ." His words almost tailed off, when he saw that of the entire circle, fifty-four stones were still unclaimed. "You need seventy to complete . . ."

"The circle *must* be complete," Lady Langdon intoned.

"So that . . . that monster can be brought through? Is this what you want me to do?"

"You must go to him," the woman replied, "to be anointed, to receive your gift of rage."

"No," Nick said, shaking his head. "No way!"

As one, however, the women began to chant. Nick clapped his hands to his ears, but the dirge rose, and he could see them swaying where they stood, rippling . . . like creatures of liquid. Even as he stared, their outlines began to dissolve, their flesh to mutate, to flow outward in protoplasmic tentacles. Sacrificial robes fell away as bodies twisted and contorted, as limbs melded together. Lady Langdon alone retained human form. She joined her hands and closed her eyes, her face written with bliss.

"*No!*" came a frenzied voice, and a rifle shot split the air.

Nick turned sharply. A figure in khaki was approaching

across the meadow. It was the drunk from the Packhorse, the one called Kurns. He didn't seem so inebriated now. When he came close, Nick saw that his eyes burned with rage; he also saw the big rifle in the man's hands. It was a huge, lethal-looking affair, a Dragunov in fact, and it was trained firmly on Lady Langdon.

"You said it would be *me!*" the man roared. "You promised *me* the gift!"

The cop glanced back at the women. Every one of them had resumed her earthly form, though several were nude, and one or two clad only in tatters.

Lady Langdon was glaring at the intruder. "You will never understand, James Kurns. This man has been chosen . . . sent to us."

Kurns could only sneer. "Is that so?" Then he raised the rifle to his shoulder, took careful aim at Nick . . . and fired.

8

When Nick came around this time, he was in a world of pain. It burned in the middle of his chest, intensifying with every breath. If he moved so much as a muscle, it wracked him head to foot, though his movement was largely restricted. He was fastened to a bed, a belt buckled tightly across his thighs, another one across his neck. His arms were loose, but it hurt like hell even to twitch his fingers.

He rolled his eyes left to try and view his surroundings. It was a spacious bedroom, nicely furnished. The curtains were drawn, but pale daylight came through them. Then Nick sensed a presence . . . this time to his right. He rolled his eyes that way and saw a man in his shirtsleeves scrubbing up at a washbasin. Beside him, on a small table, there was a black bag with a stethoscope hanging out of it.

"Dr. Death I presume?" Nick groaned.

The man glanced around. As the cop had guessed, it was Cusani, and as usual he wore a vexed expression. "I'm not enjoying this, you know," he said.

"My heart bleeds for you," Nick retorted.

The doctor reached to the sideboard and lifted up a heavy gray object. Nick immediately recognized it as his armored undervest. A flattened hunk of metal was embedded in the very center of it.

"Ingenious," the doctor said. "Expecting trouble when you came to Barrowby?"

"I always expect trouble," Nick replied, flexing his hands, finding that pain-free sensation was slowly returning. "Ever since a maniac had a crack at me with a shotgun, about twenty years ago."

The doctor pulled on a pair of latex gloves, snapping them into place on his fat wrists. "You've only delayed the inevitable, I'm afraid. And in the meantime you'll have to endure three cracked ribs and a fractured sternum."

Nick acknowledged this with a wince of fresh pain. He didn't even want to look down at his chest; he knew it would have bruised blue-black, probably over an area the size of a dinner plate. Cusani came and stood next to him, gently probing with his rubber-clad fingers.

"You'll never be able to fight them, you know," he muttered. "And at the end of the day, why should you want to? They're offering you the chance to be much more than you are now."

"Is that what they told *you*? Yet here you are . . . an ordinary G.P., probably with fewer patients than the average vet."

Cusani looked at him pityingly, as if he, too, had once thought that way. "You're either with them or against them. . . . It's that simple."

"They must have a weakness?"

"Well, of course. Everything has a weakness. But I doubt *you'll* be able to take advantage of it."

"What is it?"

The doctor laughed and turned back to the sink.

"Damn it . . . tell me!"

Cusani laughed all the more. "It's no secret," he said over his shoulder. "Deprive them of the one thing they need . . . the portal. In other words, the circle. Break that, and their cause is lost."

Nick considered, but quickly realized how futile this was. Even the smallest of the megaliths was immovable. They must weigh five tons each, at least.

"You wouldn't be the first to try, actually," the doctor added. "An attempt was made in the eighteenth century, but according to tradition, a sudden and terrifying storm put the demolition team to flight. Still"—and he turned back to his patient, now with a full hypodermic in his hand—"it hardly matters."

"What's that?" Nicked tried to shy away, but the belts held him in place. "What is it?"

"Secobarbital." Cusani depressed the plunger slightly and a jet of fluid spurted from the needle point. "It's a mild barbiturate. Just a little something to put you out. Lady Langdon's orders."

The doctor leaned over, but Nick lashed out with his elbow, catching the guy full in the groin. Cusani fell forward over his patient, dropping the hypo, which landed point-down on the mattress. Nick grabbed it, yanked it free, then stabbed it fiercely into the doctor's left buttock, flushing out its contents in a single massive injection.

"You fool!" Cusani choked, tottering back to his feet, his face a livid purple. He felt around for the syringe and tore it out. When he saw that it was empty, he went white. "You . . . *bloody fool*, you might have overdosed me!"

"I'll be sure to send flowers to the funeral," Nick replied, struggling with his bonds, though the effort sent flashes of fire through his entire chest cavity.

Cusani wheeled and lurched toward the washbasin, on the side of which there was a small bottle with a printed label. Already, however, the sedative was taking effect. He stumbled and slipped down heavily to his knees, his forehead banging on the porcelain bowl. He stayed in that position for a moment, breathing deeply, groping blindly around with weakening hands, before finally toppling sideways in a dead faint.

Nick was relieved by that, but still fought to get free. The crushing pain made it difficult—as he twisted and turned, he actually heard the grating of cracked bones inside him—but several minutes later he'd succeeding in getting his legs loose. After that, he was able to shift over onto his stomach, lever himself up with his knees, and drag his head under the neck restraint.

He sat there for a moment, wheezing, listening to see if the sounds of the fight had alerted anyone. Several moments passed, bringing no response. At length, the cop stood up and hobbled to the sideboard, where he retrieved his ragged sweatshirt. As he put it on, he noticed the empty hypodermic on the carpet. He picked the instrument up, then checked the label on the bottle by the sink. As he'd suspected, this, too, contained Secobarbital. It took only a moment to refill the syringe to its maximum capacity.

A minute later, he'd let himself out onto the upstairs landing of a large, well-appointed house . . . almost certainly Halkin Grange. He listened for a moment, and still hearing nothing, advanced along the corridor, passing portraits, vases of flowers, the occasional antique. The more he saw of the place, the more incredible it seemed that these people were mixed up in such ghoulishness, yet he'd seen the evidence with his own eyes. As if that wasn't enough, however, he suddenly *did* hear something. Something curiously repulsive, like a throaty gurgle, like a long, gelatinous groan.

Nick's ears pricked up. He glanced around. There was a

door quite close to him, firmly shut. Nick heard the noise again. This time it was more like a choked keening, as if something which had never been intended to talk was trying desperately to do so. Mystified, but with a growing sense of dread, the detective put his ear to the door. Someone or something was burbling away in there, in moist and miserable fashion.

Nick couldn't resist. Turning the handle, he found the door unlocked. Slowly, he pushed it open. What he then saw in that room was bizarre beyond his dreams, an image of madness perhaps drawn from the deepest nightmares of Picasso. The room was empty of furnishings—only blood streaked the otherwise bare floorboards and plaster walls—but it wasn't empty of furniture. For in the very center there was a chair. A *chair that had once been a man.*

The mans' tibias and femurs, stripped clean and gleaming white, had been torn loose from their original joints and, with long lines of tendon, fastened as chair-legs to the four corners of his horizontal pelvis, which also had been cleared of fleshy tissue, but was now smartly upholstered with the soft and palpitating air sacs of his lungs. These in their turn were attached through a gristly tube, which wound its snakelike way around the upright spinal column, fitting neatly between the splayed and sawn-short rib bones now providing struts for the chair's backrest—framed, by the radius and humerus, broken square and tied off with sinew—to the shaven cranium, upper jaw, and popping eyes of James Kurns . . . located in a place of honor at the very top of the macabre throne.

Nick would normally have called it impossible for a human being to survive such a transformation. *Normally* . . . but now, with the eyes still rolling in Kurns's distended sockets, with the chewed-off stub of tongue flicking in the deep crimson cavity that had once been his throat, with the mass of pink and reddish organs dangling below the seat—tucked well below it so as not to inconvenience a sitter—dripping fresh blood and bile, and clearly connected to the head through various pipes and arteries wound unobtrusively through the framework, but subtly translucent so that the labyrinthine passage of life-giving fluids could clearly be seen . . . he didn't think he could call it anything.

"Are you tired?" came a voice to Nick's left. The cop turned, but only slowly. He was so shocked that even the sight of Jenny, the estate manager, standing in the doorway, her eyes like onyx orbs, almost failed to register. "Why don't you sit down?" she said, with a demented grin, which exposed yards of sharklike teeth.

That was enough. As ordeals went, this one had gone off the Richter scale. Something inside Nick snapped.

"Why don't you fucking *lie* down!" he bellowed, thrusting at her with the hypodermic, jamming it into her neck and flushing it out.

The woman was taken by surprise. She gave a frenzied squawk, then went thrashing to the floor. Nick jumped out of the way as she threw herself across the room, writhing like a dervish and colliding head-on with the human chair, smashing it to pulp and bone-splinter. Still-living organs squashed and burst, blood and membranes splattering against the walls. Nick back unsteadily away, nauseated beyond description. He didn't know if the drug would have the desired effect upon her, for already her screams and snarls had taken on a bestial, demonic quality. But even then he was unable to flee. . . . He just watched, in appalled disbelief.

Only when the female finally began to change—black-green blubber bulging out from her clothes, tentacles unravelling, toothed maws springing open on every portion of her body— was he able to get his feet to obey . . . was he able to turn them and steer them out onto the landing.

The din that emanated from that room was frightful, bass roars shaking the walls to their foundations. It seemed impossible that anybody else in the house would fail to hear, but as he staggered down the main stairway, clutching his agonizing chest, Nick saw nobody.

Below, the front door stood open. He tottered down the last few stairs and across the hall carpet, hardly daring to believe his good fortune. Still no alarms were raised. It could only be a matter of seconds, though his good fortune persisted, for once outside he spied the Toyota SUV. What was more, the keys hung from its ignition. He clambered in and started the engine. Still nobody came.

Nick put the vehicle in gear and slammed his foot down. A moment later, he was driving at full throttle. In the rear-view mirror, he watched the palatial residence fall away and be swallowed by trees.

"Keep going," he muttered to himself. "Just keep going."

The narrow lane unspooled before him, and at length he reached the huge wrought-iron gates, now closed and padlocked. But he had anticipated this. He slowed the Toyota down but didn't stop. The heavy vehicle was doing about five miles an hour when it made contact with the gates. There was a shuddering clang and a mild shock of collision, but Nick kept his foot to the accelerator. The gates swung outward as far as the chain and padlock would permit. Nick stood harder on the gas. The engine began to rev, and the SUV's wheels were soon spinning, pouring smoke. Then, with a sudden *twang*, the chain snapped and flew away. The gates, which had begun almost to buckle, were violently flung outward, and the vehicle roared through.

Nick glanced again at his mirror as he drove. There was still no sign of pursuit, the lane deserted in his wake. He accelerated all the more; getting to Barrowby was imperative . . . *or was it?* All at once, it struck Nick that Barrowby was no longer synonymous with safety. Andy McClaine might be there, but so might Toomey, Miranda, et al. It was a bewildering moment. Thickets and hedgerows flickered past as the SUV roared along; shafts of setting sunlight broke in mellow spears across the road ahead. But where was he going? Where *could* he go?

At the very next junction, the question seemed to answer itself. It was a T-junction, with two road signs pointing in opposite directions, one indicating three miles to Barrowby, the other that it was five miles to Gilderdale. That struck a chord with Nick, and almost immediately he remembered why. The open-cast mine, the quarry . . . they had been blasting up there, which meant there'd be explosives.

Cusani's words came to him: *Break the circle, and their cause is lost. . . . Break the circle. . . .*

Nick wrenched the wheel over and turned left. The tires screeched, plumes of dust were thrown up behind. It couldn't be this easy, of course; there had to be a catch. Certainly, he'd have a difficult time getting the workmen at the open-cast to do what he wanted. He slapped at his tracksuit pants pocket, to confirm that he still had his warrant card. But even with that he'd have to be at his most convincing.

He glanced into the rear-view mirror a third time. There was still nothing behind him. Ahead, the road wound steadily on. And then . . . everything seemed to happen at once. Nick detected movement in the corner of his eye and glanced sharply left. Through breaks in the trees, he saw an alarming shape bearing down over the sloping meadowland toward him. It was a horse, a fine roan mare, with a girl on its back . . . a girl in boots, riding slacks, and a white silk blouse, blond hair streaming behind her. She was carrying something. It looked like . . .

There was a loud crack, a deafening whine . . . and the passenger window exploded inward.

Nick felt the bullet zip past his ear. He jammed his foot

down as hard as he could, though on a winding road like this, that in itself was perilous. The SUV screamed and skidded along the curbs, dragging vegetation with it. A second shot struck it in the flank. The entire chassis shivered. The horsewoman now came into view behind. She was framed perfectly in the mirror, galloping furiously. Clearly she was an expert, for even at this speed she was in full control of her animal and again taking aim with the rifle.

Just at the wrong moment, the SUV ran onto a straight and open stretch. Frantically, Nick hauled the steering wheel right, then left, zigzagging. The rifle bucked in the girl's grasp, but the slug whistled harmlessly past. Unfortunately, the tricky maneuvers also cost Nick speed. The huntress had been forty or fifty yards when she'd fired the first time; now she'd closed the gap to twenty. She wouldn't even have to be a good shot from that range.

Again Nick straightened up and floored the accelerator, pushing the needle toward fifty. Again the horsewoman fell behind, but he knew it wouldn't last . . . not on this road, unless he did something quick.

The chance came sooner than expected. He'd no sooner taken a tight leftward bend and briefly lost sight of the girl, when a road sign came up, indicating a right-hand turn to the Gilderdale Mining Company. It was a dusty access road, leading away into the woods, but it had been widened to accommodate trucks and heavy machinery. And it would serve.

Nick jerked the wheel over and yanked at the hand brake. With a screech of tortured rubber, the SUV lurched right and spun around on its axis almost 180 degrees. Checking his seat belt, he knocked the car back into first and hit the gas as hard as he could. Ten seconds later, when the horse and its rider rounded the bend, the SUV was in fourth and blazing at fifty. A collision was inevitable.

The cop caught a fleeting glimpse of the rider's panic-stricken face, her rifle spiralling from her hands, before the horse reared, and the speeding vehicle smashed headlong into it. The shock was phenomenal, the impact like a hand-grenade detonating. Nick was thrown against his seat belt with neck-jarring force. Shattered glass exploded in on him. Then he was upside down, sliding at terrifying speed into the road-side undergrowth. There was a crack of branches, a rending and tearing of metal. A welter of leaves and mold poured in, enveloping him, filling his eyes and mouth. More bangs, more jolts, another frightful impact as the slewing vehicle struck some unyielding object . . . in the event of which, incredibly, it righted itself onto its tires again.

Nick sat there, dazed, clutching the steering wheel, his face filthied and riddled with cuts. Several moments passed before he could breathe. His ears were still ringing, his hands still shaking. Warily, he began to feel up and down his body, not yet convinced he was totally intact. It was quite a surprise to find that, aside from the nagging pain in his chest, and now a grow-ing stiffness in the neck, he was relatively unharmed . . . which was more than could be said for the SUV. On all sides of him, it was bashed in; every one of its windows broken; the driver's door, crumpled out of shape, would only open half a foot or so, and Nick had to squirm his way out, snagging his clothes on shards of twisted metal. From the outside, the vehicle proved to be in an even worse state, the once-gleaming bodywork pul-verized, the hood almost torn from its hinges, though astonish-ingly, the engine was undamaged and chugged happily away as the man stood gazing at it.

A moment passed, then Nick looked back over his shoulder. His passage through the undergrowth was clear . . . a meander-ing alleyway of flattened stems and crushed leaves. He walked cautiously along it until he reached the road, where the horse and its rider lay still, about twenty feet apart. The animal was clearly dead, its legs broken and tangled in knots, its neck at a grisly angle. Cora Maynard wasn't so visibly injured, though she appeared to be unconscious. The rifle hung by its strap from a roadside bush. Nick strode over and took it. It was the Dragunov that Kurns had been using.

As a rule, Nick hadn't carried firearms during his career, but he was well enough trained to identify and use them. The Dragunov was a case in point. Russian-made, it fired a lethal 7.62 round and was ideal for the urban warzone. What it had been doing in the hands of a drunken headcase like Jimmy Kurns was anybody's guess, but the thought alone sent a chill through the detective.

He looked back at the body of the girl . . . to find that she was now sitting up, watching him. Instinctively, Nick leveled the rifle on her. She smiled, toothily.

"Don't you bloody move!" he snapped, but he knew she wasn't going to listen, and indeed she didn't.

Her grin broadened further . . . and further, to impossible width, literally from ear to ear. Her eyes became black beads. There were more teeth in her mouth than it was possible to imagine. Nick felt the sweat break on his brow. Involuntarily, his finger tightened on the trigger.

"I'm warning you," he said, but she—it—wouldn't be warned.

Her entire form began to waver before his eyes. Where once she'd had fingers, now there were tendrils—suckered like a squid's, writhing frenetically. With a loud *rip*, her blouse split open, and leprous yellow flesh puffed out. More eyes opened, in her cheeks, in her forehead, but Nick had seen enough. He fired once, twice, three times . . . each payload striking the creature in the head with sledgehammer force. Her transforming skull imploded, blood and brains thrown clear across the road. As the third slug ploughed home, what was left of the head was sheared off completely, and her torso slumped lifelessly backward.

At first the hybrid thing lay still, a gory lake spreading around it, but then, before Nick's unbelieving eyes, all signs of transfiguration receded. Tentacle suckers were reabsorbed; gross, puffed-out flesh shrank back onto the human frame beneath; new eyes and new mouths closed and were sealed; the yellow-green tinge faded and ran, flowing at last into the delicate pink-white of normality. At last, nothing more mysterious than a young woman lay there. A young woman whose head had been brutally blasted to pieces . . . which, of course, was potentially problematic if someone now happened along.

Nick hesitated for a moment, then stumbled across the road, into the devastated underbrush. The engine of the Toyota was still running . . . whether the thing would drive was another matter, though. Nick threw the Dragunov into the back, then slid in behind the wheel, knocking the vehicle into reverse and applying the gas. Laboriously, with much shaking and grinding, the SUV began to move. More twigs snagged on it, but at last it was back on the road. Warily, Nick put it in first, then accelerated slowly up the access road to the quarry.

He'd traveled about a mile when he came to a clutch of dingy prefabricated buildings, with several trucks and muddied bulldozers parked to one side of them. Further along the road, Nick saw the tall framework of an open-cast washery, though padlocked gates closed off access to that area. He slowed and braked, the SUV rattling as if fit to fall apart. In fact, there were dropped-off pieces trailing all the way behind it down the access road. A workman came curiously out from the first building. He was a broad, burly character in boots, jeans, and plaid shirt, with a beefy red face under his white hardhat.

"What the hell happened to you?" he said, staring at the trashed car.

Nick climbed painfully out, fishing his warrant card from his tattered pocket. "Police officer. I've got a serious emergency. I need some explosives."

The workman looked stunned. "Eh?"

"I need some explosives," Nick replied. "Look . . . you must have plenty here?"

The workman shook his head, bewildered. "I can't give it to you just like that."

"I told you I'm a police officer."

"I don't care who you are, you'll need proper authorization."

Nick leaned back into the car, grabbed the Dragunov, turned around, and leveled it on the workman's chest. "How's this?" he said, and to emphasize the point, he cocked the weapon.

The workman swallowed. He looked hard at the gun, then glanced up at Nick's bloodied face. It was a toss-up which was the more intimidating. "Just—take it easy," he said.

"Don't give me advice; give me the explosives," Nick replied quietly. "Believe me, I'm desperate enough to use this thing."

The workman nodded. He eyed the gun again, then turned and led the way into the prefab. Five minutes later, they were in an outbuilding at the rear of several cluttered offices. The workman opened a small safe and handed Nick two cubes, each one about the size of a tea caddy, both clad in waxed paper.

"That's Noma 4ED dynamite," said the workman. "It's all we've got at present, but it's a high-density gel. There's enough there to shift a mountain."

Nick nodded and licked his broken lips. Even after everything else he'd been through, he was wary of handling material like this. "How volatile is it?" he asked.

"It isn't," the workman said. "It's nitroglycerine-based, but it's specially compounded to be shockproof. That's why we use it. You need to fire an electric charge through it to create ignition."

"So how does it work?"

"They'll string me up for this. . . ."

"No one's going to get hurt," Nick assured him.

"Even so, I'm breaking every law there is. . . ."

"I haven't got time to argue!" the cop cut in. "I think you can see I've got a real crisis on my hands."

The workman gazed at Nick, not sure what to believe.

"If it makes you feel any better," Nick added, "the moment I've gone you can call the police. In fact, call the army as well, and the air force, call everybody. Get the world and his brother here. I think we're going to need them."

"What the hell's happening?"

"Never mind that—just tell me what I have to do to set this thing off."

The workman turned to a cupboard on the wall. Opening it, he took out another object, this one sheathed in hard, clear plastic and shaped roughly like a car battery. "You need a full detonator assembly," he said, handing it over. "This is the charge box, and these—" he also handed over a reel of red and blue cable "—these are your fuse-cords. You'll need both."

"Positive and negative, yeah?" Nick said.

The man nodded. "It's like jumper cables on a motor. Red's positive, so plug the red socket pin into the positive port on the charge box, and the blue into the negative."

Nick examined the two cables. The socket pins were visible at one end; at the other, there were two small electrodes. "Presumably these go in the gel?"

"Yeah . . . but listen, you make sure the charge box is switched off while you're inserting them."

"Or else boom?" the cop said.

The workman nodded. "They're water- and static-proof, but to be safe, keep them dry and away from any other electrical source." Again, extreme doubt appeared in his eyes. He reached out halfheartedly, as if to take the items back. "Look, mate, give 'em back, hey? I can't let you walk out with this gear. . . ."

"You haven't got a choice," Nick replied, stepping out of reach. "Interfere and I'll shoot you. What I'm doing here is going to save *all* our arses."

The man just shook his head, perplexed but also horrified at what he was party to. In fact, his ruddy features were draining of color, a milky pallor replacing them. The muscles in his neck were visibly tensing. Nick realized the guy was about to try something. And why not? In this worrying age of random gun massacres, anything was better than letting some maniac walk off with an armful of high explosives.

Nick considered this, and nodded. Then he pulled the trigger.

Just once.

A single slug ripped through the workman's right thigh. The guy went down in a heap, with a strangled gasp. Immediately, blood came pulsing between his clawing fingers.

"Sorry about that," Nick said, "but at least no one can blame you now."

9

An eerie dusk had settled on Long Meg and Her Daughters. The woods and hills were turning purple, the sky a misty metallic-gray. The great stone obelisks became twisted, tortured shapes as a spectral miasma rose from the surrounding grassland. There was neither sound nor movement.

Nick stood silently by the wrecked Toyota, watching. It was miraculous the SUV had gotten him this far, though he doubted it would go any further. Not that it mattered. Only one thing mattered now: The gateway was still closed, and that was how it had to stay, by fair means or foul. He moved forward, the rifle slung at his shoulder, his arms loaded with the explosives and their detonator kit. A moment later, he was kneeling beside the inside face of the nearest megalith. *Break the circle,* Cusani had said. *Break it.*

As carefully as he could, Nick peeled the waxed paper away from the two blocks of dynamite. A brownish black substance was visible beneath, clammy and plastic to touch. Nick wiped a sheen of sweat from his brow, then gingerly compressed the blocks together, melding them into a single glutinous blob. Once he had done that, he pushed it into place at the base of the megalith. God alone knew how much the piece of granite weighed, but his much dynamite ought to blow it to smithereens, to completely erase it from the English map.

Next he unraveled the detonator leads. There was more of them than he'd imagined . . . eighty yards at least, which gave him some idea how far away he'd have to stand once he threw the switch. He checked to make certain the socket pins weren't in contact with the charge box, then inserted the two electrodes into the gel, and, paying out the cable as he went, began to retreat across the circle.

He'd reached halfway when something stopped him.

A voice.

"Nick?" it said, baffled.

Nick turned sharply. Andy McClaine was standing there, hands in his coat pockets, gazing at his colleague with something like total bewilderment. "What's going on?"

Nick walked around him, continuing to lay out cable. "Can't tell you, Andy. Just trust me."

It briefly occurred to him that he must look an incredible sight . . . wild-eyed, filthy, ragged, bleeding from a dozen gashes. It was obvious that Andy's incredulity was growing steadily. He was gazing at the detonator cords. "There's been a nasty robbery," he said slowly. "The watchman at Gilderdale Quarry got shot, the blackguard made off with a pile of . . ." His words trailed away.

"Good news travels fast," Nick grunted. "Came over the air, did it?"

"Mel . . . Mel Toomey told me."

Nick laughed crazily. "Don't trust a word that bitch says!"

"Nick—what the fuck's going on?"

"What do you think?" Nick snapped. "While you've been swanning around the country, I've been trying to sort things out." He continued to lay out cable.

"What . . . er, what's this for?"

"Just get over there to the SUV, where you'll be safe."

"Why shouldn't I trust Mel Toomey?"

"Why don't you ask her?"

Andy nodded. "Alright. Why shouldn't I trust you, Mel?"

It took a second for that to strike Nick, then he whirled around . . . to find the policewoman standing directly behind him, a thin smile on her pretty lips. "Killing Cora Maynard was a mistake, Sergeant Brooker," she said quietly, drawing her cuffs and baton. "I'm going to have to take you in."

Nick threw the charge box down, grabbed the rifle, and aimed it between her eyes. "How about if I kill *you?*"

"Nick!" Andy protested. "What the hell . . . ?"

"You've got to trust me, Andy!" Nick roared, his finger tense on the trigger. "Well?" he said to the woman constable. "What if I kill *you?*"

"You can't kill her, Sergeant," came an imperious voice, "not with so puny a weapon. Surely you've realized that by now?"

All three turned . . . to find Lady Langdon on the outer rim of the henge, framed between the two slabs that formed its entrance. Unlike Toomey, she still wore her white druidic robes. Her eyes still shone blissfully. Almost casually, in a nearly Christlike gesture, she held out a hand . . . and from around the left slab came a stumbling, jerking, and truly hideous figure: a body without a head, a girl's body, naked, grimy, streaked with clotted blood, its neck terminating in a jagged crimson stump.

Andy McClaine's jaw fell open, a scream of disbelief locked in his throat.

Nick, on the other hand, knew that he was unlikely ever to

disbelieve anything again. Swiftly, he turned the rifle from the policewoman to Lady Langdon.

"So what about *you?*" he shouted. "You're *human*. One shot will drop you like a blade of grass."

The priestess gave a careless smile. "I've performed my task. Once *you* are fully anointed, my earthly use will be finished."

"Let's test the theory," Nick said, but before he could fire, Toomey lunged, flinging her baton in a blurred flash of movement. What it had in speed, it lacked in accuracy. Too fast for the eye to see, the missile spun clean past Nick and hit Andy square on the temple. Nick whirled around, pumping the trigger. Five shots tore into the policewoman, sending her tottering backward. In the same instant, the Cora-monstrosity came lumbering forward. Nick swung the rifle round again, still firing. Another three rounds slammed into the creature, punching fist-sized holes in its chest, hurling it to the ground. The moment it struck the grass, however, it began to quiver and writhe and . . . slowly to transform.

Nick glanced back to Toomey, who was also changing, formless feelers of protoplasm slithering out from her deflating uniform. He winged another couple of shots into the pair of them, then sensing his magazine was spent, flung the Dragunov aside, snatched up the detonator assembly, and continued to unravel it. Seconds later, he'd passed beyond the stones. He was panting with effort now and staggering, hot sweat stinging his eyes. He could hear slobbering snarls as, somewhere close by, multiple mouths yawned hungrily open.

"J-Jesus!" he stammered. "Jesus . . . help me, please. . . ."

At that moment, the fuses went taut in his hands. Thankfully, he hunkered down, slipped the pins into the correct ports, then looked back to the circle, his finger on the switch . . . and that was when he saw Andy's prone body, thirty yards at most from the dynamite.

For a second, Nick was convinced he couldn't go back to

help his friend. Andy was already a goner, he told himself . . . probably dead with his skull crushed. But even if he wasn't, to either side of him, separated by only a matter of feet, the two Shoggoths were rising on their haunches. The cop didn't understand how he knew that word, but all of a sudden he did, and not only that, he comprehended it. Shoggoths, shapeless netherbeings, foul creatures sprung from daemon sperm, hunters and killers of the infernal realms, fathered by the Old Ones as slaves and soldiers . . . as advance guard for the great reconquest.

Yet even in the face of such evil, to leave a comrade helpless wasn't an option Nick could countenance. Swallowing his fear, he placed the charge box on the ground, then, stiffly, like a scarecrow, he went back toward the circle. The Shoggoths gibbered and raised their misshapen heads to the sky, their many nostrils flaring, their myriad eyes rolling. Insanely, Nick persisted, walking boldly between the stones and moving out into the middle of the henge, refusing even to look at the towering abominations, focusing entirely on his fallen friend, who a few moments later was at last in reach.

Nick put a hand to his nose, for the sulfurous stench made the air unbreathable, then he took Andy by the collar and tried to haul him away. The young cop was coming around, but still heavily dazed. Half-carrying, half-dragging him, Nick moved back toward the edge of the circle, the Shoggoths watching him every inch of the way. A minute later, he'd reached the megaliths, and still they hadn't intervened; possibly the stupour of transformation had dulled their responses, but it couldn't last much longer. He knew that. *Then a tight claw caught his ankle from behind.*

Nick looked wildy back. Lady Langdon, her face still written with manic glee, had dived full-length to impede him. "You can't abandon them!" she shrieked. "They are your destiny. . . . You must help them prepare the way."

Nick kicked at her face, but she clung on with grim determination.

Then there came an earsplitting din of roars and snarls . . . as if all Hades had been unleashed. The cop glanced up. The first of the Shoggoths was approaching. Fully awake now, it swayed swiftly toward them. The woman laughed dementedly, but a moment later, that laughter became a shrill squeal . . . for the monster, having failed even to notice that she was there, rolled its glistening bulk straight over her. With a crunching and popping of bones, she vanished, her grip on Nick's ankle jerking loose.

Nick shot away like a shell from a canon, yanking his friend behind him. Beyond the perimeter of the circle should lay some modicum of safety. The colossal creatures would have to follow between the sacred stones with care, for fear they might damage the circle. Nick hoped he was right, and indeed he seemed to be, for the first of the Shoggoths slowed its pursuit as it reached the line of obelisks, and paused there for several seconds, while Nick dumped his groggy burden and fell upon the detonator like a starved wretch onto food.

Even then, he hesitated before throwing the switch, and gazed back at the daemons. Seventy of these fiends had been sought by the cult of the Black Goat. He'd seen the damage one alone could do . . . *but seventy!* And of course, these were only the daughters. *What of their father?*

The thought alone was too terrifying. Muttering a prayer, Nick hit the switch.

The explosion was more shattering than he'd ever imagined. There was a searing flash, in the very midst of which the Shoggoths seemed to simply fragment. Then the rest of the world turned upside down. A mountain of mud and rock rose and rose, blotting out the sky, a rain of stones and rubble in its wake. Pitch-darkness followed. . . .

10

And instantly he was back there, in that terrible, timeless place where the casement looked out on the deformed totems of a long-dead city, and beyond those, the blinding emptiness of the vast Antarctic.

This time however, the chill was unbearable, the wind a sword that slashed and slashed, the snowflakes like poison-tipped arrows driven into his flesh from the tautest bows. He'd have screamed and crumpled to the floor like paper, had his body not immediately gone rigid, had the ice slabs under his naked feet not burned like hot coals. But even above his ago-nized moans, above the numbing screeches of the wind, there came another, yet more dreadful sound: the dirge of a thou-sand slavering maws, snarling and bubbling and frothing with vengeful venom, approaching the throne room arch at unnatu-ral speed.

The man listened with appalled fear.

There was also a squelching and slapping, as if some vast, slick torso was being hauled in frenzy across a polished floor-way. All at once, the man wanted to flee, but he couldn't. He was paralyzed by the cold, wracked with pain. In any case, surely death by rending and tearing was preferable to death by prolonged windburn? But then again, as a monstrous shadow fell through the archway, and the squelching and buffeting and grunting and snarling grew to ear-cracking crescendo, a voice told him that rending and tearing was the *best* he could hope for. What of death by digestion? . . . Lodged for eternity in the acids folds of a great gelatinous belly. What of death by nib-bling? . . . As the symbiotes feasted night and day on his slowly melting flesh.

These horrors struck the man individually, one by one, as the reeking, gargantuan thing—the very appearance of which defied the will of God—reared in the archway . . . *only for the*

limitless space around it to suddenly implode, like a cataclysmic
volcano, to suddenly flood inward on top of itself.

The man felt the shockwave pluck at him with hurricane
force, but somehow, inexplicably, he held his ground as everything else cascaded past—ice, snow, and rock in an endless, ti-
tanic avalanche. And in the very heart of the maelstrom, the
unnameable thing . . . no longer so hungry for vengeance, now
battered and bombarded, ripped and gashed asunder, then
flung around and around in a growing vortex of destruction,
around and around and around, faster and faster and smaller
and smaller as shred by shred it drained away through the
ripped fabric of its hellish universe, its icy domain flowing in
after it, the cliffs and corries, the bergs and floes, a pouring
mass of liquified continent, the crags and glaciers and grits . . .
even Mounts Erebus and Terror themselves—those Atlantean
pillars of the Pole—one after other, sucked from sight like
hanks of meat into the throat of a ravening wolf.

For eons it lasted . . . eons, but all things come at length to
an end. And at the end of this, there was nothing. Simply that.
Nothing.

The man wheeled slowly in the awesome chasm of space.
Silent minutes passed, or were they years? It was impossible to
tell. On all sides of him, stars speckled the void. Some configu-
rations he recognized; others were new to him. But there, directly ahead, more distinctive than all the rest, the trails of
cosmic dust leading up to it like innumerable roads, was the
grand constellation of Orion, glimmering in the blackness, a
palatial framework of gems and jewels, and high on its bur-
nished shoulder, the great bronze orb that was Betelgeuse . . .
so near yet still so far, for the man suddenly longed to reach it.

As he struggled and kicked, and sought even to swim his way
there, the trails of dust—which in fact were seas—enveloped
him, and then coated him, thickly . . . packing his eyes and
nostrils, his mouth and ears, settling their litter over him in

choking layer after choking layer. His efforts became frantic but also weaker. The heavenly glow of Betelgeuse was lost in an ever-densening fog. Soon that fog was physically weighing upon him, pressing his limbs, cracking the bones inside them, threatening to crush out what little air was left in his bruised and wounded body. *And only then did salvation come.*

For a hand, torn and bloody but Godlike in proportion, came down to him, clawing away the debris in front of his eyes, unclogging the dirt from his nose and mouth.

"Nick!" said a booming voice. "Nick!"

Nick, the man realized, was his name. And now he realized something else . . . that he was coming up into air again, that the rubble strewn over him was starting to shift.

"Nick!" the voice repeated, and the resurrected man saw the face of one he knew—ingrained with dirt, streaked with gore, but laughing all the same, and joyful. "He's over here! And he's alive. . . . He's alive!"

A FATAL EXCEPTION HAS OCCURRED AT . . .

Alan Dean Foster

"He's going to post *what?*"

Hayes looked up from his cell phone. He'd known from the beginning that this was going to be tough to explain. Now that he actually found himself in the conference room with the others the true difficulty of it was more apparent than ever. Nonetheless, he not only had to try: He had to convince them of the seriousness of the situation.

Outside, the sun was shining through a dusky scrim of clouds: a perfect Virginia autumn day. The trees were as saturated with color as high-priced film, the creeks were meandering rather than running, and he would have preferred to be anywhere other than in this room. Unfortunately, there was the minor matter of a job. It was a good job, his was, and he wanted to keep it. Even if that meant commuting to Quantico from the woodsy homestead he shared with his wife and two kids.

The men and women seated at the table were sensible folk. Practical, rational, intelligent. How was he going to explain it to them? Aware that the silence that had followed Morrison's query was gathering size and strength like a quiet thunderhead, he decided he might as well plunge onward.

"The *Necronomicon*," he explained. "On-line. All of it.

Unless the government of the United States agrees to pay ten million dollars into a specified Swiss bank account by twelve P.M. tomorrow evening."

"That's not much time." Marion Tiffin fiddled with her glasses, which irrespective of the style of the day always seemed to be sliding off her nose.

Voice low and threatening, Morrison leaned forward over the table. "What, pray tell, is this 'Necronomicon,' and why should we give one of the hundreds of nutso hackers this section deals with every month ten dollars not to post it on-line, much less ten *million?*"

Hayes fought to hold his ground, intellectual as well as physical. He might as well, he knew. There was no place else to go. "It's a legendary volume of esoteric lore, thought for many years to be the fictional invention of a writer from Providence."

"Providence, as in heaven, or Providence, as in Rhode Island?" Spitzer wanted to know. Spitzer was the biggest man in the room. By the physical conditioning standards of the bureau, he ought to have been let go twenty years ago. He hadn't been, because he was recognizably smarter than almost everyone else. It was Spitzer who had solved the White River murders six years ago, and Spitzer who had deduced the psychological pattern that had allowed the bureau to claim credit for catching the Cleveland serial child killer, Frank Coleman. So his girth was conveniently ignored when the time came, as it inevitably did, to update personnel files.

"As in the state," Hayes replied flatly. It was no good getting into a battle of wits with Spitzer. You'd lose.

Chief Agent Morrison leaned back in his chair and put his hands behind his head. His bristly blond hair looked stiff enough to remove paint. "I'm surprised at you, Hayes. Unless you're trying to lighten the mood. Otherwise, I think your story makes a good item for the tabloid file."

"No." This was even harder than Hayes had imagined. "It's a

genuine threat, not a crank call. Don't you think I'd check it out before bringing it up here for discussion? Give me five minutes."

Morrison glanced absently at his watch. "Okay—but only if you make it fun."

Hayes wanted to say that it was anything but fun, but he suspected that if he did so he would lose his precious five minutes. And he couldn't afford to. "The hacker calls himself Wilbur. Don't ask me why. Maybe it's even his real name. He says he gained access to the restricted section of the special collections department at the Widener Library at Harvard, sneaked in a portable wide-angle scanner, and spent the better part of a day copying out as much of this book as he could manage."

Morrison frowned. "I thought you said it was fictional."

"No. I said it was *thought* to be fictional. Just for the hell of it, I checked with Harvard. Routine follow-up to this sort of thing. I had to go through four different people until I could find someone who'd admit to the library even possessing the volume in question. As soon as I did so, they went on-line to check my identification and credentials.

"I finally got to speak to someone named Fitchburn. When I told him the reason for my call, he got downright frantic. First he sent someone to check the records of recent visitors to the restricted shelves of the Widener. They were able to identify only three people who had been granted access to see the book in the past year. All three were well known to the staff, either academically, personally, or both. Then someone— apparently people were gathering in this Fitchburn's office all the time we were talking—remembered that a renovation crew had been in the special collections area for less than a week back in April, updating the fire suppression system. That must have been how this Wilbur guy gained access."

"He would have to have known the book is there, what to look for," Tiffin pointed out.

"Even if all of this is true, so what?" Morrison reached for the glass of ice water that always stood ready by his notepad. "What does Harvard want us to do about it? Perform an exorcism? Tell this Fitchburn to contact the local Catholic parish." Under his breath he growled, "Damn academics."

"It's not that kind of esoterica." Hayes's fingers kept twisting together, like small snakes seeking holes in which to hide. "The information in it has nothing to do with any of the major religions. It's—Fitchburn was reluctant to go into details. I got the feeling he didn't want to tell me any more about it than he felt I needed to know."

"This discussion is also woefully short on details." Morrison checked his watch again. "Your five minutes are about up, Hayes, and we have real work to do this morning. Sorry that all these kidnappings and murders and terrorist threats have to take up our valuable time."

"You remember the sinking of the *Paradise IV*?" Hayes asked him.

It was Van Wert who responded. "The cruise ship that sank off Pohnpei in that typhoon six months ago?"

Hayes nodded. "This Wilbur claims he's responsible for that. Claims he was trying out a couple of pages of the scanned book."

Morrison guffawed. "Typical nutcase. Next he'll be claiming credit for last week's earthquake in Denver."

"As a matter of fact . . . ," Hayes began.

"Five minutes are up." The chief agent shuffled the neat pile of papers in front of him, preparatory to changing the subject.

At that point it was doubtful he would have listened to anyone—except Spitzer. "A seven point one. Lots of property damage, forty-six killed, hundreds injured."

"I know the stats." Morrison growled, but he let the big man continue.

Spitzer scratched at his impregnable five o'clock shadow.

"Denver doesn't have earthquakes. It's situated in a tectonically stable region. The geologists said it was a freak occurrence. They still can't find the fault responsible for the geological shift."

"So?" Morrison groused. Time was fleeting.

"What," Spitzer continued softly, "if there is no fault?"

"Are you actually suggesting that it was somehow this Wilbur person's fault?" Tiffin gaped at the big man. "Sorry."

Spitzer looked at Hayes. "All I'm saying is that, while gaining admittance to the restricted section of the special collections department of the Harvard library may not be a federal crime, and therefore not fall under our purview, making threats against and attempting to extort money from the government is another matter entirely. Bob, I presume you've tried to trace this Wilbur person without success, or you wouldn't be here discussing the matter with us."

Hayes nodded, more grateful than he could say for Spitzer's support. "Wilbur says that if we don't comply with his demands, he'll post to the Net everything he's scanned from this book. According to him, that will let anyone from third-world dictators to role-playing-gamer teens have a good shot at destroying the world."

Van Wert pursed his lips. "Wouldn't that kind of render his ten million worthless?"

"I had the impression he's pretty desperate. Or pretty crazy. You know how hard it is to deduce personality types from e-mail." He went silent, watching Morrison.

The chief agent sipped from his glass, then set it back down in precisely the same place where it had been resting. "This is ridiculous, and I can't believe I'm wasting the bureau's time on it." His gaze narrowed suspiciously as he stared across the table at Spitzer. "If I find out that you two have conspired on this to try and put one over on me and get a couple of days off, I'll see you both tracking bank transfers in South Florida."

Spitzer folded his hands over his imposing belly. "I swear to God I never heard anything of it until Hayes started talking ten minutes ago."

Morrison grunted, mumbling something under his breath. "This 'Wilbur' isn't the only crazy person around. I ought to be committed myself for even listening to this. If any word of this leaks beyond this room, I won't be able to buy a burger in this town without people pointing at me and cracking up." His glare at that moment could have melted street grates. "All right—do a quick follow-up. A harmless ranting nut can turn into a dangerous nut. See if you can find him. We'll stop him from making threats, anyway. Hollow or otherwise." He picked up his papers. "Now then, about this new militia site on the Web. We know it's being routed through a server in Madison, Wisconsin, but after that . . ."

An hour later, puffing slightly, Spitzer caught up to Hayes in the hallway. "He doesn't buy it, does he?"

"Morrison? No. He didn't know whether to feel half-justified or half-disappointed. What about you? And thanks for sticking up for me back there."

"You're welcome. Let's say I have an open mind on the subject. What do you intend to do now?"

"We don't have much time. In between talking to Harvard and trying to calm them down, I asked them what I should do. One of their people suggested I contact a Herman Rumford in New York. Gave me his number."

"By the brevity of your response I take it you have already done so."

Hayes nodded as they strolled together down the corridor. "If anything, he sounds even weirder than this Wilbur character. But he said to come on up, bring what information I had with me, and he would see what he could do." For the first time that morning, he smiled. "Morrison as much as said you could come along on this with me. Be nice to spend a day in the city."

Spitzer nodded indifferently. "You think this guy can do anything?"

"Well, I put the usual technical people on the trace, and they haven't been able to run any surreptitious Wilburs to ground. So we might as well take a few of the people's tax dollars and head on up to the Big Wormhome. Either that, or find a way to winkle ten million bucks out of the discretionary terrorism fund."

Spitzer looked thoughtful. "I think we'd better try talking to this Rumford first." They walked a little farther. "That was very strange, the Denver earthquake. And before that, the cruise ship going down. Of course, it was caught in a typhoon. A very sudden typhoon, but not unusual for that time of year in the Pacific. Or so I've read."

"The ship was less than two years old. They're not supposed to sink," Hayes pointed out.

"No, they're not." Spitzer suddenly smiled. He had a charming, disarming smile. "We can take the eight P.M. express to Penn Station. Better not wait until morning."

"That's what I was thinking," were Hayes's last words to his fellow agent.

Somewhat to the surprise of both men, Herman Rumford lived in a fine old brownstone in a notable Upper East Side neighborhood, among which were sprinkled elegant shops, overpriced restaurants the size of shoe closets, and a smattering of celebrities. Rumford admitted them, not to a slovenly garret, but to a pleasant living room decorated with contemporary furniture and thick Chinese wool rugs. The art on the walls, however, instantly notified both agents that they were not in the presence of one of New York's ubiquitous brokers, bankers, or political mavens.

Some of the subject matter was unapologetically horrific. Some was in appallingly bad taste. Some reflected views of the world and of existence that would have seriously distressed even the most tolerant priest. Some was authentically old. And somehow it was all of a piece, as one seemingly unrelated composition flowed unexpectedly into another.

"My collection." Rumford was a short, thickset, fellow in his forties with shoulder-length hair tied back in a ponytail, dull blue eyes, and biceps that were little more than blips beneath his shirt. He looked like a human grenade and reminded Hayes of a renegade cherub. "Not to everyone's taste, I'm afraid. It's part of my hobby. And my hobby is my life. I spend most of my time studying its ramifications and variations."

"What is it that you study?" Spitzer loomed over their host like a sumo grand champion alongside a new student.

"Evil. I've made quite an analysis of it, with a view toward battling it wherever and whenever possible. You might say that we're sort of in the same business, although for me it's not a job." He gestured for them to follow. "Of course, I don't have access to the breadth of resources that you gentlemen do, but it's astonishing what you can find on the Net these days. But then, that's why you're here, isn't it?"

Leaving the pleasant living room and its disturbing art collection behind, the two agents followed their host into a smaller, book-filled study. Potted plants, some of them reaching to the ceiling, brought a touch of tropical rainforest into the city. They had been well looked after. Two tall, narrow windows looked out on the street. Queer sculptures and eccentric whatnots sat scattered about the dark mahogany shelves as if consulting the books neatly cataloged there. It was a reassuring contrast to the painted threats of the room they had just left.

"Not your usual hobby," Hayes told Rumford, making conversation.

"It does demand a certain devotion." Settling himself into a comfortable leather office chair, their host confronted an enormous LCD monitor. Not one, but several computers were arranged against the wall beside the spartan desk. It was more of a workbench, actually, Hayes thought. There were two other monitors, both presently displaying wallpaper that could only be described as eclectic, a tangle of cables, and a host of winking, humming ancillary electronics. "As I said," Rumford continued, "it's a hobby, not my business. I don't have a business, really. My grandfather left me a trust, you see. I live comfortably, but not to excess. I would rather do good deeds with my money that live to excess."

"Very philanthropic of you." Spitzer lumbered forward until he was standing behind the seated Rumford's left shoulder. Hayes took the right side. "Have you been able to find anything on our insistent friend Wilbur with the information we provided to you last night?"

"Oh, I caught up with him this morning. About an hour ago. We've been chatting." He indicated the miniature video camera sitting atop one of the nearby server boxes. "Not face to face. He's adamant, not stupid." Rumford chuckled as he did things to the ergonomic keyboard in front of him. Screens flashed and went on the huge monitor, the images large enough for both agents to scrutinize without straining. "He has no objection to talking. He just wants his ten million dollars."

"We can't give it to him. No government agency would approve it." Spitzer wanted to ask what several enigmatic metal boxes connected to the main server were for but decided he could inquire later. All of them were black, instead of the usual bland ivory-white. One appeared badly scarred and scorched, as if by fire.

"I suspected as much, but I hardly have the authority to tell him that. After all," Rumford added modestly, "I'm only helping you gentlemen out. I have no real clout here at all." Though naturally soft, his voice could take on a certain firmness when he wished it to. "I might mention that he's already threatened me."

Hayes looked alarmed. "Threatened you? But he doesn't know where you live — does he?" Glancing back through the front room, he eyed the front door uneasily.

"I seriously doubt it. I know how to cover my ass on-line. And I don't know where he is, either. Not physically. We only know where the other person is on the Net. Still," he added as he tapped a fistful of keys, "there are a few things we can try. Ah!" He indicated the screen. "Say hello, gentlemen."

The image on the monitor was a mass of writhing tentacles, bulging cephalopodian eyeballs, and slavering ichorous maws. Well done for a Java applet, Hayes decided, but not especially well animated. Words began to appear beneath the image.

When do I get my money . . . ?

Rumford glanced expectantly at his visitors. "What do you want me to tell him?"

Spitzer and Hayes exchanged a glance. They had already rehearsed a number of possible scenarios coming up on the train the previous night. Two-way audio would have made things easier, Hayes knew, just as he knew that unless he was dumber than he seemed their quarry would not risk committing even a disguised voice to storage that could be studied later. Speech patterns were too easily divined and applied to future suspects.

"Tell him it's in the works. He'll have his money before ten tonight, well ahead of his deadline. Provided we can assure ourselves of his sincerity, and that his threat is real."

Rumford typed in the response. Moments later, a reply was forthcoming.

> Actually, I'm surprised. The government usually isn't this sensible. Of course, this may be a stall on your part, but I don't care. You can't find me, certainly not by tonight, if at all. As for further proof of the seriousness of my intentions, turn on CNN and keep watching.

Spitzer shrugged. A somber Rumford directed them back to the living room and to the TV sequestered there. The big agent switched it on, found the requisite cable channel, and returned to the study. Two hours slipped by before the National Aquarium in Baltimore, an exceptionally sturdy and well-designed building, collapsed into the harbor amid much screaming and panic and death by drowning. Collapsed—or was pulled.

Ashen, Hayes relayed a response via their host.

> Enough! We get your point.

Back came the reply.

> I thought you would. There are quite a few passages in the *Necronomicon* dealing with a certain Cthulhu, his minions, and other really unpleasant ocean dwellers. Next time, I thought I might try to call up the servants of Ithaqua. The East Coast hasn't had a really good blow in five years.

Spitzer had Rumford type back.

> You've done enough. Give us till ten.

> You'd better come through,

their unseen nemesis declared on screen.

This stuff is almost too easy. Those Columbine guys could've blown away their whole state with it. Imagine Saddam's people scrolling through the file, or some of those murderous tribal types in central Africa.

At the end of the message, the on-screen cursor winked patiently back at the three men, awaiting commands.

Spitzer and Hayes caucused. "There's no way the bureau is going to cough up ten million for this weirdo on our say-so alone. No way," Hayes admitted. Despite the fact that it was very comfortable in the study, sweat was beading on Hayes's forehead. "We've got to find a way to get to him before he starts posting."

"We don't even know if he's in this country," Spitzer reminded his partner soberly. "He could have come in just to pay his visit to the library."

"I know, I know!"

With the sun beginning to set outside, only their host remained relatively composed. "I said there were one or two things I could try. I can't go ahead, I won't go ahead, without your authorization, though."

Turning, Hayes frowned down at their host. "Why not?"

Rumford's expression did not change. "There could be ancillary consequences that I can't predict."

"What, on-line? Go ahead. If there's something you can try, try it."

Rumford was very precise. "Then I have your authorization?"

"Sure, go ahead," Spitzer told him. "If a router goes down somewhere, or you crash an ISP, we'll take responsibility. We have to try something. Maybe you can find out where this guy is. If you can do that, and if it's on this continent, we can have people there within the hour. Overseas, within a day."

Rumford nodded. "That's not really what I intend to try, but

I'll keep it in mind." Swiveling in his seat, he turned back to his monitor.

It took less than thirty minutes. There was no shout of triumph from their host. He clearly wasn't the type. But there was quiet satisfaction in his voice. "Got him."

Both agents were more than a little impressed. "That's impossible," Hayes insisted tersely. "Our technical people at the bureau have been working on this since yesterday, and all through the night, and we haven't been beeped. Which means they couldn't locate squat." He eyed their stocky, intense host closely. "How come you could do it?"

Beady blue eyes flicked in the agent's direction. "I've been dealing with individuals of this type for some time. Let's just say I have access to a search engine or two even your people don't know about." He smiled thinly. "The Net's a big place, you know."

Spitzer loomed over both of them. "It doesn't matter. Where is he? Physically, I mean." He already had his phone in his hand, ready to transmit the vital information back to Virginia.

"Let me try something first." Without waiting for a response, Rumford returned to his typing. "If he thinks you're on to him, he can still post a lot of dangerous material before your people can restrain him physically." Both agents read over their host's shoulder.

> Wilbur: Do not post the *Necronomicon* or any part of it on-line. By doing so you're making it available to children and to people unaware of what they are dealing with. The *Necronomicon* is not a video game.

The response was immediate.

> Don't lecture me, Rumford. I know all about the *Necronomicon* and I know what I'm doing. I want my ten million! Tell the Bureau people that.

"He doesn't know you're here," their host murmured. "Probably thinks I have and am on a phone connection to you." He typed:

> If you persist in going ahead with this, steps will have to be taken.

> I'm not afraid of the government. I know how fast they don't move. By the time they find out where I buy my groceries, I can post the entire contents of The Book. They'd better not try anything. Tell them that.

Rumford didn't have to. Hayes could see it for himself.

Their host looked up at the agent. His expression was set. "Hand me that disc box, will you?" He pointed. "The one in the open cabinet, over there."

Hayes fetched the indicated container. For a disc holder, it seemed excessive. Solid steel, with a tiny combination lock. Returning, he tripped on a roll in the throw rug and nearly fell. Their host's reaction was instructive.

"For God's sake, don't drop that!" Rumford's round pink face had turned white.

Hayes frowned at the metal box, infinitely sturdier than the usual plastic container. "Discs are tougher than that. What's the problem?"

"Just don't drop it." Carefully taking the container from the bemused agent, Rumford opened it slowly. Spitzer was surprised to see that it contained only one silvery ROM disc. Mumbling something under his breath, Rumford slipped this into the appropriate drive on his main machine. It was not, Hayes observed, self-running.

A couple of clicks and a macro or two later, the monitor filled with a jumble of symbols and words that were unintelligible to the two agents. Working with grim-faced determination, their host began to use his mouse to methodically highlight specific sections. These were then cut and copied to another page, where he proceeded to carefully position them over an intricate mosaic of symbols. After some twenty minutes of this he sat back and double-clicked. Immediately, the monitor began to pulse with a rich red glow.

Spitzer observed the vivid visual activity with interest. "Java applet?" he wondered aloud. "Active-X?"

Rumford shook his head. "Not exactly."

"Nice animation," the agent continued, watching without understanding what was going on. "Bryce, or something from SG?"

"My own code. I correspond with people with similar interests. There's a guy in Germany, and interestingly, a woman in R'lyeh—sorry, Riyadh. We play around with our own software. It's kind of a hobby within a hobby."

Hayes indicated the monitor. The intense, swirling, necrotic colors had given way to the more familiar instant-messaging screen format.

> What do you think you're doing? You think you can trouble me with this?

"What did you do?" Spitzer leaned even closer, dominating his surroundings. "Send him a virus?"

"Something like that," Rumford replied noncommittally. In his server, the ROM disc drive continued to whirr softly even though no eldritch colors or patterns were visible any longer on the monitor.

> Wait . . . what's going on?

A pause, then:

Stop it . . . stop it now! You can't block me . . . I'm not
waiting any longer. Just for this, I'm going to post the first
chapter *right now*!

Hayes tensed, but their host did not appear overly concerned. He just sat staring, Buddhalike, at the screen.

What is this? . . . Make it stop. . . . Stop it now, I'm warning you! Rumford, make it stop! You sonofabitch bastard, do
something! . . .

A chill trickled down Spitzer's broad back as the words appeared on the screen. The ROM drive, he noted, had stopped
humming.

Make it go away! Rumford, do something now! I won't
post. . . . I'll do anything you want. . . . Make it go away!
Rumford, please, don't let it . . . oh god, stop it now. . . .
Please, do someth

No more words appeared on the screen.

Sighing softly, Rumford leaned back in his chair and rubbed
his forehead. He looked and sounded like a man who had just
run several laps around an especially bumpy track. "That's it."

Hayes made a face. "That's it? What do you mean, 'that's
it'?"

Turning away from the monitor, their host looked up at him.
"It's over. He's not going to post anything. Not now. Not ever."

The chill Spitzer had been experiencing deepened. "What
did you do? Where is he? *What did you send him?*"

Rumford rose. "Something to drink? No? Well, I'm thirsty.
Nasty business, this. You need to tell those people at Harvard to
be more careful. They really ought to burn the damn thing,

but I know they won't." He shook his head dolefully. "Book people! They're more dangerous than you can imagine." He eyed Spitzer.

"It doesn't matter where he is, or was. I took care of the problem. He can't post a 'you've got mail' note, much less an entire book. Much less the *Necronomicon*."

Realization dawned on Hayes's face. "You got into his machine! You wiped the copy!"

Rumford nodded. "In a manner of speaking, yes."

Spitzer was not impressed. "Unless this Wilbur was a complete idiot, he made at least one duplicate and stored it somewhere safe."

"It doesn't matter," Rumford reiterated. "He can't make use of it. Just take my word for it."

"That's asking a lot." Spitzer studied the smaller man. "How can we be sure?" He indicated his partner. "We have responsibilities, too, you know. This isn't a hobby for us."

Their host considered. Then he pulled a disc from a box in a drawer. An ordinary box full of ordinary discs. Slipping it into an open drive, he entered a series of commands. In response, both drives began to hum efficiently. Moments later, they ejected. Carefully, very carefully, Rumford removed the second disk, slipped it into a plastic case, and handed it to Hayes.

"Here's a copy of the program I used." His eyes burned, and for an instant he seemed rather larger than he was in person. "You might think of it as an antivirus program, but it's not intended for general use. It's very case-specific. You'd be surprised what can be digitized these days. If someone like this Wilbur surfaces again, you can utilize it without having to come to me."

Hayes accepted the disc and slipped it into an inside coat pocket. "Thanks, but I couldn't make sense of anything you put up on screen."

Rumford smiled humorlessly. "Just press F1 for help. There's an intuitive guide built in. I had it translated from the German." He brightened. "Now, let's have something cold to drink!"

Later, in the cab on the way back to Penn Station to catch the express back to Washington, while their Nigerian driver cursed steadily in Yoruba and battled Midtown traffic, Hayes pulled the ROM disc from his pocket. It was a perfectly ordinary-looking disc, rainbow-reflective and silvery. Their host had hastily scribbled a few explanatory notes on the inside of the thin cardboard insert.

"You really think he dealt satisfactorily with this Wilbur person?" Spitzer asked his partner and friend.

Hayes shrugged. "Unless it was all some kind of elaborate hoax."

The other agent grunted, and his belly heaved. "Better not let Morrison hear you say that. Not after we pressed for the time and expense money to come up here and do the follow-through."

Hayes nodded, absently scanning the insert. "If it wasn't a hoax, at least we won't have to come up here again. The instructions for making use of this are pretty straightforward." He had no trouble deciphering Rumford's precise, prominent handwriting, which he proceeded to quote to his partner.

"To download Shoggoth," he began thoughtfully. . . .

DARK OF THE MOON

James S. Dorr

"Houston," the voice crackled, "we've completed our separation. We're starting our descent to Tsiolkovsky now." Tasha monitored the transmission, only half-glancing at the flickering control panel screen as she fired her own rockets. She didn't need to follow it word for word, any more than she needed to check the adjacent monitor's feed from Earth with its predawn view of the moon's hair-thin crescent—the dark of the moon— just above the horizon to know, more than anyone else, what was happening. The voice was that of Gyorgi, her husband.

"Commander Sarimov, we read you in Houston. All systems A-OK?"

"Gyorgi Sarimov here. Yes, Houston. Tsiolkovsky's below us, brighter than Tycho on your Earthside. Its central mountain— you'll see for yourselves once Natasha has brought her c.m. to a higher orbit. Meanwhile, to north, we can see the sun glinting off the peaks of the Soviet Mountains while, southeast of us, Jules Verne Crater, the Sea of Dreams . . ."

Tasha heard NASA's reply, mostly lost in static, perhaps a result of her shifting orbit or, more likely, because the command module that she now piloted alone was itself passing behind the moon. It would store the pictures that Gyorgi sent to it, waiting until it passed once more into sight of the Earth, when she could transmit them to the International Space Station and thence to Houston. But for now, all she could hear was Gyorgi's voice.

She shut her eyes. Listened.

. . . fancies such as these were not the sole possessors of my brain. Horrors of a nature most stern and most appalling would too frequently obtrude themselves upon my mind, and shake the innermost depths of my soul. . . .

Why had she thought that?

She thought instead of when she had first met Gyorgi, at what they then called the Baykonur Cosmodrome, over tea at the enlisted men's mess. She was technically a civilian and he still in training, so the officers' section was barred to them. Back when the U.S.S.R. still existed.

Horrors as she herself had experienced that dark night when she'd felt a loneliness such as she felt now—separated from her then future husband, with nothing that she could do. The night of the accident.

And then she chuckled. Gyorgi had found the words now to speak to her, just in a whisper over the uplink. For her ears only.

And Gyorgi remembered. He quoted to her not the words that she had thought during the accident or words of his own, but those of an American author, Edgar Allan Poe, from a story she'd shown him in Florida after he'd started his training with NASA.

The story had to do with a balloonist who'd gone to the moon.

When she began the transmission again she already knew of the lunar module's safe landing, of Gyorgi's careful step out onto Tsiolkovsky's smooth floor. She had seen, as if through his eyes, the other two follow: one man American, one a Frenchman. There would have been another American, too, in orbit in the c.m. had he not taken ill just before their launch window. She had been a last-minute substitute for him. In her mind's eye she saw herself still on Earth, standing outside in the dim winter air to watch the nearly invisible moon rise, where she *would* be had it not been for Gyorgi's powers of persuasion. And she thought that in the imagination of another Frenchman, Jules Verne, not far from where she and her husband had lifted off scarcely four days before, other lunar cosmonauts had launched themselves in a shell from a huge gun.

So many authors, and not just Americans and Frenchmen, had been enamored of the moon for centuries. Even the namesake of her husband's landing site, their own Tsiolkovsky, had written among his scholarly papers a novel, *Outside the Earth*. Others too—Oberth, Goddard, the Englishman H. G. Wells—wrote fact and fiction about lunar travel or travel to planets beyond the moon. Or, in the case of Wells and another American, Lovecraft, of alien beings beyond the moon who, turning the premise on its head, came to Earth to do evil.

Horrors most stern and most appalling . . .

Tasha shuddered. As if mankind couldn't do evil enough itself.

She thought of Russia. Its people. Its sorrows. Its myths also, though that, like the Western science-fictional myths filled with their own wonder, had helped bring her and her husband together.

And now *he* had landed, part of the first expedition to the moon's far side. The side that was dark when you could look up and see the moon—always faced out to space. And light when you couldn't, so that now, when the moon was hidden from Earth, Gyorgi had light by which to explore.

". . . we're setting the cameras now on the crater floor." This she brought up on the c.m. monitor to watch for herself, to compare the camera-eye "reality" with such deeper truths as her mind's eye might show her, again almost as if she might see through *his* eyes. So well did she know her husband by now, and his way with descriptions.

And she saw a graveyard. . . .

Her mind snapped back to the Baykonur Cosmodrome. To a metal table and glasses of hot tea. "You," Gyorgi had said, "you know the myths, too, then?"

"Yes," she answered. "The sun and the moon. The stars, their children. You, cosmonaut-in-training Sarimov, brought up in Krasnoyarsk"—they'd known each other that well by then—"are the image of Dazhbog, of the sun."

He chuckled. She gazed at his sun-bright hair—her own was pale brown, at best its dim shadow—as he smiled and answered, "Then you, mechanical engineer Tasha, must be that strangely named beauty Myesyats. Named as a man, yet entirely a woman, the Goddess-Moon." He chuckled again. "You know, they were married."

She blushed. By then they *had* slept together, but still . . . talk of marriage? She frowned as she answered. "True. They were married. But then he abandoned her."

Gyorgi laughed. "Yes. But the following springtime . . ."

And then, a week later, he *did* leave her, though not by his own choice. The KGB was still to be feared then, and when, one evening, he didn't show up with the others at the mess, she imagined the worst. She knew what he had been trying to do for her, to get her into the cosmonaut program. Fearing, to be sure, that as an engineer she might at any time be reassigned to some other location, something she didn't want to happen either. But she knew, too, that while Gyorgi had a way with his superiors, a way of usually wheedling successfully what he asked for, one could not push the system too far before it would push back.

And that's when she'd found out how much she really loved him.

"Houston, do you read? The cameras are working, but possibly we've made a miscalculation. We've set down on the southern side of Tsiolkovsky's central peak since that's where the ground seemed the smoothest, but as a result our landing site is in shadow. Perhaps in a few days, when the sun has shifted somewhat . . ."

She watched the pictures on the TV monitor and saw what Gyorgi meant. When they turned away from the mountain they were to explore, she could see the far crater wall, brilliant in sunlight, and the l.m. itself, where it sat on its landing struts, half lit, half shadowed.

But back toward the mountain, the strange jagged peak that, so the scientists said, could prove that Tsiolkovsky itself was an impact crater—and what an impact, the scar it left nearly three times as wide as the Earthside's most prominent feature, Tycho!—back that way all that the cameras could pick up was darkness.

She *looked* through Gyorgi's eyes. . . .

Darkness. A jumble. Shadow and darkness—the realm of Chernobog. And yet, in the darkness, this side of the mountain, what looked like small hillocks, but pointed and craggy.

"The central peak's children?" she whispered, half to herself. Realizing, of course, that even if she were trying to contact him, Gyorgi, outside the l.m., couldn't hear her.

She watched as if through his eyes, as if her sight, too, were confined by his helmet as he and the others peered into the darkness.

The hills were still far away from the l.m. and the men wouldn't go to them until the next morning—Earth morning, that was, after they'd had another sleep period. The hills looked a little like gravestones.

Huge, sharp gravestones, patterned in rows. And between them — did she see what Gyorgi *really* saw? — what could almost be mist if the moon had an atmosphere.

Shadow and darkness. Her thoughts went back once more to that evening in Baykonur when all her inquiries about Gyorgi had turned up nothing. She'd lain in bed in her room that night, claiming she felt ill, and tried to concentrate on Gyorgi.

She thought of the sun and the moon and their mythic love — the cause of the seasons. Dazhbog and Myesyats. Thought of their quarrels that, so the myths claimed, also gave birth to earthquakes. Dazhbog's abandonment of his moon-bride every winter, but — here she concentrated the hardest — his coming back each spring. And . . .

She joked about it afterward, saying it must have been the special sensitivity of her Russian woman's soul. Or perhaps just stress. But she *had* seen it.

. . . the vision . . .

. . . white walls. An accident ward in a rural hospital, outside of Baykonur where Gyorgi had crashed his motorcycle. The doctors hadn't yet informed the officials — or, rather, as her vision widened, she realized they *had* told the cosmodrome's commandant but, although she'd asked, he had not told *her.*

The shadow. The brightness. The earlier myths of primeval man, of evil and goodness. Chernobog and Byelobog, gods of the Dark and Light. Light of truth, withheld even when she had asked . . .

Gyorgi had come back the following morning, little the worse for wear. And, of course, what she thought she'd seen could have been a coincidence — she knew he drove too fast. She had even argued with him about it. But in the meantime, she'd made two decisions. The first was to officially ask for a transfer to the cosmonaut program, to become a cosmonaut-in-training. This, she knew, was what Gyorgi had wanted, but up to this moment she had always held back.

And the other, when Gyorgi was better, was to insist that they get married.

She lay on her couch remembering now, while, on the moon's far side, Gyorgi was sleeping. She had read the Western myths. Fantasy.

Science fiction. Books she had purchased to read alone, in the Florida nights while Gyorgi had been away on training.

She knew about training and nights spent alone, even after her and Gyorgi's marriage. Even though by then she was a cosmonaut, too, "to follow in the footsteps of Tereshkova," as her husband had put it to those in command, there still was no question of her being actually sent into space herself. Even Valentina Tereshkova had been a symbol, making that one flight in 1963, but, as a woman, thereafter perpetually grounded—so, too, her own job had continued to be primarily that of a mechanic.

But then the Soviet Union collapsed and they'd moved again, first to Luga, where her family came from—there *she* could find work, whereas he was idle—and then to America as a package with the great *Energia* rockets that NASA had bought from the Russian Republic to help in the rebirth of its moon program.

And while Gyorgi learned the ins and outs of American space capsules, Tasha had read Western authors and wondered. She'd wondered at all the authors' obsessions with reaching the moon. For all, it seemed the ultimate mystery, especially its dark side. And even, for some, it seemed also the key to a deeper mystery.

The Russian myths, before the sun and moon, spoke of gods of light and shadow. Of Byelobog and Chernobog. She wondered if Lovecraft had known the Russian myths—

Why had she thought of Lovecraft? Rather than Verne or Poe or the others?—yet surely he had known, if not directly, as they all had. His vision sharper perhaps in some respects, just as the others' was sharper in others. It was her belief that all human thought was ultimately based on identical truth, on some all-but-forgotten memory of mankind.

Yet the myths were, at base, simply metaphor. The evil of shadow was surely *man's* evil. That she believed, too. Just as the *Energia* rocket was her metaphorical child—she and Gyorgi had proved unable to have their own children, despite the myth of the union of Dazhbog and Myesyats spawning the stars. But she'd helped assemble the *Energia* on its new American launchpad so Gyorgi could ride it, and then, when Captain Brechner came down with the flu and she was assigned to the c.m. in his place, they *both* could ride it. . . .

The ship to the moon's far side—*through* its darkness. Opening mysteries to reach to the stars beyond, past the planets; stars shrouded, yet burning bright in their own darkness. The children of sun and moon.

God and Goddess, one in the other.

Tasha dreamed of the moon and stars, her mind metaphorically one with Gyorgi's. It was while she slept in that way that she often felt she understood the most.

Tasha dreamed of the following morning—no need for TV now—as the l.m. opened and three men dismounted, bulky in spacesuits. She walked with the first of them into the shadows.

She saw the balloon first, the one Poe had dreamed of in his chronicle of the Hollander-Cosmonaut Hans Pfaall. She saw its bent hoop, its tangled netting, its bag-covered gondola—

more than even her husband could see because her eyes were clearer. She saw the projectile that Jules Verne envisioned, fired from the giant Columbiad cannon, which, even if it had not achieved touchdown, still lay on its side in the shadow before her.

She saw other shapes, too, arrayed in long rows. Rows that converged on the central mountain. A bicycle-like frame surrounded by skeletons of long-dead geese; another surrounded by metal spheres. The V2-like slimness of Robert Heinlein's and Willy Ley's coupled dream, made into cinematic flesh in a film she'd seen once when she was a child, *Destination Moon*. And yet other shapes too, saucer-like nightmares, the visions of men like Jessup and Scully that lay, side by side, with truly *non-human* dreams. Shapes to fit truly nonhuman proportions . . .

She blinked.

. . . and yet all dead. The ships crushed and broken . . .

She *heard* Gyorgi thinking:

. . . *let us put bones then. This plain would be nothing but an immense cemetery, on which would repose the mortal remains of thousands of extinct generations. . . .*

She woke. Yes, a graveyard. A graveyard of spaceships. The words were not Gyorgi's, though, but—she thought back— those of Michel Arden. The French adventurer in Jules Verne's novel.

She blinked. On Earth, in Houston, the sun would have just gone down—she'd slept the whole day through. Far to the west, the moon would be setting, too; this time she wouldn't see even a sliver.

The TV monitor was still on, the equipment functioning automatically. She heard its static. She sat up to look at it, seeing the images, shadowy, fleck-filled.

". . . tomorrow we'll rig lights that we can take with us," her husband was saying. NASA was gentle, unlike the Cosmonaut Corps of her own nation—first they must have rest. "Those, with the portable camera we have now, may give more information on those oddly shaped rocks we've found." Then he had *not* seen.

She sank back to the couch as he gave his description. A cemetery, yes, laid in rows, but still *only* stone and dust.

Only she saw what was buried beneath it.

"Gyorgi!" she screamed (knowing he couldn't hear her, not outside), watching her husband step from the l.m. the final time. Half dreaming, half waking in front of the monitor, she waited as the three astronauts, in blazing light now, walked through the ships' graveyard, her own spacecraft having swung back around the moon too late to do anything more than just watch them. She saw, with her vision, the l.m. itself, in the line of corpses. The crushing of men's dreams.

But Gyorgi could *not* see.

During the night she'd recalled, in her mind's eye, those last days before the launch. Her husband's arguments with NASA that not only had she had cosmonaut experience—something of an exaggeration at best—but also that, as a woman, with a woman's patience and natural steadiness, her presence in orbit around the moon would impart a steadfastness in those who were on its surface. But he had been wrong. She did not have patience. Not for the sort of waiting she did now, wanting to see, *straining* to see, what, even with the aid of their cameras, her husband could at best describe only dimly.

Except . . .

Except that she *did* see. The loneliness and stress produced visions in her mind. She'd looked to her instruments first, of course, the "Christmas tree" panel lights all still glowing green, just in case it might be some bad mix of air. She'd checked and rechecked again, thinking at one point she might call NASA to ask *their* opinion, but, no, she had best not—why cause needless worries? It was only the loneliness, after all, that and the fit-fulness of her sleep habits, despite the schedule of sleep-times NASA had asked her to follow.

But how *could* she have slept otherwise, now that Gyorgi and the others were on the moon's surface?

And so the visions came, from the books she had hoarded that autumn. The dreams of Heinlein, naive and hope-filled, mixed with the more cautious, Gallic optimism of Verne. And the darker, although still ambiguous, visions of Wells and Poe— Poe with his bleakness, his soul-searing horror, still having his astronaut dream, too, of fields of Selenite poppies. Of lakes and forests.

But, then, Lovecraft's *colors*. His dreams of far Yuggoth. Her own dreams, no less terrible for their having been lived once, of Hitler and Stalin, of KGB horrors. Poe at his worst still fore-saw *some* brightness, some faint trace of Byelobog. While the other, his fellow American prophet of darkness . . .

She didn't complete the thought. Something was happen-ing. Lights played on rock spires—spaceships as *she* saw, but still looking stonelike to the others. And now behind them as they climbed the talus of Tsiolkovsky's mountain.

"Over here, quickly!" The voice wasn't Gyorgi's. Rather, the Frenchman's, also with an accent. She watched as the camera panned, saw his lights sparkle. And then . . . deeper darkness.

"I don't know, Gyorgi." The voices crackled. "What do you think then?"

"A cavern of some sort."

No, Gyorgi! she thought. But he could not hear her. Nor could she call down to the l.m. to warn them, because there was no one inside to receive the call, and their suit radios were designed only for communications between one another.

And so she could only watch as they entered. Half see-ing, half dreaming—was it a cave mouth? Some huge sort of airlock?

She still heard their voices, that much of her still tracking them on the monitor.

"Sloping down . . ."

"Smooth-floored. Almost circular in its cross-section . . ."

"Almost—what do you think?"

"Almost as if it were artificial . . ."

She dreamed of Gyorgi, her vision widening, while at the same time she still stared at the TV. The sudden swirling beneath the men's feet, as if their descent took them into a mist . . .

"Some kind of gas, maybe. Do you know what this means?"

"That the moon has an atmosphere of sorts. But so thin, so tenuous, that it exists only beneath the surface. Look, you go out—check the wire antenna. Make sure we're still broadcasting up to the c.m. Then bring back a container of some sort for a sample."

She dreamed of Gyorgi, her vision widening. She saw a huge comet, and yet not a comet. A spaceship itself, crashing into the moon.

Blasting a crater two hundred and more kilometers wide— the aftershock throwing up its central mountain. The occupant, wounded . . .

Byelobog shattered. Dead. Chernobog crawling out, once the moon's floor had cooled, finding a cleft in the newly formed mountain. A hole to bore into. To bide its time . . . hiding.

And on the TV screen, the mist coalescing. Shadowy, whirling.

Forming tendrils.

The vision of H. G. Wells's *War of the Worlds.* A hollow stone turning, revealing metal. Tentacles reaching out. Except . . .

Except *much* vaster.

Edgar Allan Poe's *horrors most stern and most appalling,* yet vaster and darker still.

What she saw now, her mind's grasp expanding . . .

To bide its time from the time the moon was young, over the eons, until it was stronger. And while it was waiting, to draw others to it.

The children, perhaps, of spores it had scattered on its mad journey—some, even, that came to Earth—to draw their strength back into its own body.

And even it, perhaps the *smallest* of entities . . .

Coalescing. She *saw.* In her dream, she tried to *send*—somehow—some warning to Gyorgi.

That *something* stared back at her.

Knowing. Not knowing. The myths *were* metaphors. Human and nonhuman, all of the same spawn. Dazhbog and Myesyats. Byelobog. Chernobog. All of them part of the same dark evil . . .

Tasha woke, crying, to NASA's frantic calls via the space station, demanding to know why she had stopped transmitting. Outside she could see the Earth, bathed in full sunlight. Yet cold and colorless.

On the TV, static. There was no picture.

She closed her eyes, *straining.* Trying to dream again. Trying to find some trace of her husband.

Then, slowly, she sat up and straightened her clothing and opened the c.m.'s own, separate transmission link, wondering as she did what exact words she could use to tell NASA.

There would be no springtime.

RED CLAY

Michael Reaves

The grave lay in a tiny meadow halfway up one of the many sawtooth ridges that overlooked Harron's Notch, far from the town's cemetery and the quiet dead who rested there. No headstone or cross marked it; legend had it that the grave had once been so adorned, but not within the memory of any living man or woman in the small town. Whether the marker had been taken away or had simply been shattered by one of the many lightning storms that raged around the summit, no one knew.

Nor did anyone know who was buried there, so far from the Christian graveyard that lay behind the sturdy three-room chapel of whitewashed pine. But where history was silent, legend spoke volumes. Some said it was the grave of one of the witch folk—those shapechangers able to fly as eagles or bound as cougars from crag to crag in the dark of the moon—who had been struck down by silver and prayer and buried in unhallowed ground. Others spoke of a man who foolishly thought to deal with Mister Scratch and come out of it with both his soul and wealth intact. And there were those who insisted that a Yankee soldier, shot in the back during a cowardly flight from battle, had been interred there, and that not even the grass of this Southern soil would grow on his grave.

This last bit of legend was due to a fact easily verified by those brave enough to climb the ridge and see for themselves: Although the meadow grew high in spring and summer with flowers and grass, not a bit of green ever took root on the six feet by two feet that marked the grave. And neither snow nor frost settled there in autumn and winter. It remained the year around a raw wound of red dirt.

One theory offered around cracker barrels and potbellied stoves as to why the grave stayed naked was that it was hot with the fires of perdition, hot enough to melt snow and sizzle unwise flesh. It was also said that once a mountain man, more brave than prudent, tried to dig up the grave, but the instant he thrust his spade into the clay soil he was fried black, as though struck by one of the high-tension lines that hummed above the trees down near the highway. It was generally agreed by young children and old folks alike that anyone with the sense the Almighty gave a moonstruck possum steered clear of that unnamed and unmarked grave.

Zeb Latham was, they said, smarter than a moonstruck possum, though not by much. A massive scion of hillbilly stock, with wiry black hair that grew rampant over his skull, cheeks, and chest, and brooding gray eyes that peered out from beneath sheltering ridges of bone, Zeb had, for most of his twenty-odd years, supported himself in a life that was marginal even by backcountry standards. He lived on the edge of the Notch, in a one-room hovel made of unstripped logs, with a leather-hinged door and no floor but the ground itself. He eked out his survival mostly by foraging, hunting, and fishing; in the winter he chopped wood and did other odd jobs for the townsfolk in exchange for food and clothing.

While no one was his enemy, neither was anyone who knew

him particularly willing to call him friend. Having been raised by an abusive mother who abandoned him at the age of ten, Zeb was by nature suspicious of humanity in general and women in particular. His speech, when he was forced to communicate with others, was curt and monosyllabic but always stopped short of active antagonism. Some of the townsfolk considered him a powder keg, but most dismissed him as harmless, and some even felt sorry for him: a piece of poor white trash, doomed no doubt to an early death from malnutrition or exposure.

For his part, Zeb gave these matters little, if any, consideration. The past and future weren't things he cared to dwell on— the present he dealt with day by day.

On this particular day he had ventured far up the steep slopes of the Notch, following a flight of bees in hopes of finding their nest. He was successful, spotting the bees swarming around the stump of a lightning-blasted pine. The next step was to locate a deposit of the thick red clay so prevalent in those parts and coat his face and hands with it for protection while he scooped out part of the comb. Zeb could almost taste the thick, syrupy spoils of his hunt, spread over the loaf of bread Aimie Meechum had given him as payment for digging those rocks from her truck patch.

He pushed his way through a thick patch of brush and into a small clearing. It was one of the many leas that pock the sides of the mountains. At the far end a cliff opened onto a vista that most city dwellers would pay dearly to see from their windows, but which Zeb hardly noticed. His attention was concentrated on the patch of red dirt in the middle of the grass.

He headed for it but stopped halfway there. The meadow was oddly silent. He could hear no insects singing, no birds trilling; only the soft whisper of the wind through the tall grass. This in itself was enough for only a moment's notice, but combined with the strange barren patch of ground that lay before him, it was enough to give him pause.

In the three years of schooling he had had as a child, Zeb had heard vague stories about the mountain grave, but he did not connect those tales with what was before him now. His sudden apprehension was of a more primal sort; he sensed a wrongness here, the same way a game animal might intuit a trap laid in the woods. Zeb rubbed the black bristles of his beard uneasily and shifted from foot to foot, an ungainly dance of mental conflict.

Then a shift in the breeze brought from back in the forest the faint buzzing of the bees, which reminded him of his purpose. He crossed the last few feet and dropped to his knees before the patch of dirt.

Again he hesitated, feeling oddly nervous; then, with a scowl, he plunged both hands into the dirt at the edge. And pulled them back almost as quickly, with a grunt of surprise. There was an odd tingling transmitted from the soil up his arms, almost like a low-grade electrical shock.

Zeb reached one hand out again, cautiously, and placed it flat, fingers splayed, on the clay. The tingling was still there but not as pronounced as before. Certainly not painful. Almost enjoyable, in fact.

The other interesting thing about the clay was its consistency. Zeb worked his fingers into it, feeling the soft marl ooze between them. It was the texture of dough, with no hard or crumbly bits. He put his other hand into it, kneading it, making patterns with his fingers. There was an almost silken homogeneity to it, like long-churned butter. It was decidedly unnatural, and yet at the same time a pleasing sensation.

He pulled two handfuls loose with a sound like a cow

pulling her feet out of mud. He brought the mud up to his face and sniffed cautiously. It had the familiar damp rich odor of clay, but there was another scent underlying it; Zeb could not decide if the smell was faintly spicy or like the coarse odor of decay. The tingling had become so subtle as to be almost unnoticeable.

Zeb's original plan to use the clay for protection against the bees was forgotten. He rocked back from his knees and stood, still holding the two handfuls of red earth. He stared at them, vaguely puzzled. Then he turned and lumbered back toward the forest.

It was dark by the time he got back home. He stoked a fire in the massive brick fireplace—he had built the cabin around it, the only part left standing when a wood-frame house had burned down twenty years before—and by its flickering light sat at the rude wooden table, looking at the clay.

In the uneven radiance it seemed almost alive, with subtle shades of red washing over its surface like oil over water. Zeb stared at it for a long time, his brow furrowed in unaccustomed concentration. Twice he reached toward it, and twice he drew his hands back. The third time he took hold of it almost gently, as though it were a newborn child.

His fingers were thick stubs with hornlike nails, unaccustomed to any action more gentle than wringing a chicken's neck or wielding the shaft of an ax. But now he stroked the yielding clay lightly, almost lovingly. At first his movements were tentative, but as the minutes passed they became more assured. He molded and prodded, his face a mask of concentration. The fire began to die, but he didn't notice. He worked on in increasing darkness.

At last he stopped and sat back. It was almost too dark to

see the thing he had created. Zeb rose stiffly and put another log on the fire. The hungry flames blazed up, and he carefully lifted the small object and put it near the fire where it could dry.

Then he turned and stumbled to the straw tick mattress in one corner of the room, where he immediately fell into a deep and dreamless sleep.

The next day, when the sun was heading toward noon, Walker Burnett came to knock on Zeb's door. There was no answer, but he noticed the door was ajar and so he pushed his way in.

The morning sun illuminated the interior, showing Zeb sitting at the table, staring at something on it. "Zeb!" Walker said with some asperity. "Here you still sit, when you was supposed to be cleanin' my chicken coop as soon as those hens left the roost!"

Zeb turned, blinking in the light. He seemed even more slow-witted than usual to Walker. "Guess I forgot," he said. "My 'pologies."

Walker stepped closer to see what Zeb was looking at. The door swung wider in a gust of air and sunlight fell across the table, revealing the object. Walker's breath caught in his throat. "God, Jesus, and Mary," he said. "Where'd you find such a thing, Zeb?"

Zeb looked back at the statuette on the table. "Didn't find it," he said, with a trace of pride. "I *made* it."

Not likely, Walker thought, regarding the statuette. It was perhaps six inches high, and rudely shaped, but undeniably the work of an artist. Walker had had a year at the state college and he had been to the art museum in the capital, and though he'd be the first to admit he was no expert, he felt certain that this piece of work would not be out of place in a city gallery.

Its subject wasn't particularly impressive: a dead tree, its branches raised in vaguely humanoid shape. But there was something to it—a strength, Walker allowed, that made it impressive. Something about it was unsettling; looking at it, Walker knew he would not want to be trekking through the woods late at night and come suddenly into view of that tree, its branches upraised against a full moon like something about to attack.

"Well, Zeb," he said slowly, "never knew as how you could do somethin' like this. Right impressive. What called on you to take up sculptin'?"

Zeb shrugged, looking uncomfortable. "Just . . . thought I'd try my hand at it." He seemed somehow embarrassed.

"Well, you might could do worse than try it again. Could be you have hold of somethin' there," Walker said. Then he added, "But not till you've taken up and cleaned that henhouse o' mine."

Zeb stood hastily and headed for the door, with Walker following. "Yessir," he said, "I'm pleased to get right on it." He seemed anxious to leave the cabin. Walker followed him, turning at the door to get a last look at the clay sculpture.

Lord call me home, he thought. *Zeb Latham an artist.*

It was past noon when Zeb received his payment from Walker for the job—ten dollars and a jug of Walker's blockade whiskey. Normally Zeb would have hastened back to his cabin, where a considerable portion of the jug's contents would have disappeared before the following dawn. Zeb was no tosspot, but he did enjoy a touch of the creature when it came his way. Today he paused at his cabin only long enough to deposit his earnings there, and then turned his face toward the winding trail that led up the ridge.

Since he had awakened he had felt an urge to return. It was like the tingling he had felt in his hands, only now it seemed to be in his blood, moving within him; a restlessness that he knew could be soothed only by returning to the high meadow and the red clay that lay there.

This time he brought as much clay as he could carry in his hands back down the hill, enough for two sculptures. He stayed up all night completing them. Then, as before, he collapsed into a slumber that was deep but still not restful.

As the days passed, some more of the local folk had occasion to drop by Zeb's cabin: Gussie Peterson, in an effort to do the Lord's work, brought him a pot of beans and rice; old Jackson Pharr stopped to ask Zeb to pour gasoline on the fire ant nests around his trailer; and Lionel Rampling, on a drunken toot, stumbled into the cabin mistaking it for an outhouse and nearly peed in the iron cauldron near the fireplace before discovering his error. The first two were astonished and somewhat disturbed at the growing number of statuettes that Zeb had created; Lionel was too drunk to notice them at the time, but later memories of what he saw were so unsettling that he went on the wagon for a record sixteen days.

Word of Zeb Latham's unlikely talent quickly spread throughout Harron's Notch and the surrounding countryside. People began to show up for the express purpose of viewing the sculptures. In some households Zeb's work was condemned as satanic, and this was sufficient to warrant a visit by the Reverend Coombs. He pronounced the collection of artwork, which by the time of his visit had grown to nearly a dozen statuettes, as the work of a disturbed mind, but not demon-inspired.

Zeb paid no attention to the curious visitors at first; later, when people like Frank Cornell, who owned the grocery and filling station and was the closest thing to an entrepreneur the town had, began urging him to sell his artwork (or, in Frank's case, offering to be his agent), he discouraged visits by the simple tactic of not answering the door. This proved surprisingly effective, since most of the population of Harron's Notch viewed Zeb somewhat askance anyway, and his disturbing creations had only enhanced that impression. After a flurry of interest that lasted a couple of weeks, Zeb was largely left to himself once more.

Only Walker Burnett continued to show interest in Zeb's new avocation, partly because he had been the first to discover it and felt a certain proprietary sense. But after a few more days even his visits to the cabin began to wane, because Zeb, never the most congenial host, had grown increasingly surly and uncommunicative.

The necessity of dealing with an outbreak of hoof-and-mouth among his small herd of cattle kept Walker busy for the better part of a week. Then one evening, nearly a month after his initial visit, he determined to drop by Zeb's cabin and see if the latter was still pursuing his hobby.

There was no answer to his knock. The property was even more overgrown than usual with jimsonweed and oak scrub. Flies buzzed around the partly open door, and from within a strange musky smell issued. Walker called Zeb's name twice; receiving no answer, and becoming somewhat concerned, he pushed open the door and went inside.

The smell was much stronger inside, strong enough to cause Walker to wrinkle his nose in distaste. It spoke of dampness and mold, of blind writhing worms and long-decayed flesh. At first Walker's heart nearly jumped out of his chest because he thought he would find Zeb dead and bloated in this stifling hovel. But after his eyes adjusted to the dimness Walker saw Zeb sitting on a split-log bench by the fireplace, which was full of cold ashes. A quilt had been hung over the only window, plunging the room into shadow.

Walker was shocked by Zeb's appearance. He had never known him to pay attention to personal hygiene overmuch, but the mountain man was in far worse shape than Walker had ever seen him. His filthy hair was matted with clay, and clay was smeared as well over the stiff and crusty garments that he had obviously been wearing for days. His eyes were filmed and bloodshot, and he seemed to have lost at least thirty pounds. Such a large weight loss in so short a time was unnatural, Walker knew. For a moment he suspected illness, but some dim, fearful voice in the far darkness of his mind whispered that the cause was much more sinister.

Thus far his attention had been focused on Zeb. Now Walker glanced about the rest of the one-room shack, and was barely able to stifle the exclamation of horror and disgust that rose in his throat.

Zeb's home was filled with clay sculptures. They crowded the few wood shelves on the walls and were arrayed in ranks on the floor and table. For one terrifying moment, in the murky light, they seemed to be alive. Then he realized that this illusion was caused by the uncertain light and the lifelike quality of Zeb's skill. But it was not a thing to admire now. It was a quality to dread.

Their subject matter was varied: more of the twisted, skeletal trees that had been Zeb's first endeavor, as well as plants, oddly sinuous and lush of blossom; snarling wildcats, backs arched, claws unsheathed; bears and wolves rearing on hind legs; coiled snakes with fangs bared, ready to strike; and other things, things which, by the grace of the Almighty, had never stalked any forest during the time of modern man. Walker's nervous gaze passed over a saber-toothed cat, muscles bunched and rippling, fangs like daggers protruding from its upper jaw. There was a mammoth, its beady eyes full of animal hate, its tusks twisted like arthritic fingers.

And there were other creatures as well, creatures that Walker did not recognize. He thanked Providence for his ignorance, for he felt instinctively that they were forms of life that had never existed in any sane universe; things born of mad, fevered dreams, perverted visions made solid in clay. He shuddered and averted his eyes from one such abomination: a bat-winged, claw-footed monstrosity whose face was filled with worms or tentacles that seemed to writhe sluggishly as Walker watched. He told himself again that it was an illusion caused by the dim light. But he did not look closely to make sure—to do so, he somehow knew, would be to risk having his sanity crumble like a levee before a spring flood.

All of these creations, even the recognizable ones, were unsettling in the extreme because of the subtle poses and expressions that somehow infused them with sinister purpose—a malice, deep and implacable, toward all humanity. Looking at them, Walker felt confronted by the utterly alien life-forms with which man had shared this planet in uneasy coexistence. A memory from his childhood rose within him, nearly causing him to break into hysterical giggles: a cartoon seen in flickering black and white of some hapless soul lost in darkness, surrounded by peering, malevolent eyes of all shapes and sizes. That was how he felt staring at Zeb's creations.

Walker took as deep a breath of the foul air as he could stomach. There was no question that Zeb's newfound talent had gotten the better of him; the man's mind had been unhinged by it. So Walker told himself, ignoring the deeper, certain knowledge that it wasn't that simple. He turned back to Zeb, intending to try to convince him to leave the house, to go with him to see the town doctor. . . .

"I cain't," Zeb said in a husky, lifeless voice, as though sensing Walker's intentions. "I cain't stop. I get that clay, and I jus' *haveta* mold it. . . . Cain't sleep nor eat without I do it . . ."

He struggled to his feet. "It's almost gone now," he said, his dried lips cracking in a caricature of a smile. "Maybe when I've dug the last of it, I c'n rest. . . ."

So saying, he lumbered past Walker and out into the purpling dusk. For a moment Walker was frozen with horror; he could not shake the feeling that he had just seen a dead man rise and walk. Then he realized that he was alone with the statuettes, and he nearly tripped over his own feet in his haste to exit.

Outside he saw Zeb disappearing into the woods, heading up the mountain. For the first time it occurred to him where the poor damned soul must be getting the raw material for his work. The horror that Walker Burnett had felt inside the shack was nothing compared to what filled him now.

He turned and ran back down the slope toward the town.

Zeb pushed through the brush and clawed his way up the steep rocky slopes, heedless of thorns and scrapes. There was nothing in him now but the need; the driving desire to plunge his hands once more into that silken-textured mud, to shape it, feel it come alive in his grasp with baleful, corrupt purpose. Why he was so driven he could not have begun to articulate; he felt no pleasure, no sense of creation in this work. On the contrary, the compulsion was a black and frightening thing, an overwhelming force that blotted out all other thoughts. Whatever meager peace there was in that was mitigated by the horror and loathing he felt for his creations. Each new one was more fearful than the last; each sculpture he completed seemed to leach from him more of his strength, his thoughts. And yet he could not stop.

Full night was just beginning as he stumbled into the small meadow. Before him yawned the pit—the patch of clay that he had, over the past several weeks, mined away until he had been forced during the last few visits to lie flat and plunge his arms into it full length to scrape up the hideous substance.

This he did now, sprawling on the thick grass at the edge of the grave, stretching his arms down until it seemed his shoulders must dislocate, clawing up the last vestiges of the red dirt with his fingernails. He couldn't see what lay at the bottom of the pit, for darkness pooled within it, thick and tenebrous, seeming to flow up his arms as he worked.

At last he could tell by touch that he had amassed enough for another sleepless night of fevered work. But he found himself unable to rise. He lay in a position which required him to use his arms to lever himself up, yet he could not do so without letting go of the clay he had so laboriously gathered. He lay there in a quandary, sobbing dry, harsh sounds. The eerie stillness of the meadow intensified his cries.

Zeb did not know how long he laid there in a semi-conscious state. Gradually he became aware that his fingers were moving as though independent of his will; smoothing and shaping, forming by touch, while he lay with his face pressed into the damp ground.

He managed, with a great effort, to raise his head; it seemed as if all his strength had flowed into his wrists and hands, leaving the rest of his body leaden and useless. Silvery light flooded his eyes; for a moment he was confused, and then he realized that the moon was rising.

At that moment Zeb felt strangely content. He sensed a nearing completion, a feeling of accomplishment that was unlike any he had ever felt before. A sense of having done something *worthwhile*. His life had been shallow and meaningless, making no more of an impact on the cosmos than the life of a woodchuck or squirrel. But now, in these final few days, he had changed that. He had made a difference. Just how this had been accomplished wasn't quite clear, but it had something to do with the statues . . . something to do with creation, liberation.

His tears flowed again, moistening the dirt, but now they were tears of gratitude.

He could no longer feel his hands; could only vaguely sense that the work continued. Zeb managed to look up again and found that the moon was halfway toward zenith. And now a sudden terror seized him, as abrupt and intense as his happiness and gratitude had been moments earlier. He realized that the moonlight was gradually creeping down the side over which he was hanging, moving slowly down his arms. Soon it would illuminate the entire pit.

He did not want to see what was in there.

Zeb tried to pull back, to worm himself away from the darkness below. But he could not move, except for his helpless and frenzied thrashings. He had no idea whether or not the sculpture in the pit was finished, or what held him there. He only knew that the moonlight, creeping inexorably down the sides of the pit, would soon reveal its depths to him.

He became aware that he was screaming, pleading, gouging the ground beneath his face with his teeth. It did no good. He was caught like an animal in a snare. At last, exhausted, he was still except for waves of trembling.

"Why?" he moaned, barely aware of his voice. "Why? I did what you wanted. Why . . . ?"

The silence held no answer. The moon continued its climb, seeming to balance, for a moment, like a silver ball on the branch tips of an old dead tree.

As the cold white light reached the bottom of the pit, Zeb moaned one final word.

"Beautiful . . ."

Walker Burnett was able to persuade only three other men to come with him to the gravesite, and none of them would go until the morning sun was high.

What they found would be food for hushed discussion in Harron's Notch for years to come. Zeb Latham lay dead at the edge of the grave, which had been dug clean to a depth of nearly four feet. His mouth was full of dirt and roots, as though in his final struggles he had pitched a fit.

What they found in the pit was even more disturbing: a small amount of clay, sculpted by Zeb into a statuette. There was disagreement among those who saw it as to exactly what it was. One said it was the image of an old crone, hideously ugly; another said it was a young beautiful woman; and Walker said it was the icon of something not even remotely human. He refused until his dying day to describe it. No one else ever saw it, for the statue crumbled when they tried to pry it from Zeb's fingers, locked around it in the rigorous grip of death.

PRINCIPLES AND PARAMETERS

Meredith L. Patterson

The fluorescent lights are blinding me, and I'm walking through the largest toy store I've ever seen. If I don't look up, the light isn't quite as strong, so most of what I see are people's knees and shoes. Beside an endcap of bicycle tires, a cluster of children are playing a card game on the floor, and it occurs to me: There are an awful lot of adults here. Some older kids, teenagers, but a surprising number of twenty- and even thirty-somethings, arguing over movie action figures and who gets the next turn at testing a video game. I keep my head down. When I look up I can see their eyes narrowing: What the hell are you doing here?

I don't want any of this. Why am I here?

Farther back in the store, now, the crowds are just as thick but the toys are different. Through a knot of guys in suits, I can glimpse a flash of shiny rubber and gleaming red fiberglass — a sports car? *Just beyond them, damp sand spills across the scuffed linoleum, spreading into the distance off to the left of me, and tall middle-aged women in bathing suits and enormous sun hats walk back and forth across it, barefoot.*

It's all boring as hell and I need to find the bathroom.

There's not going to be one on a beach, so I head to the right instead, ducking and weaving through aisles full of golf clubs, stereo speakers, expensive kitchen gadgets . . . nothing that I want. It's hard not to bump into people, and every time I do I get another angry look. But no one talks to me.

Finally, just past the end of the aisle, in what must be the far right corner of the store: a stairwell. I brush past the shoppers at a display of boat horns, head down to the first landing and follow it around.

Sixty-eight, sixty-nine, seventy steps to the bottom. And in fact there is a door, complete with woman-slash-man silhouettes, and it's even unlocked. Probably the employees'—

Or possibly not.

Bathrooms usually echo when the door bangs into the wall. This one booms, reverberates. I flinch and let go of the door. The wall it hit is like all the walls—either uncut or badly cut rock, greeny-grayey-brown. Around the corner to the left, where I'm still thinking there should be stalls, something must be casting the orange glare that lights up the—some part of my brain insists—bathroom.

Okay. I'll go with it. It's a bathroom.

Such a simple realization, but such perfect sense. At least from where I'm standing. So I head into the (cavern? bathroom!) proper. And stop just before walking face-on into a column of fire that reaches from floor to ceiling. Not a column of burning wood: a translucent flaming cylinder that burns without heat, without sound.

"K'neseshti, kulayr," says a man's voice coming from just past the pillar. I look up: no, not a man, two men, in layered, flowing robes and small, flat caps. With long, oily-shiny beards, tied with cords partway down and again at the ends. Egyptian?

"Ph'n elukuri v'ni trl' tsak'n?" says one of them, extending a hand, and I don't know what to say.

He's just looking at me, they both are, as if they're expecting me to tell them something, but that language doesn't register as anything I've ever heard. Babylonian? Cushitic, maybe, but the morphology's all wrong. . . .

Is it getting hotter in here? The room's starting to swim, but I don't feel warm.

The vowels sound like Greek; I suppose it might derive from Indo-European, though with all the glottal stops I'd think it would have to be Semitic in origin. . . .

"Putoru, nasht," says the second man, shaking his head. He looks disappointed, like an upset teacher, but he also looks so insubstantial, as if he's mapped onto the wall behind him. I sidestep around the column for a better look—or try to, but it seems to follow me. The whole room does, and the only change in my perspective is that everything looks flatter. I try running forward, toward the men, but my steps take me nowhere while the figures flatten out more and more, pasted on the wall now, like portraits, stretching rubberlike into caricatures, icons, meaningless markings on a sheet—

And then I woke up.

Which was why I was doing my damnedest to catch at least a little nap during my office hours the next day. For once, none of my Introductory Theoretical Linguistics undergrads felt compelled to try to talk me into just a few more points on the last pop quiz, nor did any of the educational sciences graduate students need a shoulder to cry on about the strict department regulations that forced them to take either Fundamentals of Propositional Logic or my generative-syntax course.

Even the one applied-linguistics Ph.D. candidate who genuinely *enjoyed* my Thursday morning computational methods seminar had disappeared right after class, rather than dropping by for a chat like he usually did. Which was a shame; last week we'd had a really interesting discussion about language acquisition and whether, as Chomsky argued, it would be impossible for a computer or a nonhuman species to fully understand human language, or for us to understand a nonhuman one. But he'd just smiled and said, "Catch you next week," leaving me to enjoy a quiet afternoon.

So I was awfully proud of myself for not screaming when Dr. Latour barged in without knocking.

"Oh, did I catch you with a few minutes free? That's great!" she crowed. She had a bulging manila envelope with her, and wore a far too friendly smile. "I'm flying out to Orlando this afternoon for the Women in the Humanities conference, so I wanted to pass this on to you before I left." She pushed a stack of *Lingua* back issues off to one side of my desk and spread the folder out in front of me. It was open to the middle of a manuscript printout. From the top of the page I read

> which signify the not dichotomous, but rather holistic hermeneutics of the pre-Aryan indigenous people. In specific, the author posits the use of a nonbinary logic which was later suppressed by the patriarchally imposed social constraints. The author's methodology will be substantiated with exemplary passages drawn from the heretofore unsuccessfully translated documents which . . .

Then Dr. Latour picked up the first half of the manuscript and flipped it to the top of the stack. The new face-up page was covered in hand-copied symbols, interspersed line-for-line with characters from the International Phonetic Alphabet. The symbols looked vaguely familiar, but not exactly like any script I'd ever seen before. At the top of the page was the title "Pnakotic Manuscripts."

"Sanskrit?" I guessed.

She wrinkled her nose. "Nothing so passé, Claire. It's in

Brahmi script, phonetic, with an interlinear for you. I need you to translate it."

This was a new one on me. "Why me? You know I don't do Dravidian." Her shoulders dropped, and she looked disappointed. She'd played this game with me before—most of the department had. She knew perfectly well what I was working on. In academia, you keep tabs on your neighbors, so that when the tenure-track appointments come available, you're ready to snap them up. That was probably why I was still just an instructor, with no real way to say no to Latour, the department head.

Not Aryan and not Dravidian. "Tocharian?"

This time she smiled. Patronizing, or pity? Probably both. "Ooh, closer," she said. "Same area, the Taklimakan desert. I'm sure it predates the Aryan invaders, though. Bill Pinckney transcribed the syllables into IPA when I gave it to him a few months ago. He only just now got it back to me." She flicked a glance across the hallway to Bill's office door, which was covered in clippings from *The Nation* and the *Times Literary Supplement*. "He swears he doesn't recognize the language, though he says the phoneme set is right for Tocharian. But you can decode it, right? With your computers?"

I sighed and pushed the folder back. "Jane, you need a cryptologist. I can give you a syntactic pattern analysis, *if* there's enough material for Alex P. to sort through. But Bill's our expert in Proto-Indo-European derivative languages, and if he couldn't parse it out . . ."

That sweet smile came back. "Maybe your theory needs room for different ways of knowing, Claire."

That's what she was up to.

I shoved my chair back, stood up, and picked up the folder. "Don't give me this postmodernist crap again, Jane," I snapped, and held it out to her. "You can't conclude that just because our so-called poor benighted Western civilization doesn't have an immediate answer to every mystery, it's incapable of finding an answer at all. If human beings spoke the language, then as long as we find enough evidence, we can figure it out. Period. We may not know where Basque came from, or Finnish, but that doesn't mean they operate on a completely hypothetical system of logic." I shook the folder toward her again. She didn't take it.

"Two theories. Both unproven." She looked down, brushed at a fold in her skirt, then glanced up at me. "I'm just looking for evidence to fit mine."

"But that's not the way to —"

"Thanks so much, Claire!" she announced before I had a chance to go on. "I *really* appreciate your input on this, however it turns out. Gotta go, though! Keep me posted!" She turned and walked away. I was left holding the folder.

God*damn* her.

I plopped back into my chair, sending it rolling backward, and ran straight into a box of audiocassettes, which fell over.

"Shit," I said, and spiked the folder onto the floor. Pages spilled out across the carpet, along with a floppy disc.

I was beyond caring.

She had me over a barrel. On the one hand, if I couldn't translate the language, she'd hold it up as "evidence of a thought system unfettered by our binary-logic constraints." And on the other, if I could, she'd doubtless find some passages to take out of context, explain as "holistic hermeneutics" (whatever that meant) in practice, and thereby skew the mind-set of everyone who read her work thereafter. Either way, it meant a lot of work for me, and not toward anything I'd take any pride in having my name on. Computational linguists look at watertight reasoning as a mark of prestige, and having my name associated with an essay that spat in the face of formal logic could be a black mark on my career for years. I didn't have many pa-

pers published yet, and I knew Jane would take a perverse pleasure in giving me contribution credit on an article that would
do nothing but *dis*credit me in the eyes of the rest of my field. I
didn't want to give her any grist for the mill, but still, I didn't
want to wimp out on the challenge, either.

About the only scrap of silver lining was that this would be
perfect for testing Alex P.'s capabilities. I had designed it—the
Advanced Lexical Processor—in lieu of a doctoral dissertation,
testing the program using reams of data from generative and
computational linguists. After three years of work, I had a piece
of software that could analyze a passage from virtually any language in the world's major language families, identify its formal characteristics, determine the language of origin—*and*
provide a detailed diagram of the passage, just by analyzing the
ordering patterns of sounds, words, and parts of words. If all the
vowels were nasalized, there was a good bet it was French; if
most sentences placed a verb-inflected word at the end, chances
were it was German; and so on. With about 92 percent accuracy. Maybe it wasn't the same thing as a program that could
really *comprehend* human language, but it certainly looked
like it so far. Still, all we had comprehensive data for was the
Indo-European family. So if the language of the Pnakotic Manuscripts belonged to the Semitic family, or Sino-Japanese, or one
of the dozen other families for which I only had partial analyses, it would be a crapshoot.

Hell, it was a crapshoot anyway. But the program might
pinpoint a language for which I could track down a human
translator. A *reliable* translator.

I swiveled my chair around to face the workstation kitty-
corner to my desk, shuffled the printouts sitting on top of the
keyboard into a more or less coherent stack, and added them to
the stack already on top of the monitor. While it powered up, I
chased down the disc that had fallen out of the folder and
slipped it halfway into the floppy drive. The screen read:

> DEC/Alpha Personal Workstation 500au
> Digital UNIX rev4.0d
> Copyright 1984-2000. All rights reserved.
> #/alexp/>

I pushed the disc the rest of the way into the drive and hoped I wouldn't have to scan the entire document into a format that Alex P. could use.

> #/alexp/> chdir floppy
> #/alexp/floppy/> ls
> Path: /alexp/floppy/
> [.]   [..]   pnakotic.txt
> 799048 bytes free.

> #/alexp/floppy/> vi pnakotic.txt

Score! Bill had done me a hell of a favor by translating the original phonetic script into the International Phonetic Alphabet, then copying the IPA material into a plain-text file. That was all Alex P. needed to begin tagging the Manuscripts into a file that it (or any other corpus-analysis program) could use to look for phonetic and morphological patterns. I closed the editor and exited back into the shell.

> #/alexp/floppy/> chdir ..
> #/alexp/> ./alexp/process /floppy/pnakotic.txt
> Advanced LEXical Processor v0.87a
> Reading into memory . . . All text read.
> Option? <Press H for a list> _

I set it to perform as exhaustive an analysis as it could, marking recurring words and morphemes and attempting to identify any basic syntactic patterns. With 700 kilobytes of raw ASCII to work on, though, that would take a while—overnight, at least, even on a high-efficiency UNIX machine.

It occurred to me that we probably weren't the first to have run across this manuscript. I might not have kept the closest eye on Jane's world-traveling, but I'd think the department would have made a bigger deal about it if she'd discovered an entirely new language artifact all by herself. If it *had* come from somewhere else, there had to be some previous information on it—journal articles, an announcement in one of the archaeology trade rags, the name of the discoverer, anything. Maybe someone who wanted to see the Manuscripts translated for their own sake, rather than to make some pseudophilosophical point.

So, off to the library it was. I rummaged briefly through the papers on the floor to find the first few pages of the Manuscripts, in case I needed to compare them to something from an article, and headed out.

It was about three in the afternoon when I left the building. Outside it was hot and damp, the kind of sticky-humid that makes you feel like you're being squeezed dry to make the air even wetter. I could have gone straight to my car across the humanities quad, if I'd really wanted the air-conditioning, but I figured it'd be better not to lose my parking space. Instead I took the shadiest route I could find, under the cypress trees that grow in front of the steam tunnels in the little park next to the overhangs of the administration building. It was even wetter there, thanks to the fountains that fed into the screened-off tunnel openings, but green and cool. The mockingbirds that frequent the area have sounded like car alarms for as long as I could remember, but I noticed they were making a different call now.

It sounded a little like *meep!*

. . .

It's true what they say about libraries: You really *can* find every-thing you need if you look long enough. Sometimes "long enough" is as short as fifteen minutes. I didn't even have to check in Archived Journals to find a decent body of research on the Manuscripts, already in book form.

So much for revolutionary new discoveries.

A catalog search across the Georgia Library Exchange turned up four texts: one published in 1895, another in 1922, followed by a 1931 monograph and the most recent work in 1958. Only the 1922 edition was in our catalog, so I copied the titles of the others onto the back of the first page of the Manu-scripts, filled out an interlibrary loan form at the circulation desk, and joined a crowd of students waiting for the elevator up to the humanities wing.

Once it arrived, we all squeezed in. Buttons lit up for every floor — not surprising — and I stayed wedged at the back, pick-ing at the splintering fake-wood panels on the elevator wall, as the car creaked its way up all five stories. Finally it let the last of us out, and I headed for the stacks.

The book wasn't too hard to find. In a larger library, a tiny — almost paperback-sized — blue cloth–covered volume might have disappeared on the shelves, but here it stuck out in con-trast to the glossy folio editions of *Poststructuralism Today*. I pulled it off the shelf and looked at the cover. The gold leaf was almost entirely chipped away, but I could still make out the title: *The Pnakotic Manuscripts: A New Revised Study*. I flipped it open, skimmed the table of contents, and checked out the introduction:

In the analyses of our collective mother-tongue, under-taken by notables such as Drs. Berthold Delbrück and Karl Brugmann, much attention has been given to the idioms of western Asia, namely the languages of India and its environs;

but little study has been devoted to dialects native to farther Eastern climes. One such language, records of which
are preserved on wood-and-palm-leaf tablets known as the
Pnakotic Manuscripts, had been the object of extensive studies by Dr. J. T. Schwarzwalder, who in 1895 compiled his
Analysis of the Manuscript of the Pnakotoi. As I shall demon-
strate, however, his characterization of the Manuscripts' language as an offshoot of Greek proves highly inadequate. . . .

In other words, it was a response. Not the sort of thing I
wanted to start out with; it wasn't much good to me unless I
had the original book for comparison. So I wasn't going to get a
whole lot done today.

Before I closed the book, I flipped to the very back to check
the withdrawal record. The little paper pocket was there, dingy
and worn like the book itself. So was the withdrawal record. It
had never been stamped.

So much for academic rigor, too.

I took the stairs down this time, checked the book out at circulation, and went home early.

*The sun is almost all the way down and I'm drenched with sweat
from having walked so far. My parents are going to have my
head for this, whether they believe I missed the bus or not. I
could just kill Jimmy Esterhaus.*

*One more block to home, and then I can at least sit down.
The streetlamps are coming on, turning the road and sidewalk
hazy orange. Up the front walk of one of the houses, a pool of
yellow light spills into the half-darkness: Somebody's front door
is open.*

*My front door is open. And my parents are standing there
waiting for me. With someone behind them.*

"Where've you been, Claire?" my mother demands, arms crossed over her chest, as I blunder into the yard. This backpack is killing me. "Rebecca says she saw you go off with James Esterhaus this afternoon after school."

Is that Jimmy in the front hallway, then? I can't see. "We didn't do anything!" I shout, jockeying with the straps of my bag to lift some of the pressure off my shoulders. "Jimmy came up to me at the bus stop and said there was something he had to talk to me about, but not in front of anyone, I don't know why. So he made me follow him out behind the gym, and he just stood there stuttering for, like, fifteen minutes, until he finally asked me if I wanted to go to some stupid homecoming dance with him. And I said I'd think about it 'cuz I knew I had to get to the bus, but when I got back it had already been and gone. None of the teachers would let me use the phone or anything, so I had to walk. But we didn't do anything!"

"Why not?" asks my dad, his thumbs hooked through his belt-loops. Is he kidding? He must be.

He's not smiling, though.

"We're worried about you, Claire," my dad goes on. My back hurts so much. I don't want to be standing here any more. "It's not like a healthy teenage girl to be alone all the time. Rebecca's three years younger than you are and she's never had this sort of problem." It's not her back there, is it?

"What are you talking about? I don't think Rebecca wants to sit at a lunch table all night watching all the other kids dance country-western while Jimmy Esterhaus talks about Star Trek, either."

"Oh, Claire," sighs my mother. "All we want is for you to have a normal, happy life. Would that really be so bad?"

"Mama, I'm tired. And I have a paper due next week. Can I please just come inside?"

She steps to one side, and for a moment there's that figure

again, but it moves off behind her, and I can't make it out. But I take the opening and stumble up the front steps and through the door, sweat dripping into my eyes so I can barely see. My mother stops me in the foyer and rests a hand on my shoulder while I blink the salt away. "There'll be plenty of time for that," I hear her say, sweet and reassuring. "But we've got a visitor here for you. Your dad was over reviewing Chief Harland's life-insurance policy this afternoon, and they thought it'd be so nice if you and Richard were to spend some time together. . . ."

I shake my head fast and my vision clears up. Richard Harland? Starting lineman Richard Harland, the guy who's taken out every dancer on the drill team—with all those things written about him on the girls' bathroom wall—is standing just behind my mother. And staring at her butt. Then he glances over at me with a weird sort of smile on his face, just as my mother says, "Why don't you take him up to your room while I get dinner ready?"

"What the hell are you talking about, Mom?" I start to backpedal, but her hand closes on the strap of my backpack. Fine. I shrug the damn thing off and let it fall, ducking forward past her and Richard Harland while she fights with my ton of books. Serves her right—he's the last kind of guy I'd want to hang around with.

An idea pops into my head: Find the basement. Let 'em all act nuts somewhere else. So I dash past the staircase and around to the other side, yank open the door beneath the second-floor stairs, and barrel down the wooden basement steps as fast as I can.

Sixty-eight, sixty-nine, seventy steps to the bottom—and this is definitely not my basement. Even before I reach the ground, I realize that, even if these are my family's old moving boxes and our gardening equipment, the walls are wrong: that greeny-gray rock (again?).

The moment I set foot on the floor, the furnace erupts into a giant pillar of orange flame. I flinch back against the wall, wrapping my arms around my head, and it takes me a second to realize that there's no heat.

"K'neseshti, kulayr," *says a voice—a voice I know.*

I peer out from between my crossed arms. Two robed and bearded men stand to either side of a column of flame. The rest of the floor is empty now.

"Who are you?" *I ask, glancing back at the stairs, which are now made of marble.* "What's going on?"

One of the men spreads his hands, palms up. In every language I've ever heard of, that means Don't ask me.

"Who are you? Can you understand what I'm saying?" There's got to be a way to communicate with them. Sign language? *Helpless, I gesture at myself, then back up the stairs, and look around and shrug my shoulders.* Where am I? How did I get here?

A sorrowful look passes over the face of the one whose hands are open, and he opens his mouth as if to speak, but the other hisses "Nasht!" *and glares at him. Then he turns, regards me for a long scornful moment, and waves a hand.*

And then I woke up. Again.

Lucky for me, it was Friday, so I only had an early-morning intro linguistics lecture to give. I'd woken up from that weird dream around four-thirty A.M., then just stayed up and read a little more of *The Pnakotic Manuscripts: A New Revised Study* until it was time to shower and get ready for work. I purposely got to campus early, so I could drop by my office to find out what kind of headway Alex P. had made.

The hard drive was chattering away when I opened the

door, so I turned on the monitor to see what was up. According to the progress bar on the bottom of the screen, it was only 67 percent done. That struck me as more than a little weird. It had had over eighteen hours to work on the problem already, on a powerful UNIX machine with nothing else running to eat up CPU cycles, and it was still only two-thirds of the way through? If this had been a language Alex P. had the rules for, a tagging operation for a file that size should have taken maybe ninety minutes at the outside. Even an unfamiliar language shouldn't have needed more than four or five hours; there are only so many ordering patterns a human language can take. Once Alex P. had figured out which pattern the Pnakotic Manuscripts followed, it should have been able to apply the rule set relatively quickly.

All things considered, it looked like I had a lot more programming to do before I could even think about taking Alex P. into beta-testing.

I switched the monitor back off, then cleared some student exams off the extra chair beside my desk so I could set my briefcase down. I rifled around in it for a while, looking for the papers I needed to hand back to my intro students, then realized I hadn't graded them yet. *Damn* Jane and her stupid agenda. At this rate, neither my undergrads nor I were going to learn anything this semester.

After that, though, class went smoothly enough. I walked back to my office afterward—70 percent complete, the progress bar read—and plowed through some more of the little blue book. After about an hour, thanks to the dense prose and the lousy sleep I'd had, I was feeling pretty draggy, but it was eleven A.M.: time to meet my friend Chandler from the art history department in the park for our usual Friday lunch.

He was sitting on a bench by the time I got there, with a brown paper bag beside him and a huge gray cloth–bound book spread open across his lap. The mockingbirds were meeping like crazy in the trees, flitting between the branches and the grates over the steam tunnels. "Hey!" I called, and he lifted his head, sunlight glinting off the thick silver frames of his glasses.

"Better timing than usual!" he shouted back, and waved. "My, you're looking perky."

"Har har," I said, drawing up to the bench, and plunked down near him. "Take it up with my subconscious and get back to me. I woke up from this really creepy dream, about my parents setting me up on a blind date, and couldn't get back to sleep."

"Ew. You have my sympathies." He wiped his forehead with one sleeve. "Anything like that time you told me about, when they dragged you to that restaurant with your sister's boyfriend's brother?"

"Kinda," I answered lamely, and left it at that. "Anyway. What've you been up to?" The fountains burbled and gibbered, echoing through the tunnel entrance.

"Oh, the usual. The department's getting ready to do a retrospective on the early Expressionists, so I'm preparing the gallery catalog, including revising it every time Parker and MacAdams have another argument over who they want to exclude *this* week." He shook his head glumly. "On top of that, Pride Week is coming up soon, and elections for next year's Faculty Senate. Who's running from your department?"

I looked down, trying to appear interested in the book on his lap. "I don't know. I don't pay much attention to those things. Probably won't even vote."

He chuckled. "Claire, I'll never understand you. I've never met a professor so completely uninterested in university administration."

I forced a smile and peered at the color plate he'd turned to. It was a painting of the inside of a tumbledown building, with some shabby-looking figures lurking around. His arm covered most of the page. "I dunno. Office politics just bore me, I guess." I leaned forward and reached for the edge of the book. "Hey, what are you looking at?"

That brightened him up considerably. "Oh! This showed up from one of the publishers up north." He turned to the title page and showed me: *New England Gothic Artwork, 1830–1930*. "Miskatonic University Press. There's some fascinating stuff here, early Hudson River School up through the Roaring Twenties realists."

I paused. "Weren't you saying most of the big artists around that time were Impressionists, though?"

"Most of them, certainly." Now Chandler was really in his element, paging back and forth through the book to point out full-color illustrations. "Absolutely the case in Europe, and for the most part in America, but there was a regression in Massachusetts for a little less than a decade." He stopped at the same plate he'd had open before and pointed at the text beneath it. "Mostly involving this guy, Richard Upton Pickman, and a few people who took after him. This book calls them the Macabres."

Without his arm in the way, I had a much better view of the painting. It was a nearly photorealistic view of a run-down interior wall, with a gaping hole in it and water pooled in front. The hunched-over figures hovered around the edges of the painting, facing the hole. Something was emerging from within; it was still too far back to see, but the artist had captured its reflection in the water. All I could make out was the outline of the body and a snoutlike face. Below was a caption: "*Ghouls, Emergence I* (of a series)."

"They were a strange bunch," continued Chandler. "More of an outgrowth of the Impressionists than a backlash, according to this. They claimed they were also painting exactly what they saw, and insisted it was vital that their work be as realistic as possible—'the awful clarity of human perception.' That's a quote from one of Pickman's letters included here." He pointed at the excerpted passage on the page opposite the plate. "Except that just about all their work contained blatantly imaginary beings—goat-headed men, people with gigantic doglike teeth carrying chewed-up bones, all kinds of strange, bestial stuff."

I'd been thinking about opening my lunch bag, but suddenly I found I wasn't so hungry anymore. "How lovely. I can see why it was a short period."

He chuckled again. "Indeed. Not exactly a commercially viable movement. Apparently Pickman himself quit painting around 1926, and the last of his imitators moved on to other things in '28."

"Does it say what they moved on to?"

"Let me check." He turned the page and skimmed the first few paragraphs. "Ah. Expressionism." He sat up, closed the book, and set it aside. "I guess by then they had decided there wasn't much of a career in giving a straight picture."

"The more things change," I said, and spent the rest of the hour watching Chandler eat and listening to the meeping sounds echoing off the steam vents.

After Chandler went back to his office, I hung around the park reading until about three in the afternoon. By then it was getting oppressively hot, so I packed up my things and headed to the English building to check on Alex P. When I got upstairs, there was a note tacked to my door: The 1958 book had arrived via interlibrary loan. I unlocked the door, stepped in, and noticed that the hard drive wasn't making noise anymore. Great.

I set my briefcase down and moved a stack of library books out of the way of the printer tray. I turned the monitor on, chdir'ed over to Alex P.'s output directory, and typed "ls" while the screen was still warming up.

As soon as the directory listing appeared, I realized I was going to need a lot more paper.

The output directory showed not one, but *five* syntax-tagged files in it, each one almost a megabyte long. Instead of something simple, like "pnakotic.svo.txt," which would've meant that Alex P. had come to the conclusion that the language followed subject-verb-object word order, it had given me "pnakotic. svo.txt," "pnakotic.osv.txt," "pnakotic.vso.txt," "pnakotic.vos.txt," and "pnakotic.ovs.txt." For some reason, Alex P. hadn't managed to work out a verb-subject-object interpretation.

One by one, I opened the files and checked through the header information that Alex P. had prepended. "Probable language of origin: Variant of Mongolian," said one. "Variant of Romany," read the next. "Inuktitut," a third concluded. *Inuktitut?* Not only had it managed to jump from central Asia to the Yukon, it was *positive* that was a correct interpretation! Yet, according to the fourth one I opened, the program was equally convinced that the language was a variant of Cornish. Almost any other result it could have given me would've been better than this.

I got up, stalked over to the door, and banged it shut. One of the thumbtacks fell out of my world map, which curled halfway up the wall. *Shit.*

This was worse than bad. Obviously I'd screwed something up and put a critical bug somewhere in Alex P.'s code. Why else would it feed back such absolute crap? Alex P. had a far better than average chance of recognizing any major human language, and an awful lot of minor ones. All I could conclude from the evidence at hand was that the Pnakotic Manuscripts belonged to a culture that had been extremely isolated, bad about keeping records, and dead for a very, very long time.

Which meant that Jane, who took the phrase "absence of

evidence is not evidence of absence" to the extreme, would find nothing in my work to conflict with whatever she felt like concluding. Baffling language? "Alternate modes of thinking." Obliterated civilization? "Victims of patriarchal oppression." It wasn't an *im*possibility, yet it wasn't the *only* possibility, either. But that didn't matter in the rat race to tack your name onto a theory that might make you famous. She could propose something that made about as much sense as believing that Sir Walter Raleigh was Shakespeare—but there'd been *New York Times* bestsellers proclaiming just that.

I might even have laughed if I hadn't been the one whose hands were tied.

Then I remembered the book. I looked over the note again—*interoffice package for you at the library,* it read, in bubbly cursive handwriting on the department secretary's personalized notepaper. I shut down Alex P. and left to pick it up, hoping it would suggest a good place to start over.

I could've sworn I was just lying in bed reading the book, but my memory's so foggy. I remember going through the first three chapters, where the author attacked the previous attempts to translate the Manuscripts . . . something about the undeciphered Indus Valley scripts . . . strange how everyone keeps trying to push closer to the cradle of civilization. I'd like to read more, but the book's gone. I'm gone. I was only about sixty-five pages in, give or take a few, and now I'm blundering around in the dark.

Literally, I realize. All around it's pitch-black, but my feet are on something solid. I inch forward, socks on the cold hard floor, and the back of my neck goes all prickly as my toes slide past an edge where there's not a floor. My breath catches in my throat and I step backward. Whang!

Now I'm seeing light—from the stars shooting across my field of vision after my heel slammed into a hard shelf behind me. I crumple, biting back the pain, and squat on the narrow ledge where I'm standing. One leg slides out and skips off the edge — and then another edge.

Stairs. Again.

Hell of a difference four inches makes, in the dark.

I scoot forward and lower myself a step. It may be unceremonious, but it works. One bump, two bumps, then my foot lands again on something solid-and-not-an-edge — and then it's light again, the hazy orange flicker of the cavern of flame. My head ducks toward the wall, dizzying me with afterimages.

"K'neseshti, kulayr," says that voice I'm really getting to know. I unsquint one eye, blinking to clear out the ghost-images. Just as I'd figured, it's the two robed men again.

"Hello?" I call, picking myself up off the floor. No answer. "Wie geht's du?" Nothing. "Quo vadis?" One of them might have flinched at that. Random phrases start pouring out of my mouth: Gaelic, Tagalog, Japanese, Cherokee, greetings and questions and simple textbook sentences I don't remember having picked up intentionally.

"Ura'n tlu nekophori tok'ari li nakotos!" I blurt out, and stop there, trying to figure out where that sentence came from. It takes a moment to hit: It's the first line of Bill's IPA transcription of the Manuscripts. This is the first time I've said it out loud.

As I'm staring, surprised, at my own feet, a flat clapping erupts from the other side of the room. I look up. One of the robed men is applauding.

"We had wondered when you would begin using it to communicate," he says, in perfect BBC English.

A good couple of seconds go by in silence. "I've got to be dreaming. You mean you've understood what I've been saying all along?"

"Correct on both counts," replies the other, in a graver voice. "We speak all the languages of dream."

"Who are you?" I step to one side, putting the cavern wall behind me.

"I am Nasht," the first one says, folding his hands, and inclines in a bow from the waist. *"My companion is Kaman-Thah."* Kaman-Thah bows, too.

Nasht. *I've heard that word before. I heard it here.* "And you've been . . . calling him by name, this entire time?"

Nasht's beard dips below his clasped hands when he nods. "So he has. And you as well, Kulayr."

Okay. Now I really feel dumb. "What am I still doing here, though? Don't you wake up when you hurt yourself in a dream?" *My heel's still smarting from the whack it took.*

This time Kaman-Thah lowers his head, turning toward the column of flame. "Indeed. But not at the Gate of Deeper Slumber, or beyond it. From this point onward, it is in your province to remain within dream until something sends you away." He pauses. "Or you question the dream and send yourself away."

That sounds fishy. "Then what is this Gate? What's on the other side?"

Neither one of them moves to answer. Seconds go by, then minutes. Did I do something wrong? Am I questioning the dream?

A ripple goes through the room, like a TV with bad horizontal hold. "Wait!" *I shout.* "Let me try that again. Please!"

Nasht's face is so patient. "There was nothing wrong with the question you voiced, Claire. It is a question for you to answer, though."

"I don't get it."

"Dreamers come to the Gate because something on the other side draws them in. It is simply our task to guard the Gate, and let the worthy and willing cross over."

"But how am I supposed to know what's—"

"Three times you have come before us, Claire Meyer," interrupts Kaman-Thah, "and twice you have not deigned to tell us why. So now we shall ask of you: What is it you want?"

That stops me cold, and when I start to speak I have to fight for the words.

"I—I don't know. It'd be nice to know what's in that manuscript, I guess, but . . ." I just know my face is going red. "That's not it. I'm willing to put in the work to figure it out on my own, but I want—I want—" My fists are in tight little balls, and I smack one into the wall behind me. "I want to not have to defend myself, goddammit. I want to ask questions and look for answers because I can, not because they're a part of some grand scheme. I want to not have to be for anything."

Nasht and Kaman-Thah gaze at the column for a long moment, until Nasht finally breaks the silence. "Ulthar."

"Beg pardon?"

"What you seek is in Ulthar. It is within our privilege to send you there, if that is indeed what you wish. We have faced far more forbidding requests before this."

Don't question the dream.

"All right," I hear myself say, the same way I heard myself say the words from the Manuscripts. "I'll go to Ulthar."

"So be it," Kaman-Thah pronounces, and gestures toward the pillar of fire. "To the Great Library at Ulthar we send you. What you seek will be deeply buried, but not beyond your grasp." And before I have time to second-guess myself, I step forward to the column.

"Go on," Nasht whispers, and points an ancient finger at the flame that does not scorch. I reach toward it, sinking my hand in up to the wrist, and there's no pain, no burning. Just a door, like any other.

And like that, I'm through it, out the other side, and standing on a cobblestone plaza in a city like I've never seen before.

It's a bit like the agora in Athens, I guess, a huge open-air square, although this one is ringed by buildings. Most of them are small, maybe one or two stories, with low half-walled porches, each of which looks to be the preferred sleeping ground of its own complement of cats. A full side of the square belongs to the dark stone facade of one immense building. Two columns *rise up from squared-off pilasters on either side of a staircase leading up to a pair of double doors. And one of the doors is open.*

It can't hurt to look, I guess.

I pace across the plaza, feeling cobblestones under my socks, and up the stairs to the door. It's incredibly thick wood, banded with iron, but it's open wide enough for me to get a look inside. So I poke my head through the entrance.

There's absolutely no way this building could be anything but a library.

A short foyer opens to the left and right, each exit leading under impossibly tall peaked and buttressed archways. Through either vault, even from my place outside the front door, it's easy to see rows upon rows of packed, towering bookshelves, some wall-mounted and some free-standing, stretching into the distance as if reflected in a facing pair of mirrors. Brackets off the sides of the shelves hold glowing clear-glass spheres, lighting the entire place with a crisp, fresh gleam. Above the shelves, there are even more—at least three more floors, so far as I can tell, of open-air galleries likewise replete with bookshelves. Human figures pace along the balconies, poring through books.

I guess they decided to send me someplace where I could find a translation of the Manuscripts after all.

So I slip inside, feeling awfully underdressed in sweatpants and a T-shirt, and scout around for some sign of an information desk. Or at least a filing system. Aisle after aisle of shelves carry books of every shape and size, some with titles in Roman characters, some Cyrillic, some Arabic, some in alphabets that don't look even remotely human. Not a one of them has a tag on the spine, either, and I can't imagine they're in alphabetical order if they're not even in the same alphabet. The patrons look completely absorbed in their business, and there's no one who could pass for a librarian.

I look down the shelf-delineated corridor, trying to see the end of the building, but it doesn't look any closer. Yet when I turn around and look back to the entrance, it's farther away, too. Looking up is no better; there are only six more floors, but the galleries line the room on both sides, and they also stretch off as far as I can see.

That can't be right.

The room wavers, and one of the patrons nearby thumps his book closed and looks around, angrily. I flinch and duck into an empty row of shelves, looking left and right. One possibility duly presents itself: It looks like there's another archway in the wall opposite the entryway. No, not just an archway.

I make my way over to it, and sure enough, it's a staircase. Detailed marble steps lead up in a graceful spiral, and there's also a narrow, straight flight heading down.

What you seek will be deeply buried, *said Kaman-Thah.*

So I plunge forward and down the stairs, counting as I go. I'd expected seventy, but it's more than that—more than twice seventy. I lose track before I reach the bottom floor, and I'm kind of glad to see that it isn't a cavern. It's stone, but it's dark, smooth stone like the rest of the building, and the floor is made of huge regular slabs. It's a big room, but not dizzying like upstairs. The lit globes here are frosted, and dimmer, too, illuminating the vaulted ceiling better than the floor. Shelves line the walls, a long stone table takes up much of the floor space, and one plain doorway leads out at the far end. Over by the door, there's a wiry, blond-haired man browsing through a row of books.

"Need something?" *he asks, not turning around.*

Something in here smells *really* ripe.

"Uh," *I manage, genius that I am.* "I don't guess this is where I could find . . . um . . . a copy of the Pnakotic Manuscripts? In English?"

"Can't do English," *he says, still facing the wall.* "Greek okay?" *Goddamn, he's having a hard time pronouncing* rs *and* ls, *but that's nothing to complain about!*

"That's fine," I blurt out, not caring so much about seeming geekily eager anymore. "Which shelf is—"

"Table," he cuts in, and waves at the end nearest him. I skirt up the other side, breathing through my mouth, and indeed there's a collection of pages there—a proper manuscript, not bound into a book. A heavy paper—papyrus?—cover sits to one side. The title reads Pnakotoi.

I turn to the open manuscript and begin to decipher the lines, word by word:

> . . . Thus do the ancient ghùls, eaters of the dead, keep their counsels in the lightless vaults far below the surface of the world. There do they meep and glibber to one another, amid their collections of human bones and flesh. They delight in pools of standing water, mounds of reeking filth, and the hoards of mysteries they scavenge from human lives. The brave man who descends to the ghùls may bring back secrets, but not without some change to himself. . . .

"Who translated this?" I ask aloud. The man at the bookshelves grunts.

"Nah. Dictated. Long time 'go."

I turn the page and keep reading, though I wish I had some notepaper with me. The manuscript goes on to talk about ghouls preserving meticulous records of writings from all over the globe—from some places with names I recognize, like Thera and Pompeii, and others, like Lomar, that I've never heard—but as I read further, it's hard to remember what I saw on the previous pages. "From a language that died out before Classical Greek?"

"Nah. Not dead. Just real old." Owd, *he says, like a Yorkshire-man or someone with a full mouth.*

"How do you know it's not dead?"

His shoulders shake, and he lets out a whuffy sort of chuckle.

" 'Cause I'm not."

I set the page down a little too quickly and stare at him. "You speak this? What language is it?" My head feels awfully fuzzy all of a sudden. "Is there a copy in the original? Can you show me?" I've got to remember it all, but it's so hard to keep it all sorted out in my head! I flip the papyrus sheets back and forth two or three at a time, searching for key phrases to remember, but the world is swimming before my eyes and it's hard to make out the words. "Please!" I call out. "Please, I just want to under-stand how it works, that's all I care about!"

Reeling, I lean against the table for support, but it sags like modeling clay under my weight. "I have to learn what I can be-fore I wake up!" I shout, while the room twists and warps around me. Two images pass before me, so quickly I can barely tell them apart: high up against one of the vaults, a painting of a wall marred by a gaping hole surrounded by half-human creatures; and, turning toward me to see what's wrong, the blond-haired man, a puzzled "What?" escaping from his impossibly canine jaws.

Somewhere beyond the dark doorway, there erupts a chorus of frenzied meeps—

And, once again, I woke up.

Fifteen minutes. It was only 11:49 P.M. I couldn't have been asleep longer than fifteen minutes. Half an hour at the outside. Such an incredibly vivid dream, yet it already felt like it took place decades ago. All I could still recall clearly were the sounds—deep grandfatherly voices, that rough guttural speech, the wild meeping noises.

Then the connection went *click* in my head.

Mockingbirds don't make their own calls. They have to mimic something.

Deep . . . buried . . .

It was completely impossible, of course. It *couldn't* be the call of an actual living thing. Especially not with those teeth, all I could remember of the face in my dream.

But Pickman was a realist. . . .

I lay back down and closed my eyes; better just to go back to sleep and forget about it. Time passed while I listened to the crickets outside. Looking at the inside of my eyelids was getting really dull.

I glanced over to the clock again. Five after midnight. Lying in bed wasn't getting me anywhere, particularly not back to sleep.

"Fine, then," I said, throwing the covers back and getting up. I dragged a pair of hiking boots and a big Mag-Lite out of the closet, pulled on the shoes, shoved the flashlight into my satchel, and headed back to campus to shut up my overactive imagination. Maybe then I could go back to bed.

The tone of the meeping was different when I got to the park: deeper, more resonant, not so birdlike anymore. I slung my satchel over one shoulder, pulled out the flashlight, and played the beam over the trees and benches. Those looked the same, but one of the tunnel grates was swiveled out of alignment, leaving a crack just big enough for a person to get through. Holding the light like a police baton, I dragged a bench one-handed over to the open vent, climbed up, and shone the light down.

Something down there leaped away into the darkness.

"Hey!" I shouted, waving the light around the bottom of the shaft. "Who's there?" *Must be some kids from the dorms,* I thought, but then another sound welled up from below: a burbling, trilling sound undercut with low grumbles. All in all, *glibber* wasn't a bad name for it.

"Hey!" I shouted again. "Come back!" And in the single stupidest moment of my life, I clambered onto the top of the shaft, grabbed the first rung of the ladder, and climbed down.

The tunnel headed off in a straight line, vaguely toward the admin building. In the distance, by flashlight, I could still see something loping away. "Come back, dammit!" I called one more time before chasing after it, satchel knocking against my legs as I ran.

It wasn't quite as fast as me, but it had a good lead, and more than once I thought I'd lost it around a corner. It ducked right, then right again, then left in quick succession, and I realized two things: One, it was following a pattern, and two, the tunnels were sloping downward. It turned again, sharply, down a fetid-smelling tunnel—this one with no overhead steam pipes. I rounded the corner after it, maybe only twenty feet away by now. It didn't run like a human.

"Slow *down*!" I called, just as it turned once more. This time it spun left instead of right—straight into a blind alcove. I trained the flashlight on it and sprinted up to look at it. Him. He was blond. His face, the part he wasn't shielding from the light, looked like someone had grafted a dog's lower jaw onto it. His teeth were enormous. I'd seen him before.

"Turn it off," he whimpered.

"And have you rip me open and eat me? Not hardly." I gripped the barrel harder.

"Won't." He rubbed his lips with one wrist. "You're too fresh."

. . . amid their collections of human bones and flesh.

"I'm remembering the dream from last night," I said, trying to hide the note of surprise in my voice. "You were there. Tell me what you said. Prove it's you."

"The records. Showed them to you in Greek. Didn't have

English." His voice was muffled against the wall from trying to cover his eyes. I twisted the nose of the flashlight just a little, to diffuse some of the spot of light on him.

"I couldn't remember what I read after I woke up. Why is it coming back to me now?"

He peered back at me with crimson eyes. "You followed me. Down a bolt-hole." I jiggled the flashlight, and he hissed. "Through steam tunnels, back into the dream."

"So I'm dreaming now?"

"No."

"Then where are we?"

"Going to the vaults."

What am I even doing here? I asked myself, fully expecting the scene in front of me to waver away into nothing again. *I'm not really underground, am I? Isn't this just a recurring dream?*

The world refused to spin.

"I don't understand what's happening," I said, reaching for my satchel with my free hand. "It started with that manuscript, all I wanted was a proper translation, and I haven't found a single person who could do that."

He crossed his arms, still squinting. "People can't."

"Then was the version in Greek a fake one?" He shook his head once, hard. "So who dictated it?"

"Ghouls."

As Chomsky argued, it would be impossible for us to understand a nonhuman language.

Thus do the ancient ghùls, eaters of the dead, keep their counsels in the lightless vaults far below the surface of the world. . . .

"And you're a . . ."

He nodded.

"Do you have a name?"

"Oous."

"Come again?"

He slipped a paw into his back pocket and pulled out a

beat-up cloth wallet. He opened it under the light and pointed
to a Georgia driver's license — unexpired. *Lewis Wilson*, it read.
The face was perfectly human.

"Where'd you get this?"

He snatched it away and stuffed it back into his pocket.
" 'S been mine." I looked hard at his face again. The hair was
right, as were the eyes and ears. If it weren't for the impossibly
large fangs and jaw, it would have been the exact same person.

"And you're saying you used to be a . . ."

He nodded again.

"How?"

He pointed to the flashlight. "Turn it down? I'll show you."

Ghouls could read the Manuscripts. They could even show
me how. And if all of them were this light-sensitive, the flashlight was insurance that would get me back to the surface. I
nodded slowly and dimmed it.

He reached out a hand. "Hold on. Gets slippery from here."
So I did, and along we went, deeper into the bolt-hole into
dream.

"Why're you so interested?" he asked as we walked.

I thumped my satchel with the flashlight handle. "I've got
my copy of the Manuscripts with me. I want to find out what's
really in it."

"Whafor?"

"Just . . . to know what's really there," I said. "I can't think of
anything I'd do with it, except that."

He glibbered something softly, and we kept on going.

Finally, after what felt like miles of walking through silent,
ripe-smelling darkness, the tunnel opened up into a small den
of a cave. Lewis squeezed my hand and stopped, then let out a
series of meeps. Seconds later, crimson eyes blinked into view
in the shadows. I shrank back, tripped over Lewis, and scrab-
bled with the flashlight. Something hissed as the beam passed
over it. "Shh." Lewis found my hand again and helped me up.

"Guides." I took a deep breath and pointed the flashlight down again. Two voices meeped back.

"C'mon," said Lewis, and led onward.

The rear of the cave narrowed into a passage only wide enough for one person. Three sets of glowing eyes moved single-file into it, and apart from the rocks lit by ambient flashlight glow, they were all I could see. We moved about thirty paces along the rough floor, and then I saw dim light and felt smooth stone under my feet again. "Here," said Lewis's voice, and he stopped. I blinked, looked around, and saw chiseled floors, ceiling vaults and crammed shelves, just like the basement of the library at Ulthar.

And ghouls by the dozens, all of them more or less dog-faced, some glibbering quietly in small groups, some reading alone by candlelight, some gnawing on lumps of meat. I couldn't smell anything at all anymore. Our guides meeped softly and trotted off to the back of the gallery.

" 'Scuse," said Lewis, and let go of my hand. He loped over to one of the others, glibbered briefly, picked up a meat-covered bone and went after it teeth-first, even though it was the size of a human arm. When he came back, carrying the remains, he looked brighter, more refreshed—maybe also a little more flat-nosed and pointy-eared, too.

"That's how you . . . become like this? Eating raw meat?"

"Dead. For a while now. Grave meat. 'S good."

I shuddered slightly, though less than I expected myself to. "That's inhuman."

"Yup."

Something else clicked into place then. "Then you can't show me how this language works, after all."

Lewis cocked his doggy head to the left. "Can translate it for you . . ."

I shook my head. "It's not the same, though. I want to know

how it functions—what all the rules are. Like in school. Is that something you can explain in English?"

His face twisted into an impossibly large, thoughtful frown. He pursed his lips a few times, as if about to speak, but finally shook his head no.

So this was what it had come down to. Perhaps Lewis and his fellow ghouls weren't quite human anymore—but they were still human enough to retain a command of English, not to mention dozens of other human languages, judging from the books I'd seen last night. Yet they were not-human enough to understand a communication system that a mind specialized for human speech could never grasp.

And, the thought occurred, not-human enough in other ways, if the Manuscripts were right. Being a human scholar meant claiming an agenda and clinging to it tooth and claw— had meant that for centuries, though it seemed so much worse these days. There just wasn't room for someone who only wanted to learn, collect, and preserve. Not on the surface, anyway.

That's not what I want; I thought. *But there's more. I know what I do want, now.*

"It's all right, Lewis," I told him, putting a hand on his forearm. "Don't feel bad. I still want you to show me. It's just going to take a while." And I patted his wrist for comfort, took the meaty bone from his hand, and raised it to my lips.

ARE YOU LOATHSOME TONIGHT?

Poppy Z. Brite

When Elvis was first cutting records in Memphis, back before pills and Colonel Parker really got their hooks into him, he used to shop at a black men's clothing store on Beale Street. The store was owned by a black man, and the clothes were aimed at young jiveass black men: ruffled shirts in painful colors, wide-legged pants with glittery stripes, jackets decorated with a king's ransom of rhinestones. Blue suede shoes.

No other white people ever shopped there. Elvis never forgot the fact that the owner had let him take clothes on credit back when his tastes outstripped the size of his wallet, and he patronized the store until it closed in 1968. Bought the owner a Cadillac, too.

Of course Elvis loved the clothes at this store, but there was another thing that fascinated him: an eight-foot albino python the owner kept in a tank near the shoe display. Elvis could never quite get it through his head that the snake wasn't poisonous. "Looks just like a big ole worm," he'd say. "But if it bit you you'd fall down dead in two seconds."

"Naw, Elvis," the owner kept telling him, "only way that snake could hurt you is to get 'round your neck and squeeeeeeeeeeeeze."

Elvis never listened. Well, maybe he did just a little. He'd always had a taste for things that made him feel endangered without truly being dangerous, movies with plenty of blood and guts, books by men who'd traveled through deserts or to the North Pole and written down every awful detail, snakes that weren't really poisonous but could still squeeze you to death.

After his momma died, though, Elvis no longer cared so much whether things just *seemed* dangerous. For years now he has been edging closer to real danger in ways he can still deny from day to day. Pounds, *kilos* of bacon. Peanut-butter-and-banana sandwiches fried in butter. Dilaudids and Seconals and Nembutals and Placidyls and Quaaludes . . . the names themselves are soporific to him now, making the back of his brain seem to lubricate with anticipation, much as his mouth waters when he smells food.

There was never a time in his life when Elvis couldn't get all the drugs he wanted. But sometimes even he has to level off a little in order to enjoy the next ride down. When that happens, when he begins to crave his handful of pills, the desire is like a big white snake moving slowly in his gut.

He loves the pills so much that the man who supplies them, Dr. Nick, was recently able to talk him into lending the Presley name—previously unsullied by product endorsement—to a chain of racquetball courts. Even in his fog, Elvis can see the pathetic humor in that idea, which fortunately never came to fruition. He loves the pills so much that once, when a doctor tried to talk him into cutting down, he threatened to go out and buy his own damn drugstore.

Onstage in Vegas in 1974, Elvis told his audience, "In this day and time you can't even get sick—you're *strung out*! Well, by God, I'll tell you something, friends: I have never been strung out in my life except on music. When I got sick here in the hotel, from three different sources I heard I was strung out on heroin. I swear to God. Hotel employees, Jack! Bellboys! Freaks who carry your luggage! Maids! If I find, or hear, the individual that has said that about me—I'm gonna break your neck, you sonofabitch! That is *dangerous*, that is *damaging* to myself, to my little daughter, to my father, to my friends, to my doctor. I will pull your goddamn tongue out by the roots! Thank you very much."

Then he sang "Hawaiian Wedding Song."

These days Elvis spends most of his time in his bedroom and adjoining bath. When maids come in to clean these rooms, Elvis sits awkwardly in the chintz- and doll-filled chamber that is always kept ready for Lisa Marie's visits. The maid has to open Lisa Marie's windows afterward to get the lingering smell of him out of the pale pink room: a heavy smell of hair oil and sweat, for Elvis has a lifelong fear of water and hates to bathe. Often there is a faint chemical edge to his odor, the excess nostrums and toxins coming right out of his pores.

He is supposed to leave on tour tomorrow, twelve days, twelve shows without a night off. The list of cities alone would be enough to kill a lesser man: Utica, Syracuse, Hartford, Uniondale, Lexington. Fayetteville, Tennessee. And more. He doesn't want to be anywhere but this bathroom. He's told everybody he's not going, but nobody believes him. The colonel says he can't afford *not* to go, and the hell of it is that this is true: Elvis spends so much, and his money has been so poorly managed, that he'll be broke within the year.

By the mid-seventies, the snarling voice that ripped through "Heartbreak Hotel" was gone, and there was only a touch left of the "Love Me Tender" croon. Now he has lost it all completely: no control of his breathing, a strain to hit the notes, a thick druggy glaze over the emotions that used to seethe just below the surface. He performs songs like "Unchained Melody," songs he can just belt out from deep in his considerable gut. He talks to the audience, particularly when they are unresponsive, trying to win them over. He has given away thousands of dollars' worth of diamond rings and guitars to strangers in Vegas nightclubs, just trying to rekindle that look of unconditional love he used to see in all their eyes.

It's all Elvis has ever wanted, really, unconditional love from everybody in the world.

Sam Phillips had Elvis's first Sun records pressed at Plastic Products, a vinyl plant and warehouse in a bleak part of Memphis. "That's All Right" was pressed there, backed with "Blue Moon of Kentucky." Thousands of black circles dripping with sex, menace, and magic rolled out of Plastic Products and into the clamoring world. Today the building stands vacant and derelict, humpbacked like a giant barrel half-buried in cement, a footnote of corrugated steel behind high chain link.

> When rattlesnakes convene for denning, they first form a bolus—a ball-shaped cluster, like a collection of rubber bands. Every member of the bolus keeps moving, the pulsing amalgam growing as more snakes arrive. One man peered into a cave and saw a bolus more than four feet thick. There are bigger claims, too, if you want to believe them.
>
> Writer J. Frank Dobie reported the story of a hired man sent to bring in two grazing mules. The man's boss heard a scream, then a fainter one. He found the body in a gully amid hundreds of rattlers. The snakes were forming a bolus. The man, who must have stepped into the gully without looking, was already dead.
>
> —GORDON GRICE, *The Red Hourglass: Lives of the Predators*

Elvis sleeps through the day (rising usually between four and eight P.M.) and cannot abide the least sliver of light, so his bedroom windows are shrouded in musty cloth. The bathroom, though, is a shag-carpeted chamber of light with a big black toilet, modular and low-slung, that Elvis privately thinks of as the Toilet of the Future. He spends a good bit of time leafing through girlie magazines on that padded throne, not masturbating—he hasn't had a hard-on in months—but just looking. He's sitting on the Toilet of the Future right now, reading not *Penthouse* or *Cheri* but a book about sexual astrology. Elvis is a Capricorn and supposedly likes to be aggressive. His worst quality is an inability to take no for an answer. And that used to be true, actually, back when anybody still dared to tell him no.

Right now the only thing telling him no is his own bowels. He's been sitting here for hours, it feels like. Sometimes he has to take an enema or soak in a hot tub until his belly softens up. His digestive tract, slowed to a crawl by downers, cannot handle the massive amounts of soft processed food Elvis shovels into it each day.

He strains, feels something deep in his gut stirring but refusing to dislodge itself. And then the pain tightens around his heart and begins to *squeeeeeze*.

Elvis hopes there will be peace in the valley for him, but he fears there won't be.

    The colon is approximately five to seven feet in length in a person Elvis's size and should have been about two inches in diameter. By [Shelby County M.E.'s investigator] Warlick's estimate, however, Elvis's colon was at least three and a half inches in diameter in some places and as large as four and a half to five inches . . . in others. As [pathologist] Florendo cut, he found that this megacolon was jampacked from the base of the descending colon all the way up and halfway across the tranverse colon. It was filled with white, chalklike fecal material. The impaction had the consistency of clay and seemed to defy Florendo's efforts with the scissors to cut it out.

— CHARLES C. THOMPSON II AND JAMES P. COLE,
The Death of Elvis

Atmosphere is the all-important thing, for the final criterion of authenticity is not the dovetailing of a plot but the creation of a given sensation.

—H. P. LOVECRAFT, *Supernatural Horror in Literature*

THE SERENADE OF STARLIGHT

W. H. Pugmire, Esq.

> *I see the stars have spelt your name in the sky.*
> —Boy George

1

We walked arm in arm beneath the humped moon, and I smiled at Stanley's frowning face. He held a piece of paper up to an arched streetlamp.

"She said it was around here somewhere, at the top of the hill. Curse the woman for not coming with us." I watched him search the crooked old streets that twisted before us, saw his frown deepen. I pushed him against the ancient brick of the building near us, took from his shirt pocket a pack of cigarettes, and placed one of the thin cylinders between his lips. Breathing deeply, he lit up.

"This is certainly a very charming section of your antique city," I told him. "One can sense within one's soul its agedness. Why, even the hoary darkness seems more venerable than ordinary shadow."

Stanley groaned wearily. "Please, Willy, don't wax poetic. It gives me gas when you start talking like an Oscar Wilde fairy tale."

Leaning next to him, pressing my back to the cool brick, I gazed toward heaven. "Ah, my dear boy, that's not a fairy-tale moon. That is the moon from *Salome*, casting its edacious light upon the doomed and the dead."

"And the dizzy," he sardonically replied.

Shrugging off the implied put-down, I took from my pocket a gold compact and a tube of lip gloss. He pushed away and began looking into the windows of the buildings that lined the street.

"Here," he shouted suddenly, a noise that echoed loudly in the silent street. I went to him and looked at the small sign above a door. I could barely make out the dark letters. GIL-MAN'S, it read.

"You are certain this is the place?" I asked hesitantly.

"Of course it is. There's Eve's sculpture."

I joined him and squinted through the murky glass of the shop's display window. The work in question stood one foot in height. Composed of smooth gray clay, it depicted two nude and hairless creatures standing near an *outré* skeletal tree. The human figures were squat, their bald heads oddly formed. The facial features were amorphous and amphibian. Each of the tree's sinister branches ended in a serpent's head.

"In the image of Frog created He them," I chuckled. As if in reply, an amphoric wind echoed in the gables above. Gazing through the cloudy window, I thought I could discern a faint illumination from within, and shadows that crept through deeper darkness. I went to the door and turned its chilly knob. The fragrance of antiquity, of dust, of shadow, wafted toward my painted face.

I entered in, followed by my companion.

We left fuliginous night behind and walked into a different realm of twilight. The glow within the shop was misty and muted. It fell upon the items of the shop with a kind of ethereal grace. It seemed, this light, as dusty and old as were most of the contents upon which it rested. It felt warm and ancient on my eyes. I felt it oddly clothe my tingling flesh. My lungs breathed it in deeply, and in so doing I could actually taste the dead aeons of forgotten time.

"I'm gonna look around. If I find any cool jewelry, I'll howl," my friend informed me. I raised my hand in reply, dimly aware of the sound of his moving away from me. I looked above me to one cobwebbed corner, from which the dry husk of some creature was suspended on wires. Surely it was a fantastic fake, this creature. The dry, dead countenance was that of a hateful hag. A cruel mouth snarled open so to reveal rows of sharp, twisted fangs. The thin arms were raised as if poised for attack. The mauve flesh revealed a cavity shaped of bone at the chest. The torso contorted, ending in the tail of a fish.

I moved onward, past pillars of brittle books and pieces of old furniture. I ran my fingers across the dust that covered a brass lamp, then smoothed the heavy residue into my hair. I felt slightly uneasy about the silence of the place, about there being no anxious shopkeeper eager to make a pitch and sell to us his antique gems. Looking at Stanley, I thought to voice my curiosity on this matter, but he was intrigued by some faded piece of Egyptian statuary, and I hesitated, not wanting to break his obvious spell of rapture. Still I could not stop from letting my eyes wander into darkened corners, expecting to find some form of an owner smiling expectantly at me. Silently, I moved past a wall of faded photographs, watched by a myriad of dead eyes.

I came upon a small alcove and stepped within. Before me was a curious display. I gazed in delight at the armlets of white gold that sat upon velvet of deep purple. But it was the necklace of black pearls that literally made me gasp. It took no especial sensitivity to beauty to fully appreciate their unearthly splendor. How queerly the pearls seemed to catch the obscure light of the little room, to catch it and transpose it to a different order of spectrum. I could feel its weirdness reflected on my eyes, could feel it sink beneath my jellied orbs and find my pulsing brain.

I took my eyes from the necklace and studied the statuette that sat upon a brick of polished black glass. It was the image of some wild monster of nightmare, a winged beast that squatted on humanoid legs, whose pulpy tentacled face wore an aspect of age-old evil. What was strangest of all, however, was that this fearful entity seemed vaguely familiar, as though I knew it from some pocket of forgotten memory.

"Entrancing, isn't he?"

I turned and looked at the handsome young man who stood just behind me. I had a kinky thing for those skinhead types, and he was a beautiful example, a beauty that hinted of danger. I gazed into his wide aqua eyes.

"As entrancing as sin," I said, simpering. He smiled in return, and I looked once more at the thing of stone. "It seems to be waiting. . . ."

"Perhaps he waits for you." He reached toward a shelf that had been built into the wall by which he stood. From it he took a large, pale seashell. He held it fondly, then placed its cavity to my ear. "What do you hear?"

"An echo that mocks the song of waves on sand," I replied quickly; then paused as another sound, a dim vibration of humming, came to me. I frowned, and the sound faded. I was not certain that it had been more than imagination.

The young man studied my face with his fascinating eyes. I felt a shiver and turned to study once more the string of black pearls.

"You seem hypnotized by that necklace."

"Indeed, it is exactly what I'm looking for. I'm going to a ball, and I need a piece of jewelry, something simple yet stylish. Those onyx gems would do perfectly. But I sense that they are not available."

"They are not for sale. This case is for display only. But I could loan them to you."

"My dear boy, you can't be serious! You know nothing about me."

He stepped closer and spoke in a soft low voice. "I know that you are a creature of fancy. You are a dreamer, and a poet. The wings of vision have brushed your brain. You have seen things in slumber that you vaguely remember, misty visions that fill you with fanciful fears, with curious longings. No matter the society you are in, you are always an outsider."

I arched an eyebrow. "We've met before?"

"Not in the waking world," was his enigmatic reply. His thick lips formed an esoteric smile. I suddenly felt as if I had known him from some forgotten moment of my past. Everything about him seemed suddenly familiar, but strangely so. I watched his graceful hands as they reached for the necklace. I trembled slightly as he came behind me and placed the string of pearls around my throat. His solid body, with its queer and sweetly sour aroma, leaned heavily against mine as he fastened the clasp. How cold were his hands against my skin. How colder still the onyx gems.

"Will?" Stanley entered the alcove and frowned at the scene before him. I felt deliciously wicked.

"What do you think, my dear?" I asked, fingering the pearls.

"Oh, very nice. And how clever of you to find a color that matches your soul."

I faintly smiled. "Do they make me look regal?"

"Every inch a queen. All you need to complete the illusion is a crown."

"Excuse me, gentlemen," whispered the young proprietor. He vanished for a moment, long enough for my friend to give me a naughty look, which I superbly ignored. When the shopkeeper returned, I gasped in wonder at the object in his hands. "It's been in my family for generations. As you can see, it's

composed of the same material as the other items. You'll notice the identical pictorial motif, those curious aquatic creatures." He spoke this in his low, hypnotic voice, never taking
his eyes from me. I sensed that his every word was pregnant
with hidden meaning that I was somehow supposed to understand, but what he was trying to communicate I could not say. I
sensed a kind of urgency in his look, his tone of voice.

I reached for the tiara of white gold, shivered at the chilli-
ness of its surface, gazed intently at the bizarre motifs. I sensed
that I had seen their likenesses before, in that elusive pocket of
memory that had suddenly begun to beckon my brain. My
hands trembled as I slowly brought the thing to my dome.

"It must have gotten damaged in shipping," said Stanley.
"Look at how it's bent. It'll never fit."

He proved correct. And yet, as I placed the magnificent
work of beauty upon my head I was overwhelmed with an uncanny sensation. How can I describe it? It was similar to what I
felt when entering my grandmother's old house. The moment
I entered, certain smells and shapes brought to vivid life long-
buried memories from childhood. A teacup with a windmill
painted on its delicate surface brought to me a certain afternoon when I was dining on toast and tea with Granny and my
aunt Josephine. As I reached with a wee child's hand for the
container of cream, my aunt said, frowningly, "Boys don't put
cream in their tea, unless they're sissy-boys." Oh, how defiantly
I poured cream into my teacup. How delicious it tasted, laced
with my innocent sense of challenge.

As I placed the golden tiara on my head, I sensed things that
were both alien and familiar, I could feel the coldness of its
metal sink beneath my flesh and chill my brain. I closed my
eyes and seemed to hear once more the *outré* echo of song that
I thought I had detected when the seashell had been placed at
my ear. Softly, I hummed the uncanny semi-melody. I sensed

the movement of watery waves and swayed to their flow and ebb. I felt myself suddenly tilt and start to fall.

He held me in his strong cold arms. His wide unblinking eyes wore a trace of triumph. I removed myself from his embrace and took from my head the thing of gold. I studied its eccentric shape. Certainly, the large and curiously irregular periphery seemed intended for a head of freakish design. However, the rim did not, as Stanley had suggested, appear bent or damaged—its metal was too perfectly smooth, unmarred in any way.

Sadly, I returned the thing to the handsome young skinhead. Reaching for my wallet, I took from it my photo I.D. and a twenty-dollar bill. "This is to assure my return of your wonderful necklace." I noticed Stanley's forehead fold in confusion. "This delightful young man is allowing me to borrow these onyx gems for the ball. Isn't he divine?"

The proprietor took my hand and kissed it, then waved away my offering. "My payment is the joy I see in your smile, and the knowledge that my grandmother's necklace will be seen again on a person of exceptional beauty. Wear it to your ball, and then return it. I'll be here, awaiting you."

I stared into his eyes, those blue eyes that seemed to contain within them a wisdom and patience of the ages, the liquid shadows of unfathomable secrets. I thought that I could gaze into their beauty forever, and did not want to pull myself away. Grabbing my sleeve, Stanley muttered our thanks and dragged me to the door.

2

Waves of incoherent sound washed over me. He held before me the large sea conch. As I gazed into its circular aperture, I felt myself enter into its swirling obscurity, become one with a cryptic darkness. All around me throbbed the sound of storm, of water, of electric air. Curling shadow slithered to embrace my soul, a blackness I could taste. The ebb and flow of sound became a riot of vociferation. And underneath the noise I could hear echoed one fantastic name:

Y'ha-nthlei.

I whispered the strange and beautiful word as his thick wet lips pressed against my throat. I did not close my eyes, but rather stared steadfastly at the idol of chiseled stone that oddly wavered in the black space before us, at its texture that seemed to glisten, its eyes that seemed to gleam wetly. I felt the tongue at my throat play with the pearls that pressed against my neck. He kissed the midnight gems as they broke free and fell into his hand. I madly laughed as he pitched them into the sky, and howled as they blossomed like aphotic blooms that revealed the ruins of an ancient city spread before us, a city of pillars and gigantic steps that led to a monolithic crypt. And I shuddered in ecstasy as a liquid voice from beyond the sculptured mass of door called my name.

"Willy?"

I awakened to the loveliest pair of eyes I had ever seen. Indeed, the entire face was composed of breathtaking beauty; and not merely the beauty of youth, but rather a loveliness that was ageless. She brushed her auburn hair away from the smooth and perfect complexion of her face, smiling with full rose-tinted lips.

"You asked me to wake you up before I left for the studio."

Wearily, I stirred beneath the bedclothes. "Ah, yes, darling. Thank you. What time *is* it?"

"Three in the afternoon. That bearded beast had you out all night. Whatever were you two up to?"

"Well, he had to take me to his favorite local bar, although he well knows that I abhor the stench of booze. Then we went looking for your friend's delightful shop." I gazed for a moment at the foot that peeked from the corner of the rumpled coverings, at its scarlet painted toes. Bravely, I threw the blankets from me and met the bracing air that cooled my nudity.

"So, what did you think of Ian?"

"Is that his name? I never asked. Oh, my child! He made me so dizzy I nearly swooned. It was rather peculiar, really. I almost seemed to remember him from somewhere else. . . ."

"Perhaps he's the man of your dreams."

"Of my wet dreams, certainly," I intoned, dramatically fanning my face with a hand. Blinking, I glanced about the room, until my eyes rested on one of Eve's works. "And, speaking of liquid dreams, I've had a most curious vision about that piece of art."

She looked to where my polished nail was pointing. "Really, you've been dreaming of *The Vault of Time*? That's cool. I'm flattered."

Reaching for my robe of magenta silk, I rose and crossed to where the thing of stone sat upon a small stand. It was the twin of the ruins I had beheld in slumber, a thing of pillars and oddly formed steps that led to a kind of crypt. Eve had created a semblance of seaweed from some kind of cloth, with which she had dressed portions of the pillars. It was impressive.

"What, exactly, does it represent?"

She joined me and linked her slender arm with mine. "Well, the odd fact is that it's something *I* saw in a recurring dream, a vision I had during a special organic high."

"Oh, my—narcotics."

"Purely organic, freak boy. Don't be such a prude. If you're a good girl I'll share with you before you leave our lovely old town and return to your mad city life."

"Whatever." I traced the path of steps with a timid finger, then pressed a hand to my suddenly painful head.

"What?"

"My head feels rather queer, darling. Have you any aspirin?"

She took my head into her hands and softly stroked my hair. In a low and lovely voice, she hummed a melody, a tune that seemed slightly familiar. My flesh prickled. I gazed into her eyes, those golden eyes flecked with green and blue. "Before you leave us, I want to do your head. You're so gorgeous."

Smiling, I bent to her and bit her bottom lip. Her balmy breath fanned my visage. She moved her mouth to my ear and sighed into its cavity the strange song. Her strong hands pushed against my dome. I imagined that I could feel my skull expand with shifting shape. The pain was delicious.

Her fingers combed my flowing hair. With eyes closed, I dreamed of young Ian, and suddenly it was his hands that loved me. I saw him twist the necklace until it broke. Catching the pearls that spilled into his hand, he tossed them above us. I watched as they formed a cluster of midnight stars that glistened as darkly as an idol's jeweled eyes. A cosmic wind rose in melody, accompanying the song that was blown into my ears by a hungry mouth. It was a song to cold black starlight, and as I eagerly listened to it I watched the dead stars crawl across the sky and form an esoteric signal.

"I'll see you tonight," Eve whispered. I smiled but did not open my eyes. Lost in trance, I found my way back to bed. When again I awoke, the light of day had departed. Early evening graced the clear heavens. Staggering to the bathroom, I washed my numb face. My head still ached, and as I looked at my reflection I frowned in confusion. My face seemed subtly altered, as did the shape of my head. I lifted a strand of yellow hair, suddenly loathing how it felt to my touch, hating the sickly shade of it. I searched Eve's toiletries until I found the razor. Oh, how cool and smooth the blade felt as I slid it across my scalp.

My head still ached with dull pain, and my eyesight was blurred. I did not care. I filled my hands with warm water and washed it over my shaven head, felt the sting where tiny cuts bled minutely. I gazed at my reflection for a long time, smoothing my hands over my soft dome. How wonderful it felt. I leaned closer to the glass so as to see more clearly the shape of my altered eyes. Then I noticed Eve's reflection joined with my own.

She smoothed powder over my scalp. How cool and soothing was her touch. "I've been waiting such a long time for this moment. I've suspected for ages that you were kindred, ever since you first came to visit staid old Stanley. It's wonderful how we sometimes know our own. Your transition is occurring far faster than mine. You can see it in my eyes alone. Sometimes in the shape of my mouth. I've too much bloody human in my genes. But not for much longer, praise Dagon."

"Honey, whatever are you talking about?" She was still behind me. I could feel the fullness of her breasts pressing against my back. She began to take her wonderful hands from my head. Raising my own, I placed them upon hers, then leaned my head against her sleek hair.

She chewed upon my earlobe. "We share a genetic history that predates humanity. We are of the Deep. You cannot remember because of our soiled heredity, but I know that images and sensations are swimming to your cells and awakening memory. Ian has told me much that I did not understand. He's taken me to Innsmouth, the seaport wherein we once thrived."

"And how did he know that you were a part of this culture, or whatever it is that we're a part of?"

"Because of my art. And because of where we first met. I'll show you on our way to this ball that Stanley insists we attend. Let's get ready for that."

She dressed me and did my makeup. I delighted in the touch of her hands upon my face. I gazed into her eyes and studied their shape, seeing for the first time how widely round they were. As she dressed me in my flowing gown, she hummed a weird tune that was strangely familiar. Smiling, I hummed with her. She laughed and kissed me, then went to fetch the necklace. I watched her press the black pearls to her mouth, watched as she placed them at my throat and did the latch.

She took little time in getting ready, and I saw that she was not dressed for the ball. Rather, she wore a simple dress of green silk, her black cloak, and a felt hat. Around her throat was a clasp of smooth stone upon which alien symbols were embossed. As we walked to our destination, I kept looking at her astonishing beauty in the light of star and moon. Her eyes especially fascinated me. I saw a hint of this *outré* look of which she had spoken, and my sense of kinship blossomed.

She led me to a derelict section of the ancient downtown area. We walked through what I suppose was meant to be a park, although now it was the sleeping quarters of sad, homeless humans. Eve linked her arm in mine as we approached a kind of alcove. I heard the light music of tinkling water. Before us was a very strange sight. Together, the tilted columns composed a fountain, where water fell from various tiny holes.

Beyond the dripping columns was a wall of water. Slipping off her shoes and motioning for me to do likewise, Eve led me into the shallow pool of cool water. As we passed beneath the columns I noticed that upon their surface had been chiseled symbols that were similar to those on Eve's necklace.

We stopped before the granite wall. I watched the flow of water that covered it. "This is where I met Ian, when I first came to this city. I've told you a little of my upbringing, of my strict Christian family with their unimaginative ways. The one member of my family I felt close to was my crazy aunt Alison. She was deemed 'mad' because she made it no secret that she was a lesbian. She dressed in black, and so hated daylight that she came out only at night. She would read to me by candlelight. She hinted of a curious heredity that was dormant in all but a few of us. She would smile at me and say that I wore the taint."

I watched the wall of water as I listened. Beneath its liquid surface I began to see the mammoth visage that had been subtly carved upon the granite wall.

"I escaped my horrible family at an early age. One day I came to this New England town and felt—I don't know, a sense of destiny. I had been sculpting for a few years and had a sketchbook filled with imagery found in dreams. You can imagine how stunned I was to find this neglected civic work of art, for it corresponded so amazingly with my dream visions. It was created during the spring of 1925, at a time when artists and madmen all over the world shared a vision of cities beneath the sea, of the slumbering titan housed therein."

I walked toward the wall. I placed my hand upon the cool, wet surface. Closing my eyes, I saw the face that had been carved into the wall, but I saw it as a living entity. It was my destiny, this being. I would not call it a god, for gods are a creation of human ego. This thing was beyond squalid humanity. I felt my knees bend in ecstatic supplication.

My head writhed with numbing pain. I felt my skull stretch and bend with new shape. Eve's lovely hand soothed my dome. As I opened my eyes, I saw that she was kneeling next to me. Before us stood Ian, looking magnificent against a background of dark sky and starlight. Oh, those cosmic gems, those stars that shaped themselves into archaic symbols that named my kismet.

Reaching into his shoulder bag, Ian took from it the tiara of white gold. I trembled as he placed it upon my head.

It was a perfect fit.

OUTSIDE

Steve Rasnic Tem

I know always that I am an outsider.
—H. P. LOVECRAFT, "THE OUTSIDER"

Three months after his wife died, and once the youngest of his three sons had gone off to college, Malcolm closed up their beautiful house by the sea and wandered the coastline in a beat-up van he'd bought especially for the trip. He had no intention of returning, but he did not tell his boys this. He didn't sell the house, although he'd been sorely tempted to just rid himself of the memories it embodied—and God knows he needed the money; but he knew one or more of the boys would want that fine old house someday and he couldn't find it in himself to deny them. He loved those boys, even though they had never felt much a part of him.

Of course, he had never felt a part of anything.

Janet had understood that, accepted it, and with that poor material had worked miracles. She'd made them a family despite him. She'd made him love her despite his fear that she could not be what she seemed, because no one could be what they seemed. Not in this world of secrets and horrors.

If she had died from an accident, of anything besides the leukemia, he might have chanced a belief that she had escaped the dark plot of humanity. But she hadn't escaped, and on their last visit with their oldest son, Bill, and his wife and their baby girl in their home in Cincinnati, Janet's blood flowing full of its poison, Malcolm recognized that his brand-new grand-daughter was looking a bit—he had no word for it. Froglike would do.

No one escapes. As the T-shirt says: NO ONE GETS OUT OF HERE ALIVE. He'd known that since he was a boy—it shouldn't have been any surprise. But Janet had brought a phenomenal amount of hope into their relationship, into his life.

He could almost hate her for it. At least he could hate him-self, as he lay beside his beloved wife night after night while she died, and instead of comforting her he struggled *not* to imagine what was happening inside her lovely shell: the way the cells were changing, the way the darkness might spread, the invisible tendrils and vague pseudopods and questings and encroachments of beings far older than humankind, but who had given to us our blood and the dark ancient closets within our poorer, smaller brains.

He'd never felt a part of anything. No one gets out of here alive. The whole blasted world was looking a bit—froglike.

As a boy his deepest fear had been that he would miss some-thing. Every day there were opportunities to be left out, to be forgotten, unheard, to remain uninvited at the end of the day as everyone else went to the game, the club, the party at the friend's house.

And, of course, that was exactly what happened. "You wear your difference on your sleeve," a short-term girlfriend had told him once during his college years. Although he'd pretended to be insulted, she couldn't have been more correct. He had his badge of freakiness, his authorization of solitude, even though it was not readily apparent when he looked into the mirror.

To recognize this quality, however, wasn't necessarily to understand it. Parsing the dynamics was quite beyond his capa-bilities. He had no idea what the rules were. He was clueless as to exactly what it was he lacked.

As a young adult, working a standard nine-to-five office job — not that he enjoyed it, but it seemed the very definition of normalcy and beyond all else he did appreciate that — he spent no time at all at coworkers' homes. He ate his lunches alone at his desk. In his suburban neighborhood he didn't know his neighbors, but they appeared to throw good parties.

He would not feel sorry for himself. It was a pitiful line he refused to cross.

All those years he lived this way. He lived this way with little understanding.

What little he did understand, however, was that sometimes the world operated outside the world, that some of the rules were subtle and written down in out-of-the-way places, that each and every day there are things, vast and complicated things, which we miss.

"Just let me take care of it, Malcolm. Just leave it to me. You really don't need to bother." Janet always said it like a prayer, and although he recognized it as a kind of dismissal — what kind of adult would you say such things to? — she made it into the most wonderful thing anyone had ever done for him. She'd made him a part of the world without his having to be a part of the world. She handled him, and he adored her for it.

With three active boys there had been athletic meets and parent-teacher conferences and ceremonies. He had not participated because he could not participate. He distrusted the smell of teachers and coaches and all the other child-care professionals. That oh-so-earnest smell. Of course he understood that his absence bothered his boys but he spent copious amounts of alone time with them, far more time than a normal father might. Eventually they appeared to understand that a trade had been made, a bargain, and seemed to appreciate what their father *would* do in lieu of what he *could not* do.

After a time they took care of him in their way, just as Janet had taken care of him.

"Here, Dad, let me do it," Bill had said, taking some prescription down to the pharmacist's to be filled. He'd been only thirteen, but quite the responsible young man. He knew how uncomfortable his father was in the drugstore, buying things to keep imperfect bodies running, buying things to manage their smells and infirmities, having to talk to the little man in the white coat who appeared to know everyone's infirmities.

Joe and Richard had been helpful in their own ways. Richard would talk to the postman if Janet wasn't around, or any service people who came to call with their tools and their incomprehensible conversation. Joe was good for food shopping, or when Malcolm needed a paper or magazine from the newsstand several blocks away.

Lovely boys, he'd felt so blessed to have them, so that he pretended not to smell them or hear the strange sounds their bodies made at night when he watched them in their sleep from the door. He never told them about the ugliness he occasionally saw in their eyes or in their eager faces.

He drove carefully down the long, narrow coast road, making sure that the police would have no reason to stop him. It wasn't that he distrusted police officers over any other group—his distrust was democratically distributed. But the police had the power to lock you away—at least for a time—if you were breaking the rules. And Malcolm imagined that he was *always* breaking the rules, not really understanding what the rules, in fact, were. Other people seemed to understand them without even talking about them. But in his younger days his attempts at action and conversation had so often been met with stares and awkward silences it had become painfully clear that he had no understanding.

Janet had not treated him with silence and if for no other

reason than that kept him devoted to her a lifetime and beyond. His sons did not treat him that way to his face, but he had no doubt things were different when they were with friends. He could forgive them their secret complaints about the eccentricities of "the old man."

It pleased him to no end that his admirable sons had always had so many friends, that they were, in fact, far better at the sport of being human than he had ever been. Surely someone in the family besides Janet had to deal fully with the world.

The coastal towns were few and far between, just as he remembered them from when he used to travel. But the individual towns were far larger than he remembered from his time among them. In fact, tremendously larger, with an especially unplanned, chaotic growth on the outskirts — endless shopping malls and complexes and townhouse communities. Like fat creatures spilling out of their clothes in all directions, threatening to capture the unwary passerby in some entanglement whose laws were not immediately discernible to those who hadn't lived there for some time.

But in each case he drove straight through the town, murmuring, "I live here, as well," to himself with a microscopic sense of triumph.

After Janet's death, he might well have remained in their fine old house by the sea forever, and not had to face these rules and expectations and stares and silences ever again. And some who knew him (but, of course, there were none) might wonder why he had decided to leave his safety and undertake such a journey.

Simple enough, he thought, almost grinning for the first time in months. *I wouldn't want to be trapped there once humanity decided to pay me its long overdue visit.*

Malcolm understood perfectly well that some might label such an attitude paranoid, delusional, something-or-other ideation. Humanity had developed an entire vocabulary for dealing with its outsiders. But he wasn't about to be trapped. Better to be a moving target than a hibernating one. Better to take to the coast road in a rusty nondescript van.

The other issue, of course, was that their house was so close to the sea, and he could not look very far into the sea, he could not tell what had been covered by its dark, oily waves. Each night in that house he could hear the whisper the waters made along the shore, but he could not understand what it wanted, what it expected, what it said.

Now and then he passed hitchhikers, their thumbs wavering hopefully as if attached to palsied limbs. Much to his own surprise he was tempted to stop each time and offer his door to some gentleman or lady with a knapsack and a quiet, desperate air. Somehow he imagined that a hitchhiker was much like himself, forced to put a thumb out in order to travel through a world in which he or she was an outcast. But as he slowed the van at each vagabond he discovered he could not trust the look of them: the eager eyes and smiling mouths and skin no doubt salty and damp from the ocean. Each time he sped away, chased by their whining and imprecations.

He had to eat, of course, and periodically replenished his supplies at some roadside stand, not in some brightly lit warehouse of bargains and massed humanity. And now and then he had to fill his tank and check the oil—preferring the last pump in the row, payable by credit card (although it was Janet's card, not yet canceled, and he felt ill with guilt each time he slid its magnetic strip through some slot and waited as faraway computers read his every thought and secret before flashing the "Approved" message).

He slept in the van, among pillows and comforters gathered at the last minute from the bed he'd shared with her for more than thirty-five years. He wore one of Janet's old bathrobes to sleep in, for its warmth and fading Janet smell. Each night he parked the van as far away from the sea and the main road as he could, the doors securely locked and with little Christmas bells attached to the handles to warn of intruders.

At sundown on his sixth day on the road he drove into a town that had been consumed by some manic and far-ranging celebration. Signs everywhere proclaimed FESTIVAL! but none seemed to specify what the festival was for.

Revelers with bright clothes and bare limbs, armed with glasses in their hands, swirled uncomfortably close to his vehicle. He rolled his windows up quickly but not before their distinctive odor filled the interior. He imagined the sides of his van smeared with their bodily oils. He thought of how the paint might react and determined that when he left this town he would need to check the finish for damage.

He thought of something Janet had asked him to do, years ago, something for her, and she had so rarely asked for favors from him. She had wanted him to go with her to a party at the neighbors'.

"You might have fun. I'm told that the Galloways always throw a good party." The eagerness in her voice had made him both sad and fearful.

He could not help himself. He'd said, "Honey, you know how I hate a good party," and the hurt in her face had reduced him.

As suddenly as the revelers appeared they were gone again, and it seemed that he might continue on his way. But it bothered him that they could appear and disappear so quickly. Some great accident was happening, some great catastrophe, some powerful and evolutionary celebration.

So Malcolm began to turn the van onto street after street, down a succession of narrow and fetid alleys, catching now and then a glimpse of bright shirts and darkly tanned bodies, the flesh shiny with oils, the music loud and archaic and incomprehensible.

They were always just a few blocks ahead of him—this great mass of smiling and joyful people, this grand party that went on all day without him—always just a chance few moments away.

Then after a time Malcolm grew alarmed that he had no idea where he might be, that the sunset had long passed and without even thinking about it he had switched on his headlights and continued the search, that he was not sure if he could find the coast road ever again. The streetlights here were sparse, the houses quickly glimpsed with a flash from his lights distressingly shabby and poorly constructed. Now and again some vague, drunken shape—no doubt someone struggling home from the celebration that surely must have ended by now—brushed against the van, bumped it so strongly he feared he might have run them over. He could not bring himself to stop, to get out and search for the body.

His tires began to squeal and slip as the streets deteriorated, vast potholes gleaming from too much moisture. The ancient ocean air had a corrosive effect on everything. It did not do to breathe it, and yet he and Janet and the boys had breathed it every day of their lives together. There had been times when he had suggested that they move, but Janet had been resistant—the boys' friends were all there (certainly not Malcolm's friends, Malcolm had no friends)—and he was not competent to pursue such a major undertaking as selling one house and buying another and managing a move, much less persuade his family to feel good about it.

Suddenly he saw the colorful crowd in his windshield, approaching him, arms waving as if they had been searching for *him*, and having found what he had been looking for Malcolm panicked and threw the van into reverse, backing hard into darkness, hitting things, crashing into shadow shapes he was almost sure must be people. But he could not stop, and he continued this way until he came to another intersection of wet, gleaming streets and threw the van into forward again and tried to make his escape down a lane that wound into tall, leaning homes along his right.

He continued for several blocks before the celebration surrounded him once again, the bodies pressed close to the van, mashed into the glass, and he was amazed by their elaborate masks, the effort that must have gone into fashioning such fantastic visages, when he realized these weren't masks at all but people's faces, perfectly ordinary people's faces with mouths grinning and mouths open in laughter, eyes winking and eyes closed and the skin moving the countenance into a complete and joyful rapture.

Then the people parted for a small space, just enough to allow passage for the van, and Malcolm roared through the crowd, again feeling the thumps and crashes, but he did not care, he could not stop, he had to get away, he could not breathe.

Moon glistened off the black ocean waves. The passage the crowd had created for him had led to a beach.

He moved the van slowly over the sand, peering into his rearview window at the steadily dwindling crowd. They were not following him. He stopped when the waves began lapping his front tires.

He cut the engine quickly, compulsively needing to hear the ocean, needing to hear the crowd. He heard nothing, even after rolling down the van's windows. He looked into the rearview mirror again. There was still no sign of movement. He opened the door and stepped down into the soupy sand. A smell of rotting fish filled the air.

Malcolm turned and gazed at the crowd. Behind them an incredible vision: layer after layer of ancient, decaying buildings, jumbled together and spread across the horizon, rising as far as he could see. Bits of cloth moved, curtains in windows, and other things he could not think about. The crowd still remained motionless, watching him with a kind of awkwardness, as if waiting to see what he would do. He imagined that they did not know what to make of him.

But eventually they did begin to move toward him, one at a time, then two, then increasingly larger ragged bits of the crowd, their smell wafting over to him to blend with the odor of ocean and fish.

As Malcolm walked out into the sea he could feel the moisture climb his clothes like some insistent and sumptuous aquatic creature. He could feel it sliding across his skin. He could feel it ease into his pores. He could feel his own blood grow eager for some kind of reunion.

When he turned around he could see that some members of the crowd remained hesitant, waiting on the shore. Others entered the water eagerly, eagerly. He could not decide whether he was leading or being chased.

He simply knew that once you were Outside, all things were possible.

NOR THE DEMONS DOWN UNDER THE SEA

Caitlín R. Kiernan

(1957)

The late-summer morning like a shattering bluewhite gem, crashing, liquid seams of fluorite and topaz thrown against the jaggedrough shale and sandstone breakers, roiling calcite foam beneath the cloudless sky specked with gulls and ravens. And Julia behind the wheel of the big green Bel Air, chasing the coast road north, the top down so the Pacific wind roars wild through her hair. Salt smell to fill her head, intoxicating and delicious scent to drown her citydulled senses, and Anna's alone in the backseat, ignoring her again, silent, reading one of her textbooks or monographs on malacology. Hardly a word from her since they left the motel in Anchor Bay more than an hour ago, hardly a word at breakfast for that matter, and her silence is starting to annoy Julia.

"It was a bad dream, that's all," Anna said, the two of them alone in the diner next door to the motel, sitting across from each other in a Naugahyde booth with a view of the bay, Haven's Anchorage dotted with the bobbing hulls of fishing boats.

"You know that I don't like to talk about my dreams." Anna

pushed her uneaten grapefruit aside and lit a cigarette. "God knows I've told you enough times."

"We don't have to go on to the house," Julia said hopefully. "We could always see it another time and we could go back to the city today, instead."

Anna only shrugged her shoulders and stared through the glass at the water, took another drag off her cigarette and exhaled smoke the color of the horizon.

"If you're afraid to go to the house, just say so."

Julia steals a glance at her in the rearview mirror, wind-rumpled girl with shiny, sunburned cheeks, cheeks like ripening plums, and her short blond hair twisted into a bun and tied up in a scarf. And Julia's own reflection stares back at her from the glass, reproachful, desperate, almost fifteen years older than Anna, so close to thirty-five now that it frightens her; her drab hazel eyes hidden safely behind dark sunglasses that also conceal nascent crow's feet, and the wind whips unhindered through her own hair, hair that would be mouse brown if she didn't use peroxide. The first tentative wrinkles beginning to show at the corners of her mouth, and she notices that her lipstick is smudged, then licks the tip of one index finger and wipes the candypink stain off her skin.

"You really should come up for air," Julia shouts, shouting just to be heard above the wind, and Anna looks slowly up from her book. She squints and blinks at the back of Julia's head, an irritated, uncomprehending sort of expression and a frown that draws creases across her forehead.

"You're missing all the scenery, dear."

Anna sits up, sighs loud, and stares out at a narrow, deserted stretch of beach rushing past, the ocean beyond, and "Scenery's for the tourists," she says. "I'm not a tourist." And she slumps down into the seat again, turns a page, and goes back to reading.

"You could at least tell me what I've done," Julia says, trying hard not to sound angry or impatient, sounding only a little bit confused instead, but this time Anna doesn't reply, pretending not to hear or maybe just choosing to ignore her altogether.

"Well, then, whenever you're ready to talk about it," Julia says, but that isn't what she *wants* to say; wants to tell Anna she's getting sick of her pouting about like a high school girl, sick of these long, brooding silences and more than sick of always feeling guilty because she doesn't ever know what to say to make things better. Always feeling like it's her fault, somehow, and if she weren't a coward, she would never have become involved with a girl like Anna Foley in the first place.

But you are a coward, Julia reminds herself, the father-cruel voice crouched somewhere behind her sunglasses, behind her eyes. *Don't ever forget that, not even for a second,* and she almost misses her exit, the turnoff that would carry them east to Boonville if she stayed on the main road. Julia takes the exit, following the crude map Anna drew for her on a paper napkin; the road dips and curves sharply away from the shoreline, and the ocean is suddenly lost behind a dense wall of redwoods and blooming rhododendrons, the morning sun traded for the rapid flicker of forest shadows. Only a few hundred yards from the highway there's another, unpaved road, unnamed road leading deeper into the trees, and she slows down and the Chevrolet bounces off the blacktop onto the rutted, pockmarked logging trail.

The drive up the coast from San Francisco to Anchor Bay was Anna's idea, even though they both knew it was a poor choice for summertime shelling. But a chance to get out of the laboratory, she said, to get away from the city, from the heat and all the people, and Julia knew what she really meant. A chance to be alone, away from suspicious, disapproving eyes, and besides, there had been an interesting limpet collected very near there a decade or so ago, a single, unusually large shell cataloged and tucked away in the vast Berkeley collections and then all but forgotten. The new species, *Diodora thespesius*, was described by one of Julia Winter's male predecessors in the department and a second specimen would surely be a small feather in her cap.

So, the last two days spent picking their way meticulously over the boulders, kelp- and algae-slick rocks and shallow tide pools constantly buried and unburied by the shifting sand flats; hardly an ideal place for limpets, or much of anything else, to take hold. Thick-soled rubber boots and aluminum pails, sun hats and gloves, knives to pry mollusks from the rocks, and nothing much for their troubles but scallops and mussels. A few nice sea urchins and sand dollars, *Strongylocentrotus purpuratus* and *Dendraster excentricus*, and the second afternoon Anna had spotted a baby octopus but it had gotten away from them.

"If we only had more time," Anna said, "I'm sure we would have found it if we had more time." She was sitting on a boulder, smoking, and her dungarees soaked through to the thighs, staring north and west toward the headland and the dark silhouette of Fish Rocks jutting up from the sea like the scabby backs of twin leviathans.

"Well, it hasn't been a total loss, has it?" Julia asked, and smiled, remembering the long night before, Anna in her arms, Anna whispering things that had kept Julia awake until almost dawn. "It wasn't a *complete* waste."

And Anna Foley turned and watched her from her seat on the boulder, sloe-eyed girl, slate-gray irises to hide more than they would ever give away. *She's taunting me*, Julia thought, feeling ashamed of herself for thinking such a thing, but thinking it anyway. *It's all some kind of a game to her, playing naughty games with Dr. Winter, and she's sitting there watching me squirm.*

"You want to see a haunted house?" Anna said, finally, and whatever Julia had expected her to say, it certainly wasn't that.

"Excuse me?"

"A haunted house. A *real* haunted house," and Anna raised an arm and pointed northeast, inland, past the shoreline. "It isn't very far from here. We could drive up tomorrow morning."

This is a challenge, Julia thought. *She's trying to challenge me, some new convolution in the game meant to throw me off balance.*

"I'm sorry, Anna. That doesn't really sound like my cup of tea," she said, tired and just wanting to climb back up the bluff to the motel for a hot shower and an early dinner.

"No, really. I'm serious. I read about this place last month in *Argosy.* It was built in 1890 by a man named Machen Dandridge who supposedly worshiped Poseidon—"

"Since when do you read *Argosy?*"

"I read everything, Julia," Anna said. "It's what I do," and she turned her head to watch a ragged flock of seagulls flying by, ash and charcoal wings skimming just above the surface of the water.

"And an article in *Argosy* magazine said this house was *really* haunted?" Julia asked skeptically, watching Anna watch the gulls as they rose and wheeled high over the Anchorage.

"Yes, it did. It was written by Dr. Johnathan Montague, an anthropologist, I think. He studies haunted houses."

"Anthropologists aren't generally in the business of ghost-hunting, dear," Julia said, smiling, and Anna glared at her from her rock, her stormcloud eyes narrowing the slightest bit.

"Well, this one seems to be, *dear.*"

And then neither of them said anything for a few minutes, no sound but the wind and the surf and the raucous gulls, all the soothing, lonely ocean noises. Finally the incongruent, mechanical rumble of a truck up on the highway to break the spell, the taut, wordless space between them, and "I think we

should be heading back now," Julia said. "The tide will be
coming in soon."

"You go on ahead," Anna whispered, and chewed at her
lower lip. "I'll catch up."

Julia hesitated, glanced down at the cold salt water lapping
against the boulders, each breaking and withdrawing wave
tumbling the cobbles imperceptibly smoother. Waves to wash
the greenbrown mats of seaweed one inch forward and one
inch back; *like the hair of drowned women*, she thought and
then pushed the thought away.

"I'll wait for you at the top, then," she said. "In case you
need help."

"Sure, Dr. Winter. You do that," and Anna turned away
again and flicked the butt of her cigarette at the sea.

Almost an hour of hairpin curves and this road getting narrower and narrower still, strangling dirt road with no place to
turn around, before Julia finally comes to the edge of the forest
and the fern thickets and giant redwoods release her to rolling,
open fields. Tall yellowbrown pampas grass that sways gentle in
the breeze, air that smells like sun and salt again, and she takes
a deep breath. A relief to breathe air like this after the stifling
closeness of the forest, all those old trees with their shaggy,
shrouding limbs, and this clear blue sky is better, she thinks.

"There," Anna says, and Julia gazes past the dazzling green
hood of the Chevy, across the restless grass and there's something dark and far away silhouetted against the western sky.

"That's it," Anna says. "Yeah, that *must* be it," and she's
sounding like a kid on Christmas morning, little-girl-at-an-
amusement-park excitement; she climbs over the seat and sits
down close to Julia.

I could always turn back now, Julia thinks, her hands so tight
around the steering wheel that her knuckles have gone a waxy

white. *I could turn this car right around and go back to the highway. We could be home in a few hours. We could be home before dark.*

"What are you *waiting* for?" Anna asks anxiously, and she points at the squat, rectangular smudge in the distance. "That's it. We've found it."

"I'm beginning to think this is what you wanted all along," Julia says, speaking low, and she can hardly hear herself over the Bel Air's idling engine. "Anchor Bay, spending time together, that was all just a trick to get me to bring you out here, wasn't it?"

And Anna looks reluctantly away from the house, and "No," she says. "That's not true. I only remembered the house later, when we were on the beach."

Julia looks toward the distant house again, if it *is* a house. It might be almost anything, sitting out there in the tall grass, waiting. It might be almost anything at all.

"You're the one that's always telling me to get my nose out of books," and Anna's starting to sound angry, cultivated indignation gathering itself protectively about her like a caul and she slides away from Julia, slides across the vinyl car seat until she's pressed against the passenger door.

"I don't think this was what I had in mind."

Anna begins kicking lightly at the floorboard, then, the toe of a sneaker tapping out the rhythm of her impatience like a Morse code signal, and "Jesus," she says, "it's only an old house. What the hell are you so afraid of, anyway?"

"I never said I was afraid, Anna. I never said anything of the sort."

"You're *acting* like it, though. You're acting like you're scared to death."

"Well, I'm not going to sit here and argue with you," Julia says, and tells herself that just this once it doesn't matter if she sounds more like Anna's mother than her lover. "It's my car and we never should have driven all the way out here alone. I would have turned around half an hour ago, if there'd been enough room." And she puts the Bel Air into reverse and backs off the dirt road, raising an alarmed and fluttering cloud of grasshoppers, frantic insect wings beating all about them as she shifts into drive and cuts the wheel sharply in the direction of the trees.

"I thought you'd understand," Anna says. "I thought you were different," and she's out of the car before Julia can try to stop her, slams her door shut and walks quickly away, following the path that leads between the high and whispering grass toward the house.

Julia sits in the Chevy and watches her go, watches helplessly as Anna seems to grows smaller with every step, the grass and the brilliant day swallowing her alive, wrapping her up tight in golden stalks and sunbeam teeth. And she imagines driving away alone, simply taking her foot off the brake pedal and retracing that twisting, treeshadowed path to the safety of paved roads. How *easy* that would be, how perfectly *satisfying*, and then Julia watches Anna for a few more minutes before she turns the car to face the house and tries to pretend that she never had any choice at all.

The house like a grim and untimely joke, like something better off in a Charles Addams cartoon than perched on the high, sheer cliffs at the end of the road. This ramshackle grotesquerie of boards gone the silvergray of old oyster shells, the splinterskin walls with their broken windows and crooked shutters, steep gables and turrets missing half their slate shingles, and there are places where the roof beams and struts show straight through the house's weathered hide. One black lightning rod still standing guard against the sky, a rusting garland of wrought iron filigree along the eaves, and the uppermost part of the chimney has collapsed in a redgreen scatter of bricks gnawed back to soft clay by moss and the corrosive sea air. Thick weeds where there might once have been a yard and flowerbeds, and the way the entire structure has begun to list perceptibly leaves Julia with the disconcerting impression that the house is cringing, or that it has actually begun to pull itself free of the earth and crawl, inch by crumbling inch, away from the ocean.

"Anna, wait," but she's already halfway up the steps to the wide front porch and Julia's still sitting behind the wheel of the Chevy. She closes her eyes for a moment, better to sit listening to the wind and the waves crashing against the cliffs, the smaller, hollow sound of Anna's feet on the porch, than to let the house think that she *can't* look away. Some dim instinct to tell her that's how this works, the sight of it to leave you dumb-struck, vulnerable, and *My God, it's only an ugly old house,* she thinks, *An ugly old house that no one wants anymore,* and then she laughs out loud, as if it can hear.

After she caught up with Anna and made her get back into the car, and after Julia agreed to drive her the rest of the way out to the house, Anna Foley started talking about Dr. Montague's article in *Argosy* again, talked as though there'd never been an argument. The tension between them forgotten or discarded in a flood of words, words that came faster and faster as they neared the house, almost piling atop one another toward the end.

"There were stories that Dandridge murdered his daughter as a sacrifice sometime after his wife died in 1914. But no one ever actually found her body. No, she just vanished one day and no one ever saw her again. The daughter, I mean. The daughter vanished, not the wife. His wife is buried behind the house."

Only an ugly old house sitting forgotten beside the sea.

". . . to Poseidon, or maybe even Dagon, a sort of Mesopotamian corn king, half man and half fish. Dandridge traveled all over Iraq and Persia before he came back and settled in California. He had a fascination with Persian and Hindu antiquities."

Then open your eyes and get this over with, and she does open her eyes, then stares back at the house and relaxes her grip on the steering wheel. Anna's standing on the porch now, standing on tiptoe and peering in through a small, shattered window near the door.

"Anna, wait on me. I'm coming," and Anna turns and smiles, waves to her, then goes back to staring into the house through the broken window.

Julia leaves the keys dangling in the ignition and picks her way toward the house, past lupine and wild white roses and a patch of poppies the color of tangerines, three or four orange-and-black monarch butterflies flitting from blossom to blossom, and there's a line of stepping stones almost lost in the weeds. The stones lead straight to the house, though the weedy patch seems much wider than it did from the car. *I should be there by now,* she thinks, looking over her shoulder at the convertible and then ahead, at Anna standing on the porch, standing at the door of the Dandridge house, wrestling with the knob. *I'm so anxious, it only seems that way,* but five, seven, ten more steps and the porch seems almost as far away as it did when she got out of the car.

"Wait on me," she shouts at Anna, who doesn't seem to have heard. Julia stops and wipes the sweat from her forehead before it runs down into her eyes. She glances up at the sun, directly overhead and hot against her face and bare arms, and she realizes that the wind has died. The blustery day grown suddenly so still and she can't hear the breakers anymore, either. Only the faint and oddly muted cries of the gulls and grasshoppers.

She turns toward the sea, and there's a brittle noise from the sky that makes her think of eggshells cracking against the edge of a china mixing bowl, and on the porch Anna's opening the door. And the shimmering, stickywet darkness that flows out and over and *through* Anna Foley makes another sound, and Julia shuts her eyes so she won't have to watch whatever comes next.

The angle of the light falling velvetsoft across the dusty floor, the angle and the honey color of the sun, so she knows that it's late afternoon and somehow she's lost everything in between. That last moment in the yard before this place without even unconsciousness to bridge the gap, then and now, and she understands it's as simple as that. Her head aches and her stomach rolls when she tries to sit up to get a better look at the room and Julia decides that maybe it's best to lie still a little while longer. Just lie here and stare out that window at the blue sky framed in glass-jagged mouths, and there might have been someone there a moment ago, a scarecrow face looking in at her, watching, and there might have been nothing but the partitioned swatches of the fading day.

She can hear the breakers again, now only slightly muffled by the walls, and the wind around the corners of the house; these sounds through air filled with the oily stench of rotting fish and the neglected smell of any very old and empty house. A barren, fishstinking room and a wall with one tall, arched window just a few feet away from her, sunbleached and peeling wallpaper strips, and she knows that it must be a western wall, the sunlight through the broken window panes proof enough of that.

Unless it's morning light, she thinks. *Unless this is another day entirely and the sun is rising now instead of setting.* Julia wonders why she ever assumed it was afternoon, how she can ever again assume anything. And there's a sound, then, from somewhere behind her, inside the room with her or very close;

the crisp sound of a ripe melon splitting open, scarlet flesh and black teardrop seeds, sweet red juice, and now the air smells even worse. Fish putrefying under a baking summer sun, beaches strewn with bloated fishsilver bodies as far as the eye can see, beaches littered with everything in the sea heaved up onto the shore, an inexplicable, abyssal vomit.

"Are you here, Anna?" she says. "Can you hear me?"

And something quivers at the edge of her vision, a fluttering darkness deeper than the long shadows in the room, and she ignores the pain and the nausea and rolls over onto her back to see it more clearly. But the thing on the ceiling sees her too and moves quickly toward the sanctuary of a corner, all feathered, trembling gills and swimmerets, and its jointed, lobster carapace almost as pale as toadstools, chitin soft and pale, and it scuttles backward on raw and bleeding human hands. It drips and leaves a spattered trail of itself on the floor as it goes.

She can see the door now, the absolute blackness waiting in the hall through the doorway, and there's laughter from that direction, a woman's high, hysterical laugh, but so faint that it can't possibly be coming from anywhere inside the house.

"Anna," she says again, and the laughter stops and the thing on the ceiling clicks its needle teeth together.

"She's gone down, *that* one," it whispers. "She's gone all the way down to Mother Hydra and won't hear you in a hundred hundred million years."

And the laughing begins again, seeping slyly up through the floorboards, through every crack on these moldering plaster walls.

" 'I saw a something in the sky,' " the ceiling crawler whispers from its corner. " 'No bigger than my fist.' "

And the room writhes and spins around her like a kaleidoscope, that tumbling gyre of colored shards, remaking the world, and it wouldn't matter if there was anything for her to hold on to. She would still fall; no way not to fall with this void devouring even the morning, or the afternoon, whichever, even the colors of the day sliding down that slick gullet.

"I can't *see* you," Anna says, Anna's voice but Julia's never heard her sound this way before. So afraid, so insignificant. "I can't see you *anywhere*," and Julia reaches out (or down or up) into the furious storm that was the house, the maelstrom edges of a collapsing universe, and her arm sinks in up to the elbow. Sinks through into dead-star cold, the cold ooze of the deepest sea-floor trench, and "Open your eyes," Anna says, Anna crying now, sobbing, and "Please, God, open your *eyes*, Julia."

But her eyes *are* open and she's standing somewhere far below the house, standing before the woman on the rock, the thing that was a woman once, and part of it can still recall that lost humanity. The part that watches Julia with one eye, the desperate, hatefilled, pale-green eye that hasn't been lost to the seething ivory crust of barnacles and sea lice that covers half its face. The woman on the great rock in the center of the phosphorescent pool, and then the sea rushes madly into the cavern, surges up and foams around the rusted chains and scales and all the squirming, pinkwhite anemones sprouting from her thighs.

Alone, alone, all all alone . . .

And the woman on the rock raises an arm, her ruined and shellstudded arm, and reaches across the pool toward Julia.

Alone on the wide wide Sea . . .

Her long fingers and the webbing grown between them, and Julia leans out across the frothing pool, ice water wrapping itself around her ankles, filling her shoes, and she strains to take the woman's hand. Straining to reach as the jealous sea rises and falls, rises and falls, threatening her with the bottomless voices of sperm whales and typhoons. But the distance between their fingertips doubles, triples, origami space unfolding itself, and the woman's lips move silently, yellow teeth and pleading gillslit lips as mute as the cavern walls.

—murdered his daughter, sacrificed her—

Nothing from those lips but the small and startled creatures nesting in her mouth, not *words* but a sudden flow of surprised and scuttling legs, the claws and twitching antennae, and a scream that rises from somewhere deeper than the chained woman's throat, deeper than simple flesh, soulscream spilling out and swelling to fill the cave from wall to wall. This howl that is every moment that she's spent here, every damned and saltraw hour made aural, and Julia feels it in her bones, in the silver amalgam fillings of her teeth.

Will you, won't you, will you, won't you, will you join the dance?

And the little girl sits by the fire in a rocking chair, alone in the front parlor of her father's big house by the sea and she reads fairy tales to herself while her father rages somewhere overhead, in the sky or only upstairs but it makes no difference, in the end. Father of black rages and sour, scowling faces, and she tries not to hear the chanting or the sounds her mother is making again, tries to think of nothing but the Mock Turtle and Alice, the Lobster Quadrille by unsteady lantern light, and *Don't look at the windows*, she thinks, or Julia tries to warn her. *Don't look at the windows ever again.*

Well, there was Mystery. . . . Mystery, ancient and modern, with Seaography: then Drawling—the Drawling-master was an old conger-eel . . .

An old *conjure* eel—

Don't ever look at the windows even when the scarecrow fingers, the dry-grass bundled fingers, are tap-tap-tapping their song upon the glass. And she has seen the women dancing naked by the autumn moon, dancing in the tall, moonwashed sheaves, bare feet where her father's scythe has fallen again and again, every reaping stroke to kill and call the ones that live at the bottom of the pool deep below the house. Calling them up and taunting them and then sending them hungrily back down to hell again. Hell or the deep, fire or icedark water, and it makes no difference whatsoever in the end.

Would not, could not, would not, could not, would not join the dance.

Julia's still standing at the wavesmoothed edge of the absinthe pool, or she's only a whispering, insubstantial ghost afraid of parlor windows, smokegray ghost muttering from nowhen, from hasn't-been or never-will-be, and the child turns slowly toward her voice as the hurting thing chained to the rock begins to tear and stretches itself across the widening gulf.

"Julia, *please.*"

"You will be their queen, in the cities beneath the sea," the old man says. "When I am not even a *memory*, child, you will hold them to the depths."

. . . And they all dead did lie, And a million million slimy things Liv'd on—and so did I. . . .

"Open your eyes," and Julia does, these sights like the last frame of a movie or a dream that might never have ended, and she's lying in Anna's arms, lying on her back in the weedy patch between the car and the brooding, spiteful house.

"I thought you were dead," Anna says, holding on to her so tight she can hardly breathe and Anna sounds relieved and frightened and angry all at once, the tears rolling down her sunburned face and dripping off her chin onto Julia's cheeks.

"You were so goddamn cold. I thought you were dead. I thought I was alone."

Alone, alone, all all alone . . .

"I smell flowers," Julia says, "I smell roses," because she does and she can think of nothing else to say, no mere words to ever make her forget, and she stares up past Anna, past the endless, sea-hued sky, at the summerwarm sun staring back down at her like the blind and blazing eye of heaven.

A SPECTACLE OF A MAN

Weston Ochse

"Such a leisurely way to die, don't you think?"

Alvin Samovich couldn't help but pause at the spectacle of a man with his feet nailed to the side of a building as if he had been tacked there by some collector. So queer, the angled perfection of the railroad spike pinning him to the crumbly mortar so far away from the nearest train.

So queer, indeed.

"I know what you're thinking. There must be a better way? Of course, one can always second-guess or attempt to promote his own methods, but for me, I believe this is the best. Yes. In fact, would you believe that I feel no pain?"

Alvin had taken a shortcut—an alley he had traversed a hundred times before. Sure, he could have bypassed the dark slit of emptiness, but his alternative was to travel around the wide city block where his shoulders and elbows would be accosted at each brush of a stranger, where his breath would mingle with others as they ingested one another in furious combinations, where he would need to pause continually as people who were not him crossed, blocking his path as if they were made to detain him.

Is it any wonder why Alvin chose the privacy of a dark alley? Is it any wonder why he had chosen this *In Between* as an avenue to allow him a protective ignorance of the sweat and smell and insectile life of those who proposed to be his peers?

But never had he ever imagined this upside-down spectacle of a man.

"Come on, cat got your tongue? What do you think? Did I do it right?"

Alvin opened his mouth to answer, then closed it as he realized he had nothing to say.

The hanged man before him was obviously a businessman, as was Alvin. Some middle manager at some middling company whose existence was defined in the promotion of the economic dogma of an unseen board. Even though he was now clad only in paisley boxers and a white T-shirt, the carefully folded blue suit beside him indicated he had once been a man of substance, perhaps even a junior executive who commanded dozens. "Don't get the wrong idea," said the hanged man, his arms crossed over his chest. "This isn't forever. They told me I could be helped and fixed of my proclivities, so to speak. There's even a chance I may live. Now, wouldn't that be something?"

Alvin spun and stared out the mouth of the alley. It was only six feet away, yet the eternal flow of shakers and movers appeared to be blithely unaware of this peculiar fellow, possibly the victim of some human vandalism.

As if the man wasn't real at all, but a figment of Alvin's little-used imagination.

As if he was finally going insane.

As if . . .

He felt a hand reach out and grasp at the creases of his trousers. Spastically, Alvin stepped back, checking for the dirty residue of this unclean man, wiping frantically at the assaulted material.

The temerity of the man to attempt to touch him.

Yet it was this very touch that proved it all real.

"Come on. No reason to be afraid of little old me. I'm just getting a little education. Just a little is what they said. I was smart, they said. I was salvageable, they said. Ha ha. That's why I'm here and not there," he said, pointing a manicured finger at a muddy puddle beneath him.

Alvin shuddered, gripped his briefcase more tightly, and prepared to move on. He had wasted far too much time dawdling with this clearly insane person. He had tried to help the hanged man, but it was plain that help wasn't part of the grand scheme.

"You know the pain isn't too bad, actually. I mean sure, I said before it didn't hurt. To tell you the truth, it hurts like hell, but you get used to it. And like they said, from this perspective the world looks different. And it is all a matter of perspective."

Yes. Totally insane. The man had probably been an accountant who became too entranced by the numerology of prime numbers upon a balance sheet. Alvin turned to leave.

"Ahhhh. That's it. Just a little lower please."

Alvin glanced back to see what had been the impetus of the strangely sensuous comment and felt his jaw strike the ground.

The hanged man had his hands interlocked behind his head and was smiling with an almost sexual satisfaction. His eyes were glazed, closed to mere slits. But that wasn't what was so shocking. What was irrevocably the most disgusting sight Alvin had ever seen was the tentacle teasing the surface tension of the puddle of piss and mud and urban sewage, rising and sliding beneath the white T-shirt. Green with brown splotches, it held dozens of pale blue eyes along its length. Several attended Alvin, their unblinking focus unnerving, while the rest appeared to be examining the hanged man. The claw-shaped tip of the tentacle could be seen nuzzling the man's left rib cage beneath the white cotton of the T-shirt, as if it was there to scratch an itch and not rip out a lung.

Alvin began to tremble and backed away until his back touched the opposite wall. He spun, bringing his briefcase up as a shield, but was confronted only by an empty brick facade. The man cooed behind him and Alvin spun again.

This was far too much.

Either an interactive insanity had become Alvin's new reality or the hallucinatory terrain he was presently traveling upon was the result of an imbalance of ingested chemicals or . . .

Alvin mentally inventoried the foods he had recently consumed.

Perhaps poison.

Maybe ptomaine.

Or botulism.

Or one of those mushrooms that are like LSD.

Or worse even.

Alvin reminded himself to immediately call the doctor for a checkup as soon as he arrived at his office. It would be the second time this week, but the persistent vision of the hanged man was proof that one couldn't be too careful.

Or maybe it was a reaction to one of the medications he had taken last year. Alvin had read in *Woman's Day* that more than half of the FDA-approved drugs produced unforeseen side effects—which, of course, was the main reason he had begun to see a Chinese herbalist.

No FDA.

No profit margin.

The Chinese had been working at their science for thousands of years and were the only experts he was willing to trust. And trust he did, even if some of their ingredients were on the low end of the Good Taste Scale.

Like brown bear liver . . .

. . . or rhinoceros horn . . .

. . . or dehydrated elephant urine.

His stomach tumbled twice as he thought what he promised himself he wouldn't think. He fought down a sliver of bile and returned his attention to the insanity at hand.

Alvin did allow himself a grin, however, as he realized that he had shown enough sense to not speak with his hallucination. Not mumbling like so many on the street. He had always been intelligent and hadn't been one to fall for the demented normalcy of his fellow human beings. It was one of Alvin's greatest virtues, and it had allowed him to elude the pitfalls that were apparently common to the masses.

Hurrying his feet into motion, he resumed his trip to work. He hadn't traveled a dozen feet, however, before he heard the voice of a woman speaking on his left.

"He may be a strange old goat, but he knows what he's talking about."

The voice was slow, smooth, and filled with the sexy syllables of an expert. There was only a hint of the bourbon that had forever flavored her voice, and it stopped him in his tracks. Even though this new fantasy meant touching, Alvin felt himself becoming hard, his excitement lifting the tweed of his pleated pants. In a combination of dismay and interest he turned to the product of his strange desire.

Again, he felt displaced as the impossible sight that presented itself to him.

The woman was rigid. The tentacles of yet another unseen creature rising out of yet another putrid puddle had wrapped her in a state of statuesque stillness. Three, no, four of the green lengths wrapped and rewrapped themselves around her, pinning her legs and her arms until finally twining up to cover her eyes, the tentacle ends twitching above her like alien antennae. Where the other man's tentacles had eyes, this one had thorns and, at small intervals, rivulets of blood on the woman showed the placement of the otherworldly injections. These tentacles pulsated slowly, making him wonder if they were delivering some kind of strange sustenance or perhaps removing something critically human.

"Tell me, sir. What do you look like? Are you a blond? I do love my blonds, you know."

She squirmed as the tentacles undulated. A sigh escaped her lips, tinges of pain and pleasure mingled and drifted across the space between them.

Sweat beaded upon his forehead as he noticed that the undulation had revealed the dark brown of a swollen nipple. His throat dried and his breathing hitched. He pulled his spare handkerchief out of a back pocket and wiped slowly at his face.

Alvin so much wanted to tell her he was a blond.

He could do it too. Just to see what she would do. What it would do.

What she and it would do.

His imaginings became too much. Alvin had never been a brave man. He forced himself to look away, shielding the side of his face with his hand in the event his eyes turned traitor. He rushed further down the alley, his distress and eagerness to return to the sanctity of his office evident in the clipped notes of his shoes against the alley floor. According to his watch, he was going to be late—something that had never happened before, and an event that would certainly send the others in the office buzzing around the water cooler, discussing his failure.

I bet they even have a pool, he thought.

The alley was a gauntlet, however, and Alvin did his best to ignore the sights and sounds.

He did his best to ignore the man held several feet above the ground. A tentacle had pierced his throat and by the bulging in the neck it was evident that the stomach was the destination.

What was at the end of this one? Was it a hook, raking the intestines? Was it an eye to examine, to see the internal man? Or was it a feather to tickle where no itch could be scratched?

Whatever it was, the round protrusion at the man's center moved as if a newborn something was about to hatch.

He did his best to ignore the man in the wheelchair whose legs were pumping at the instigation of the tentacles that ensconced the ankles as if he were competing in a marathon for one.

He did his best.

He did his best to ignore the many others that he hurried by.

He gathered speed and determination as he passed each, until Alvin was running pell-mell down the alley, the echoes of his retreating shoes lending an undertone to the moans and groans and questions from the tentacled proselytizers.

Alvin controlled the urge to vomit until he reached the end of his once-favorite shortcut and again entered the stream of commuters. He fell to his knees and retched across the milling feet of the masses. Screams and curses struck as the stench of his own vomit and the sight of the green oatmeal spew made him sick anew.

He was a spectacle but he didn't care. Between heaves he laughed, urging forth the visions of tentacles and their impaled victims among the chunks of bile.

He giggled.

. . . and for the first time in an age he was actually pleased to have the company of strangers.

The air was filled with a buzzing. The sound was everywhere but refused to coalesce. Like the sound of a million bees, but wherever I turned, they seemed to be just out of sight. I couldn't turn fast enough. The air was liquid and my movements were slow-motion echoes of what they should have been.

I was on a hill high above a plain. The heaviness of everything blurred my vision, but even with the vitriolic lens of this reality, I could make out the squarishness of buildings.

Of a city.

Distant mounds shifted in my blurred vision. Moving mounds of what could be people. Or bees. Thousands of them moving toward me. Toward the light.

I stared at my hands and allowed my vision to follow my arms and my chest. And then to the rest of me. I was naked. Completely naked. But that wasn't what had caught my attention.

It was the light.

The tremendous light.

I appeared to be at the epicenter of an unknown radiance. The pinkness of my skin had been washed out by the whiteness.

As if . . . as if I was the reason for the light.

As if the moving things were drawn to me like a swarm of earthbound moths.

I turned to flee and found myself in a slow-motion sprint to freedom.

It was then I realized the light wasn't coming from me. What had been behind me was brighter.

Blindingly brighter.

An oval orb of white that possessed luminescence beyond vision, as if my insides were as bathed in the brilliance as was my skin.

I fought to turn away, to spare my burning eyes. I felt as if my brain was on fire.

Melting my heart.

But the longer I stared the less bright it seemed. Whether it was dimming or whether my eyes were boiling, I couldn't tell. I felt heat but no longer any pain.

Just the all-encompassing light.

Just the persistent buzzing.

With the dimness came an eternal shape. It was a cross that rose high.

Higher than the hill.

Higher than anything.

The shape was the highest thing in the world, the pinnacle of

*all attention. With the coalescing of the cross came the shape
upon it. A tall man, his legs pinned. His arms were spread as if he
was waiting to embrace the world. His head was raised skyward.*

I found that I had moved closer and I could make out that his
lips were peeled back, the muscles of his neck bulging as if he
was screaming, begging, crying. But whatever sound that might
have emanated was smothered by the eternal buzz that thickened the air.

I wanted to reach up and draw his head to my ear.

I wanted to hear his words.

I wanted to listen to what he was saying.

As always, however, he was too high above to understand. Instead, I reached out my arms, begging them to elongate. Stretch
those many impossible feet so that I could touch him. Touch him
like the tentacles that were intertwining themselves around the
wood and his bloody feet.

They rose from the pink puddle like living vines, their genesis
founded within a commingled mess of blood and tears. But more
than vines, they were limbs of a much larger creature—or creatures. Each an appendage with purpose beyond my imaginations.

Some with thorns.

Some with eyes.

Some with wicked, serrated teeth.

Each one different from the others as if created for a specific
purpose.

All originating from someplace beneath the undulating surface tension of the puddle.

All becoming more and more frenzied, reaching higher and
higher, until they were caressing the length of the crucified
man's body.

Tracing the curve of his jaw like a mother would a wounded
child.

I spun, seeking help.

I sought to save him.

Behind me, the blurred shapes that had previously been so far away had come upon me. All eyes were on the figure. Every mouth was open.

It was then that I realized what I had mistaken for buzzing was the murmurs of a thousand throats.

Voices, old and young, rough and pure all chanted the same strange words. Each person rapid-fired:

Gog-Hoor . . .

Gog-Hoor . . .

Gog-Hoor . . .

For the hundredth time in seven days Alvin awoke screaming.

He had dreamed again, and his body begged for respite. For seven days, since his trek through the gauntlet of the strange, he had been virtually without sleep. When his body was finally able to comply with the natural order of things, the inevitable dream followed, leaving him haunted by the visions and no less tired.

Visions of Christ on a cross with tentacles.

Inexplicable tentacles caressing, terrorizing the Man, the Son, the God.

The first three days Alvin had managed to actually go to work. The necessity and his obsessive compulsiveness still ruled his life. Yet on the third day, after he had fainted twice and fallen asleep in a conference only to awake screaming much to the chagrin of the young executive giving a presentation, Alvin had been ordered to take a leave of absence.

But the worst occurred after he had been escorted from the conference room, when his boss had commented, "You know, your work has been suffering lately."

The words were daggers, cutting large swathes through his fortified confidence. The pain of it sent him shaking as he packed his briefcase with half a dozen unfinished projects.

With his chin sunk to his chest and his briefcase barely grasped in his weak hands he shuffled to the elevator. He pressed the button for the ground floor and with the passing of each level he became more and more depressed. He barely registered the pause of the car, the *ding*, the *snick* of the door opening, and the passenger who joined his descent. He felt the man's eyes upon him but was unwilling to look up and stare into the eyes of a successful person. He was afraid to confront someone who was descending by choice and not by order.

All his life Alvin had fought the chaos around him . . . within him. He had challenged himself and conquered every task until his life was the paradigm of order and perfection. People called him compulsive, but he merely smiled at their comments, knowing, as a dog could smell disease, that their very lack of understanding had already determined their fate, their destiny to die in the chaotic squalor that was everyone's secret challenge.

All yet with all of his perfection, he had been the one to fall.

"I've been where you are."

Alvin's heart nearly stopped as the man spoke. The voice was firm, filled with the rigid discipline of confidence that Alvin had so recently known himself. It was a voice he would follow.

A voice that brooked no hesitation.

A voice he had heard before.

Slowly, his body quivering with an apprehension he had never anticipated, Alvin stared into the face of the man and saw confidence and concern and wisdom upon a face that had so recently been upside down, feet pinned to an alley wall with a railroad spike.

Alvin was saved from a reply by the *ding* and the *snick* of the door as it arrived at the bottom. Shifting his eyes back to his feet, Alvin hurried out the elevator door. He was almost able to ignore the words that rushed after him.

"Have they spoken to you yet? Have you listened to them? Have you listened to the Gog-Hoor?"

That had been Wednesday and he had believed it to be the worst day of his life.

Until Thursday, that is, when he ran out of furniture polish and found himself unable to leave his apartment for fear of what he might see . . . or actually encounter.

It wasn't that Alvin had never listened to the battalion of therapists he had engaged; it was just that he had never believed in their institutionally learned dogma. How could they possibly understand a person's wish to control?

They called it a bad thing.

They called him obsessive-compulsive.

They said he was on the edge of insanity and needed a formulated, dedicated life of good therapy and better drugs.

What did they know?

Then on Friday, trash day in his building, he found himself unable even to open his door. He had sat the entire day with plastic-gloved hands in a kitchen chair, staring at the perfectly sealed, triple-layered white plastic that contained a breeding ground for an entire universe of bacteria, which left to its own devices would most certainly begin a plague. Drifting in and out of sleep, he fought his fear and begged his limbs to move the few feet, lift the bag, walk to the door, open it, drop the bag, close it, and be free from the impending doom. It was as if this simple task was beyond him, as if the bag was a ticking bomb that he was unable to disarm.

It was like his therapists had said.

"First it's the little things, Mr. Samovich. A clock in a perfect place, rearranging the silverware at every meal until the angles are perfect, continuous dusting, always ensuring that everything is in its place . . ."

It was like his mother had said.

"Yer a rare boy, Alvie. You'll be somethin' special someday. Somebody of means and substance."

It was like his mother's boss had said.

"Who the hell do you think you are? A man? Someone who can beat me? Get the fuck outta my way, boy," said Frankie the Fly, his mother's pimp, who continually stormed into their flat to batter his mother for holding out.

It was like his own boss had said.

"I think you need some time off to work out a few problems."

Alvin's head hit his chest and he again succumbed to the dream. . . .

. . . I found that I had moved closer and I could make out his lips peeled back, the muscles of his neck bulging as if he was scream-ing, begging, crying. But whatever sound emanated was smoth-ered by the eternal buzz that thickened the air.

I wanted to reach up and draw his head to my ear.

I wanted to hear his words.

I wanted to listen to what he was saying.

As always, however, he was too high above to understand.

He returned from a swoon only to be assaulted by the vision of the bag. Standing shakily, he plodded around the five rooms he called home. At each surface he winced as he saw specks gath-ering, one every second, piling up, until soon his entire exis-tence would be covered in a thick blanket of dust.

He remembered screaming and falling and twitching in a combination of anger and frustration and fear until his body fi-nally fell still. All he heard was the beating of his own heart and the strange words flowing through his veins.

. . . *Gog-Hoor!*

. . . *Gog-Hoor!*

. . . *Gog-Hoor!*

The only truly clean and perfect place was the bathroom. When he had moved in, there had been an insidious array of gold and green tiles. Matching yellow stucco forever dripped from the ceiling, and Alvin couldn't help but be reminded of a sky of snotty discharge. The mere sight had made him sick. He had even retched, later in the hotel room. It wasn't until the landlord had removed the offensive tile, replacing everything with the perfect abstinence of white enamel that he had finally moved in.

And on the sixth day, he rested within the confines of the clean walls and floor and ceiling of the bathroom . . . within the clean clear water of the bathtub, the whiteness of the room the only thing that could dull the color of his unblemished skin. It was the whiteness that settled his raging mind and let him keep whatever slim grip on sanity he was able to maintain. Everything was fine except the minute rippling of the water. He tried to control his breathing. He ignored itches. He fought the urge to urinate.

Yet each miniscule movement, each twitch of a muscle, each minute shift of an elbow sent the water undulating . . . quivering.

It was seven P.M. when he finally shot out of the tepid tub imagining each tiny wake as the precursor for a tentacle. The nasty appendages that so defined chaos and imperfection had been haunting him, laughing at him, making him afraid of life. Those damned tentacles that were so much like the swinging arm of the pimp or the wagging tongues of the therapists or the chained wrists of his mother as she discoed atop yet another john.

If it was all in his mind, he could fix it.

If it was the devil he could beat it.

If it was a chemical imbalance, he could purify his body.

Alvin would not, could not be defeated by apparitions that were begging his attention. He would fight them. He would challenge their vision and prove his superiority. He would fight for himself and the perfection that was his life.

That is . . .

That is, if he only knew how.

The rage he had been forging dissipated into the water. His chest expanded until it threatened to burst, the static pain of isolation and the irreconcilable fact that he was adrift and about to die filled him. A lonely sob escaped into the white room.

He descended into himself and once again fell prey to the dream.

. . . the shape was the highest thing in the world, the pinnacle of all attention. With the coalescing of the cross came the shape upon it. A tall man, his legs pinned. His arms were spread as if he was waiting to embrace the world. His head was raised skyward.

I found that I had moved closer and I could make out his lips peeled back, the muscles of his neck bulging as if he was screaming, begging, crying. But whatever sound emanated was smothered by the eternal buzz that thickened the air. . . .

Alvin awoke screaming . . .

. . . shivering.

Instead of lying within the water of the tub, he found himself standing in the kitchen. Water dripped from his thighs and arms and torso. Rivulets slid down his body, forming a puddle upon the floor.

He was groggy from a hundred dreams. Seven days of assault. Each blink of an eye, a nightmare. It was time to end it.

He reached and opened the silverware drawer to his right. His eyes were upon the growing puddle below him. His impeccable organization allowed his hand to immediately grab the boning knife and he withdrew it from the drawer. He shifted his glance slightly and admired the slim Italian blade. He knew how sharp it was, for he had spent many nights filleting pork loin, removing the skin from his chicken breasts and de-marbleing his steaks.

Alvin marveled at his own fearlessness as he dipped the blade into one of his naked thighs and then another, slicing two perfect six-inch seams, revealing pinkish white-lined muscle. His blood quickly ran in small rivers down his legs, mixing with the clear water in reddish clouds.

Almost absently, he dropped the knife and stared upward, his eyes seeing past the ceiling, past the sky, searching for the God he had so long ago turned away from. As his bladder released, the warm trail descending and commingling with the water and the blood to form a fetid brew, he began his chant:

. . . *Gog-Hoor!*

. . . *Gog-Hoor!*

. . . *Gog-Hoor!*

It began as a mumble, his mouth fumbling over the words his mind had found so familiar, but soon rose to a shout as he became more used to the alien sound, until finally, he was belting the syllables in rapid-fire reverie. So engrossed was he in his cries for salvation, it wasn't until a tentacle danced across his knee that he realized that the creatures of his nightmares had arrived.

His voice became a fevered moan as he fought both the fear of the unknown and the ecstasy of the Gog-Hoor's touch. He stared and watched as the single tentacle was joined by another and then another and another, until seven brownish tentacles were wrapping and rewrapping him in alternating embraces. They were tasting him. Loving him. Testing him, waiting to see if he bolted.

From the moment he had grasped the knife, he had known that he would stay. He had seen their victims and knew that there was no limit to their painful ministrations or their creative solutions. He moaned again and barely registered a tentacle piercing and ripping the plastic bag of garbage. It thrashed within the detritus, sending offal flying throughout the kitchen and into the living room.

But he was already changing. Instead of a cringe, he shuddered in anticipation, wondering what his sentence would be.

He didn't have long to wait.

Alvin rose into the air and was shoved roughly against the cupboards, the antique brass knobs he had picked up at auction digging wickedly into this back. Two tentacles rose side-by-side in front of him, each gripping the T-shaped bone of last week's steaks. His body arched as the bones pierced his wrists, pinning him to the cupboards. He screamed as he was crucified, his arms wide as if embracing the world. He screamed again as his feet were pinned to the wall by the screwdriver he had thrown away, the Phillips head spinning as it entered his skin, sinking through bone and plaster. His head was raised skyward. His lips peeled back as the agony shot through his bones.

He was Jesus.

He was the man in the dream.

The Gog-Hoor was attending him.

His shrieks changed to giggles as the tentacles began to rub the trash upon his body. Coffee grounds, rancid butter, beef fat, spaghetti noodles, used tissues, eggshells scoured his skin.

Alvin laughed louder, remembering playing in the mud as a child, making mud pies, eating them, smearing them over his body. He remembered his mother skipping down the stairs to join him, the brown earth immediately dotting her face, adding to the many freckles that made her so beautiful.

The dirt and grime became more a part of him as the tentacles began to speed up. Soon each one was sliding across the slick coating that had been created like a cocoon atop his skin.

He stared at his body, simultaneously hating and admiring the melange of colors that he had become. He watched as the tentacles disappeared beneath the surface of the puddle, and his gaze followed . . .

. . . and it was like staring into the face of God.

The thing beneath the puddle, the Gog-Hoor, stared back at him.

Its head was immense. More than a dozen wide blue eyes watched him, expectant, loving and patient. Bullet shaped, the mouth was more a proboscis that opened and closed in such a regular motion that it seemed to be speaking to him. Beneath the enormous head stretched a body that disappeared into eternity. It was as immense as the universe was immense. The size was unfathomable and seemed able to wrap the world if necessary.

Alvin tried to lower his head, ignoring the blood as the skin and muscle of his wrists ripped around the steak bones.

He desperately needed to hear the submerged words of the Gog-Hoor. He needed to know the answer. He began to struggle, begging to be freed so he could dive and become one with the Gog-Hoor.

Finally, a single word bubbled forth.

"You."

And with that word came knowledge.

The Gog-Hoor was there for his sins.

Alvin was special. He was different. He was rare.

The Gog-Hoor had chosen to salvage him rather than allow his existence to continue.

He would live.

He would change.

He would become something he had never imagined.

Maybe even normal.

Alvin raised his head and laughed. The muscles of his neck bulged with the effort and very quickly he lapsed into the peaceful darkness of a dreamless sleep.

THE FIREBRAND SYMPHONY

Brian Hodge

> *I believe that sound is a powerful tool to investigate the cosmos*
> *because it reflects the properties of celestial objects. . . . Socrates*
> *thought that the movement of celestial bodies generated music. But*
> *even though man is born with the music of the spheres in his hearing,*
> *man doesn't hear this music anymore.*
> —Dr. Fiorella Terenzi

1

I couldn't fight it: I am definitely more my father's son than
my uncle's nephew, even though I was raised mostly by the latter. The two of them were as unalike as any pair of brothers
could be—twelve years apart in age, with my father the younger
of the two, and operating from opposite halves of the brain.
Their life-paths skewed in such divergent directions that it's
a wonder my uncle took me in at all after I no longer had parents . . . although a part of me wonders if to him I was some
sort of noble experiment in the realm of those endless nature-
versus-nurture hagglings that seem never to be satisfactorily
resolved.

My father, if you must know, was an irresponsible hedonist
who held every credential required to live a tumultuous life
and then die young. Ordinarily that's as secure a career path as
any to insure a kind of immortality, but he was no Jimi Hen-
drix or Jim Morrison, even though he *was* their contemporary.

Every now and again, in a used record shop, some twisted sense of nostalgia will get the better of me, and I'll flip through the bins of musty, dusty vinyl and find a sad castoff or two from my father's band. They look embarrassing now, artwork choked with puffy lettering in Day-Glo colors and swirling with psychedelia. It looks silly and naive. Some styles of music and their trappings age well. Acid rock did not. Turn the album sleeves over and there he is, my father and his guitar and his bandmates, and in these pictures he's usually standing beside a tree or some eroded hulk of statuary, striving hard to look British because that was all the rage then, but mostly appearing unkempt and ill-bathed and very much a trendy product of his time. I'll look at his pictures and just barely remember the guy who would try to get me stoned when I was four or five; yet, too, I'll remember us at a lake — exactly where, who knows? — his hair and beard streaming gallons of water, and the infinite patience he showed while teaching me to swim. I'll look at the pictures and wonder what it was about him that drew my mother to him above all the rest. And what it was that made her different from the multitudes of other skinny, starstruck groupies who must have come to him with flowers in their hair and, probably, a willingness to dispense blow jobs like M&Ms. I'll wonder whose idea it was that she get pregnant, or if it just happened that way. I'll imagine them loving and touring, and fighting because he couldn't stay faithful, or sober when it mattered, and I'll wonder why she continued to choose that life instead of raising her son, even after my father overdosed in a rented Vermont farmhouse where a new album was to be rehearsed and recorded.

Unanswered questions, all. Because he was dead in his so-called prime, and soon she was gone off with another one just like him, never to be heard from again, and my sixth birthday was still months away.

Over these last several years, it's always been strange to think of myself as being older than he ever got to be. Almost as strange as it was, growing up, to look at my uncle and think *They were* brothers, *those two?* Because my uncle was a professor of anthropology at the University of Chicago, and perhaps under all that hair my father might have resembled him, but as it was, my father looked more like something Uncle Terrance would've studied rather than admit to being related to.

So, knowing that much, at least, you can imagine my surprise when, given the hundreds of esteemed colleagues my uncle must've worked with and associated with over the decades, it was *me* he chose to give that enormous skull to after he learned he had only a few months left to live.

2

Conventional wisdom would hold that Uncle Terrance shouldn't even have been traveling, but I suppose there's little enough about our family that has been strictly conventional. Besides, he was doing practically none of the driving himself, and admitted to me that he longed to see the Pacific Northwest one final time.

It hurt to hear that. Not only because it drilled in the idea of *his* imminent demise, but because it emphasized that everything we most enjoy doing is done a finite number of times, and, whether or not we realize it at the moment, one of them will be the last. The last time we hear the opening bars of Beethoven's Fifth. Or see the full moon. Or kiss the person we love most in the world.

So. My uncle wanted to see the Northwest again before he died.

And, as I was to realize, people with agendas have a remarkable way of seeing them through regardless of how sick they are, and maybe even because of it.

For the past few years I've lived and worked in the forested hills of Oregon's Cascades. If you were to pin me to it, I would have to admit that probably I became the son of two fathers — although I distinctly recall Terrance admonishing me as a young boy that I was never to call him "Dad." From my father I inherited a love of and talent for music (well, noise and structure, if you were to nitpick), and from Uncle Terrance I inherited (if belatedly) a use for stability. I suppose I'm one of the lucky ones who eventually figured out a way to indulge most whims and meet most needs under the same roof.

Even so, the path here, to our six thousand square feet on five acres, wasn't without its share of sordidness, violence, starvation, and drama. Fifteen years ago Terrance would've had every reason to write me off as a lost cause, settling on the more distressing answer to his nature-or-nurture conundrum.

So I suppose what I was feeling most while I showed my uncle and his assistant/companion/lover around was a sense of smug but still affable pride. I'd succeeded in *his* world, but on *my* terms. So there.

He stood in the center of my studio, which takes up a full fifth of the house, and nodded with bemusement at the vast arsenal of electronics. Keyboards. Synthesizers. Samplers. Sound processors. Racks of arcane gear with more tiny lights than a Christmas tree. Twenty-four-track mixing board. Three pairs of reference monitors. Computers. Microphones on boom stands. Plus strange hunks of iron that hung from welded frameworks like mangled gongs.

In technical terms, I'm what's known as a gear slut.

"What are you working on now — anything I can hear?" he asked, and then amended: "Anything I'd *want* to hear?"

I sat at my main desk and grabbed a CD-24 that I'd burned the night before but hadn't yet sent down to Los Angeles: a rough mix for the film I was working on at the moment. I popped it into the workstation and routed the audio to the

Mackie HR824s and the subwoofer, and when I potted up the volume, the effect was like a punch to the gut that radiated throughout the entire body.

It's not music, per se. It's sound design, a logical extension of the discs I've recorded under the name Megalith that are themselves mostly sonic sculpturing. Had this epiphany long ago that if I wanted to sustain any kind of music career, the only way to do that would be to shun trends and stick to the strange, which never goes out of style because it's never wholly *in*. Which automatically imposes a lot of *nevers*. I would never see a chart position. Never get close to a gold record. Never have the cover of a magazine that sold more than ten thousand copies, or have the luxury of destroying a hotel room. Then again, I would never have to be the subject of one of those humiliating where-are-they-now? documentaries on VH-1. Or find myself on a packaged instant-nostalgia tour with two metric tons of flabby, forgotten flavors of the last decade, trying to fake excitement for a crowd of balding one-time fans.

Fortunately, the same conclusion was reached by an early sometime-collaborator of mine named Graham Pennick, who made the peculiar but lucrative transition from ferociously clangorous industrial music to scoring film soundtracks. And who was eventually able to start hiring me, on the strength of those first couple of Megalith recordings, to create ambiences and sonic textures that aren't part of the musical cues, yet are still an essential component of film soundtracks.

Uncle Terrance listened to several moments of my past weeks' work with an expression of increasing distress: deep, murky drones that roiled in and out of one another's grasp like a tangle of vast worms.

"Good God," he said. "It sounds so much like the movements of giant bowels that I think it's moving mine right where I stand."

"Terrance," chided his friend Liz. "Try harder not to be disgusting." But she obviously adored him. My aunt had been dead for a dozen years, and I was glad Liz had taken her place in his life, in a relationship that had evolved from professional into the personal. She was years younger, in her late forties, while Terrance was just over seventy, but he had aged nicely, into one of those trim gents who had more than enough intellectual curiosity and just enough physicality to give them a vigor that some women find appealing.

"Well," he said to her, "it'll never be confused with Chopin."

I clicked ahead to another track and the oppressiveness lifted into a mood of hushed mystery, with the subtle, low chiming that might be made by stalactites if they could in fact sing. I explained that these were for a film entitled *Subterrain,* set largely beneath the surface of the Earth, about a hidden civilization there.

The look on Terrance's face was that of a rational and rigorously analytical man who, in the twilight of his life, has been forced into submission, and forced to admit that there is no such thing as coincidence.

"I brought you a present, you know," he said, with that kind of impishness some people develop when they grow old. He nodded around the studio. "Little question as to where you'll keep it. By the sound of things, I suspect it'll be quite at home right here."

He began by asking me if I was familiar with the phrase *erratic enigmatics,* and I had to confess that I wasn't. At least not by that terminology. By examples, of course I was. Most people have heard of a few.

"It's any kind of anomaly, most often archaeological," he said, "that makes orthodox scholars profoundly uncomfortable, if not outright hostile, that it's been found in the first place.

Physical remnants of one kind or another that appear either in geological strata before they should or in places they shouldn't be appearing at all. The earth coughs them up with surprising frequency. Most of them you never hear about, and the ones you do are often minor. But the worst of them threaten to completely topple conventional views on human civilization and prehistory."

By now we'd gotten off by ourselves, just the two of us. Liz was still inside, where my wife, Sonja, was showing her the rest of the house and, I learned after, lending an ear as Liz broke down with the need to talk to someone about what it was like to travel with and deeply care for someone who wouldn't be seeing the change of more than the next season or two.

For his part, Terrance seemed content enough, and I suppose that he would be — death makes the smallest things significant. Draped in a thick, colorful sweater that seemed vaguely Andean, and drinking whiskey-laced coffee, he sat with me on the cedar deck overlooking forested hillsides and, in the distance, the triple peaks of the Three Sisters. At the moment he appeared as if nothing could've given him greater pleasure. You would never guess that the tendrils of a tumor were slowly choking off the length of his spine and the base of his brain.

"Now, very often, finds that may seem like world-shakers can be dismissed as mere curiosities, since it's the geologists who should be embarrassed rather than the rest of us. For instance, objects that are obviously man-made sometimes turn up in coal. Seldom can they be absolutely dated, but an instance where one could occurred roughly a century ago. An Englishman found a coin imbedded in a chunk of coal, and the coin bore a clear date: 1397. A five-hundred-year-old item inside a material formed supposedly millions of years previous. Which leads us to two scenarios: Either time travel was involved, and our traveler dropped this rare coin in some primeval swamp . . . or coal can form much faster than is generally believed. Well then, if you apply the principle of Occam's razor, that the simplest explanation for something, with fewest assumptions, is more likely to be the correct one, we can toss out time travel. And it's true, that under the right circumstances, geological processes can take a fraction of the time they're thought to. Sandstone has been observed forming in as little as twelve years. Quartz crystals in fifteen.

"But then," he said, shifting gears, "there are those rude bits that turn up and don't remotely fit in *anywhere* with what we think we know."

With that, Terrance asked me if I would accompany him on a short walk to the truck that he and Liz were using for their travels. Around the house we went, on a path softly paved with cedar chips. He unlocked the Explorer's rear gate and swung it up, and pointed to a padded crate the size of a cooler. Its lid was secured with dual padlocks. He had me drag it closer, then dialed combinations and opened the lid.

We both hoisted the heavy, stonelike thing from inside and set it out for a better look. He peeled away the concealing cloth. The best I could do at that point was stare and tell myself that, no, the Earth wasn't really tilting underfoot.

With an affection that its appearance hardly seemed to encourage, Terrance patted the top of the fossilized skull.

"I can't begin to fathom the assumptions that William of Occam would've had about *this* brute," he said.

The human mind is perhaps the greatest of paradoxes. For all its power to explore and explain, to comprehend and codify, it is a fragile thing, ill-equipped to withstand assaults on the schematics it holds dear. When it sees too much, in too great a violation, the mind grows forgetful, or blind; it turns defiant, attempting to squeeze out the offender the way the body may reject a transplanted organ.

Rarely are we granted the opportunity to come, literally, face to face with such unassailable arguments that what we know isn't the half of it. That we're like arrogant children, stumbling around in the darkness of our ignorance. That we are, as I've heard remarked before, a species with amnesia.

Seeing this thing thrilled me, and terrified me, and filled me with the kind of wonder I probably hadn't felt for thirty years.

It was human, this brownish skull, or at least humanoid, but it was huge, nearly half again the size of a basketball, if not quite the shape. Because it wasn't a roundish skull, with the sloping forehead and lesser brainpan of our alleged early ancestors; instead, it was as high-domed as our own. The cranial capacity must've been immense. The eye sockets were caverns, the cheekbones prominent and cruel. The jaws were crushingly massive, and just as unsettling as the skull's size were its remaining teeth, like a blend of primate with something from even earlier along the evolutionary scale: incisors and cuspids in front, wide grinding molars in back . . . but in between were carnassials, those long, razored teeth that fit together top and bottom like meat shears. You'll find them in the jaws of any dogs or cats you might have around the house.

"Tough to find the words, first time you set eyes on him, isn't it?" My uncle seemed to be enjoying this, in an ornery way.

"How old is it?" I asked. Four words, the easiest start I could make.

"This one's been dated at about three hundred fifty thousand years."

"Is it . . . maybe . . . some kind of *Gigantopithicus?*" I tried. First thing that came to mind. You can't live in the Pacific Northwest without hearing about Bigfoot now and again, and I knew enough from TV documentaries that there was a theory that Bigfoot, the Yeti, Sasquatch, call him what you will, was a surviving lineage of gigantopithicines.

"Nice try," said my uncle, "but he's of a lot more advanced

design than that. Put him side by side with one and you'd see there's about as much comparison as there'd be between you and a gorilla. And that extends on down to the hyoid bone." Terrance tapped his throat. "How much he utilized it I couldn't say . . . but this fellow had the power of speech."

"I wonder," I said, rather haltingly, "what he would've had to say."

"I would hope it might have something to do with why his ancestors keep popping in and out of the fossil record," Terrance said. "This one? The chronology on him's just an eyeblink, by comparison. In one version or another, these fellows have been found going back as far as thirty million years. *Ten times as old* and *three times as tall* as that runty little skeleton in Africa that Johanson named Lucy and crowned as the mother of us all."

The queen is dead, I thought. *Long live the king.*

We got ourselves situated once more on the deck, where there were normal things like chairs and mugs and bird feeders. After I'd had some time to let this all sink in, I learned about an uncle I'd never realized I had, although he was himself quite late in coming to these . . . growth spurts, I guess you'd have to call them.

It began twelve years ago, not long after my aunt Genevieve died from being struck in the head by a mugger armed with a brick. I suppose at a time like that any distraction is welcome, and the more out of the ordinary the better. Maybe that was how Samuel Charlton, a former colleague from my uncle's department, saw it, too. Years earlier, Charlton had left Chicago for New England to take a position with Miskatonic University. Which hardly enjoyed the most sterling reputation within academia; Terrance had regarded the place as little better than a haven for fringe types . . . or, in the preferred slur of his own devising, "quackademics."

That summer following my aunt's death, my uncle was invited, on Samuel Charlton's recommendation, to accompany an archaeological dig in Norway as, so they told him, the resident skeptic. Which appealed to him, in a curmudgeonly way, and the prospect of a cool summer in Scandinavia handily beat the soggy heat of Chicago with no debate at all.

As Terrance told me this, I began to suspect the same thing he'd concluded on his own: that, valid though it might've been for them to want him to subject their findings to his scrutiny as a respected physical anthropologist, his resident skeptic status was still only a pretense. A way of bringing him on board, gradually. From the way he spoke of the place, it doesn't take much time at Miskatonic for someone to turn too insular for his own good, and they periodically feel the need for fresh perspectives, as well as to broaden their cabal . . . and they can't trust just anyone.

"My impression is that in past decades, certain circles there tended to regard themselves as keepers of a flame," Terrance said, "but more lately this has reduced itself to a siege mentality. They've spent decades quietly—well, *usually* quietly— gathering information and cataloging archaeological finds that the rest of the scientific and academic worlds would still like to burn them at the stake for, if they could get away with it. And I should know, because that's the side I used to be on, even though I like to think I kept a more open mind than some.

"When it comes to our own history, there's a tendency for anything that doesn't fit accepted paradigms to get swept under the rug. Because it's a threat to an entire web of assumptions that are in turn the foundations of solidly entrenched careers. Oh, so the Sphinx exhibits clear evidence of water erosion? No, wait—it can't, because that would mean the Sphinx has to predate Egyptian civilization by thousands of years. And we can't have that, because then all the books would be wrong . . . along with the whole picture we have of ourselves.

"So I was actually quite flattered when I was asked to go to Norway, because I thought it meant that these much-maligned diggers and scrapers from Miskatonic weren't averse to letting the enemy keep them honest. But then—" he patted the lid of the crate we'd brought up from below "—look who we pulled out of the ground. And guess who'd seen his kind before."

"How many times?"

"They're rarely complete, but Miskatonic has skeletal and fossil remains of fourteen individuals more or less like this, found since the 1880s. Some variations, depending on age, but basically the same. Correctly or not, they've dubbed the species *Homo sapiens primoris*."

"But with fourteen," I said, "it seems like any arguments against them would have to be null and void."

Terrance was shaking his head. "Numbers really don't matter. First, there's the source. It's practically a slogan: 'If it says Miskatonic, it must be fraud.' The implications here would be lost immediately, because for decades the debate would focus instead on how they'd pulled off such an elaborate hoax. Piltdown Man, times fourteen. Again, it goes back to contradicting those assumptions that are held so dear. The same archaeological find that can *make* a career can also *destroy* one if it's found, say, thirty feet lower. It's happened. Careers in ruins because the person dared to base conclusions on where the rogue evidence led. People see that happen once or twice, and they learn to keep their mouths shut.

"And," Terrance said, "things like our friend here have a way of disappearing without a trace. The antiquity of *Homo sapiens primoris* is another matter, really, but much more recent giants have been found all over the world. And not isolated flukes, like circus folk, but what appear to have been whole races of them. And quite often there are obvious differences in the dentition—twin rows of teeth, like that. But if there's a single one of them in a public museum, I don't know about it. Late 1800s, around Death Valley, prospectors pulled out a whole caveful of mummified, red-haired giants. The area Indians knew all about them. Terrified of them, just from oral tradition and legends. Said they were cannibals. But where are they today? What's happened to them? Who knows. Same thing that always seems to happen: They get lost, get misplaced, their paperwork gets misfiled, they never existed in the first place, and you can't find a soul who knows otherwise."

"Does Miskatonic have any of those, too?"

"None of the ones from Death Valley, no. But similar, yes." When he smiled, his eyes lit up with enough wonder to shave ten or fifteen years off him. "They have things *I* haven't even seen. But maybe I will before I—" He stopped, looking his age again. "Before I lose my tenure. That's how I've taken to referring to it."

And then he mentioned, with obvious regret, obvious anger, that Miskatonic had also had things in their possession that neither he nor anyone else would get a chance to see, ever, because they'd been destroyed. Starting fifty or sixty years ago, a series of fires—arson, all—had ravaged some of the university's halls that had never been open to the general public, or even most students, and where artifacts of unimaginable age and value had been stored.

"Unsolved, every single fire, but *that's* the kind of hostility that has greeted what they do there," Terrance said. "Obviously some people take it as a clear threat."

Hence Miskatonic's latter-day policy of scattering its collection far and wide, rather than housing it in a vulnerable central location where a truly organized assault might succeed in wiping out everything. Which settled my curiosity as to why Terrance—who wasn't the type to abscond with antiquities—possessed this skull in the first place . . . if not why he was bequeathing it to me.

He smiled toward the deck, then those distant triple peaks, as he thought about it, and in the air of gentle sadness that descended upon him, I sensed that it had less to do with his death than with his life.

"Whatever we've gained in technology," he said, "it's come at the expense of a word I had no use for at all fifteen years ago: soul. There's so little soul left to learning and discovery anymore. It's all been sliced down into such narrow ribbons of speciality. Which ultimately mean almost nothing beyond themselves, since they all exist in their own vacuum-sealed capsules."

"The gestalt is gone," I said.

"Exactly." He grinned, but it was still a sad thing to see. "Lately I've found myself wondering what it might've been like to have been born in the past. Say, anywhere between the time of da Vinci and the Victorian era. When there were no boundaries between disciplines, and science was the province of leisured gentlemen who were just curious about the way it all works . . . this piece with that piece. And in the evening they were talented enough to sketch lovely pictures of it all. Those would've been the days, I think."

"For you, maybe. I would've been stuck with a harpsichord."

"Poor you."

"I *can* play Bach," I reminded Terrance. Then grinned myself. "I'm just more interested in what he might've sounded like . . . decomposing."

My uncle groaned. "Good God—so the conversation's degenerated to *this*." But then he brought it back up, with a look of warmth and forestalled farewells. "It's why I'm giving you the skull. When Miskatonic demands it back, as they surely will someday, you should of course give it to them. But for now I think it's time that something like *Homo sapiens primoris* is allowed to be appreciated by someone in the arts."

"Even mine?" I said. Because he'd be the first to admit he once thought I had no future. Just as I'd be the first to admit I once probably agreed with him.

"Even yours." He gazed down at the crate, seeming suddenly ill at ease, and what he said next was the first time I wondered if the tumor in its higher reaches wasn't playing havoc with my uncle's mind: "Besides, there's another reason why he seems rightfully yours. He sings. I swear that, on occasion, he sings."

3

Terrance and Liz stayed with us for a couple of days, then continued north, their next destination Vancouver Island. The good-byes were agonizing in a way I never thought they could be, because while I hoped so, I honestly didn't know if I would ever see him again, or at least see him lucid, still in control of himself.

But I was glad it had come to this, to pain, because we both remembered a time when I was much younger, when I hated him for not being my father, and hated my father for not being at all. When I took a perverse delight in making my aunt Genevieve cry, because my mother wasn't there to shed those tears instead. When Uncle Terrance, I'm sure, regretted ever taking me in and saw within me as I grew only the most contemptible reminders of his brother, and probably worse — because unlike my father I had no illusions of Day-Glo utopias, only an inclination to destroy them if they dared exist at all.

Yeah, there was a time I wanted to burn the world.

A time when my greatest fascination lay in what certain extreme frequencies, creatively applied and embellished with hypnotically pulsating strobes, might do to human minds; to see if I couldn't amp them up and then send *them* out to do my bidding . . . to set the fires, to smash the windows, to tear down whatever they could.

I used to perform, you know. Back in my Angry Young Man days. These events were staged more like exhibitions of guerrilla warfare than real concerts in venues with proper plumbing. Old warehouses, empty factories, unused airplane hangars . . . We'd come in and set up, and word of the location would've gone out only hours before, and for me it was always an expedition to see how much damage I could inflict via sonic terrorism. Pack together a bunch of sweaty malcontents just like me, then turn the high-volume electronics loose on them. Shred their inhibitions, fry their nerve cells, pierce their eardrums, jar loose everything that was still connecting them to civilization. I wanted to hear bones break. I wanted teeth crunching underfoot. I wanted frenzy. I wanted an army, if just for a few hours each random night, leaving destruction in its wake.

And after I got it enough times, I just wanted to know why.

Because my mother and father didn't love me enough to stay? *That* clichéd whine? It didn't feel like enough; it seemed that the answers and the wellspring of all that anger against general humanity had to lie much deeper than my having been abandoned by a pair of slovenly twits whose parenting skills I was better free of anyway. I liked to think I hadn't even *needed* parents, that I'd been found under rocks; that I could've raised myself in a Dumpster and turned out just as well.

A place like that, in your heart and soul, you can never stay there for long. You either grow out of it or stay until it kills you.

And now that I'm able to look back on that time from the vantage point of a cedar deck and mountainside trees, I feel gratitude that I grew. But I still can't decide whether or not I miss that more savage era. On the days when I think maybe I do, it's usually because I've let myself remember that I never learned the answer to a single question that mattered. . . . I'd just left them as better off unasked.

Uncle Terrance was right, of course. There was only one place to display that ancient skull: my studio. I cleared a space in the center of the speaker deck above the mixing console, where he would sit gazing with empty sockets through the sweet spot of the stereo field or seem to stare down at me as I tweaked faders and knobs. Because he needed a name, I defaulted to Goliath, and as a constant companion for my work on *Subterrain*, he was so perfect that it bordered on predestination.

Sonja of course found him equally fascinating—welcome, even, because Goliath validated her own suspicions that the common knowledge of our remote past is patchwork at best. She also enjoyed no end of amusement at his discovery site among her one-time neighbors to the west. There's always been this thing between Swedes and Norwegians. They'll tell the most vicious jokes about one another. Same jokes, a lot of the time—they just switch the nationality.

"I think he predates the borders," I told her.

"Maybe so," Sonja said. "But I can still smell the herring."

Things like that, she would say, then she'd laugh, and I'd remember how lucky I was. If I told you she was blond and cruelly beautiful, would it surprise you? I doubt it, because that's what we've come to expect from Swedes, and they rarely disappoint, even when they don't work for airlines.

We met years ago when Graham Pennick and I were touring Europe together, in an actual organized fashion, if still in a low-rent, scuffling sort of way. Sonja was a Stockholm music journalist who'd come to see what was up with these American electro-savages known for inducing headaches on a good night and small-scale riots on a better night. There was also the tie-in with my father's history, which I wasn't above exploiting whenever it served, and which I immediately saw appealed to her as perversely ironic.

"Who are you trying to kill?" she asked during the interview after the show. "His memory, or yourself?"

Sonja had, I was astonished to realize, picked out in our maelstrom of sound a few samples from my father's vinyl legacy that I thought I'd mangled beyond recognition.

Whatever callous armor I was wearing over myself in those days, I was glad she saw through it, since by then—after enough melees and one-night stands and one-week girlfriends—I'd gotten it in my head that I could never spend my life with an American woman, because in my experience, or at least in my strata, I felt they didn't have enough of a sense of where they'd come from and who they really were . . . and these things were becoming important to me.

After our tour ended in Germany, Graham returned to the States, but I went back to Sweden, since when we'd left three weeks earlier, Sonja had dropped a strategic promise to show me more of her country the next time I came. So I made a strategic reappearance to take her up on it, staying long enough to see both the midnight sun of summer and the near-perpetual night of winter.

And I would have to say that my work as Megalith was born directly out of that sojourn. It did something to me, my time on this peninsula flanked by the cold North and Baltic Seas. The mists and fog seeped past my skin and dampened some of those fires that burned inside me, smothering them to smoky billows. As we sat and watched the bellies of low gray clouds scrape over mountain peaks, I would feel swallowed by the mystery and timelessness of the moment. Where I'd once sought the voices inside the rust and girders of Chicago, I could now sense an infinitely more ancient call from huge stones, righted and carved by hands that had themselves long since returned to the soil.

So I listened, and, when shortly afterward Sonja finagled me some time in a friend's studio, I tried to echo. It felt like rebirth. As if I were finally channeling the sounds I'd always been meant to make.

Then there was Sonja herself, quick-witted and coolly impassioned, blue-eyed and with hair like the sun shimmering on ice. She knew who she was and what she desired out of life . . . and one of those things was me. I'd been in lust before, often, and even in mutual loathe a few sick times. But at last I could say that I was in love.

Of course, if I'd known then what I know now, I might've killed her years earlier.

Because of their mood and atmosphere, the CDs I've recorded as Megalith seem to attract an inordinately high percentage of fans who are into occult practices to one degree or another. These are *not* the same people who are listening to Cher. Some of those I've met or have otherwise been contacted by seem to have come from, or at least belong on, another planet. Others really do strike me as being on to something.

One motif that I've found recurrent among them, from pagan celebrants to ceremonial magicians to worshipers of devils, is a conviction that simple belief is the single greatest step toward being met halfway by the powers they wish to contact. And that as soon as they're ready, someone or something appears in their life to aid and guide them. Events transpire, or seem to *con*spire, that only later reveal the symmetry of some grand design, not unlike the Nazca lines in the high Peruvian desert: meaningless as long as you're too close to them, but full of purpose and pattern when viewed from a broadened perspective.

He sings, my uncle told me. *I swear that, on occasion, he sings.*

So was it Terrance's telling me this that made it true for me, as well—the force of suggestion an induction into the possibility? At the time, I thought maybe it was a delusion manifesting as the first outward symptom of his illness. But because he remained so clearheaded about everything else during their visit, I wondered if instead he wasn't turning poetic in these final months of his life, and describing the skull's impact on his soul and imagination in similar terms as I'd used for my own time in the Scandinavian countryside, the call that I sensed there. When you're touched by something that has its roots in the infinite, rational language is of little use; you can speak of it only in the figurative. So I decided that perhaps Terrance had at last discovered a need for such an expansion of his vocabulary.

Yet there it lay within me:

He sings. I swear that, on occasion, he sings.

Were these words, however unlikely, my first seed of faith toward making it happen? Did they usher me to a state of mind in which I could hear it, too?

All I know is that the threshold was crossed in a moment when it was the last thing on my mind. Like most creative types, I can utterly lose myself in my work, and Goliath was just another quirky item of studio decor that had become invisible. But late one night, while sculpting the imagined sound of vast subterranean walls, I found myself growing cranky when no adjustment of volume faders or console buttons could isolate a track that had generated the unexpected artifacts I was hearing. Processed sound does that sometimes: combines to generate something unforeseen. Occasionally it's useful, other times not. But first you have to find it . . .

I found it only when I'd turned the playback off, and the speakers went dead silent.

He sings.

It wasn't an intrusive sound or even a direct one. It seemed to come from more than one place in the room. If it had been coming from something with flesh on its bones and air in its lungs, I would've guessed that it was made high in the being's throat, but bifurcating somehow . . . a denser fundamental tone paired with a higher trilling harmonic. Yet still they clashed, these tones. They rubbed and abraded against each other; they made the hair on the back of my neck prickle. They moved in tandem, but slowly, lingering long on some notes, with much shorter duration on others; the rhythm was hard to pick out, and the scales or modes like none I'd ever heard before.

But the longer I listened, spellbound, the more apparent it became: There *was* structure here. Deeper insight came when I heard a strange flourish that briefly reminded me of vocal ornamentation in Gregorian structure.

No, not singing, I decided. Or intuited.

He's chanting.

It didn't even occur to me right then to wonder to whose glory the chant was being offered.

Of course not. Because I was too busy attaching a contact microphone to the skull itself, and setting up others within the studio to record the impossible.

Late the next morning it seemed important to establish that I wasn't losing my mind, or at least letting it play tricks on me. Goliath had been silent for hours, and I'd managed a little sleep to clear my head, so I called up the half-hour's worth of that strange keening drone I'd recorded to see if it really was there.

I still heard it. But since some delusions can be persistent, I called Sonja down to the studio.

"Do you hear that?" I asked her, cautiously.

"Why shouldn't I?" she said. A little furrow creased between her brows. "It's very creepy. How did you *get* this? It sounds like a duet between a hippo and a lark."

I told her she was close, that it was animal sounds after lots of processing.

Few were the lies I'd told her over the years, and they were nearly always to spare her a worry or keep a surprise. But this was different. I couldn't tell her the truth and expect her to believe it, at least not without Sonja hearing it happen for herself. I wasn't sure I could tell her even with this dark miracle furnishing its own proof. Having heard it in the dead of night, I felt it to be a secret thing, an aberration of time and space, matter and energy, that wasn't meant to be acknowledged widely, because building up a shared awareness of it would give it more power, creating templates of expectation for it to follow, meet, surpass. It would broaden the portal for whatever primeval echo this was.

So I kept it to myself . . . and before long it was as though we began working together, Goliath and I.

Very late, after the house was silent and the forested hills were hushed with the chill of autumn nights, I would listen to the recordings. I would play them through each different pair of monitors, through headphones, listen while striving to grasp it on a deeper level. If it was a chant, that implied language . . . but words and syntax eluded me. Whenever I'd get close to syllables, they would slip from my grasp. And throughout, it seemed at once both remotely alien and tantalizingly familiar, as though I *should* know it if I would only listen a little harder.

Which sounds obsessive, and I suppose it was, but not debilitatingly so. To the contrary, because I have no other explanation for the enormous burst of new ideas that were sparked during the next couple of weeks.

Over the years I've collected a diverse library of sound sources, and one morning I awoke with the idea of taking radiation waves recorded from deepest space and converting them down into the spectrum of human hearing. The "noise" emitted by celestial objects consists of the same basic two components as the sounds we hear every day—amplitude and frequency—but the frequencies of stars and galaxies range from one to one thousand gigahertz. Fractionalizing the data into something audible to human ears—between a mere twenty and twenty thousand hertz—is mostly a matter of number-crunching, and computers excel at this. The resultant stream of digital data I could then use to trigger software oscillators.

On my shelves were CD-ROMs of data recorded by the radio telescopes at Kitt Peak in Arizona; near Socorro, New Mexico; at Germany's Southern European Observatory; others. I had my pick of several but found myself drawn to the disc of Sirius A, the "Dog Star" of the constellation Canis Major, and its twin, Sirius B. A binary pair, their frequencies would be close, but not exact; the sounds they made would flutter and beat against each other, like the thrumming of two guitar strings tuned microtones apart.

And slowly, as the ancient skull of *Homo sapiens primoris* watched on, I began to decipher the music of distant stars.

Now, of course, I freely admit that there was a greater design to even this.

I'd thought my idea was my own. And that I was making a choice for Sirius based on sonic needs, the tension inherent in the detuned frequencies of binary stars. Consciously at least, the other matter hadn't occurred to me or factored in as part of the appeal, even though when I'd read about it years ago in a book by a writer named Robert Temple, I'd found it wholly fascinating.

Do you know the secret of the stars called Sirius? Probably not.

For millennia, only one was known to exist, Sirius A alone visible to the patient eyes of astronomers who knew the night skies better than they knew their own families. By the mid–nineteenth century, an unseen twin was suspected because the Dog Star showed effects of an unexplained gravitational pull. Sirius B, no larger than Earth itself, wasn't seen until 1862 and wasn't understood in detail by science until the 1920s, when Sir Arthur Eddington posited the theory of those collapsed stars now known as white dwarves.

Except this minuscule star, invisible even to early telescopes, had already been known about by uncountable generations of a West African tribe called the Dogon. They also possessed sophisticated knowledge of our own solar system long predating the first efforts by Copernicus and Galileo. They knew of the moons of Jupiter and of the rings of Saturn. They knew of the elliptical shape of the orbit of Sirius B, and of A's off-center position within it . . . even that the length of a single orbit takes fifty Earth years.

The Dogon knew all this, they claimed, because it had been told to their early ancestors by gods who had come from a watery world lit by these mated stars.

I've sometimes wondered why it is that skulls seem to grin.

Now I think I know.

It's because of all the secrets the dead are at last allowed to remember about who and what they really are.

4

Marriages often do their floundering when you're too busy looking the other way. Mine, I discovered, was not immune to this.

For years I've considered it a luxury to only rarely need to know what day it is. In the studio they're all the same, time melting like the watches of a Dalí painting. And when the days run together and I run out of steam, there's always the couch along one studio wall. It can be a long time before I have to come up for air.

I'd always thought Sonja indulged me in this. But the note left behind on the kitchen counter set me straight on *that* fallacy:

Maybe we need to spend a little time apart.
Not that we haven't already been doing that under the same roof.

What scared me—well, even more than seeing myself in the mirror—was not being able to pinpoint on which of the past three or so days she would've written it.

You could say I'd spent that time off in my own world, but then the same thing could be said about every project of mine as it neared completion, and there was no reason to have expected my work on *Subterrain* to prove any different.

But it *was*. Because this most recent world in which I'd lost so many days wasn't mine, I was coming to realize. I'd never created it, only permitted it. Only tuned it in and turned up its volume.

It poured from the speakers around me, thick swirling textures like veils of mist from distant aeons, pulsating with colors that weren't part of any nature familiar to us from equator to poles. There were deeply hidden rhythms in it, too. Sometimes I used the frequencies as a modulation source, rather than audio, driving banks of my own sounds and hearing them reborn as percussion, like batteries of drums made from the resonant skins of animals glimpsed only in the most fevered of dreams. The polyrhythms astounded in their complexity. The louder I turned them up, the deeper they reverberated in bone and brain, and I understood more completely than I ever had why the martial cadences of vast drums have always stirred men to war.

He sings, my uncle had told me.

He chants, I had decided.

Could I really have discovered the source of Goliath's rhythms in so little time, without . . . help? Or had I known them all along, at a level air and daylight never reached?

Late one night, my third alone, so far as I knew, I decided that the house was insufficient to contain such primal orchestrations. My studio has a pair of sliding glass doors that overlook the hills and sky and woodlands—which destroys any hope of soundproofing, but it's more inspiring than four solid walls, and we're remote enough that it's rarely a problem. I pushed those doors wide and hauled speakers through the opening, snaking out cables that hadn't budged for years. I set them facing the world of streams and leaves and mossy stones, then walked back inside to the master volume fader on the control board . . .

And let the worlds collide.

How would *they* react, I wondered, everything that lived out there in the night—the creatures who still carried on the primal legacy endowed them by their ancestors? Answers came soon enough, with the screeching of birds awakening and bursting into panicked flight, and the shrill cries of things I couldn't quite identify, and finally, from far out in the darkness, the escalating snarls and wailing of coyotes pushed beyond mere savagery. I imagined, from such a din, that they must've been rending one another to pieces.

So I ducked back inside one more time and toted out a portable DAT and a few omni- and unidirectional mics, thinking, What the hell . . . I'll record this, too.

· · ·

I'm not a complete hermit, you know.

Even in the midst of my dour funk over Sonja's getting away by herself (at least I hoped it was by herself), I still maintained routine contact with Graham and the director of *Subterrain* and a few others involved in the soundtrack. Movies are made by nothing if not committees, often in conflict. Post-production, from my perspective and since it's all I've ever been involved with, is the worst—okay, we've got a bunch of raw footage. . . . Now what do we *do* with it? Needs can change on the momentary whims of any of a dozen or more people. Oh, so you're using the underwater sequence after all? Sure, I can come up with something for that by next Tuesday.

And then there was Uncle Terrance, who, after a few days in Alaska, had had to cut short their trip because the rigors of travel were getting to be too much for him. He and Liz had returned to Chicago so he could rest and, I suppose, try not to lie there imagining he could feel the growth advancing inside him like vines. We were on the phone with each other at least every other day, and at first it was as though he'd never left off that crate and its contents. He didn't even mention it the first time or two we spoke, but then, almost tentatively:

"Have you heard him yet?" my uncle asked. "Has he sung for you?"

I told him yes, along with my theory that it was actually a chant.

"I never thought of that. I'll have to pass that along."

"Terrance," I said. "Since there are other skulls, do they do the same thing?"

A pause; then, cautiously, "So I've heard."

"Do they have any explanations for it?"

I could hear him laughing softly, almost derisively. All the answer he'd give.

"Well over a century's worth of skulls," I tried next. "Have they done this all along? Or is this something new?"

"I really can't speak on behalf of them all, and because Miskatonic's finds aren't as centrally stored as they once were . . ."

"Just yours, then," I said. "Ours. When did it start?"

"Two years ago, perhaps a little less."

"Why? What happened then? Why would it suddenly start up then?"

"You must understand, Miskatonic often shares information on a need-to-know basis—they've learned the wisdom of that the hard way—and, well, thus far . . ."

"Do you know that its rhythms perfectly sync with emissions from Sirius when they're converted into audio range?"

"Good God," said Terrance. "However did you discover a thing like that?"

And I stood there holding the phone, shaking my head. Having to tell him that I didn't know, because I *couldn't really say* where those ideas had come from and what had guided my hands toward the Sirius data.

"The Dogon tribe," I said. "They have to know about that, don't they?"

"Quite extensively."

"'Terrance, whose . . .'" And I faltered, because I found that it was requiring a surprising amount of courage to ask what I wanted to know. "Giving me that skull. Me, someone completely unconnected with Miskatonic. You made it seem like this soulful gesture. But whose idea was it for you to do that? Was it yours?"

Silence. Then, "No. Theirs."

"Toward what end?"

"I really don't follow . . ."

"You must've thought it was strange. You *had* to. Because you don't just take an artifact like that and treat it like a family heirloom. So what was giving it to me supposed to accomplish?"

"It was discussed among the committee that oversees the business to do with *Homo sapiens primoris*, and what I understood is that there was interest in seeing what someone of your background in sonics would make of the phenomenon. Your work isn't unknown to them. Surely you're aware that your own work has been used for group rituals, for trance inducement and other consciousness alterations."

Judging by some of the fan mail I've received from such people, I wasn't sure how much importance could be placed on *their* conduct.

"Why not just be up front about it?" I said. "Why the charade?"

"I suppose," he mused, "for the same reason that wildlife filmmakers tend not to interfere in what they're documenting: to let nature take its own intended course."

So maybe it was cruel, but I had to ask: "Terrance, are you even dying?"

"I deserve that," he said. "Much to my chagrin, let me put it this way: If there's a black suit hanging in your closet, don't get rid of it anytime soon."

It was something I'd been taking for granted: that when I first heard from Sonja after she left, it would be with a phone call. Which was why I'd been taking the cordless into the studio, something I ordinarily never did. Or she would just reappear, having gotten over the worst of her frustration with my monomaniacal work habits, and I would hear her car, or the door, or the sound of her voice calling to announce her return. I was ready for any of these, hoping for one, so we could at least start to negotiate some sort of compromise between what I was and how I worked, and whatever needs of hers had evidently begun to conflict with that.

What I didn't expect was a postcard. Or where she'd mailed it from. Or what she'd written on it.

The front of the card showed a simple, boring shot of the

capitol building of Vermont, in Montpelier. The postmark had been stamped in a small village to the southeast, in the farm country where . . .

Well, you know.

I suspect there are things about your father's death that you've never come to terms with, Sonja had written. *Maybe the time has come for you to do that.*

Except for signing her first name, this was all she'd written. Evasive, concise, cryptic . . . and indescribably cruel. I'd never known her to play games before. It was one of the reasons I'd been so drawn to her. After some of the psychobitch mind-fucks endured during my more tumultuous years, Sonja had seemed refreshingly free of pretense and artifice. So what was I supposed to blame for *this* shift: the cultural kinks of the country she lived in now . . . or just a life spent with me?

Because you really couldn't expect me to wonder if it hadn't been there in her all along, and I'd been too blind to notice, would you?

One phone call later and I had a ticket for a cross-country flight the next day, with a rented car waiting at the other end. After all this had been taken care of, it was only a matter of how to spend the oppressive hours between. For the first time ever, the idea of going into the studio repelled me, because I imagined the skull waiting for me down there, and the sound of it sliding into my soul the way slivered bamboo slides beneath fingernails.

When you look upon a skull, any skull, especially a monstrosity like this one, it's so easy to lose sight of the fact that this was once an individual. Who was born, who grew, who died. Whose eyes had seen creatures no longer alive today, known only by their bones, if they're known at all; whose ears had listened for them; whose tongue had tasted their flesh. And I wondered if, when he raised his eyes to the night sky, he stared in awe at its vastness, or with instinctive collusion at the glimmer of far stars, or if he roared in defiance of it all. I wondered what he had built and left behind, how he had adorned it to mark it as his own, if he knew pride. And most of all, I guess, I wondered what had become of the offspring he'd almost certainly sired, and theirs as well, and all the others down through the ages, with their savage teeth and their long long stride.

To these ancient fathers, I fear we would today seem like such a puny race.

Thinking along these lines had put me in the mood to call Terrance, and I'd already thought I should tell him that I would be away for a day or two, or however long it would be. He assumed I was flying south, something pertaining to the film, and I let him go on assuming it.

He sounded worse, his voice noticeably weaker. The cancer? Yes. And no.

It was everything.

"I feel as if a while back I started reading the most absorbing mystery in the world," said my uncle, "but now I'll never have time to finish the book."

Only everything.

"You wondered what happened two years ago?" he said. "I pressed my old colleague from here in Chicago, Sam Charlton . . . and think I may have learned of something that's at least linked to the phenomenon of the skulls. The report was initially submitted to a professor of genetics at Miskatonic by an ally in Reykjavík. Can you guess why Iceland has become a living genetics laboratory in recent years?"

"I give up," I said, weary of the way Terrance always seemed to think he was in a classroom.

"Two main reasons. First, it's been settled for roughly a

thousand years, and the influx came almost exclusively from one place: Norway. Where, you remember, we found the skull. Even today, because of its remoteness, Iceland's population remains remarkably pure. They're pretty well all descended from those original settlers. And second, from the very beginning they were obsessed with genealogies. They have unbroken records going all the way back to the Viking age. The history of its population has literally been mapped out in its entirety.

"So these factors combine to make the place a haven for genetics research, unlike anyplace else on Earth. If you have, say, the same disease or congenital defect afflicting widely dispersed members of the present-day population, it's possible to comb the genealogies and see if there's a common ancestral link between them all, even if it goes back dozens of generations. It's invaluable for helping to identify and isolate the specific genes and mutations that cause various conditions."

"And now that I know that, why should I care?" Playing hard to reach; but then, losing your wife will do that to you.

"Because, quite unexpectedly, it isolated something else. Another of those anomalies that get the official silent treatment because there's little or no basis for understanding them. Apparently there's one lineage on the island that exhibits something in the genetic structure that isn't strictly, as we recognize it . . . human. But almost without fail, the people it was found in are characterized, either anecdotally or by photographs, as being of quite large stature. Dental peculiarities, too, sometimes. As if a diluted but still viable strain of DNA had survived from that race of *primoris* we know was in Norway."

The sons and daughters of giants, I thought, and flashed on the old European legends of such unsavory folk as ogres.

"And soon after this was noticed, and the tests were run and rerun to confirm that the results weren't contaminated, the test subjects themselves disappeared. *All* of them."

"What do you mean, 'disappeared'? You mean, poof, you blink once and they're gone?"

"I mean homes abandoned, jobs vacated, money left in bank accounts and untouched ever since. I mean a mass exodus of hundreds of men, women, and children occurring within a week's time, with no trace of them since."

"Your choice of words," I said. "Exodus implies a destination. So where to?"

"Since there were no indications of flights booked or any other kind of travel arrangements . . . ? Presumably the Icelandic interior. The country's populated only around the coast— a lot like Australia, just different extremes of temperature. The place is a cold waste that was deforested by the original settlers. Most of Iceland's uninhabited. Uninhabit*able*, by almost anyone's standards. Geologically the place is quite young, spit up by volcanoes when the rest of the Earth was already old. Not much in the interior but calderas, crags and flows of black lava, barren land, and glaciers."

"Sounds like a time capsule," I said. "The prehistoric world condensed down to . . . how big is it?"

"Forty thousand square miles," he said. "And you're not the first to make that observation."

"So these latter-day giants disappeared, and then . . ."

"And then the skulls began to sing."

"So what happened there?" I asked. "Your Miskateers must have all sorts of ideas about that, don't they?"

"Well, what occurred implies a kind of group consciousness. Whether or not its members were aware of it before, in their everyday lives, they must've possessed it. So if they encountered one another on the streets, maybe there was an innate recognition in passing, even if it left them puzzled. At night, perhaps they dreamed of one another. So, just speculating, it's possible the threat of discovery, of further examination, awoke . . . something. A flight response. A homesickness predicated more on *time* than geography."

"So they retreated to . . ."

"The replication of their ancestors' world. They went home."

5

If I've given the impression that I'm completely callous about my original family, that's not the case. There isn't much I have pertaining to the first five years of my life, but what there is I've kept in a lidded wooden box, except for my father's record albums, which won't fit. Most of my family photos aren't originals, but are on the glossy inner sleeve of his final album. You know how bands used to do with their packaging— take a scrapbook's worth of candid photos and reprint them scattered on top of one another to show the world how much fun they had every day. Here's the lifestyle you fans are paying for.

So I've always known what it looked like, the place where my father died. The band had rented the same Vermont farmhouse before as a songwriting retreat, and there was a shot of it in that final album. In my early teens, I'd done enough digging to know how to find the place, always intending to go there, but by the time I had a car of my own, my interest in making such a pointless trip had already begun to wane.

Besides, it was probable that I'd been there before, maybe even was there that mid-October night he'd died. If I had, though, I'd blocked it from memory. Terrance and Genevieve had always been vague on the subject, claiming that by the time I was old enough to seek answers about it, they were no longer sure what these were.

So if I was expecting a flood of memories to be unleashed as soon as I stepped from the car and onto the grounds, it didn't happen. A hazy familiarity, nothing more, which may have been as attributable to the old picture as genuine memory. Or suggestibility, because here it was October again, October in Vermont, and the leaves of the maples were searingly red, and the oaks a merry orange and yellow.

Since the place was deserted, and had been for a long time, it was easy to imagine that everything had been left just as it'd been back then, the austere charms of this white two-story farmhouse allowed to rot day by day. The windows, knocked out perhaps by stones flung by boys from neighboring farms, never replaced. The boards of the porch, sagging underfoot, never repaired. Nearly thirty years of dust, never swept aside. Graffiti, never scoured away.

It was strange to see them, these sentiments of strangers wrought in paint that had been sprayed and slopped by long-ago fans of my father. In the years following his overdose, this place had drawn them . . . the fanatics who couldn't let go of the dead, the delusional who'd dissected his dippy lyrics and concluded he was speaking just to them, the losers who'd decided to make their own lives a eulogy for the life he had squandered. I assumed this was why the place had gone to seed—his death had doomed it to become a morbid road-side attraction for just the kinds of tourists you wouldn't want: the kind who traded in a currency of broken dreams instead of cash.

Most of what they'd left behind was still legible, although waterstains down the walls had rippled away parts of it. Some of the mourners pledged eternal devotion, which I wondered if they remembered now. Others promised to see him again one day in Narnia or Middle-Earth, fantasy lands that he'd lyri-cally appropriated from richer imaginations than his own. Still others, more ambitious, had reproduced album artwork on a wall-size scale.

Pathetic, just pathetic. All of it. Whatever Sonja could have possibly thought I needed to come to terms with, I couldn't see how she'd gotten the notion it would happen here.

As I walked through the derelict house, its musty damp chill heavy in my nose and the gritty crunch of my footsteps unnaturally loud, I realized that I didn't know specifically where he'd died. Down here on the first floor, or upstairs, or . . . ? I'd always imagined it happening in whichever bedroom he and my mother had been staying in, but for all I knew, it could've happened on the flagstone path out back, or the hayloft of the barn, or the bank of the brook that was supposed to flow past the treeline.

Would I know it when I stood on the spot? Would *they* have known, these sorry pilgrims from another age who'd been left unmoored by his unceremonious junkie's death?

It appeared that they had, once I'd climbed the stairway to the moldering second floor. All graffiti led here, to a room at the end of a hallway whose floor was a hazard zone of warped boards. A corner room, with windows on two sides, where nothing remained in the way of furnishings, only what the grieving and the curious had brought with them and left behind— bottles and candle stubs, empty packages of rolling papers and used condoms as dry and brittle as cicada shells. More faded paint, expressing more of the same . . . except for one inexplicable sentiment that brought on a momentary frown:

NO ACCIDENT, it read, in block letters that were strangely ornate. HE KNEW WHAT SHE WAS.

A few inches below that, a much sloppier, hurried attempt to establish some sort of dialogue:

OH YEAH & WHAT WAS SHE???

It had, after all these years, gone unanswered.

You can waste a lot of time after seeing something like this, hunting in vain for anything else that can illuminate it—it has to be there, you've just missed it. Every square inch becomes important. But eventually I surrendered. There was no more, just the watercolor residue of old dried tears.

She . . . my mother? I couldn't think of anyone else it might be referring to. He wasn't faithful, and they weren't even married, but still I sensed that this had to mean my mother, if only because she'd been by all accounts the main woman in his life. Mother of his child. They can draw a lot of flak, the mates of coveted men, so maybe this was no more than the aching bitterness of some lovelorn schoolgirl who by now had short, practical hair and teenagers of her own.

He knew what she was.

But *I* didn't want to know, because wanting to know would mean I cared. And all I cared about now was this strange and lonely turn my life had taken, the void in our bed left by the woman I *had* married.

Sonja had been here. Certainly in the state, but closer still. *Here.* This house, this room. Why refer to it otherwise, alluding to it with a veiled invitation?

I stayed in the house for hours, until nightfall, then gave up for the day and drove off to find a motel, where I slept so little it seemed a waste of money. But at least I was showered and fresh the next morning before going back to the farmhouse to wait again, certain that whatever was to happen next, it was meant to happen here.

The day was altogether more dismal than the sunny day before—the darker side of October was showing now, the October of spirits and Samhain, the October that blusters gray skies above your head and drags at your bones with a misty rain. I roamed the house and listened to it creak, and tried without success to recall the place from another time, to remember running happily through its well-kept halls.

I was sitting halfway up the staircase to the second floor

when she came that afternoon—first the sound of a car stopping on the weed-choked gravel drive out front, and then footsteps, too light to be those of some deputy arrived to run off a squatter. Her hollow tread on the porch, the painful rasp of the front door hinges.

And then, for the first time in nearly two weeks, we were looking at each other, here on the other side of the country.

The normal instinct you ordinarily have at such a moment is to run and hold the other person. That the impulse was suddenly squashed within me is the best testament to how unsettling the moment truly was. It was Sonja and then again it wasn't. It was someone wearing Sonja's face. It was Sonja after she'd removed a mask I'd never noticed. And it might've even still been love with which she looked at me, but no kind of love I would ever knowingly seek.

"You *must've* been upstairs, at some point," she said.

"This is ancient history," I told her. "It's been years since what happened here meant anything to me."

"Years and meaning have nothing to do with each other." Blue eyes and total conviction. "Besides, how can you say that if you don't even know what really did happen?"

"Oh, and you do?" I challenged, but she didn't answer, just moved to the stairs and ascended, one hand on the dingy banister, brushing my shoulder with the other as she glided past.

I rose to follow. You *know* where we went.

"It happened right here," she said, this stranger I'd loved—hadn't I? She was pointing to a spot along the floor, a few feet from one set of windows. "The bed was here, and he sat on the floor and this is where he slid the needle in his vein. A few seconds later he tried to stand but he fell back on the bed and never got up again. He died staring at the ceiling. But what he was *looking* at, who knows?"

"So what. So fucking what. You're an obsessive fan who

somehow managed to hide it until now. *You're* the one who needs to come to terms." Telling her this, but thinking now that it was never me she'd loved, it was him all along—the image of him, the stupid fantasy of him, because she'd been three years old when he died, and I was just the consolation prize.

She ignored me entirely, moving now to the other wall's windows. "But he'd looked at enough for one night."

Gaze out these particular windows and you had an excellent overview of the farmhouse's backyard, long since overgrown and wild; once it must've been lush and mown, the flagstones to the far barn like a curving archipelago.

"He watched it happening from here," Sonja said. "She thought he was asleep and so he wasn't supposed to see it, but he did, and that must've been why he killed himself. But he didn't do it right away, because she was finished already and he was still alive, so he probably wanted to make sure he wasn't just hallucinating. He killed himself in front of her, you know—he didn't die alone."

"You can't know these things," I whispered.

She merely smiled. You can argue with anything but a smile.

"Watched *what* happening . . . ?" I asked, crumbling the way she knew I would.

"Do I have to say? It can be enough of an insult to tell a man what his mother did with other men . . . let alone something very tall that walked out of the woods late at night, that she was waiting for . . . because unlike so many she always knew who and what she was . . ."

And I suppose it was right about then that my head began to pound—

"She was such a tall woman, do you even remember that about her?" Sonja said. "You can't really tell so from any of the pictures you showed me, but she was uncommonly tall. Maybe why you don't remember is because all little children think their parents are tall. But . . . where do you think you got *your* height?"

—and I felt that I was about to scream, because I wasn't supposed to care.

"Do you even remember her name?"

And I stammered out that it was Gudrid, something like that, a name I'd never even thought was real, because it sounded like one of those fantasy names that counterculture airheads were fond of using back then. But no, Sonja said, it was my mother's real name.

"I should know—it's Icelandic," she said. "They've told your uncle about what happened in Iceland by now, haven't they?"

And Sonja stood before me with her cold beauty and her hair like the sun shimmering on ice, so much more in control of herself than I was as I pleaded to know who she really was, where she had really come from, who had really sent her to meet me so many years ago, if it had to do with these people at Miskatonic who had drawn Terrance in . . . but her inarguable smile was sad in its refusal, and all she would say was that there was science, and there was worship, and sometimes, if very rarely, they overlapped.

"I could worship *you*, too," she said, "if it wasn't for your ignorance."

But why would she ever want to, I wondered, but didn't want to know, either because of what it would say about her or imply about me.

"So I'll settle for this. . . ."

And I swear it was Sonja who picked up the discarded bottle, heavy old thing long drained of wine, and put it in my hands, then knelt before me and tossed her head back and looked up at me with the kind of expectation you might expect in the transcendent eyes of sacrifices who willingly laid themselves beneath the obsidian knives of Aztec priests. Giving themselves to a higher cause.

"If it helps you to know, to *awaken*, then *do* it . . ."

And here I was, years later, back with the sick mind-fuck games all over again. No different than with the unhealthy women I swore I never wanted to meet again, who'd wanted me to cut them, to whip them, who weren't happy unless they were hurting—did they smell something on me?

"Do it!" she shouted, beautiful Sonja whom I'd never known, who'd come to me for reasons I'd never suspected. "*Do* it . . . or I'll tell you about your *real* father."

That did it.

It's astonishing how sturdy thick glass can be, how hard and how many times it can be swung before breaking.

It looked far too time-worn for Sonja to have brought it here herself during the past days. Whoever had left it, years ago, decades even, I wondered what dim impulse they'd obeyed, if they had the faintest sense the bottle was meant to be left here for just this day.

To kill the future daughter-in-law of their fallen god.

For the trip home, I ignored the airlines and took Sonja's car, in part because I didn't want to leave it behind to be found. To possibly be linked with the remains of the unidentified woman that were sure to be discovered sooner or later. Most of her I left in the cleansing waters of the woodland brook near the farmhouse. The rest, which might have established her identity from fingerprints or dental records, went elsewhere, many elsewheres, for more thorough concealing.

I found it amazing, the survival instincts that welled up

within me. I did these things as if the self I'd always known was watching them be done by another self who had assumed command. Another self I'd never realized was there, buried deep in bone and DNA.

And afterward, Sonja's car and solitude across a continent's worth of roads. I felt so numb that I had hardly any sense of seeing the eastern third of the country, able only to drive and sleep and, just barely, eat. I would drive late into the night and the frosty black breath of its dampened autumn chill, and sometimes I would stop on a desolate stretch of highway and stand beneath the frozen light of stars, listening for their distant music.

On the third night I was finally able to sit awake with myself and my deeds in the cheerless cubicle of a motel room. Nebraska, this was in. On the bed, I opened the lid of the wooden box containing what little I had to remember my earliest years by. I'd packed it for the flight to Vermont without really knowing why, only that it seemed fitting, full circle.

Inside were the worthless, priceless treasures of a young boy. Trading cards, seashells, those few faded family photos. Guitar picks. A little pistol that must've belonged to a toy soldier, long gone. Two Matchbox cars. A bone, small but strangely dense, from nothing I could guess. A magnet. Stuff like that. I held it all, piece by piece, and marveled at how small our worlds are when we're young.

At the bottom lay a brown envelope, a tiny thing really, two inches by four. Small as it was, it had been rubber-stamped with the name and office address of a dentist; the town, I was surprised to see, was just a few miles from the farmhouse. Pencilled notations, too, in what might've been my mother's hand—my first name and an October date only two days before my father had died. I had to smile at this unexpected evidence of maternal responsibility, my mother taking me in for a checkup.

I opened the envelope, probably *un*opened since I was ten, and slid out the only thing inside: a pair of dental X rays, ghostly blue-white on black. When I held them up to the light of the motel lamp, they were clearly a child's, the baby teeth grown in, the adult teeth in their hidden sockets above, awaiting their turn.

But above *those*, there were more.

Along each side, high in the bone of the upper jaw, deep in the bone of the lower, they abided even then . . . wide teeth down the center of each side, long and razored, that looked made to mesh together top and bottom like meat shears.

Whether they had implications for a future still to come or were vestigial leftovers from aeons ago, I couldn't begin to guess.

But no wonder they were in with the family photos.

6

So I returned to my home in the mountains, and to the one thing that had always helped me find purpose: my work with the sounds of other worlds and of other people's dreams and nightmares.

I had a film to finish up, and came through for the studio and its deadlines, and the day after the package of my sound design arrived down in Los Angeles, to be layered into *Subterrain*'s soundtrack, I got a call from Graham Pennick, who had no reservations in proclaiming it the single most unsettling work he'd ever heard me, or anyone, do. Parts of it really got under his skin, he said, although he couldn't say precisely why, and of course asked what I'd done, what my sources were.

"A little of this, a little of that," I said, elusive. "From here and there."

Which he respected, of course. Trade secrets. There was no need, really, to mention how far away some of it had come from in time and space.

And it was around then that Uncle Terrance lost the power of speech, so we communicated by e-mail for a short while, but by now there was little more to share than his own misery.

This thing growing inside is eating me alive, he wrote in the final missive I received from him. *If it's true we were made by conscious design, we still were not made in benevolence. There can be nothing crueler than an evolving world.*

I believe you have a point, I wrote in reply. *Just look at the teeth that rise to the challenge.*

But I don't know if he received this, because the next thing I heard—from his companion, Liz—he was dead. He'd been squirreling away painkillers until he had enough of a cache that would rob the cancer of its last laughs. The unspoken implication was that she'd helped him make his exit. For which I thanked her.

But while I know she made him happy, I had to wonder if Liz was really who he thought she was. Or if she was with him according to dictates other than those of her own heart. You'll naturally understand my paranoia, since I have to wonder when all this *really* started. If my aunt Genevieve's murder truly was an unsolved mugging or only looked like one. The surest way of shaking up Terrance's life, getting him to Norway and to the skull, which then made its way to me. The surest way of bringing in Liz to ease the fresh loneliness of his life . . . and make sure certain things got done.

I have to wonder if his colleagues at Miskatonic were players or mere pawns on a much grander scale of dominion. Because, as Sonja had said, there is science, and there is worship, and sometimes they overlap.

Or maybe it all began earlier still, with my birth, or my father's death and my abandonment, so that someday I could more easily receive this legacy of chant and bone. Marked for this, perhaps, even while in Gudrid's strange womb, then once I was free, imperceptibly guided the rest of the way.

Years ago, it occured to me that when you can barely remember your own parents, you can hardly know who and what you are.

And now, while I still agree with this, it occurs to me that *discovering* such knowledge, rather than growing up with it, means it's much less likely to be taken for granted. Or rebelled against.

I think of another conversation Terrance and I had while he was here, the day after he'd given me the skull. I was intrigued by those huge intervals in the geological levels at which the various specimens of *Homo sapiens primoris* had been found. It wasn't a smooth, continuous fossil record. Instead, they'd been found in four distinct strata—from roughly thirty million years ago, eighteen million, six million, and, like the skull he gave me, just 350,000. Mostly consistent in form, but separated by vast gulfs of time.

"What do they make of that at Miskatonic?" I'd asked.

"The natural inference drawn is that something periodically seeded the Earth with these . . . beings," Terrance had said. "And long after they went extinct, tried again, until maybe, finally, they flourished."

"Are they us?" Something I would know better than to ask now. "Are they any part of us?"

"I'm not even sure what 'us' means anymore," he'd said. And wouldn't look at me. "But if we really were created in some other being's image, I'm no longer sure I like the prospect of who or what that might've been."

. . .

News will periodically come to me that I'm now much better equipped to know what to make of, how to read between its lines, than I would've been before receiving my birthright.

When I first heard about a tiny town in Iceland that had been mysteriously burned to the ground, every last inhabitant slaughtered, I immediately knew what to make of it. And understood instinctively that the world is poised to embark upon another cruel path.

When similar events occured in Canada and Germany and Brazil, I saw the same hand at work and didn't even need the affirmation furnished by the large footprints found.

But news comes from much closer to home, as well.

The soundtracks of films are generally mixed by three or so audio engineers working at a large digital board. When word got back to me of the strife between the trio who mixed *Subterrain*, and how they twice had to be replaced, I thought back on my late-night experiment that had caused coyotes to tear one another to pieces.

When a couple of weeks later I learned about the arrest of two of the studio executives who'd sat in on the screening of a preliminary cut of the finished film, I understood *why* they might've gone on their killing spree afterward.

The prerelease buzz is that it's an extremely powerful movie.

A major holiday release, it premiers nationwide in another week, in more than two thousand theaters. I look forward to opening day with great anticipation.

Once I wanted to burn the Earth, remember? Never dreaming I would be handed the chance, in the service of ancient gods whose names I don't yet know, but whose titan souls I suspect I've always heard.

I began by telling you that I'm more my father's son than my uncle's nephew, and surely this is more true now than I ever fathomed it could be, if Sonja's final words really were spoken from knowledge:

Do it . . . or I'll tell you about your real *father.*

But until he makes himself known to me, I will above all regard myself as the son of my mother, and yearn to see her one last time. . . .

If only to show her how I've grown.

TEETH

Matt Cardin

> *For in much wisdom is much grief:*
> *and he that increaseth knowledge increaseth sorrow.*
> —ECCLESIASTES 1:18

> *Consciousness is a disease.*
> —MIGUEL DE UNAMUNO

1

My first and decisive glimpse into the horror at the center of existence came unexpectedly during my second year of graduate school. I was pursuing a doctorate in philosophy, and I had stopped by the library in between classes for some quick research. As I was searching out a copy of the *Enneads* of Plotinus I came upon my friend Marco hidden away among the second-floor stacks at a small table near the south wall.

"Marco!" I said with genuine pleasure, flashing a smile. "Hello, Jason," he murmured, without glancing up from his books. He was surrounded by piles of them, so many they were almost spilling off the table. He appeared to be copying a passage from one of them into a notebook, and I stood by uncertainly while he continued writing.

Marco was a visiting student from Guatemala, though he had only a slight Spanish accent. His auburn skin, coal black hair, and muscular physique gave him the air of a Third World revolutionary. He was also the most brilliant person I had ever met, a savant who was triple-majoring in physics, philosophy, and history. We had met at the beginning of the fall semester, and I had quickly learned that his chic-terrorist look concealed a fierce intelligence. Now, at the end of the spring term, I was still amazed at his vast knowledge. He could discourse at length on almost any subject, and in the process usually would make anyone else feel woefully ignorant. The books now spread out on the table before him were enough to dizzy the average mind. He was only twenty-six, and I could never figure out how he had gained so much knowledge in such a short time.

As I stood by in silence I began to wonder what was wrong. Our meetings usually consisted of a perennial philosophical conversation, but today Marco had nothing to say. I studied his face as he wrote, and saw that he looked exhausted and even depressed. There was something else, too: a queer haunted, almost hunted, look around his eyes.

"How are classes?" he asked, startling me.

"Some good, some not," I answered nonchalantly. "Teaching philosophy to disinterested freshmen is like asking your cat to come to you. They just don't give a shit."

At this he paused in his writing and seemed to smile to himself, but his expression bespoke more bitterness than amusement. "Philosophy," he murmured. "The crown of the intellectual disciplines. The one discipline whose goal is to comprehend all the rest." He seemed about to say more, but then a troubled look crossed his face and he returned to his writing, leaving me to wonder why I was suddenly uneasy in his presence.

At length he set his pen down. "Do you have a few minutes before your next class?"

"A few. What's up?"

He hesitated, then said, "I want to show you something. Something I think will interest you very much."

"Very mysterious," I said.

He didn't laugh. Without a word he stuffed his books and notebook into his bag and we headed for the stairs.

2

In his eight-by-twelve room on the sixth floor of the dormitory, Marco held out a spiral notebook to me. I looked at him cautiously.

"Take it," he said. "Look on the forty-sixth page."

I took the notebook and examined it. It appeared to be nothing special, just an ordinary seventy-two-page spiral notebook with a red cover. In fact, it was the same notebook I had seen him writing in earlier, and I wondered why he hadn't shown it to me then.

The first page was crammed with his minute handwriting, and from the snippets I caught before turning to the next page I could see that the notebook was some sort of personal journal filled with Marco's thoughts on quantum physics, history, and other subjects I couldn't even identify. The pages were hand numbered in the upper right-hand corner.

Remembering that I was supposed to be looking for page forty-six, I began to flip slowly through the notebook. Although the primary subject of the notebook was obscure to me, I discerned that he was conducting his own private inquiry into a certain matter, an inquiry that encompassed ideas from fantastically diverse fields of knowledge. He made great use of quotations from other writers, and I caught snatches of a theoretical treatise on quantum physics by Niels Bohr, a monograph by an obscure astronomer, the Vedanta Sutras of Sankara, and the writings of Schopenhauer and Nietzsche.

On page forty-five were two quotes, one from a book with a strange name that was vaguely reminiscent of Hindu deities, and the other from a story by H. P. Lovecraft. I had heard of

Lovecraft, even though I had never read any of his writings, but this other work was completely unfamiliar to me.

"What is all this?" I asked, forgetting to pretend I wasn't reading as I turned the pages. "What are you getting at here?"

"It will help you to understand if you turn to the next page," he said, and something about his voice caused me to look up at him. His face and body were tensed, and I saw a bead of sweat run down his temple. The expression in his eyes was unreadable. I stared at him for a long moment before finally looking back down and turning the page.

I don't know what I was expecting, but it was most certainly not an elaborate drawing. Rendered in the same blue ink Marco used to record his thoughts was an incredibly intricate mandala, with shapes and forms and shadings so lush and vivid they seemed to reach out from the page. I knew that the creation of mandalas had been developed into an exquisite art form in many eastern religious traditions, but the one I was seeing now was even more breathtaking than those I had encountered in my studies of Buddhism and Hinduism. I stared at it for a moment with a feeling of wonder and admiration. Was this yet another talent of my amazing friend? If so, he was an artist of genius.

I was about to ask him to explain himself when the lines along the outer edge of the mandala began to blur. Thinking my eyes must be tired, I blinked twice and was astonished to see that the blurring had now become a shimmering. Like waves from a stone thrown into a pond, the shimmering began to spread in concentric rings, moving not outward but inward, converging toward the mandala's central point. In a few short seconds the effect had taken over the entire picture, so that I seemed to be seeing it through ringed waves of summer-pavement heat.

Dumbfounded, I tried to look up at Marco but found that I

couldn't. My eyes were locked against my will on the increasingly obscene drawing, and without warning I felt a wave of revulsion wash over me like rotten seawater. The sensation was so strong that I felt I would vomit, yet struggle as I might, I could not look away. The nausea increased when I saw dark, angular shapes begin to appear at the edges of the drawing and move back and forth like tiny fangs.

Then in an instant all motion stopped. A dark spot no bigger than a pinhead formed at the center of the picture and began to grow, appearing to eat away at the very page, until I felt I was actually looking *through* it into a black abyss seething with half-seen forms. Living forms. *Hungry* forms. I could see sharp protuberances, points, spikes, in all directions, and I heard them clicking and grinding together. Beneath this sound was another, a firm, monotonous undertone that seemed variously to be a gibbering, a hissing, a screaming, a roaring. Suddenly a flash of comprehension that seemed more like a darkness than an illumination blossomed somewhere in the tiny corner of my mind that I could still call my own, and I realized that I was staring into a nightmare abyss of endless teeth.

Then I felt the attention of a massive and malevolent intelligence turned upon me, and as the first of trillions of teeth began to sink into my mind, I knew with absolute, horrible certainty that this nightmare abyss was also staring into me.

3

"What the hell happened?" I gasped. I was lying on Marco's bed as he looked for something in his medicine cabinet. He ignored me as he brought out a plastic container, uncapped it, and shook two tiny white pills into his hand.

"Take these," he said, handing them to me with a bottle of water from his refrigerator. I swallowed them without thinking and repeated my question. "What happened, Marco? What happened to me?" We both knew my anger was a defense against the fear I didn't want to acknowledge.

I was terrified, in a true, deep sense of the word that I had never imagined. Marco had grabbed the notebook out of my hands just as I was on the verge of being swallowed by whatever was reaching out for me.

He explained that he had been obliged to rip it from my grasp, even though I was making horrified, guttural sounds of revulsion at it. The room and the normal world had come back quickly, but as if from a great distance, rather like those occasional mornings when I wake to the feeling that yesterday was aeons ago.

Marco sat down at his desk and looked at the notebook that lay there, now closed. "Stupid, stupid, stupid!" he hissed to himself. "It might have killed you!"

"*What* might have killed me!" I yelled. I could hear the hysteria rising again in my own voice.

"Just calm down," he said, turning his full attention upon me. "I gave you a couple of muscle relaxers. You'll feel more calm in a few minutes." He took a deep breath and let it all out, sinking deep into his chair. Even in my near-shock condition I could sense the hopelessness he radiated.

After a long silence he started to speak, his gaze on the far wall. "Jason, do you think people want truth? Do people truly want to know the reality of their lives?"

Conversations of this sort made up much of my life at that time, and either the familiarity of a philosophic discussion, or perhaps the drug Marco had given me—or perhaps a combination of the two—began to have a calming effect. I opened my mouth to say something, anything, but he went on as if I weren't there.

"To know why we are here, why we live and die, why it thunders and rains? Most of all, to know who and what we are. Is this not the primal human motivation?" My head was still clearing, and I had no idea what he was getting at.

"I've tried for many years," he said quietly. "I've devoted myself to the search for truth. A noble pursuit, to be sure. We all say we want it. Even nihilists think their insight is better than ignorance. But what if," he said, turning to look at me for the first time since he had started this monologue, "what if this is all wrong? What if the thing people really want and need is *illusion?*" He warmed to his subject and leaned forward, gripping the edge of his chair. "What if the truth, the ultimate, all-encompassing truth of the universe, is unutterably terrible? *What if reality itself is evil?*"

I stared at him. Sweat stood out on his forehead and upper lip. His eyes bored into me, and for a split second I thought I could sense the same roaring black presence I had felt just moments before.

"What you're saying isn't new, and you know it," I told him. "The idea has been around for millenia. Schopenhauer and Nietzsche expressed it just over a century ago."

"So have a thousand horror writers and college students," he shot back, "but what I'm talking about isn't theory—it's *real*. You can't distance yourself from it just by recalling who first thought of it, or what he or she said about it. After what you've just experienced, you know something of what I mean."

I had no reply, because he was right. Whatever had happened to me had made me, at least for the moment, more open to strange ideas. My usual self-absorption, my narcissism, my obliviousness to my surroundings as I indulged in my own interior monologue—all these defenses had been stunned, and in the unfamiliar calm of interior silence I thought I could hear the sound of something terrible approaching.

He must have seen the confusion on my face, because he cut his speech short and handed me the notebook. "Read it," he said. "It will answer most of your questions. I probably don't need to tell you to avoid the mandala." He took my arm and gripped it so tightly that I was sure he must be bruising me. "Do not, under any circumstances, look at that picture again."

"But what . . . what is it?" I managed weakly. "Isn't it yours? Didn't you draw it?"

"In a way, yes. Read the notebook. We'll talk more when you finish it."

I was in no shape to argue. I rose unsteadily to my feet and told Marco good-bye, wondering why I had the strange feeling that I wouldn't see him again. Before I really knew what I was doing, I was in the elevator and headed for the ground floor. Then I was walking out of the dormitory and across campus to my apartment. Then I was unlocking the door and stepping inside.

It was only then that I realized I was carrying the notebook. I dropped it like a snake, walked into the bedroom, collapsed onto the bed, and fell immediately asleep. While I slept I dreamed that Marco was standing outside my door talking with some strangers. I called to him that the door was unlocked, that he could come inside, but when I saw the knob begin to turn it dawned on me that he would bring the strangers inside with him, and I knew that I really didn't want to meet them.

Consciousness didn't return until the next morning.

4

The next week of my life was devoted to reading Marco's notebook, and it was the most grueling experience I have ever endured. This was partly due to the fact that the speculations on astronomy and physics were practically incomprehensible to

me, but there was another reason as well: a new sense or faculty seemed to have been opened within me, a sense that was
distressingly responsive to the dark suggestions unfolding on
the pages before me. As I read, I began to understand the oppressive weight of the worldview under which Marco labored. I
also noticed that the very same despair seemed to have taken
root in my own heart, and was in fact being nourished by my
reading.

Much of the notebook was filled with long quotations carefully transcribed by Marco from a wide array of books. Schopenhauer figured highly, as did Nietzsche. I had first encountered
their harsh and bitter philosophies during my undergraduate
years, but now it was as if I were truly understanding them for
the first time. Recorded here was Schopenhauer's famous criticism of the assertion, so common among a certain variety of
philosopher, that evil is merely the absence of good: "I know of
no greater absurdity," he wrote, "than that propounded by most
systems of philosophy in declaring evil to be negative in its
character. Evil is just what is positive; it makes its own existence felt."

Also recorded was Nietzsche's amplification of this idea:

> Nobody is very likely to consider a doctrine true merely
> because it makes people happy or virtuous. . . . Happiness
> and virtue are no arguments. But people like to forget—
> even sober spirits—that making unhappy and evil are no
> counterarguments. Something might be true while being
> harmful and dangerous in the highest degree. Indeed, it
> might be a basic characteristic of existence that those who
> would know it fully would perish, in which case the strength
> of a spirit should be measured by how much of the "truth"
> one could still barely endure—or to put it more clearly, to
> what degree one would *require* it to be thinned down,
> shrouded, sweetened, blunted, falsified.

The quotes went on, page after page, interspersed with Marco's own notes and observations, and after two days of reading I began to despair of making heads or tails of it all. The notebook seemed to be merely a particularly pessimistic collection of aphorisms and observations. But then I came to a quote from the Indian philosopher Sankara, and the outline of the puzzle began to take shape in my mind. Sankara wrote, "With half a stanza I will declare what has been said in thousands of volumes: Brahman is real, the world is false, the soul is only Brahman, nothing else."

I had long been acquainted with the Hindu idea that the material world is actually *maya*, illusion, a mirage resting upon the absolute reality which the Vedantic Hindus call Brahman. But the Eastern philosophies all teach that release from illusion and the subsequent realization of ultimate reality is a wonderful experience. The very word *moksa*, which the Hindus use to refer to this experience, means "liberation." Marco, on the other hand, seemed to be perverting the Eastern beatific vision by positing that the uniform reality underlying physical existence is an utter nightmare. And if "the soul is only Brahman"—I couldn't bear to follow this line of thought to its conclusion.

Of the scientific line of thought interwoven with the philosophy, all I could comprehend was that Marco was struggling with some unresolved issue in quantum physics. The mathematics was beyond me, but from the sparse text notes I could gather enough to grasp the bare essence of the matter, which had something to do with the philosophical implications of quantum mechanics. I read that the equations used in quantum mechanics *work*— everything from television to the hydrogen bomb attests to that—but no satisfactory explanation for their *meaning*, for their implications at the macroscopic level of existence, had yet been established.

On the subatomic level, I read, particles flash into and out of existence for no discernible reason, and the behavior of any single particle is apparently arbitrary and usually unpredictable. If there is a cause or "purpose" behind this behavior, it is one that the human mind is perhaps not structured to comprehend. In other words, for all we know, the only ruling principles at the most basic level of physical reality may well be what we call madness and chaos.

This predicament of knowledge had remained essentially unchanged for seventy years, and Marco had the audacity to believe that he'd begun to solve the riddle that had haunted the keenest scientific minds for nearly a century. Unfortunately, his ideas were mostly expressed in mathematical terms that were incomprehensible to me, and so I was left with a tantalizing glimpse of what might have been a revolutionary theory.

As I read through the notebook I could feel revulsion rising inside me. At times it became so strong that I was forced to stop for several hours; once for more than a day. Finally I realized that what I was feeling could only be described as *horror*, a word whose referent I had never really known. Marco's comment about the human need for illusion began to make sense to me, for if this puzzle pointed to reality, then I would rather be deceived.

It was with great trepidation that on the sixth day of reading I turned to the forty-fifth page of the notebook, the last page before the one containing the drawing that had begun this nightmare. Slowly I read through the first of the two quotes, the one from the book with the Hindu-sounding title (whose name I have long since forgotten). As its significance became clear to me, I felt the words themselves begin to sink into my mind like barbs.

> Foolish soul, wilt thou comprehend the All, the great Central Mystery? Man's place is the middle. Thou approachest the Gate in both the Greatest and the Least. In

the face of the night sky, at the core of a dust mote—the same One. Wretched is he who hears the call, but more wretched still the one who answers it.

The final quotation was from a story by H. P. Lovecraft, and in the margin beside it Marco had written, "The Capstone."

The most merciful thing in the world, I think, is the inability of the human mind to correlate all its contents. We live on a placid island of ignorance in the midst of black seas of infinity, and it was not meant that we should voyage far. The sciences, each straining in its own direction, have hitherto harmed us little; but someday the piecing together of dissociated knowledge will open up such terrifying vistas of reality, and of our frightful position therein, that we shall either go mad from the revelation or flee from the deadly light into the peace and safety of a new dark age.

5

After this my nerves could stand no more. I shoved the notebook far back into a drawer and for several days tried to forget that I had ever seen it. But its dark secrets were working their way inward, ever inward, toward my deepest self. My teaching and class schedules were mercifully light, but even the slight strain of conducting a freshman philosophy class was almost more than I could handle. More than one student gave me a strange look as I attempted to deliver a lecture with a quaver in my voice that I could not control. I felt a trembling all the way to my core, and when I realized I was getting worse instead of better, I began to think seriously of putting my entire graduate program on hold until I could sort things out.

My immediate intention was to talk with Marco. I knew I should see him again, should talk this all out before making any rash decisions, but when my decision to see him was fully set, it dawned on me that I had no way to get in contact with him short of physically making the trip to his dorm. I didn't even have a phone number. I had never had any need for one, because he and I usually encountered each other randomly on campus two or three times a week. Under normal circumstances I would have wondered why he had been so conspicuously absent for the past ten days, but I'd been so caught up in his notebook that I probably wouldn't have noticed if the sky fell on me. Now it occurred to me that I had neither seen him nor heard from him since my terrible experience with the mandala.

I had to force myself to go to his dorm. The memory of my nightmarish encounter in that little room on the sixth floor pained me like a fresh, gaping wound, and I felt a mounting terror as I approached Marco's featureless brown door and knocked sharply. Predictably—why I should have found it predictable, I don't know, but it seemed entirely appropriate in a poetic sort of way—he wasn't home. I stood there in the hallway for a long time, staring alternately down at the faded gray carpet and then back up at the door, as I debated whether to try the knob. Every time I reached for it I felt a surge of panic, and finally, in a kind of daze at the depth of my own wretchedness, I had to give up and admit that for whatever reason, I couldn't do it.

But I was still determined to find him. I inquired of his professors and found that he hadn't attended classes since Monday of the previous week—the last day I had seen him. It was apparent from their attitudes when I spoke with them that his physics professors, at least, were not at all displeased with his absence.

Next I sought out a few of our mutual acquaintances and discovered that they had not seen him either. At a loss for what to do, I finally returned to his dorm to confront my fear. Once again, there was no answer to my knock, and before I could fall back into that awful state of panicked indecision, I grabbed the knob and wrenched it violently.

Much to my surprise, the knob turned easily and the door swung open on silent hinges. I quickly stepped inside like nothing was wrong, and indeed, nothing at all seemed to be out of order in the room. Marco's bed was made, his book-shelves were full, and upon opening his closet I found a rack full of clothes. For a moment I was perplexed; I had half expected to find an empty room, to find that he had disappeared and left no word. The other half of me had expected to be overwhelmed by some unspecified, ultimate horror.

I crossed over to the desk hoping to find a note or some other clue, and I saw that a layer of dust had settled on its surface. A quick run of my finger proved it to be rather deep, deep enough that I knew nothing had moved upon the desk for some time. Further inspection showed that the bookshelves, books, medicine cabinet, and bedside table were all covered with a layer of dust. It was obvious that nothing had moved in this room for some time, and I knew then, without knowing how, that Marco had left his room shortly after my own departure ten days ago and had not returned.

It was at that point that my last reserves of strength began to fail. I simply couldn't go on. I had been concealing it from myself, but now I admitted that I was worried as much for myself as for Marco. Far from explaining anything, his notebook had raised a host of new questions and given in return only a smattering of frightening and maddeningly obscure ideas. Nothing was clear except for the fact that I was suffering from something I can only describe as a sickness of the soul.

I sat down on his bed and felt a hot lump rise in my throat, and with something like humor I realized I was about to cry. Nothing made sense. When I tried to consider my future I saw nothing but an endless black tunnel lined with

(Teeth)

painful, meaningless events and encounters. All the purpose, all the meaning and significance, seemed to have drained out of my existence. How had I come to this in just a few short days? Up until ten days ago I had known the normal difficulties of college, work, family, and the occasional romance, but at least I had been capable of leading a life and taking pleasure in the small niceties it afforded. Now I just wanted to sink into oblivion, whether sleep or death did not matter. Was existence, was my life, nothing more than a short interval between one darkness and another, an amusing but ultimately vain respite from an underlying reality of— of what?

(Teeth)

At that moment my tenuous hold on sanity began to slip, and I felt that gaping hole in reality begin to open again, not on any page but within me. Then I felt the needle-teeth begin to sink in, and I am convinced that if I hadn't had a specific thought to engage my attention, I would have slipped off the precipice into madness.

But with an enormous effort of will I fought off the insanity and decided to do what I had put off for days: examine the rest of the notebook. I had a hunch that Marco hadn't created the mandala of his own free will or in a normal state of mind. It would have been typical of him to write about it after creating it, to make some attempt to analyze what had happened. If this were true then I might gain some understanding of my own condition from his notes. At the very least, I might find a much-needed clue to the reason for his decision to involve me in all this.

I didn't let myself consider what I would do if he had written nothing.

6

The trip back to my apartment was a scene from the darkest nightmare. The sun was shining and everyone around me seemed to be enjoying the mild spring day, but it was as if I saw these things through a dark-tinted glass. The light seemed shaded, muted, like night scenes from a movie that were obviously shot in bright daylight with a filter on the lens. I kept seeing movement out of the corners of my eyes wherever there were shadows or dark spots. In each shadow I thought I could see living forms crouched and waiting, but when I looked directly at them they disappeared. It gradually became apparent to me that I was seeing shadows more clearly than the objects that cast them.

I hurried on. Shaken, out of breath, and terrified, I finally made it back to my lonely apartment and collapsed on the couch. I knew I couldn't keep this up much longer. The strain on my nerves and body was wearing me down to the point that I feared for my bodily health as well as my sanity.

At length I dragged myself to my feet and went to fetch the notebook. It remained where I had left it, at the back of my desk drawer, and I felt a vague surprise. I had half expected it to have disappeared, like the memory of last night's dreams. Its nondescript red cover seemed to mock me, as if its very dullness represented its defiance of my understanding. I sat down at my desk and flipped through to page forty-seven, squeezing my eyes shut lest I catch a fatal glimpse of the mandala.

Sure enough, Marco had recorded his thoughts after he drew it. Writing that would normally have filled only half a page in his minute hand now sprawled across three pages. Evidently he had scrawled these notes immediately after his first experience with the mandala, while he was still in shock. That he could have written anything at all seemed a miracle to me, in light of my vivid memory of my own experience.

His thoughts were surprisingly coherent:

> Almost sucked in. It almost pushed through. God, how? The perfect sequence of shapes, the perfect placement and size on the infinite continuum of distance between points. *They* forced my hand. Would it open the gate for anyone, render all preparation unnecessary? Chance—purpose—meaning—God! What fools we are! Our damned desire for "truth." The need is for *illusion*, fantasy, dreams. What price the true vision? What must we become? Lovecraft—correct about the vast conceit of those who babble of the malignant Ancient Ones. Not hostile to consciousness, indifferent to it. "Consciousness is a disease"—oh Miguel, if only you knew! The greatest horror reserved for minds, not bodies. Azathoth not conscious, pure Being. Consciousness, intelligence, *mind* the ultimate tragedy. To be somehow self-aware yet wholly incidental to the "purpose" of the universe. Conscious only to be aware of the utter horror of consciousness. Perfect intelligence negates itself.

I sat there, stunned. Much of what I had just read was obscure, but I understood enough. Somehow Marco had been offered a glimpse into the chaos at the center of Being. For reasons known only to Itself, some power had chosen him as a conduit for the revelation of what Lovecraft had rightly called "our frightful position in the universe," and then Marco, for reasons known only to himself, had shared his madness with me.

For a brief moment I tried to gain some distance on the situation by reasoning with myself, by telling myself that this was insane, that Marco was obviously suffering a psychotic breakdown and so was I. But the speed with which my newly

454 THE CHILDREN OF CTHULHU

born intuitive faculty demolished these ratiocinations was dizzying. I simply could not deny the naked truth, the knowledge of which seemed to bubble up from somewhere deep in my gut.

I had to find him. I had to know what had become of him, for I feared that his fate, whatever it might be, would be mine. I had to know the end toward which my strange affliction was leading.

But how? I hadn't the slightest idea of where to begin looking. Marco had always been rather aloof and reclusive, and now the full depth of my ignorance sank in. I knew next to nothing about this man whom I had called friend for nearly a year.

Completely baffled, I unthinkingly reached down and turned one more page of the notebook, and what I saw triggered the final stage of this journey into madness. I froze and read the words three times while their significance slowly sank into my mind like hooks. Dropping the notebook from numb fingers, I lurched toward the door and fumbled with the knob for what seemed like an eternity before managing to turn it. Then I was outside and racing across campus, the front door still banging open against the wall and the notebook lying open on the living room floor.

What I had seen was an article Marco had clipped from the *Terence Sun-Gazette* and pasted carefully to one of the pages of the notebook.

WORLD-RENOWNED SCIENTIST TO LECTURE AT
TERENCE UNIVERSITY

British physicist and astronomer Nigel Williamson will deliver a lecture titled "Chance, Meaning, and the Hidden Variable in the Quantum Universe" next week at the Terence University campus. Williamson, a Cambridge professor who is visiting Terence as the first stop on a worldwide lecture tour, is known for his tendency to ruffle the feathers of his colleagues with his iconoclasm and unorthodox theories. His claim to have arrived at an explanation for "the seemingly causeless actions of subatomic particles" has aroused worldwide interest and much skepticism in the scientific community. He is scheduled to speak Thursday, May 2, at 7 P.M. in the Stockwell science building on the Terence University campus. The lecture is free and open to the public.

7

I reached the Stockwell science building in eleven minutes, my scholar's body exhausted from running barely a mile and a half. As I leaned against the double doors, sucking in a huge lungful of air that seemed to do little to replenish my oxygen-starved tissues, I noticed a clock on the far wall inside. It read 7:06, and I let myself feel a moment's relief. The lecture would have started by now and there was no commotion. Perhaps my awful hunch had been wrong.

Still gasping like a fish out of water, I glanced up for a moment at the twilight sky and saw a half moon shining through the branches of a scraggly tree. The once-familiar moon was now the dead, decaying fetal carcass of some unimaginably monstrous creature, and as I looked on I saw it beginning to mutate into something more monstrous still. Dread washed back over me like ice water, and with a strangled cry of despair I flung myself through the door of the science building, as much to escape the awakening gaze of the moon as to stop the tragedy I feared might be occurring within.

I burst through the doors of the lecture hall to find a small group of middle-aged men and women checking their watches and waiting impatiently for the lecture to start. Most were seated, but a few had gathered around the lectern down front, where a nervous, balding man was trying to placate them. Several people looked up when I entered, and I saw their faces tighten into angry-worried lines. I recognized the expression. As a member of white, middle-class America I had worn it many times myself when confronted with scenes of economic squalor or ethnic unfamiliarity. It was the look of a person who senses danger and withdraws into himself; the look of a woman who finds herself stranded alone in a bad part of town in the dead of night and notices a seedy-looking stranger edging down the sidewalk toward her; the look of a man who sees something alien and fears its strangeness. I knew the expression well, but I had never felt it directed at me until now.

Ignoring the stares as best I could, I made my way down to the man with glasses. He stammered when I approached, and the cluster of people turned to look at me.

"Where is Professor Williamson?" I demanded. My voice seemed to reach me from a distance, and I noticed that I didn't feel a part of the situation at all. I felt like a spectator watching a play in which I appeared.

"I was just explaining—" the man with glasses began. He was already flustered, and something about me seemed to aggravate it. Finally he gave up and gestured toward the door behind him. "He's in there."

"Is he alone?"

The man was becoming more miserable with each passing second. "Well, no. There's a young man in there with him. He showed up a while ago and demanded to see the professor. I told him we were busy, but Nigel came out and decided to talk with him. They went into the conference room half an hour ago and haven't come out."

"Have you knocked?" By this point I was almost yelling.

"Well, no," the man said. "The young man was rather . . . passionate. His eyes were wild, like—" He cut himself short and shifted uncomfortably, but I could read the unspoken words on his face: like your eyes.

I opened my mouth to speak, but a sudden loud thump from the conference room silenced us all. It sounded like a chair or table falling over. This was followed by wild, incoherent shouting that froze the blood in my veins, for even through the thick door and the hysterical tone I recognized the voice and accent of Marco. I bolted past the stunned group of scientists and grabbed the door handle, only to find it locked. Now another voice, a voice so full of fear that it almost obscured the British accent, answered Marco's.

"What are you doing?"

"You mustn't! The madness, the chaos! The Gate is in the great *and* the small!"

I redoubled my efforts on the doorknob, but then froze with fear as there was a tremendous crash and a sound of shattering glass.

"What are you doing? You're mad!" There was a pounding on the door right in front of my face. "Roger! Open the door!" The voice rose to a shriek. "*No! Stop!*" There was a noise like a knife ripping into a side of beef, and the voice turned to a gurgling, choking scream. This was followed by a sickening thud and the sound of something being dragged through glass. Then rang out the last coherent words I would ever hear Marco speak.

"The Gate above and below! The One in the many! Oh God, the teeth! The *teeeeeth!*"

Silence.

The spectator feeling was gone. I was completely, horribly present. The others in the room were in various states of shock. One woman was weeping. A man had run halfway up the stairs toward the rear exit and then stopped, standing there blinking as if he had forgotten where he was going. The rest of the group either stood or sat in stunned silence.

Then the spell broke all at once and panic set in. Some ran for the exit while others came toward me. Everyone seemed to shout something different, and finally someone ran out to the hallway, found a maintenance closet, and returned with an enormous hammer. I grabbed it from him and set to work on the door handle while someone else called the police.

The handle was strong, but it gave way after six stout blows. Clutching the hammer like a talisman, I pushed open the door and took a step forward while the assembled scientists clustered behind me like sheep.

The room I had entered was a standard conference room with a long wooden table and eight chairs. One of the chairs was lying on its back, and the floor was littered with shards of broken glass from the shattered doors of a bookcase that had been overturned. The glass was covered with what looked like gallons of blood. My gaze followed the trail of blood to the point where it disappeared behind the table, and I crunched through the glass to see what it was that I had come here to prevent.

Nigel Williamson, physicist, astronomer, Cambridge professor, would never have the chance to reveal to the world his grand theory concerning the inner purpose of the universe. He lay on his back behind the table where Marco had dragged him, the nine-inch piece of glass Marco had used to eviscerate him still protruding from his side. The expression of twisted horror on his face must have matched my own, but I didn't think about that at the time. My attention was riveted to the blood-spattered, empty-eyed face of my friend Marco as he crouched over the professor's body and mechanically devoured his innards.

8

The years since that night have blurred together until my memory has almost failed me. Shortly after the furor died down I quit my studies and moved to another town, where I now hold down an inconsequential job that provides me with just enough income to afford the squalid apartment where I hide from the world and pray for a merciful end to my own existence. From time to time I buy a newspaper or pull the television out of the closet to find out if the direction of events has changed, but I know it never will.

The world is still disintegrating inexorably into madness. The prophecies of Lovecraft and Nietzsche are indeed coming to pass. As our knowledge of the universe increases at an almost exponential rate, we continue to grow increasingly schizophrenic as a species, and it cannot be long before we inadvertently let loose Azathoth, the nuclear chaos, to consume the world. In that awful instant, not only our bodies but our minds, our spirits, our very "souls" will be annihilated as we gaze in awe and horror at the blasphemy that is the ground of our being.

I find it ironic that the man who cursed me with this vision will not even be aware of it when these events come to pass. Marco spends his days and nights screaming out his madness in an asylum. I visited him only once, when the police were still trying to discover where he had hidden himself during his ten-day absence. I almost could not bear to look at him, and when I finally met his gaze I knew my friend was dead. Some other intelligence now looked out from behind his eyes. Something had compelled me to bring the notebook, and when he saw it he rushed at me, knocking me down, and ripped it to shreds with his teeth. Then he tried to attack me, and the doctors said it would be best if I did not visit him again. I later heard that he managed to break his restraints after I left, and in the absence of another person he turned on himself. Before the orderlies could reach him he had chewed off and swallowed two of his own fingers.

What scares me the most is that the insanity gnawing at the shell of Marco is the same insanity eating away at me, and indeed, at the whole human race. I do not know why I have been spared Marco's fate, unless it is meant as a joke to amuse a power beyond my comprehension. I yearn for oblivion, but what will death bring? Only too well do I understand the wisdom of the ancient Greeks, who held that the best thing is never to have been born. Nietzsche said the thought of suicide can comfort a man through many a dark night, but I am denied even that solace. When I die I will only be absorbed back into the shrieking maelstrom from which I came, the maelstrom that reclaimed Marco even before his death.

There is only one ray of hope for my salvation. Over the years I have taken the time to read all of Lovecraft's "fiction," and I cannot understand how he saw so deeply into the truth and yet remained so sane. Perhaps this gentle New Englander knew something I do not, something he was trying to convey when he wrote of the "vast conceit of those who babble of the malignant Ancient Ones." Perhaps the horror I sense is in me, not in things. Perhaps Marco was wrong, and there is no need to fear the truth. After all, It knows only Itself, and maybe I will not perceive It as horrible after I die. Perhaps "I" will not even exist at all. If this is true, then may it come quickly.

But this hope can never sustain me for very long, because I know that I bear the evidence of damnation within my own body. The very physical need that compels me to take nourishment is the expression of the abyss to which I must return. I have gained a certain sensitivity in my mouth, a certain unpleasant awareness of the action of the protruding bits of bone that grind to a pulp the flesh of plants and animals to sustain this bodily life. From time to time I pause before a mirror to draw back my lips and gaze at the truth.

Do I seem mad? Do I seem like a man who has become lost in his own private delusion of hell? Then let me remind you that you also exhibit the truth in your own body. Show me your smile and I will show you your fate.

NOTES ON THE CONTRIBUTORS

BENJAMIN ADAMS traces his interest in H. P. Lovecraft back to an exposure at age nine to a Scholastic collection titled *The Shadow Over Innsmouth*. After that, nothing was ever quite the same again. Adams's work has appeared in anthologies such as *Blood Muse, Miskatonic University, Horror!: 365 Scary Stories, Singers of Strange Songs*, and *Return to Lovecraft Country*.

POPPY Z. BRITE is the author of four novels, *Lost Souls, Drawing Blood, Exquisite Corpse*, and *The Lazarus Heart*; two short story collections, *Wormwood* (also published as *Swamp Foetus*) and *Are You Loathsome Tonight?* (published in the U.K. as *Self-Made Man*); and a biography of rock diva Courtney Love. She wrote and illustrated the novella *Plastic Jesus* for Subterranean Press, and is at work on a new novel. She is not sure whether "Are You Loathsome Tonight?" is truly a Mythos tale, but once she got it into her head that there was a connection between Elvis and Lovecraft, she couldn't get it out again until she wrote this story.

MATT CARDIN first encountered the works of H. P. Lovecraft in high school. While in college he spent a considerable amount of time neglecting his assigned studies in favor of reading Lovecraft and Lovecraft criticism. After graduation he underwent a period of profound psychic and philosophic upheaval that led him to write "Teeth" and a number of other Lovecraftian-Ligottian stories embodying an extremely grim cosmic worldview. In recent years he has earned a minor name for himself as an interpreter of Thomas Ligotti's work among the Internet community centered around that author. Currently he is pursuing a teaching certificate for high school English and a master's degree in religious studies at Southwest Missouri State University. He resides in southwest Missouri with his wife and stepson.

MARK CHADBOURN is the award-winning author behind several critically acclaimed horror novels. His works include a dark fantasy trilogy—*World's End, Darkest Hour,* and *Always Forever*—examining how society would fare if the brutally passionate gods of Celtic mythology ever returned. Chadbourn lives in rural seclusion in the English Midlands and can trace his own roots back to the Celts. H. P. Lovecraft was his first introduction to the world of horror, at the tender age of twelve when he picked up a dog-eared copy of *The Haunter of the Dark* from a market stall. His imagination was instantly caught by Lovecraft's florid mythologies, so it was only a matter of time before he contributed to the Mythos.

Short story writer and poet **JAMES S. DORR** is an active member of HWA and SFWA, a past Anthony (mystery) and Darrell nominee, a multitime Rhysling finalist, winner of the 1998 Best of the Web award, and has been listed in *The Year's Best Fantasy and Horror* eight of the last nine years. While his present interest lies mostly in horror, Dorr's first acquaintance with H. P. Lovecraft was via "The Color Out of Space," and so he thought it especially appropriate that his offering for this volume be a piece that is also primarily science fiction.

PAUL FINCH writes: "I'm a former cop and journalist, but now a full-time writer, living in the north of England with my wife, Cathy, and my two children, Eleanor and Harry. My bread and butter these days is the British TV crime series, *The Bill,* which I've now been writing for the last two years, but dark fantasy and horror are still by main literary interests and I devote as much time to them as I can. 'Long Meg and her Daughters' was inspired by a visit to the real Long Meg site in Cumbria. The place is steeped in mysticism and is very atmospheric, and from the moment I got there, the story began to write itself."

ALAN DEAN FOSTER's work to date includes excursions into hard science fiction, fantasy, horror, detective, western, historical, and contemporary fiction. He has also written numerous nonfiction articles on film, science, and scuba diving, as well as having produced the novel versions of many films, including such well-known productions as *Star Wars,* the first three *Alien* films, and *Alien Nation.* Other works include scripts for talking records, radio, computer games, and the story for the first *Star Trek* movie. In addition to publication in English, his work has appeared and won awards throughout the world. His novel *Cyber Way* won the Southwest

Book Award for Fiction in 1990, the first work of science fiction ever to do so. What many readers may be unaware of is that Foster's first professional sale was to the venerable Arkham House, original publisher for the works of H. P. Lovecraft.

He says, "When I was a young reader, H. P. Lovecraft was the only writer who was really able to give me chills. It's ironic that my first professional sale, 'Some Notes Concerning a Green Box,' turned out to be a Mythos tale. I'm happy to return to it."

BRIAN HODGE is the author of seven published novels, including his breakout crime debut *Wild Horses* and the follow-up volume entitled *Mad Dogs*. He's also written more than eighty short stories and novellas, several of which have been shackled into the highly acclaimed collections *The Convulsion Factory* and *Falling Idols*. About his novelette here, he says, "For years I've admired the vastness and grandeur of Lovecraft's universe, but in adding to the canon it's not enough just to mimic. I wanted to do something that would resonate on that leviathan scale, but at the same time weave in layers that work on a more intimate level, as well, with matters of self-identify and family history."

CAITLÍN R. KIERNAN's first novel, *Silk*, was released in 1998 and received both the Barnes & Noble Maiden Voyage and International Horror Guild awards for best first novel. Her second novel, *Trilobite*, was published in 2001.

Caitlín's short fiction has appeared in such anthologies as *The Year's Best Fantasy and Horror* and *The Mammoth Book of Best New Horror*, and her chapbook, *Candles for Elizabeth*. Her first full-length collection was *Tales of Pain and Wonder*, followed shortly thereafter by a second volume, *From Weird and Distant Shores*.

"I'm not sure of the precise inspiration of this story," she writes, "but it may have been a sculpture of Andromeda by Daniel Chester French. Though much of Lovecraft's fiction has influenced my work, I've always felt that his stories involving the sea, and what it might be hiding from us, are the most powerful."

RICHARD LAYMON has been called "a genius of the grisly, the grotesque, and the humorously excessive." He first read H. P. Lovecraft after discovering a Lancer paperback edition of *The Colour Out of Space* in 1968. Laymon was an English major at Willamette University at the time and he has been reading Lovecraft ever since. Over the past twenty years, Laymon has authored more than thirty novels and seventy short stories. He received Bram Stoker Award nominations for two of his novels, *Flesh* and

Funland; for his short story collection, *A Good Secret Place*; and for his nonfiction book *A Writer's Tale*. His novel *The Traveling Vampire Show* received the Bram Stoker Award in 2000. Recently published novels include *Friday Night in the Beast House* and *Once Upon a Halloween*.

Laymon's books are published in the United Kingdom by Headline, and in the United States by Leisure Books and Cemetery Dance Publications. To learn more, check his website at http://www.rlk.cjb.net.

TIM LEBBON's books include *Mesmer, Faith in the Flesh, White, Naming of Parts, Hush* (with Gavin Williams), and the short story collection *As the Sun Goes Down*. Stories have appeared or are due to appear in many anthologies and magazines, including *The Year's Best Fantasy and Horror, Best New Horror, Cemetery Dance, October Dreams,* and *Last Days*. His love of horror began with *The Rats*, and his enjoyment of Lovecraft started with *At the Mountains of Madness*.

Lebbon writes: "The Cthulhu Mythos is as fascinating and relevant today as ever, because it invokes a fear of the unknown and a terror borne of our total irrelevance in the scheme of things. And whatever age you live in, that's as scary as it gets." Lebbon is a recent winner of the British Fantasy Society's award for his novella *Naming of Parts*.

L. H. MAYNARD AND M. P. N. SIMS are the authors of the hardback collections *Shadows at Midnight* and *Echoes of Darkness*. They provide regular essay columns in *At the Worlds End* and *Masters of Terror*, as well as book reviews. They publish and edit under Enigmatic Press, which has produced *Enigmatic Tales*, among other titles. Their supernatural stories of quiet horror have been extensively published in a variety of publications. Their interest in the Mythos has been active for nearly thirty years since they first discovered the Arkham volumes of Lovecraftian stories. Visit their site at www.epress.force9.co.uk.

CHINA MIÉVILLE is the author of *King Rat* and *Perdido Street Station*, as well as short fiction published in various anthologies. He lives and works in London. On his contribution to this anthology he writes, *"Weird Tales* is the church of high pulp, Lovecraft its pope, the Cthulhu Mythos his unique and astounding liturgy. I offer 'Details' to the canon, humble and grateful as an altar boy."

YVONNE NAVARRO writes all kinds of stuff, including horror, suspense, science fiction, mainstream, and weird westerns. By the end of the year 2000 she had eleven novels published, including the suspense novel *That's Not My Name, Dead Times*, and the media original novel *Buffy the Vampire*

Slayer: Paleo. She's currently waffling between several projects (just like a politician) and writing a short story now and then. She still stubbornly clings to her dream of someday living in Arizona and owning a big, congenial dog. She thinks "Meet me on the Other Side" is the first story she's written that includes tentacles; then again, she's been at this for nearly two decades and could have easily forgotten a slimy appendage or two along the way. Visit her website at www.para-net.com/~ynavarro.

WESTON OCHSE lives in Sierra Vista, Arizona, high in the mountains of the Sonoran Desert. This social deviant is an interrogation instructor for the U.S. Army at the U.S. Army Military Intelligence School and enjoys twisting young minds and teaching the finer points of low-voltage reasoning. He has been writing for four years and is the coauthor of the highly acclaimed collection titled *Scary Rednecks and Other Inbred Horrors.* He has sold more than fifty short stories and is currently hard at work on his novel, *Scarecrow Gods.*

MEREDITH L. PATTERSON graduated from the linguistics department at the University of Houston, and is doing her level best to pursue a master's degree and a writing career at the same time. A discussion with one of her professors about computer intelligence prompted her to read Noam Chomsky's remarks on cognitive specialization, and much later on, this story was the result. She has two cats, a day job, and a long-running fascination with Lovecraft's more fantastic work, like *The Dream-Quest of Unknown Kadath.* Her short fiction has appeared in *Texas Magazine, Jackhammer,* and most recently the Green Knight Publishing anthology *The Doom of Camelot.*

JOHN PELAN is the author of *An Antique Vintage* from Gargadillo Publishing. His first short story collection, *Darkness, My Old Friend,* is forthcoming from Shadowlands Press. With Edward Lee, he is coauthor of *Goon, Shifters, Splatterspunk, Family Tradition,* and numerous short stories. John's solo stories have appeared in *The Urbanite, Gothic.net, Enigmatic Tales, Carpe Noctem,* and many anthologies. John is currently working on several anthologies, including *Dark Arts* for the Horror Writers Association, and editing the complete supernatural fiction of Manly Wade Wellman for Night Shade Books and several volumes of short stories by Fritz Leiber for Midnight House. With coeditor Michael Reaves, he is assembling an anthology of Lovecraftian tales set in the world of Sherlock Holmes for publication by Del Rey Books in 2003. Visit his website at www.darksidepress.com.

W. H. PUGMIRE, Esq., began reading Lovecraft in 1972 while serving as a Mormon missionary in Northern Ireland. He began writing at that time and placed his first story with *Space & Time*. Upon returning to the States he discovered Arkham House, read the *Selected Letters*, and became an H.P.L. fanatic. At this time he met Jessica Amanda Salmonson, and it was her attendance at the Sunday School class he taught that led to his being excommunicated from the Mormon Church. Under Jessica's steady influence, Pugmire began seriously writing Lovecraftian horror fiction. A book of thirty-three sonnets and his first hardcover collection will see print this year from Delirium Books. He is the Queen of Eldritch Horror.

MICHAEL REAVES is an Emmy award–winning television writer, screenwriter, and novelist. He's written for *Star Trek: The Next Generation, Twilight Zone,* and *Sliders,* among others. He was a story editor and writer on *Batman: The Animated Series,* and on the Disney animated series *Gargoyles.* His screenwriting credits include *Batman: Mask of the Phantasm* and the HBO movie *Full Eclipse.* Reaves's latest book, *Hell on Earth,* will be published in 2001 by Del Rey Books, and he has written a *Star Wars* novel *(Darth Maul: Shadow Hunter)* for them. Reaves has had short stories published in magazines and anthologies such as *Fantasy* and *Science Fiction Magazine, Heavy Metal, Horrors,* and *Twilight Zone Magazine,* and has written comic books for DC Comics. In addition to winning an Emmy, he has been nominated for a second Emmy, an ASIFA Award, and a Writers' Guild Award. His prose fiction has been nominated for the British Fantasy Award and the Prometheus Award. In 1999 he was named Alumnus of the Year by his alma mater, California State University at San Bernardino. With coeditor John Pelan, he is assembling an anthology of Lovecraftian tales set in the world of Sherlock Holmes for publication by Del Rey Books in 2003.

JAMES ROBERT SMITH is married (to Carole Handerson), has one son (Andy), the two requisite cats, two dogs, and a job. He and his family reside happily in Charlotte, North Carolina. "Visitation" was his forty-fifth sale— this story, in various forms, had been making the rounds for more than eighteen years. Never let it be said that Smith gives up easily. His first book, a collection of twenty-nine stories, is entitled *A Confederacy of Horrors.* He's waiting for a clever editor to buy one of his novels.

STEVE RASNIC TEM's recent publications include two short story collections: *City Fishing* from Silver Salamander Press, and *The Far Side of the Lake* from Ash-Tree Press. "I'm not particularly interested in playing in other writers' universes, but I am interested in what happens when my own particular obsessions encounter those of another writer. Hidden races, secret messages in alien tongues, questionable ancestry, ancient and decaying towns, the problems of isolation, the disintegrating family, the dangers of self-delusion, traumas passed down through generations: by the time the story was finished I wasn't sure which were Lovecraft's obsessions and which were my own."

JAMES VAN PELT writes and teaches in western Colorado. He was a finalist for the 1999 John W. Campbell Award for Best New Writer. His work has appeared in numerous magazines including *Analog*, *Weird Tales*, and *Realms of Fantasy*. New stories from him are scheduled to appear in *Analog*, *Asimov's*, and *Alfred Hitchcock's Mystery Magazine*. His wife and three sons think he tells a pretty good bedtime story.

"Colorado ghost towns fascinate me," he says. "You can't walk around fallen buildings or dark, abandoned mines without thinking about what might be waiting in the shadows." His home page is at http://www.sff.net/people/james.van.pelt.